Holmes and Watson:

The War Years

A Collection of Sherlock Holmes Adventures

Kieran McMullen

Hardback ISBN 9781780923154

Published in the UK by MX Publishing
335 Princess Park Manor, Royal Drive,
London, N11 3GX
www.mxpublishing.co.uk

Cover design by www.staunch.com

To

My wife Helen
And our children, Molly, Seanan and Keenan

Contents

Introduction

Since an early age I have always found that Holmes and Watson held a great fascination for me. They are the ideal combination of the thinking man and the feeling man. But what fascinated me more than anything was where did they come from, how did they get to be who they are? Scores of volumes have been written about Sherlock. Somewhere someone has probably written a thesis on the type of frock coat he wore. Little is written about Dr Watson, the man who keeps the thinking man in check. Where did he come from, what was his early life, why the army? All good questions.

It was my interest in Watson that started me on a quest to fill in the missing information. Presented here is one possible answer to all the above questions plus some others. For example; how could Watson be in the 5th Northumberland and wounded in Maiwand when the unit was not there? Why was he with another unit? Where and how was he actually wounded? But this is just the start.

There are more questions to be answered. Crime was not the only interest of the great detective, brother Mycroft saw to that. But besides their work in *The Bruce-Partington Plans*, *The Adventure of the Naval Treaty*, and *The Second Stain* we know that Holmes and Watson took on the roles of secret agents at the start of the Great War. So is it not likely that our friends served Queen and Country in the Second Boer War as well? And why would their efforts end in August of 1914? Would they not still serve through the entire "war to end all wars"?

This volume is the story of Holmes and Watson during the troubled and magnificent times in which they lived. It is their wartime experience.

Foreword

The Three tales that I have collected here are those in which I or I and Holmes were able to serve the country in particular times of crisis. The first is my own tale. It is the story of how I came to arrive back at St Bart's, alone in London, and met my friend Sherlock Holmes. I have set down a synopsis of my early youth and those events which steered me toward my Army career (short though it may have been) and my wounding in Afghanistan. The tale may interest those curious about my time there and set at rest, once and for all, the comments about my wounds. I call it *Watson's Afghan Adventure*.

The second adventure, which I have named *Sherlock Holmes and the Mystery of the Boer Wagon*, was the second time I put on the uniform of the Royal Army Medical Corps. I had been back in rooms with Holmes at Baker Street for some time and as middle aged men do, I became restless. So, when the opportunity was presented to me by Dr Doyle to accompany the Langman Hospital to the Cape in support of the Crown against the Boers, I went willingly. My time there however, was also occupied in assisting Holmes in his task of finding spies within our ranks and searching for a large store of gold.

Many of you are aware of Holmes service at the start of the Great War. I have published it under the title of *His Last Bow*. During that period Holmes had spent nearly two years perfecting his undercover persona as Altamont, a disaffected Irish-American who was willing to work for Germany against Great Britain. But that was not his only use of the disguise he had perfected. It is only now, some years after the event, that I have been given permission by both Holmes and his brother Mycroft to make public the story I have called *Sherlock Holmes and the Irish Rebels*. It was the third and last time that I wore the uniform of the king.

I am proud of the efforts that these three tales represent. Be they successes or failures I will let the reader decide.

John H Watson
Dover
3 May 1929

WATSON'S
AFGHAN
ADVENTURE
KIERAN
MCMULLEN

Chapter 1
An Old Friend

It had been a long but beneficial day. The late April days in London had been clear and pleasant and in the parks, at least, the smell of spring was wonderful.

Holmes had concluded two rather interesting cases in the last weeks. One I had titled "The Case of the Hansom Horse" and the other "The Adventure of the Locked Tantalus". Should Holmes approve, I would put them aside for a year or two before offering them to Dr Doyle for publication.

So here I was, strolling home, sunshine, a day of rounds, my lunch at the club and now to Baker Street and a relaxing evening. Life was good.

As I approached 221, I noticed a hansom cab pulling away from the kerb and wondered if we had had a visitor in my absence. With a quickened step, I advanced to the door and trotted up the seventeen steps to our sitting room. As I entered, I saw Holmes by the bow window, pipe in hand and looking most contemplative.

"Holmes," I said as I laid down my bag and hat, "Have we had a visitor?"

"Ah Watson," said he turning toward me and moving to his favourite chair. "Yes, we or actually you have had a visitor."

"I? And who would that have been?"

"Actually, it was your old orderly, Murray," he said, sitting and propping his feet on the fender of the cold fireplace.

"I should greatly like to have seen him. Is he to be in London for a time? Where is he staying?"

"I'm afraid you've missed him, Watson. He is on his way to the train, thence to Liverpool and finally to America. I understand he is to live with his daughter and her husband in a town called Guthrie in the Indian Territory of all places. They evidently are in some kind of a mercantile business and invited him to live with them and the grandchildren now that his wife has passed."

Suddenly, my happy mood had been rained on. Feeling irritated with myself for having dawdled at the club, I sat in my chair on the other side of the fireplace. "Well I'm greatly sorry to have missed him. He and I had more than one adventure together and I'll always be in his debt. It's sad to think I'll probably never see him again."

Holmes leant forward in his chair and retrieved his Persian slipper. Filling his old clay with tobacco, he leaned back and smiled. "He did leave you something to remember him by," said Holmes. "Over there on the table, a white cardboard box. Murray said you would understand its contents. He also said he will be forever grateful to you. He did not explain why and I did not press him for an explanation."

Rising, I went to the table upon which lay a white cardboard box about six inches square, two inches high, tied with twine and unmarked. It rattled slightly when I picked it up. I returned with it to my chair and cutting the string with my pocketknife, I heard Holmes chuckle. "Preserving the knot as evidence, Watson?" I had to smile.

"I suppose you have had an effect on my habits, Holmes. But it's really just faster to cut it."

Leaning back, I opened the box. I don't know what the look on my face was but my reaction evidently startled Holmes. "Watson" he said, "Are you all right? Can I help with something, old friend?" Closing the lid on the box, I stood and leaning on the mantel, looked into the cold space.

"No Holmes, I'm quite fine. It's just that a sudden flood of emotions seemed to overwhelm me. Sorry."

"No need to apologize, Watson. Would you care for a whiskey?"

"Quite right, Holmes, I would."

A short whiskey, a deep breath and I felt myself again.

"Holmes," I said, "How do you feel about dinner at Simpson's tonight? My treat."

"Excellent, Watson, we deserve a night out. I'll inform Mrs Hudson."

We enjoyed an excellent leisurely dinner and it was near eleven when we returned to Baker Street. I was again feeling all was well with the world and had even enjoyed Holmes' constant one-sided discussion on the merits of the horseless carriage and its positive effect on the London environment. As we sat with a last evening brandy, I turned to Holmes, "I suppose you have deduced, by now, the contents of the package left me by Murray."

"No, other than it contained some memento of your time together in Afghanistan, I have no idea."

"Well, let me show you and see what you can deduce. I can believe that is should be fairly easy for you."

Taking the package from the mantle, I handed it to Holmes who put it on the edge of his chair while finishing lighting his pipe. The pipe lit, he opened the box and examined its contents. Rising, he moved to the table and one by one, removed the contents: one glass phial containing two bullets, a ruby of approximately five carats and a medal with a likeness of St. Peters Basilica on the reverse with the date of 1880 and on the obverse a likeness of Pope Gregory XVI and subscribed "John H. Watson".

For the first time, in a long time, I saw a quizzical look on Holmes' face.

"Well Holmes, what do you make of it?"

"Some of this is obvious of course, but some is curious," he said. Picking up the phial, he opened it and placed the two bullets on the table and taking up his magnifying glass, he examined them thoroughly. The ruby was next to be examined and lastly the Papal medal. Sitting at the table, he once again picked up the two bullets.

"I am of the opinion that these two bullets make my friend out to be a liar."

"Holmes!" I cried.

"These two bullets are undoubtedly the two that came from your shoulder and your leg. Why else would Murray have saved them all these years? Neither, however, was fired from a Jizail. This one here was fired from a Snider rifle," he said. "A Jizail, while sometimes rifled, is usually a smooth bore musket, and in either case will be about .56 to .79 calibres. This bullet is a .577 of about 480g with a hollow cavity, I believe it is called a Metford and it was fired by a weapon with five grooves, therefore a Snider short rifle or carbine."

Picking up the other bullet, Holmes continued, "This bullet is a pistol bullet. Probably from an Enfield Mark I. The .476 calibre and rifling are very distinctive. Neither bullet, however," he said, dropping the bullets in the phial, "is from a Jizail. And since you have always contended that you were wounded by a Jizail bullet, you have obviously lied. For what purpose I don't know, but I assume they have something to do with this ruby and an award to John H. Watson from the Roman Pope."

I was mortified and ashamed. "Yes, Holmes, I have lied to you. Those are the bullets from my wounds and while there was plenty of fighting involved, only one of the wounds ever came from an Afghan fighter. Perhaps it is time that you, at least, knew what really happened in Afghanistan."

Chapter 2
Australia

Holmes walked back to the sideboard and poured two more brandies. "You know that that is not necessary, Watson. Whatever the cause, I know that you are a man of honour and would have done nothing immoral. Illegal perhaps, as you have shared a few less than legal moments with me. Whatever happened, it was in a good cause."

"Thank you, Holmes." I replied. "But I really would like to tell you what those items represent. I'm afraid to do so though, might be a bit lengthy in the telling."

"As you know, Watson, we have no cases at the present and I, for one, am not tired and you have always been fairly closed-mouthed about the details of your Army service. I see no reason not to tell your tale right now."

"I'm afraid, Holmes, that it starts back in the days of my youth. As you know, I was born in August of '52 in Hampshire. Both of my parents were Scotch Presbyterian. Being the second son, and my older brother already named after my father, that is Henry Watson, Jr., I was named for my father's first cousin, John Watson, who was serving in the Bombay Army. He and my father had been inseparable as children. My middle name, Hamish, was my mother's father's name. All this may sound irrelevant, but it all ties into what happened to me in Afghanistan.

"Mother died when I was not quite two. In fact, it was June 24th, 1854. Father was a Railroad Construction Engineer and had been given an opportunity to work on the building of the Sydney railroad. So in August of '54, he packed up my brother and I and a nanny by the name of Eileen Duffy and off we went to Australia. There were no close relatives on my mother's or father's sides of the family living, so there was nothing to hold us here in England.

"Father completed his work on the Sydney railroad when it was opened on September 26, 1855. From then on it was a series of railroad camps across different parts of Australia and finally in the summer of 1857, two things happened. First, father took a position as Railroad Inspector for the Crown and second, as these things will happen, he married Miss Duffy, or Miss Eileen as we boys called her.

"She was a wonderful woman and Henry and I thought the world of her. She insisted that we continue to call her Miss Eileen in deference to our deceased mother. Miss Eileen not only saw to our physical needs and education, she now saw to our religious education. Father, although nominally Presbyterian, was truly an agnostic. He had little use for organized religion. Miss Eileen however was a devout Catholic and being a woman, knew how to bend her husband's will to hers. So it was that Mrs Eileen Watson and sons became regular members of the St. Mary's Catholic Church. Henry and I made our first communion two years later.

"It was also in '57 that my father and his cousin John began a communication that lasted until the death of my father. I also started corresponding with my namesake and he quickly became my hero. Lt. John Watson of the 1st Punjab Cavalry won the Victoria Cross at Lucknow during the Sepoy Mutiny.

"I was thrilled to hear of his gallant charge against a Ressaldar (that is, an Indian captain of cavalry) and six enemy sowars or troopers. Firing his pistol at a distance of three feet, the Ressaldar missed and Lt. Watson ran him through with his sabre and dismounted him. The Ressaldar was not finished though and with his tulwar drawn, he and his six sowars assaulted cousin John anew. Lt. Watson defended himself until his own men could arrive and together, they vanquished the entire rebel company. Cousin John received Sabre or Tulwar cuts to the head, his left arm, his right arm (which was temporarily disabled), a bullet through his coat and a sabre cut to his leg which left him somewhat lame for awhile.

"Here was adventure for a boy to lust after. So now I knew what the future held, the Army. As I grew, I stayed in contact with cousin John. I relished his every letter. His adventures in the mutiny, his raising of the 4th Sikh Irregular Cavalry (Watson's Horse) in '58, the Umbryla Expedition in '63, it was all a bright, shining adventure.

"Henry and I spent our days being tutored by Miss Eileen, occasionally traveling with father on a railroad inspection, exploring the Outback, learning to shoot and ride and pretending to be the conquering British soldiers in our games. This happy state lasted until my thirteenth year.

"Typhoid came in the spring of that year and with it, the death of the only mother I had really known. I watched the progress of the disease as it took her: the chills, sweating, pain, headache, fever and diarrhoea. In those days, it was called enteric fever and was treated with opiates for the diarrhoea, hot poultices for the abdominal pain, cold water sprays for the fever and turpentine by mouth for the internal ulcers.

"By the third week of her suffering, I was convinced there had to be some other treatment. I was able to find a paper by a Dr Joseph Bell of Glasgow, who as early as 1860, was successfully using silver nitrate to treat typhoid. But who would listen to a 13 year old boy anyway? And so we lost her. My only consolation was that she had seen me confirmed in the Roman Catholic faith before she died.

"I now had two missions in life. I would devote myself to medicine and the Army.

As had happened in '54, it was time for the Watson family to move on. I was sent to England to Wellington College in Hampshire. Henry however stayed with father. Henry was already 17 and knew he wanted to be a Railroad Construction Engineer. So as I sailed for England, Henry and father sailed for San Francisco and work on the expanding railroad system in America, which was booming with the end of the American Civil War.

"Life at Wellington took some getting used to. I quickly learned how alone I was in the world. With the exception of an occasional letter from Henry or cousin John, I was on my own. As you know, there were hard lesson to be learned, but I found that my outdoor life had made me capable of defending myself and my education thus far had stood me in good stead. The one thing I did learn quickly was to keep my Catholicism and my opinions on the 'Irish Question' to myself.

"Suffice it to say that I did well at my studies and excelled in athletics. I also kept up my correspondence with cousin John. I continued to thrill at his adventures and took great pride in his receiving command of the Central India Horse in '71.

"In '72, I entered the University of London Medical School and of course worked at St. Bart's. Outside of the classroom, rugby was my life. All in all, things were good. In '74, I heard that Dr Joseph Bell was teaching at Edinburgh University and since I had a great desire to meet him, I spent a year there before returning to London. Actually Holmes, you and he are very kindred spirits. He is still there and you should meet him."

"I'm quite aware of Dr Bell and his techniques, which I agree, are much like my own," Said Holmes. "Forgive me while I refill my pipe. Go on, please. This is most interesting."

"Well" said I quite pleased that Holmes should show an interest in my history, "I returned to the University and received my Doctorate in June of '78. It was at that time that cousin John sent me notice that he had been dispatched to Malta in command of all the Indian Cavalry. But he also wrote of the touchy situation in India on the Afghanistan border. He was convinced of an imminent war on the border and urged me to apply directly for a position with a regiment already in country. This I did. cousin John recommended the 5th Regiment of Foot, now called the 5th Fusiliers or the Northumberland Regiment. Their nickname was the 'Fighting 5th'.

"Everything seemed to be falling in place as far as my career. So upon leaving the University in June, I reported to Netley for the School of the Army Surgeons and it was there that I first fell in love.

Chapter 3
Two Kinds of School

Netley was not a challenging course. It amounted to four things: doctors needed to be competent (and few were), get their own men organized, get the Commanders to listen about sanitation and finally, make sure you had adequate supplies. So, for five months, I was to be as sixes and sevens, not really knowing what to do with myself, while waiting to deploy.

I decided to fill my time with a personal study of military medical issues but still had much time for my new club and one of my favourite sports, horseracing. I know Holmes; I still enjoy it too much. But at the time, besides my pay, there was still a stipend from father in America. It was on one of my track days that I met a lovely young lady named Violet Enderby. But I get ahead of myself.

I had been to the Grand National that April and had failed to place my money on Shifnal and was therefore down a bit on my funds. But in June, I was feeling good and decided to go ahead and attend the Epson Derby to celebrate my new career. It proved a most interesting day. It was there I met three people who would forever impact my life. I was just about to place a modest wager with a bookmaker when I noticed a most lovely lady walking on the arm of a man I assumed to be her father or guardian. She was about 5'2", willowy, with beautiful golden blonde hair and hazel eyes. She wore summer dress of light green with a broad brimmed hat and a parasol of matching material. Her escort wore the uniform of a Colonel of the Indian Army. It was as they strolled by that I saw this lovely creature look my way. She smiled, nodded her head and walked on. I stood there speechless and wondering how to make her acquaintance. It was then I heard a voice at shoulder, "Give it up Old Boy. Nobody gets to meet Miss Violet."

Spinning around on my heels, I looked into the smiling faces of two young men of about my age. One put out his hand and said, "Lt. Sutter Sturt, 5th Fusiliers and the grinning Irishman next to me is Lt. Arthur McMullen of the 18th Bengal Cavalry. And the delightful creature you were admiring is Violet Enderby, daughter of the most pompous ass of a Colonel in the Indian Army. No one is good enough for his daughter."

"John Watson" I said shaking hands with both, "And delighted to meet you. I've just been assigned Assistant Surgeon with the 5th."

"Well, all the better to save a fellow from certain disappointment" said Sturt. "You could have ended up like Arty here, broken heart, poorer and on the run from an angry Colonel." At this remark, the two started into a fit of laughter.

Placing his arm around my shoulder and walking toward the rail, Sturt asked if I had already placed my wager. "No." I replied. "I need to get one down quickly."

"Well" replied Sturt. "Arty and I were just about to pool our modest sum. Would you care to go in with us? Mr Cavalry claims to have a sure fire system to pick the winner."

"I've no objection as long as he's betting on Sefton."

The two laughed again and arm in arm we were off to make the wager. That night we celebrated our win at the pavilion dance. It was here that I was introduced to Miss Enderby.

The pavilion dance was a gay affair and McMullen, Sturt and I were having a wonderful time. The two of them were telling me their stories of India, and I was trying to sort truth from fiction. We danced with numerous young ladies and drank our fill.

It was about halfway through the evening that we heard a commotion coming from a far corner of the pavilion. It was followed by a call from the bandleader asking for a doctor. I immediately responded and found an elderly lady lying unconscious on the floor surrounded by people.

"Sturt! Arty! Keep these people back, please!"

The two moved the crowd back but one beautiful lady stayed, kneeling, holding the hand of the stricken woman. Miss Enderby. "Are you a doctor?" she asked.

“Yes, Miss”, I replied.

"This is my great aunt; she was standing one minute and the next she was on the floor."

"Does she have any condition I should know of?"

"No" she replied. "She is quite healthy. I can't imagine what's happened."

I quickly examined the woman and as I did, she stirred slightly. "She's only fainted" I said. "A little air and some water and she'll be fine. Is there somewhere we can take her?"

"There is a lounge just off the patio" piped up a waiter who was standing by.

We moved the lady to the lounge and the crowd went back to its business of revelry.

Having deposited the lady on a chaise lounge, we commenced rubbing her arms and she soon came round. As her eyes opened, she suddenly sat upright. "Oh, my dear! What has happened?"

Tears welled up in her eyes. "Oh! I'm so embarrassed! Violet, help me up."

"I really wouldn't advise that, Madam. You really need to just sit and relax awhile. Doctor's orders." I smiled and patted her hand.

"You do what the doctor says, Aunt Katherine. I'll stay with you. It was getting rather heated in the pavilion and it's so much cooler here."

Turning to me, she said, "I want to thank you, Doctor."

"Really" I smiled, "It was no problem. Happy to help."

At this point, Sturt stepped forward. While looking at Miss Enderby, I had completely forgotten the presence of others in the room.

"Allow me to do the introductions. Miss Violet Enderby, let me present Dr John Watson of the 5th Fusiliers. And now, if you'll excuse us, Lt. McMullen and I will retire, happy to help." Smiling, he turned and grabbing Arty by the elbow, the two of them left for the bar.

"So, you're friends with Lieutenants McMullen and Sturt?"

"Yes, well, we just met today but they seem fine fellows."

"They are. I know both of them from India. They were assigned to general staff for a short time with my father, Colonel Enderby."

"Violet," called her aunt, "some more water, please."

"I best attend to my Aunt Katherine. But once again, thank you Doctor. Perhaps we'll see each other again." Violet extended her hand and taking it, I bowed.

"It will be my pleasure." I said and as I walked out, I was nearly bowled over by the form of Colonel Enderby rushing into the room.

"Was that Lt. McMullen I saw coming out of this room?" he stormed.

"Father, he was just helping with Aunt Katherine," Said Violet.

"I'll thank him not to help with anybody in this family, and who are you, Sir?"

"Assistant Surgeon Watson, Sir. Like the Lieutenant, just helping." I said, the blood rushing to my face.

"Well we appreciate your assistance" he blustered, "but we'll take it from here. Dismissed." Turning, he walked toward Aunt Katherine. Stunned, I drew myself up to attention, "You're welcome, Sir, and good night." I turned about and left to join the others at the bar.

"Get on well with the old man?" smirked Sturt as I approached. "Have a whiskey.'

"What a pompous ass!" I spit out. "No gratitude."

"That's just his way of saying he cares" laughed Arty. "Now, what about next week? Do we roll our winnings over?"

I hesitated for only a moment. "I'll be here if you both will."

"Then it's settled. We'll see if the combined knowledge of Dr Tout and Mr Cavalry can pick us another winner," chuckled Sturt.

So the following week we met again, this time for the Oak Stakes. It was much the same as the week before, and Arty and I studied the horses. Arty really was a sound judge of horse flesh and he and I finally agreed on a young filly named Jannette. The Oaks, of course, was for three year old fillies only.

As we walked about the track that fine day, you know who we saw, once again, on the arm of her father. The difference now being I had been introduced.

"Good Afternoon, Sir, Miss. What a beautiful day for racing. I do hope your good Aunt is doing well."

Miss Enderby smiled, "Quite well thanks to you, Doctor. Isn't she, Father?"

"Yes, quite well, quite well. Hope you're not looking for new clients, young man" huffed the Colonel.

"No Sir. Just enjoying the day. Will I see you at the pavilion later?" I said, smiling back at Miss Enderby.

"Perhaps, young man" scowled the Colonel. "Perhaps. Well come along Violet. Time we got along. Oh, and thank you again young man for your help last week."

With that they went off into the crowd. "That didn't go too badly" I said, turning to where Arty had stood. There was no one there. I looked all about and saw neither Sutter nor Arty until I moved up to the track.

"John, over here" called the voice of Sutter. "Go alright with the old codger?"

"I believe so but you two certainly disappeared quickly!"

"Only for the best" laughed Arty. "Now to the bar, we just have time for one before the race."

The day went well for us. We bet individually on the early races and while Arty and I were better than even, Sutter was down not an inconsiderable amount. The Oaks went as we hoped and Jannette increased our pool of funds quite well. That evening, we adjourned to the pavilion to enjoy some of our winnings having agreed to take ten per cent for ourselves and place the rest on the St. Leger Stakes in September. Arty would hold our winnings until then.

It was another gay night and I looked forward to hopefully seeing Miss Enderby again. I was not to be disappointed. It was "Aunt Katherine" I found first. Having left my companions at the bar, I was wandering the pavilion when I heard above the throng, "Doctor. Doctor Watson, over here." As I looked toward the voice, I saw Katherine Enderby waving a handkerchief, surrounded by her friends of a like age. I smiled and went over to her.

"Not feeling ill tonight, are we Miss Enderby?"

"Please, please Doctor, you must call me Aunt Katherine, everyone does."

"Of course, Aunt Katherine" I grinned.

"I was so hoping I'd see you so I could thank you properly for your help last week."

"It was nothing really, happy to help."

"Now don't be modest, dear boy. I was just telling the girls what a fine doctor you are."

I smiled round at the "girls" and wondered if any of them was less than sixty. "Is the other Miss Enderby here tonight?" I asked.

"Why, dear boy, of course. And you shall dance with her. Now where has she gone? Oh yes, over there with her father. Violet! Oh Violet" she called. "Here's that wonderful Doctor Watson. He so much wants to dance with you, don't you Doctor?"

Miss Enderby and I both grinned with embarrassment and took to the floor to avoid more attention. She and I danced until late; she was a startling woman, beautiful, intelligent, and courteous. She had a way of looking at you that made you feel special. As the night came to an end, Violet and I were lost in conversation.

"Violet, it's time to go dear." It was Aunt Katherine. Colonel Enderby stood next to her, quite a formidable figure with a scowl under his military moustache.

"Now, Doctor Watson, I've been talking to the Colonel and you must come visit us at the Hurling House. It's all decided. Two weeks from now, we won't take no for an answer" bubbled Aunt Katherine.

"Aunt Katherine, no one could refuse you anything. I'd be delighted."

The Colonel continued to scowl as I said my goodnights and went in search of my compatriots.

Two weeks later, I had the most wonderful weekend. For the most part, the Colonel kept to himself while I and Violet (and of course Aunt Katherine) had a wonderful time. In fact, the summer and early fall passed this way and I became a frequent guest.

Other things were happening that summer too. The undersea cable and two cross continent cables gave three telegraph routes between India and England. The Russians had opened relations with Amir Sher Ali Khan in Kabul in 1877. When we had asked for representation, the Amir refused us. In '78, the Amir signed a treaty with the Russians and moved large numbers of his Afghan troops to the border of the Northwest Frontier. Everyone knew there would be war and troop movements began. Cousin John commanded a large portion of native troops. He let me know that now was the time to get to my unit, yet I chaffed under the constraints of a slow, methodical course for Army surgeons and knew it would be the end of November before we would ever set sail.

In September, McMullen, Sturt and I met in Doncaster for the St. Leger Stakes. You could tell that we all strained to be away to India.

McMullen had decided to end his six month leave and announced he would be sailing in two weeks. Sturt had been detailed to the 2nd Battalion of the 5th, while he recruited for the 1st Battalion. All our talk was about the possible coming fight. Would we be there in time?

Arty and I made the round of horses, but it was really a forgone conclusion as to how we would place our money. Jannette, the 3 year old filly who had done us so well in June was being ridden by Fred Archer. Archer was undoubtedly the finest jockey England has ever produced. The combination of horse and rider was perfect. The resulting win gave the three comrades a considerable amount of money. In fact, I will say that I have never before or since had so much in winnings as we did that day.

Of course I knew that the Enderbys would be at the gathering after the races. Arty, Sutter and I were early arrivals at the festivities and, standing at the bar, began to speak of our future plans. Sutter hoped to be on his way by the end of November.

"I shall have finished this damnable course by then. Perhaps we can travel together. I'd be grateful to have an old hand with me." I told him.

"Don't see why we can't make that work" he replied "but Arty may have the war over by then and we'll miss the fun."

We laughed, but Arty's laugh was not very hearty. "It's never much fun in the Khyber Pass" he mused. "Never know which side has paid the beggars last or best, the local tribes, that is. It's all about local gain and never about the whole picture with those boys. Oh well, I'll do what I can to save you some sport." And smiling to himself, he ordered another round.

I had made a decision over the course of the summer that I needed to come on better terms with Colonel Enderby. He was now somewhat use to me and could not find an obvious reason to stifle the relationship between myself and Violet. I had also noticed the decidedly cold stares he inflicted on Lt. McMullen and Lt. Sturt but neither of them cared to offer a reason for this and I had let that issue lay.

It was the evening of the St. Leger, about midway through the evening's festivities that I found the old Colonel alone on the patio.

"Oh, Doctor Watson, come out and join me in a cigar. Beautiful night, eh? Makes one feel young and ready to retackle the world."

"Thank You, Sir. Don't mind if I do." I took the cigar proffered and lighted it. Taking a deep draught, I looked at the old man and wondered at his pleasant greeting.

"Going back soon, Sir?"

"Yes, end of the month, be back on general staff. Can't wait. Tired of all this tommy-rot sitting around. The action is in India, well some in South Africa by the looks of it, but India is the place to be."

We stood smoking for a few minutes.

"Give you a hint, Doctor. I can see you're not a mason. Oh, don't look startled, no badge or ring, you see? Lots of young men don't think about it. But if you're going to make the Army a career, you must become one. It's part of the game as they say. All my officers are masons. Look out for each other you know. Helps you make rank when you have brothers in the right places. Oh, I know it's not as important in the Medical Department. It's not like you're a line officer or something. Reason your friends McMullen and Sturt will never get anywhere. Sturt was sponsored you know, then turned it down. Said he didn't like the holier than thou attitude, ass! And McMullen's a damned Papist. Never should have let them in the officer ranks. Oh, the Irish Catholics are alright as rankers, but they've got no place in the officer corps! And the damned impertinence of the man. Wanted to marry my daughter, can you imagine?"

I stood stunned, silent, wondering what to say, how to respond.

"Doctor," he continued, "You seem to be a good fellow. When we get to India, I'd be happy to sponsor you. Just let your commander know and we'll get it fixed up."

I had finally started to think. So this is why Arty and Sutter had made sure never to be around when Enderby was. My face started to burn and I looked at the old man in the new light of his bigotry.

"Sir, you have generously opened your home to me and for that I'm grateful." I said. "I also appreciate your advice and offer of sponsorship."

The Colonel smiled.

"But I happen to be one of those damned Papists and while I have been negligent in practicing my faith, it does preclude me from membership in an organization which hates us. As for my friends, I stand by them. Thank you for the cigar, and good night, Sir."

With this, I left the Colonel red-faced and sputtering something about ungrateful bore.

"Well you two are fine friends!" I stammered. "Let me put my foot in it with the Colonel. Why didn't you tell me?"

The two of them looked at each other and choked with laughter.

"We knew you'd get it figured out," said Sutter. "It just took you a lot longer than we thought it would."

"By God," laughed Arty. "Found out what it's like to be a "Papist", have we?"

The two of them were now slapping my back and excusing themselves from two attractive young ladies, led me to the bar.

"Three whiskies" cried Arty to the bartender.

"You should have told me! I just can't believe you didn't warn me! I thought we were friends!"

"Drink up" said Arty. "It'll all be better in the morning, and you wouldn't have believed us if we had told you, would you?"

"Well, probably not, but see here…"

"Enough" said Sutter. "You've learned a valuable lesson and we are still three comrades, with booty to split. Let's be off to London and see the town one last time before Arty sails. What about it, John?"

"Alright. But I still think you should have told me. I quite like Violet" I sulked.

Arty placed a hand on my shoulder. "Let me explain something to you, John. When you get to India you won't have a chance to worry about anything but your duties. Don't be afraid to be who you are but don't go about with a chip on your shoulder about this. The Colonel was right about one thing. Freemasons have the officer corps fairly sowed up. In fact, for a Corporal to make Sergeant means joining. Over half of the British troops in India are Catholic, most of those Irish, and yet the Army doesn't see fit to provide them a Chaplain. Only Protestants get Chaplains. Don't get me wrong, there are some good commanders who will try to get a local padre to come by and even pay a little for them, but there are few priests. That's just how it is. Now, get your hat and we're off to London."

So, in a somewhat better mood, we three started on a new adventure.

Chapter 4
Talk of Treasure

It was the 8th of October and the eve of Arty's departure. The three of us got together for dinner and a drink at Simpson's. I had spent the day at St. Bart's with some of my colleagues, going over the latest developments on the treatment of typhoid, cholera and dysentery as I knew I'd be treating more of this than I would anything else.

As we sat with our brandy at the end of the most excellent dinner, Sturt recommended that we retire to the bar at his hotel as he had some information for Arty and me.

As we sat down in the bar, Sturt called the waiter over. He arrived carrying three wooden boxes slightly larger than a cigar box.

"Thank You, Walter. Just put them down here and we'll have three whiskies if you please" said Sturt and the waiter departed.

"Here Gentleman" he continued, "is a little gift to the three of us on the eve of Arty's departure. Open your boxes please."

Inside, we each found a new Webley-Pryse, break-open revolver in .476 calibre. Each was engraved along the barrel with our names. They were fine weapons and I have used mine to good effect, I will say, ever since. These Webleys had only become available the year prior and were already quite popular because of their system for automatically ejecting the empty cartridges when they were opened. It also had a rebounding hammer. This meant that all six chambers could be loaded safely, instead of the traditional five and leaving the hammer on an empty chamber.

"I hardly know what to say!" I exclaimed.

"I hope you never have to use it John. You or Arty. But it's best to have something reliable and now you have it."

"I have more news for you, John," he went on. "Received word today that the 5th has been ordered to move from Chakrata to Afghanistan as soon as possible. Captain Beamish contacted me by wire. He's to be left at the depot with a small detachment and the women and children. He is not happy. Now, by my reckoning, there will be 27 officers, 43 sergeants, 15 drummers and roughly 690 rank and file on the march. Beamish says I'm to spend six more weeks in recruiting and then join the 5th. We'll see if we can't sail together, eh John?"

"I should enjoy that," I replied. "I'll need a hand just finding my way."

"Well here's to us and may we meet again in Kabul" said Arty, raising his glass. And so we toasted our coming adventure and the following morning Arty sailed to re-join the 18th Bombay Cavalry.

Time now started to move swiftly. I continued my studies in earnest. The full realization that men’s lives would be in my hands finally set in. I saw little of Sturt but when I did, he was always full of information. On November 7th, the 5th reached Lawrencepore and by the 20th, they were part of the Peshawar Valley Field Force assigned convoy duty for supplies going through Jamrud. On that same day, Sher Ali refused to allow the British Delegation entry into Afghanistan. The following day, the actual shooting war began as on the 21st our forces started the march for Kabul.

The 21st of November was also the eve of Sturt and I sailing to join the 5th Fusiliers. We met about nine that evening and having dispatched all but a light case to the docks, sat in the hotel bar until midnight. Sturt spent the time regaling me with stories of his family and India and he fretted about possibly missing "all the action".

As last call was sounded, we headed for the docks, Sturt had arranged an early boarding for us. We had been extremely fortunate and had gained passage on the P&O's newest liner, The Kaisar-I-Hind, which had just been christened in June. Loosely translated, it means Empress of India. She was a beautiful boat, not as fast as the trans-Atlantic kind but broader in the beam and extremely well appointed. She sported the P&O black hull, funnels and buff decks.

We sailed early on the 22nd, the same day that Lt. Gen. Sam Browne took Ali Masjid. The British field forces were losing no time on their push into Afghanistan. Sturt and I had a pleasant time and I discovered a secret known already to the regular travellers of the P&O. The secret was called the "fishing fleet".

The "fishing fleet" was made up of young ladies who were looking for husbands among the outward bound diplomats, soldiers, merchants, etc. headed for India. Should they find no likely candidates, they would make the return journey on what the crew called "returned empties". I will say that Sturt and I made the acquaintance of more than one such lovely on our trip. But it was the last evening of our voyage that was to prove the most memorable for me.

We had forgone our usual evening entertaining with the ladies and adjourned to the smoking room. Sturt was quite in his cups by now and as it was very late, we were alone.

"Never did tell you why that old goat Enderby doesn't like me, have I, Watson."

"No, not that it matters but I thought it was your refusal to be a mason."

Leaning across the table, he looked about the room and in a stage whisper said, "It's the treasure, you know." And smiling at his own cleverness leaned back in his chair and took another drink.

"What treasure?"

"The one that Enderby is after and can't have," he laughed. "One more drink, old man."

Drinks came and pulling me by the sleeve he moved me to a far corner of the deserted room.

"It's like this, old family story. Seems to be true but I can't prove it yet. Enderby wants the map, you see?"

"No, I'm afraid I don't." I replied.

"How should I tell this? How familiar are you with the last Afghan war? Well, never mind, I'm sure you know about the retreat from Kabul. In the fall of '41, the East India Company was tired of paying to keep troops in Afghanistan. The company man in Kabul was named Macnaghton, real skin flint, tried to make a name for himself by declaring Kabul tamed and cutting expenses. The Major General commanding the Army forces was named Elphinstone. Old man, fought at Waterloo. Elphinstone tried to get the Army in order and build a proper fort but Macnaghton was against spending the money. Macnaghton also cut in half the payments the company made that went to the tribes controlling the Khyber Pass. The tribes started raiding the convoys again and Macnaghton decided to teach them a lesson. He sent the 1st Brigade under Sir Robert Sale back to India, having them punish the Ghilzais on the way. Macnaghton thought he'd save some money and show the company how secure Kabul was. But once the first Brigade left on the 10th of October 1841, they found they had to fight their way through the Khurd-Kabul pass and had to hold up at Jalalabad.

"On the second of November, the British diplomatic representative, Sir Alexander Burnes, his brother and another officer were murdered and their compound set on fire. Soon the whole garrison was surrounded and cut off from their supplies which were a quarter mile outside their lines. There were several little forays out to drive off the Afghans but to no effect.

"Sales, at the time, was in Gandamak. He was five days away and unable to return because of the thousands of Ghilzais in between. Another column was at Kandahar 300 miles away and a relief expedition, if they could get through the passes, would be five weeks coming.

"By the 11th o f December, Macnaghton's position was hopeless, with two days of rations remaining, he negotiated with the forces of Akbar Khan. The deal was the British leave Afghanistan forever and in exchange Macnaghton was to get safe passage to India and rations. They were to leave on the 15th, but Macnaghton was too clever for himself. He stalled while trying to get the different Afghan groups to work against each other, hopefully to his advantage. Akbar was not to be toyed with and on a meeting on the 23rd of December, Macnaghton was murdered and all deals were off.

"On Christmas Day, Akbar offered to let Elphinstone take out the garrison with safe conduct if he left behind almost all his artillery, the military treasury and all families. Elphinstone knew he'd have to fight his way out, so on 6 January, 1842, he moved out. He abandoned the sick and wounded and with 690 British soldiers, 3,800 native soldiers, 36 British women and children and 12,000 camp followers, he started for India.

"The fighting started from the first. They fought not only hostile Ghilzais, but sub-zero temperatures and snow. By the 10th, there were only 240 Europeans, a handful of sepoys and 3,000 camp followers. On the 11th, Akbar invited Elphinstone to discuss how to enforce a safe passage. Instead, he took the General prisoner. On the 13th, the last 20 men of the 44th, the final survivors, made a stand near Gandamak, where they fought with sword and bayonet, until overwhelmed. The one survivor of the march was a Dr Boydon, a regimental surgeon, who alone, made it to Jalalabad.

"Now, here's the part you don't know. On the 8th, LT Sturt, my great uncle, was killed during one of these skirmishes and on the 9th, his wife and son, along with Lady Sale and a number of others, including Elphinstone, became prisoners of Akbar. Before he died of his wounds, LT Sturt gave his wife a map that he had been given by a friendly Afghan a few months before the siege. While the map was of the area near Jamrud, all of its inscriptions were in Latin and Greek. It meant nothing to the Afghan merchant, but LT Sturt recognized it for what it was, a map drawn by a Jesuit Monk named Benedict Goes.

"Benedict had been a Portuguese soldier in the 16th century," continued my friend. "In 1584, he became a brother of the Jesuit order in India. At the request of the Emperor Akbar in 1595 he and two others travelled to Lahore where they became fluent in Persian and learned the ways of the Saracen.

"In late 1602, he was selected to make an overland trip from India to China, at the time, no one was sure if Cathay and China were in the same place and Benedict was chosen to find out. Another Jesuit had been progressing from the China coast toward Peking, but it would take 15 years for Matteo Ricci to be allowed to reach there in 1598.

"With the blessings and financial support of Akbar, Benedict started his journey disguised as an Armenian merchant. He went from Agra to Lahore and the on to Kabul with a priest and a Greek merchant named Demetrios. The priest stayed in Kabul as did Demetrios. Benedict, calling himself Abdullah, hired a real Armenian merchant in Lahore named Isaac. Isaac would stay with Benedict all the way to China.

"While in Kabul Benedict met a lady named "Agahanem". Her brother was the ruler of Kashgaria and her son the ruler of Hotan. On her way back from a pilgrimage to Mecca, she ran out of money. Benedict befriended her and supplied the funds for her to return to her homeland. Benedict and Isaac travelled through the Hindu Kush and Northern Afghanistan and by

November of 1603, they had reached Yarkand where Demetrios caught up with them. Here they stayed for a year, gathering jade for the great caravan to Cathay.

"During this time, Benedict travelled to Hotan where the Queen Mother repaid him many times over, both in jade and precious gems. Now Benedict made a decision of great consequence. He needed the jade for his impersonation to proceed, but the casket of rubies and diamonds he did not want to risk on the trip. The treasure would do wonders for the Jesuit teaching mission and should be returned to India.

"Demetrios was assigned to start the journey back to Agra. So they parted, Demetrios to return to India and Benedict and Isaac on to Cathay. Benedict made it to China, but never to Peking, dying in Suzhou while waiting permission to continue. Isaac made it all the way to Peking, having been rescued by another Jesuit Brother, Giovanni Fernandes and taken to Ricci. Isaac returned to India by sea, but nothing more was ever seen of Demetrios. Until LT. Sturt received that map, it was thought that Demetrios had either absconded with the treasure or was killed along the way. He was killed, by Ghilzais, but not before he hid the treasure. It's this map that Enderby wants and he's not sure that I have."

"What an astounding tale," I said. "And you have this map?"

"Yes," he smiled and sat back in the chair.

"You've never actually looked for the treasure?"

"No. Never had a real chance but with the 5th moving up to Jamrud, I expect to get it."

"Best of luck," I laughed. "I expect it's long gone. Taken by the same Ghilzais who killed Demetrios and took the map."

"Think that if you want, as for me, I intend to find it."

With that, we were off to bed for a few hours sleep before arriving in Bombay. I had no idea that the treasure would overshadow my whole life.

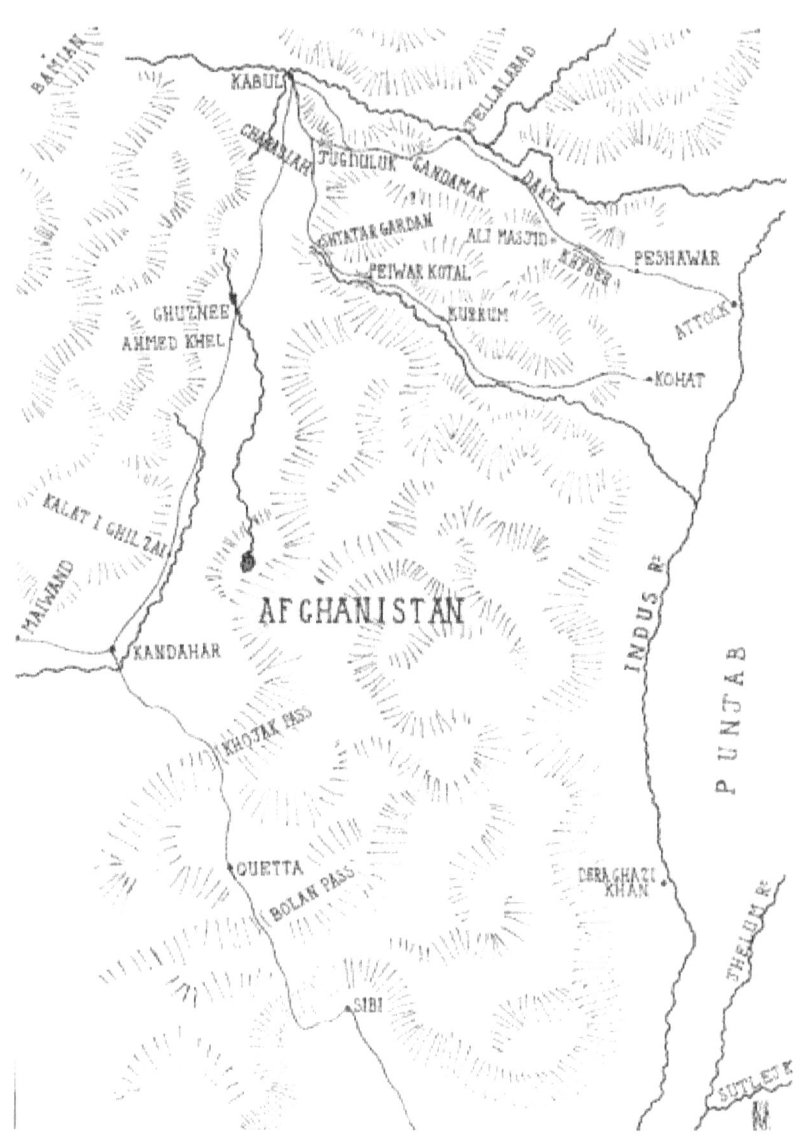
BAMIAN
KABUL
JELLALABAD
CHARASIAH
TUGHULUK
GANDAMAK
DAKKA
SHUTAR GARDAN
ALI MASJID
KHYBER
PESHAWAR
PEIWAR KOTAL
KURRUM
ATTOCK
GHUZNEE
AHMED KHEL
KOHAT
KALAT I GHILZAI
MAIWAND
AFGHANISTAN
KANDAHAR
INDUS R.
PUNJAB
KHOJAK PASS
QUETTA
BOLAN PASS
DERA GHAZI KHAN
JHELUM R.
SIBI
SUTLEJ R.

Chapter 5
India

Bombay was an amazing place. The sights, sounds, even the smells were something I had never experienced. And how fortunate I was, for not only did I have Sturt, I was met by the man who would later save my life, Private Liam Murray.

Murray was about 5'10, slender, with red hair, sunburned skin, piercing blue eyes and a military moustache. "Private Murray, Sir. Been sent to help you get to the regiment. I have arranged for quarters for you until the coastal steamer leaves on Monday, and General Watson asked if you would join him tonight at his quarters. He's leaving in the morning."

So it was that with the able assistance of Private Murray, Sturt and I dropped our kit at our quarters and went to meet my father's cousin. He's a magnificent fellow. He was in his fifties then and a more active man you never met.

Cousin John was staying at, of all places, the Watson Hotel. A beautiful five story hotel with an atrium and ballroom, the finest service by English waitresses and an excellent bar. The finest hotel in Bombay, it was built in England of cast iron and shipped to India one piece at a time. Murray left us to our own devices on the steps of the Watson, saying he would collect us on the morrow to see to improvements to our kit. With that, he was off, to a native pub, I imagine.

Cousin John was most amiable, asking questions of father and my brother and treating us to dinner and drinks. It was after dinner that he called one of the waitresses over.

"Sally, bring out that box I left with you, eh girl?"

Going to the pantry, she returned in a moment.

"Here you are, Sir."

"Good Girl, now bring another round, will you?"

"Here my boy is a little something for you. All the officers are having them made. Very helpful on campaign, called a Browne Belt. Old Sam Brown developed it, much better than issue equipment. Lost his left arm you see in the mutiny. Sabre kept banging around so he came up with this system, quite a good show.

"I see the 5th is up on the Khyber, you should see some action, but I hope you aren't kept too busy doctor." He smiled.

"Tell me, Sir. How bad is it in Afghanistan?" I asked.

"Oh, we'll pull through to Kabul. Their problem is the tribes can never unify. Each will change sides depending on the last battle. Remember that. None of these Afghans are to be trusted."

And with that small bit of advice, the evening closed. Cousin John was off in the morning and Sturt and I were back to our hotel and for two busy days occupied our time seeing what we could of Bombay and collecting additional equipment.

On the morning following my meeting with Cousin John, I discovered that Murray had taken my whites to be dyed khaki by a local merchant with the promise of a return in time for our sailing on the 9th.

So three days after arriving in Bombay, Sturt, Murray and I sailed on the British India steamer, Vingorla, for Karachi. It was a three day trip at about 8 knots. The Vingorla carried salon passengers and cargo along with deck passengers. She relied on steam and sail and her captain, J W Stuart was a young man who ran a taught ship.

While sitting in the salon on the second night, Sturt talked to me about his revelation of the treasure. As we sat smoking our cigars, I asked where his ancestor had actually come upon the map he now held.

"You may know that there is a small Armenian Catholic community in Afghanistan. In both Lahore and in Kabul, they have their own churches. The Jesuits in India had been in touch with them even in the time of Benedict, although they came under the authority of the Armenian Apostolic Church in Esfahan. They were mostly merchants but in Lahore they were fine gun makers. In 1755, the gun makers were forcibly moved from Lahore to Kabul and it is thought the map, along with their other church treasures, came with them. About 1830 these people were abandoned by the Armenian Church and no more priests were sent. The Armenians did the best they could, but many of their books and documents could not be read as they only spoke Persian and possessed papers in Greek and Latin as well.

"My ancestor became friendly with these folks in Kabul, many times visiting their church which sits in the shadow of Fort Bala Hissan. It was during one of these visits to the Church that he discovered the map. At first, he thought it only an interesting map of the Khyber area, and he was given the map by the Armenian elder as a gift for his kindness to them and interest in their community. They, of course, unable to read it, had no idea what it represented. And it was only after some months that LT Sturt was able to piece together its meaning. It was shortly after this that he met his end in the retreat. He never had a chance to look for the treasure.

"Amazing" I said. "And will you really look for it?"

"No, Watson. We will look for it! I don't suppose this is a one man job and I can't think of a better partner. What do you say, are you in for an adventure? I've already talked to Arty."

"Of course," I replied, "but where will we find the time? What with the campaign and all, we've no chance."

"Oh, we'll make short work of these Afghans, I've no doubt of that and then we'll have all the time in the world."

So we left it. We were now both Army officers and treasure hunters. First to fight the war and then to find the treasure, what excitement.

We arrived in Karachi the afternoon of 11 December, and disembarked. It was a short wait of only three days in Karachi as there were supply trains leaving almost daily to the north. It was here we met Mr Frederick Dibble, a civil engineer with the railroad who was returning from leave.

Having rested and gathered our kit, Sturt, Murray and I boarded the train that would take us north to Lahore. The train was a sight to behold, pulled by an engine that probably saw it's best days twenty years prior and made up of three coaches and a half dozen freight cars. Sturt, Murray, Dibble and I shared two bench seats in the first car. Every inch of every car was filled with all forms of freight and humanity. Soldiers, merchants, paupers, men, women and children rode in and on the cars as we pulled out of Karachi.

"You Gentlemen are quite fortunate," said Dibble. "We have made great progress on the railroad in the last few months. We will be in Lahore in less than 48 hours where we will rid ourselves of all the natives. From there to Jhelum, the railroad has been commandeered by the Army. It's the railhead at the moment but we're pushing on steadily. Tough going because of the mountains. We hope to be in Peshawar in two years. That is if you boys can keep the natives under control."

"We're going on to Jamrud. How do we continue?" I asked.

"Well, by foot, I'm afraid. It's about 180 miles to Peshawar but the military road is very good. Is that where you're headed?"

"Yes, I'm afraid so," said Sturt. "Gets kind of tough from Peshawar."

"Yes, I suppose, but only 8 miles. Your first real stop will be Rawal Pindi. It's about 68 miles. You'll get a break there. The horse carts are a little rough on the nerves. We have to change trains twice before we even get to Lahore. There are still no bridges over the Sutlej at Adamwahan or the Indus at Sukkur, but we're working on it."

So we passed the next 48 hours by rail and ferry and arriving at Lahore, connected with a troop train for Jhelum. Another day saw us at the great supply depot. Here we were met by LT Thomas Godard of the 5th who had been sent to gather supplies, recruits and horses. It was here my official duties began as I attempted to assemble three horse carts filled with medical supplies from a list given to me by Lt. Godard in response to a request of the Principle Medical Officer (PMO) Dr James Hanbury. With Murray's help and Godard's firm hand, we filled the carts.

We left Jhelum on the 20th, a caravan which included horse carts and camels, foot soldiers and cavalry and a vast assortment of camp followers trying to sell their wares. At the end of the first day, we had made 20 miles. Godard, Sturt and I had been well mounted on native ponies and so the next morning we decided to push on to Rawal Pindi and let the caravans catch up the following day. The medical supplies were left in Murray's capable hands. We arrived at Rawal Pindi to find news that General Browne had taken Jalalabad. True soldiers that they were, Godard and Sturt were both joyous at the news and disappointed not to be in the fight.

"Damn thing will be over before we're in it," complained Godard.

"Lots more to do before we get to Kabul," responded Sturt, "but I don't want to waste time here. Suppose we press on in the morning for Peshawar? We can make it in three days even with the climb."

To this proposal, I resisted. I reminded Godard of his duty to get the 5th supplies forward, and I had no desire to abandon Murray and the medical kits.

Late the next afternoon, the caravans arrived. Godard had made arrangements to secure the 5th's supply carts and I had spent the day in the local infirmary assisting on cases. Most of which were minor.

Early on the 23rd, we pushed on with the caravan toward Peshawar. Somewhere on the road, we celebrated Christmas 1878 and arrived in Peshawar late on the 27th. The following morning we joined the regiment at Jamrud.

Chapter 6
The 5th Northumberland Fusiliers

Our commander was Lieutenant Colonel Rowland. Fine fellow, well bred, who cared greatly for his men. He was the kind of commander who led soldiers, not ordered them into battle without sharing their trials. On the day we met, he had been recently back from an excursion in the Bazar Valley with 300 men. They had met little opposition.

Sturt had taken me to the headquarters directly on arriving in Jamrud and we were passed directly in to see the colonel.

"Lieutenant Sturt, reporting, Sir. Lieutenant Godard is seeing to the delivery of supplies to Commissary O'Rourke and will be along directly. And this is Assistant Surgeon, John Watson, been assigned to us, Sir."

"Good to see you Sturt. We've been a little short on duty officers. Glad to have you back," said Rowland with a smile, "and Dr Watson. I understand you have significant qualifications as a surgeon. I hope we never have need of you, unfortunately, we probably will. Murray taking good care of you?"

"Excellent care, Sir. May I say that I too hope you don't need my skills."

We all laughed and I knew this was a commander one could rely on. He would not just accomplish a mission, he would also see to the needs of his soldiers.

"Well, Doctor," he continued, "We'll let Murray see you over to the infirmary; the Surgeon-Major should be over there. As you know, surgeons and commissary officers are not normally members of the mess, but I think we're all in this together so in the 1st battalion, you're our permanent guest. We'll see you this evening. Murray." he called, "Show Dr Watson to the infirmary, will you? And Sturt, you stay here. I've some things to catch you up on. 'Till tonight, doctor." With that, I was dismissed and Murray and I went to the infirmary.

The infirmary was fairly small, 12 or 15 beds. Murray introduced me to Surgeon-Major Thomas Bennet. Bennet, I knew, had been in the Army since the mutiny and had served in posts across the world. My first impression was a little disappointing. He was short, probably 5'6" and heavy set with drooping eyes and the nose of a drinker. He looked older than his 50 odd years, but his smile was bright and genuine and I could see the orderlies thought the world of him.

"Come in. Come in Doctor," he called cheerily from a tiny closet of an office. "Glad to have you, young man. Always need help we'll have you know. Understand you've had an uneventful trip, most unusual in India to have uneventful trips. But come in, sit down and tell me about your journey."

I thanked him for his welcome and detailed my qualifications to him, which he seemed to take in with interest.

"Horseman?" he asked.

"I like to think I am."

"Good. Good, that will be helpful. Can't ride well myself anymore. Still limp from 20 years ago, stiff leg won't sit in the saddle long and we need to send someone along on some of these little forays they like to go on. Let me see, what do I need to tell you?

"Let's start with the hospital here. Just 15 beds, mostly sickness right now. Large hospital in Peshawar, 50 beds moving up to Jalalabad. Right now we are well off on supplies but our problem is people. We are understrength in orderlies, have no hospital sergeant or writer and the doolie, that is, stretcher bearers aren't much use. We just have to make do and hope for the best. Let's see. What else can I tell you?"

"What is the 5th supposed to be doing?" I asked.

"Ah, well, that's pretty simple. They provide two things. Escort of convoys between Peshawar and Jalalabad and go on little excursions around the area to punish the tribes that don't stay in line. Keeps the poor fellows moving about all the time. Still, that's better than just sitting. Less likely to malinger if they have something to do, you know. And now that the Amir has fled Kabul, with the Russians we won't be here long."

"The Amir has left?"

"Yes, yes, left his son Sadar Yakub Khan in Kabul, as I say, maybe we can make an end of this and get back. But now, let me show you around and you can get settled in."

So I started my official duties with the 5th. The next few weeks were dull indeed. Little happened at our infirmary except the constant coming and going of soldiers with the usual blisters and boils, cuts and scrapes and an occasional fever. It seems that the 5th's long time in India had indeed toughened the men, most of whom were the old 21 year enlistments.

During those weeks it was not unusual for Sutter to come visit me or I him. The boredom of convoy escort was starting to show and Sutter had once again turned his attention to the Jesuit treasure. As we sat one night in my quarters with a bottle of whiskey he took out the map and placed it on the table.

"John, the best I can tell, this village here is Kam Dakka," he said, pointing to the centre of the map. "Now look to the northeast here. It appears to be a trail leading what must be 10 or 12 miles to the base of these foothills and then to a valley, all of which is filled by bloody tribesmen. And here," stabbing with his finger, "are the words 'Confianca Sagzado', which is Portuguese for "Sacred Trust'. That must be where the treasure is."

I took out my ordnance map of the area and laid it beside the treasure map and we spent the next while comparing villages and mountain tops.

"It certainly seems to be Kam Dakkar, I must admit but it's the trail that doesn't seem right. Our map doesn't show it at all after about a mile."

"Probably couldn't take the time to survey in that direction," sighed Sutter. "We'll have to find time to scout out that way if we can ever break free of this damned convoy duty."

"Something else is odd about this map of yours."

"What would that be?"

"In the four corners are crosses, quite understandable, but three are Roman crosses and the fourth is Eastern Orthodox. Curious."

"Well, the Jesuits were Roman Church and I suppose he added the fourth in deference to the Armenians."

"Possible," I replied. "What was that noise?"

"Hello chaps" came a voice as I turned toward the door. It was Godard. "Having a conference?"

"Just looking over some maps of the area, need to know your surroundings," replied Sutter, gathering up his map as I started folding mine.

"Excellent. Just came to get you Sturt. Colonel needs you. We're to go up the Bazar again. You too, Doctor. One ambulance wagon, you and a couple orderlies, and whoever you need in Doolie bearers. Best get the word out. Later." And with that, he turned and was gone.

"How long do you thing he was listening, John?"

"Surely not, he just came with the orders."

"Maybe," he said slowly. "Maybe. Well, off to the old man. Best get your kit."

It was a hurried night. It was my first experience of a military expedition. It seemed that Major Cavagnari, the political officer, felt that good results could be made of a show of force in the valley. The Jamrud column, of which we were a part, was only one of three converging on the Bazar.

What an amazing sight it was. Over 1200 soldiers in a single column. Elephants loaded with artillery, the 5th Fusiliers, the 25th foot, native lancers and infantry and an assortment of bhisti's and doolie bearers and the like.

We left Jamrud early on the 24th. I still had my fine native horse(whom I had named Emmett) and Murray drove a four mule team from the ambulance box. We had one other orderly and four bearers.

The dust was the worst of it. The slow moving column must have been visible for miles by the dust cloud, and at the end of the day it lay heavy on and in everything. As we camped for the night, cook fires were lighted and picquets were sent out. All through that first night, and during the entire rest of the expedition, you could hear the picquets exchanging fire with the Afghans. Fortunately, the first few nights saw no work for my little section.

On the 26th of January, we met with a column from Ali Masjid, adding another 1200 soldiers. On the next day, in the Bazar Valley Plain, we camped with yet another thousand men from the Basawal Column. That night Sutter found time to stop by for a pipe. By now, I was treating cuts and bangs and blisters but nothing of significance, so we had time to sit and contemplate the massive force camped before us.

"When you look at a sight like this, you can't contemplate failure, can you?" mused Sutter.

"No, I suppose not. But what a queer question?"

"Oh, we'll win this little war, no doubt, but in the long run, I think the natives will have it all their own way. We can't stay here forever and once we're gone, well, it's back to the usual for them. Anyway, still no time for our little adventure, eh?"

"No," I replied. "But we'll get there."

For a long time that night we just sat and smoked. The next few days were filled with movement. The Zakha Khal Afridis were definitely hostile. We were fired on constantly from the hillsides but never would they come forward for a fight. They also burned their own villages prior to our arrival. It was a bad sight as we had received direct orders not to molest any of the villages. By the 3rd of February, we were on our return to Jamrud having punished the Afridis at a cost of about a dozen wounded to us. So ended my first experience on the active march.

The next few weeks were the usual dull routine. That is, until the visit of the Commander In Chief for India, Sir F.P. Haines. We had but a day's notice of his visit which would include a parade of the entire 2nd Division and an inspection of our medical facility. His trip onward from Jamrud as far as the Shahqai was protected by the 5th with a soldier on every hill.

Sir Haines' visit to our hospital was memorable in several ways. Firstly, he was well pleased with our facility, but it was who came with him, who would impact me more. As I stood awaiting Sir Haines' arrival, in walked Colonel Enderby. He appeared not surprised at all, and to his side, walked Lt. Godard.

"I see you've made yourself at home, Doctor." Smiled the Colonel. A smile of pure malevolence. "Hope you enjoy these backwaters, Watson. Could have gotten you on staff you know. Need to be more prudent how you pick your battles. Well, seen all I need to Godard. Let's move on. Good Day, Doctor."

My mouth was open as they left. But that wasn't my only surprise. LT McMullen appeared the moment they left.

"Don't let the old bastard get to you, John. He's as big an ass as ever. Doesn't mind sending other people on forlorn hopes! Well close your mouth and offer me some medicinal brandy, eh?"

“Arthur, good fellow, of course, of course! What are you doing here?”

“Oh, escort with the Commander. We’ve a squadron of the 18th at Peshawar and I’ve got a detachment with me. All pomp and show, you know. Have a detachment from nearly every cavalry and lancer regiment around traveling with the entourage. So, how have you been?”

We spent the next few moments in pleasant conversation when Arty had to leave for Ali Masjid with his detail. It was good to know there was another friend in the area.

That night Sutter and I met as usual at the mess and taking a small corner table, started discussing the surprises of the day.

“Not a shot fired from Jamrud to Ali Masjid today. They say Sir Haines was impressed. That’s good, I suppose. Saw Arty, said he talked with you at the hospital, but he wanted to pass something on to us. He said, watch out for Godard. Evidently, Godard has been down to see Enderby on at least two occasions. They’re way too chummy. Arty just has a feeling about things.”

“Have you been able to do any scouting?” I asked.

“Not much, being so far off the road, it’s not really in our bailiwick. Hard to justify the risk, you know. Been about 3 miles along the trail. It’s definitely there beyond what the survey crew put down. We’ll get a chance at it, I’m sure.”

It would take another two months but circumstances would lead us to Dakka and give us a chance to continue the search.

As the warmer weather of March started, so sickness began to take its toll. The constant convoy duty and work parties were starting to wear on the men of the 5th. It was now not uncommon to have 10 to 15 in hospital at one time. Cholera would be our constant companion. Even with my special knowledge, many would not be saved and it has always worn on me. Somehow, I should have saved them. In all, that year, we lost 2 sergeants and 35 rank and file, heart-breaking.

Around about the 1st of March, we got the news of Sher Ali’s death the month prior. Surely we could negotiate with his successor Yakub Khan. Of course, as it turned out, we could not. The fighting would continue, and soon.

Chapter 7
My First Combat

I sat writing reports on the afternoon of the 23rd when Murray came in with word to pack up the ambulance wagon and be ready to march that night. I left Murray and the doolie bearers to get our equipment ready and went in search of information.

At the headquarters, I found Surgeon-Major Bennett in conference with Major Tucker, our second in command.

"Watson," cried Bennett. "Over here. Seems you're going to a little tussle down the road. Nothing you can't handle. The Major here assures me you'll be back in a couple of days. Don't enjoy yourself too much." Bennett smiled and Tucker looked irritated. I knew there was something else and on Bennett's leaving for the mess and another whiskey, Tucker took me over to the wall map.

"Look here, Doctor," he said pointing to a point to our west. "This is where you're going. Deh-Sarakh is a plains area near our fort in Pesh-Bolak. Seems a Jemadar, that is, a native lieutenant, was leading a foraging part out there when he was jumped by about 300 Afridis. He did a fine job though, camels to the rear, retired in good order to Pesh-Bolak. Now the political officers say we need to go punish the natives. Sir Sam Browne is sending a force under Brigadier Tyler to punish the blighters. The 5th has been tasked for 150 bayonets. You're going along to patch the boys up. Don't suspect it'll amount to much though. Better you than that drunk you call Surgeon-Major! Anyway, be ready by midnight."

With that bit of information, I was off to see that Murray had the requisite supplies, when I was stopped by a call from behind.

"Dr Watson!" came the shout.

Turning, I found Sutter trotting toward me on his bay. Before he even reached me, he had leaped from his horse and ran toward me. Throwing his arm around my shoulder, he whispered in my ear, "I found it! By God, I found it!" He was shaking with excitement.

"The treasure?" I blurted out.

"Quiet, quiet," he admonished. "Well no, but a Roman cross about 3 ½ miles up the trail. Plain as day, chiselled on a rock on the side of the trail, it must mean I'm on the right track. It must! Grab your kit and we'll go back and look."

"But I can't," I moaned. "We're off on an expedition tonight. I can't leave."

The disappointment showed in his face.

"Lt. Sturt," came a voice, it was Sgt Ryan. "The Colonel is looking for you. Moving out tonight, Sir. You're to report immediately."

"Damn and bother! Alright, Sergeant, on the way. Doctor, not a word."

"Sutter, you know I won't," I complained.

"I know, must report. See you later." And with that, he was off to headquarters.

The next I saw Sturt was about one in the morning as the column started for the Deh-Sarakh plains. It was a fairly formidable force, or so I thought, of 500 bayonets, 150 lances and two cannons.

As we moved toward Pesh-Bolak in the darkness, our little ambulance choked on the dust of the column. Being mounted, I was able to, now and then, move to the upwind side of the column and avoid some of the dust. I also took the privilege of moving up the column to ride with Sturt at the head of his two companies from the 5th.

"You know, Sutter, just a cross on a rock doesn't mean you're on the right track," I said, riding up alongside him.

"John, it must!" he looked around to see that no one was close. "I have it figured out now that I've seen the cross. Remember the four corners of the map? Those Roman crosses and a Byzantine. It must mean follow those three to the one!" His face was flush with excitement.

"Yes, well, it's possible," I contemplated. "But that's an awful long stretch. That one cross may mean nothing. Quiet! Godard!"

I had noticed Godard coming up on our left out of the corner of my eye.

"Conspiring, are we?" he smirked.

"Sturt was just explaining our mission. Quite interesting. Hope the politicos are right and there won't be much action."

"Can't get promoted if there isn't any action, eh Sturt?"

"Can't take casualties if the enemy doesn't fight and that's fine with me," replied Sturt. "Best get back to your company, Godard, I can see Pesh-Bolak up in the distance." With that, Godard reigned up and turned back.

"Best do the same, John. Sun's coming up and we'll get busy. And trust no one!" he called as I turned my horse back to the ambulance.

As I turned, I could see the 11th and 13th Bengal Lancers picking up the pace and leaving the infantry and guns behind. No matter Sturt's wishes, it looked like there would be action.

We continued past Pesh-Bolak and by mid morning were into the Deh-Sarakh Plain. I was riding alongside the ambulance when Murray suddenly stood, reigns in hand, squinting into the distance.

"What is it?"

"I can hear rifle fire, Sir. It's up ahead to the south."

I now realized that besides the creaking harness and the grinding of the iron tires, there was indeed the distant pop of carbines and muskets. The column had also sprung to life. The infantry was suddenly moving at the double quick and the artillery had moved to the left of the column and was sprinting ahead.

"Stay with the 5th!" I called to Murray and spurring my horse, rode for the front. I crested a large hill the same time as the infantry and came upon Brigadier Tyler and his staff. To their front, dismounted lancers were returning fire to both a small village to our left and to the fort of Mausam about 750 yards to our front.

Sturt arrived just then with his two companies of the 5th, along with a lieutenant from the 17th Foot who also had two companies. BrigadierTyler ordered the 5th to relieve the 13th Lancers who were fighting on foot, the 17th and the two half companies of Indian troops stood in reserve.

The fortified village stood on the high ground of Safed Koh. To our right was a deep nala or drainage ditch and on the left, another. The walls of the fort and the towers were filled with Shinwaris. They had also poured out of the gate and filled the nala. Even I could tell we were greatly outnumbered.

The guns of the Royal Artillery were being unlimbered as the 11th Bengal Lancers returned from an abortive attack on the east nala. I watched the 13th remount and fall back, replaced by the men of the 5th. The 13th rode out of sight to the southwest.

The Royal Artillery guns opened fire on Mausam. Their fire was both accurate and devastating. Round after round crashed into the fort and the tower, tearing gaping holes in the walls and sending bodies to be buried under the rubble. But most impressive of all were the artillerymen themselves. Rifle fire from the nearby village of Darwazai constantly rained upon them, striking dirt and boxes and occasionally an animal or piece of equipment, yet the gunners calmly went about their duties. Their officers stood in full view, giving corrections for the firing of each shell. Truly a wonder to watch.

Murray had arrived with the ambulance and I instructed him to keep with me. The Shinwaris were now abandoning the fort, not able to withstand the cannon fire. The infantry, in mass, was now ordered to advance and our little ambulance followed at a distance of about 200 yards. Rifle fire now spit all around us as the few Afghans left in Mausam had their fire increased by the men in the west nala who could now fire on the infantry.

Springing from the earth behind the west nala appeared the 13th Lancers. Captain Thompson and his 60 men seized their chance. With 800 rifles concentrating on the infantry advance, he boldly ordered his men to charge. Completely surprised by the attack, the Afghans got off a single volley, unhorsing nine, but the surprise was so complete all resistance ceased and flight became the natural instinct. The Lancers pursued them into the foothills, killing 50, the Shinwaris did not stop until they were on the hills a mile distant.

As our infantry poured into Mausam there only remained a single Afghan locked in a tower, sniping as best he could and holding the entire column at bay. Anyone who showed his face was liable to be shot at. No one could get near the tower. As the rest of the infantry went about the business of destroying the other towers, Sturt tried to decide how to take this single man. He finally did it by climbing another tower and in an exchange of fire, killed the last defender.

Murray and I were exceedingly busy. While there were no casualties in the 5th, there were two dead Sowars and a dozen wounded. I, being the only doctor, treated each as quickly as possible. Fortunately, all the wounded but two were fairly minor. So as the infantry set about blowing up the towers, Murray and I patched and sewed and moved on to those of our enemy too wounded to be carried away by their comrades. Here I learned another lesson of war, for as I was about to amputate a leg, the call came to form up. We were retiring and the Afghan wounded would be left to their own. I couldn't take them, the ambulance was full of dead and wounded Sowars, and I couldn't stay. I left behind at least two dozen men that I knew native medicine wouldn't save.

As our little ambulance drove past the village of Darwazai, the village that had fired on us, I saw the Indian sepoys move hut to hut, burning the village to the ground and destroying the towers.

"Sir," it was Murray. "In the road there," he pointed to what I first took for a pile of rags. "I think that woman is wounded."

I jumped down from my horse and approaching, found a young Shinwari woman. She was unconscious and having obviously been caught in the crossfire, had been wounded in the shoulder. It was not a bad wound but the shock and loss of blood had done their work.

"Hold up, Murray. Let's find some room in that wagon."

Picking her up, I placed her on the wagon and handing the reigns of my horse to a doolie bearer, climbed in.

"Keep moving," I instructed. "We can't fall behind."

The moment the columns had blown the towers and evacuated Mausam, the Shinwari had swarmed back in. They were on our heels as we left Darwazai in flames and started to fill the hillsides. By now, tribesman from the whole area were assembling, perhaps 3,000 fighters now trailed our force of 700.

As we moved along, I cut the cloth from the woman's shoulder. She was lucky; the bullet had gone all the way through, leaving a clean wound. Antiseptic and bandage was the best I could do as the springless wagon continued to move. Leaving the wounded in the ambulance, I reclaimed my horse and went in search of Sutter, finding him on the left of the column.

"What the hell are we into?" I asked.

"We're alright," he replied. Suddenly, the cannons cracked and shell landed just 500 yards to our rear, scattering a large group of Shinwaris.

Coming back up from a crouch, I called to Sturt, "You're sure?"

"Yes" He laughed. "We've got Lancers caring for the flanks and we are retiring by alternating lines. The guns will help them stay back."

"Hope you're right!"

"I am, not to worry. And by the way," he said looking around, "don't flinch in front of the men. Bad form, old boy, gets them concerned."

So we continued for the next ten miles. There were 3,000 tribesmen ebbing and flowing against our flanks and rear, sometimes coming within 100 yards of our line. It was not until we reached the walls of Pesh-Bolak that they retired. We heard the next day that they had lost 160 dead and 300 wounded. But I again had learned a valuable lesson. Had the Shinwaris been well armed instead of using 300 year old matchlocks, or had the different villages and tribes been able to coordinate and form a coherent command, our little expedition would not have ended so well.

Chapter 8
Fight at Kam Dakka

It was at Pesh-Bolak that I made the decision that I must find a way to provide medical treatment to the Afghans. Following a day of rest under the walls of the fort, I saw noticeable improvement in my native patient, but I could not get her to speak. As I cleaned her wound, she would only stare in another direction, never looking at me or answering the smiles with which I tried to reassure her.

My first problem was that as a woman, she had to be kept segregated from the sowars. None of them would remain in the same room with her and would rather forego treatment than have their bodies exposed in any way to her.

My second problem was the language barrier. She spoke only Dari. I, of course, had picked up a few phrases, but nothing useful in such a situation. Fortunately there was a native orderly named Guhkta with the 27th Punjab Infantry who was in the little infirmary who could speak her language.

Guhkta had been a hospital assistant in the Indian Army back to before the mutiny. He was a kind fellow, always a smile, nothing too hard for him to accomplish. Between him and Murray, there quickly became a bond, both professional and personal. I think that for a few months, they became like the brothers that neither had.

On the second day of our stay at Pesh-Bolak, it was Guhkta who got our little patient to speak. Her name was Malalai. She was about 19 years old. She was not a native of the Darawazai village where we found her. Only the night before our attack, she had been traded by her father for a debt owed of nine goats.

"Traded for nine goats?" I exclaimed, standing with Guhkta at her cot. "Who the devil trades people for goats?"

"You do not understand, Sahib, this is most common," said Guhkta. "Women are traded among the hill tribes all the time in payment of debts. Sometimes, if one man should kill another, he will give his daughter or sister to the other family in payment. It ties the families together, or so it is supposed. Most times it ends in the death of the girl in a short time."

Guhkta spoke to the girl again and then turned back to me.

"She wants to know if she will die. I told her no, she will live, thanks to the English Doctor."

"Yes, she'll pull through all right. We can leave her here when we return to Jamrud tomorrow."

Guhkta translated my statement to the girl. She looked at me with such a sad face. She actually was quite beautiful. About five foot tall and if she weighed 100 pounds, I'd have been surprised. Dark skin, coal black hair and eyes. The kind of eyes that spoke. She spoke to Guhkta.

"She cannot be left here Sahib, she knows no one and if you send her back, she will be stoned to death for going off with the English devils. She wants to go with you."

"Bloody hell, she can't come with us. It's a military column, tell her."

"She will not listen, Sahib, and if you leave her she will kill herself rather than be stoned."

"Damndest country I ever saw. Alright, I'll do this much. I'll keep her in the ambulance as a patient until we get to Jamrud, but then she's on her own. Make sure she understands." And with those words, I turned and left.

The following morning we left Pesh-Bolak on our way to Jamrud. The sole occupant of our little ambulance was Malalai as we left the sowars in hospital. On our short journey, I wondered how I could explain my new ward to Bennett. Morning and night, I changed her bandage and we started the game of learning to speak to each other. With the help of Guhkta, I was learning to communicate and so we pointed and spoke and smiled. I became her tutor and she mine. An attachment had begun. I went to Bennett that first day back and explained what I wanted to do, start a treatment centre for locals. To my surprise, he was very receptive to the idea.

"I've thought the same for a long time, Watson. There are three of us here and we aren't all that busy. You know, of course, that Fort Dakka has already started a clinic, regular hospital there, so they have what they need."

"Perhaps I can go see what they're doing? It would give me an idea for a starting place. We'll need supplies and native speakers and who knows what."

"I'm sure that won't be a problem. Our boys travel the road every day on convoy duty. Why don't you just go with the next convoy? I'm sure I can get it cleared with Rowland."

"Well, I do have a bit of a problem I have to take care of, if I can explain."

"Whiskey?" said Bennett, offering a glass.

"No, not before morning brunch, thanks." The frustration in my voice must have showed for he put down the glass and sat back in his chair.

"And the problem is?"

I explained how I had found Malalai at the roadside in Darawazai, treated her wounds and brought her back to Jamrud.

"Yes, I see. Is she now able to leave?"

"She will be in a day or two, but who will take care of her wounds? She needs care for a couple weeks to be sure that it heals properly."

"Like her, don't you."

"No, no, it's just a case of common decency." I blustered. "I can't save her life and turn her out to die. It would be heartless. If she'd been a dog, I'd have shot her. But she's not a dog, she's a human being. Surely we can help."

Bennett smiled and looked at his glass. I could feel the heat in my face that must have shown and realized that I did like the girl. I felt sorry for her, but I liked her too.

"Let's do this, old man. She can rest until the wound is healed. Then, if you get this clinic up and running, we'll need some females to help. You can put her to work, fair enough?"

"Quite a good idea, Sir. I'll start looking for an area in the village to put the clinic. Just outside the gate would be best."

"Go ahead and look, but we need to wait for permission. Not only Rowland, but the Fort Commander will have to approve. I'll let you know."

Here the usual bureaucracy took control. It was nearly a week before Bennett informed me of the command's conditional approval. In the meantime, I had located a building not far from the gate and near an open square. My young patient was doing well also. Each day I found myself spending more and more time with her, trying to teach the phrases I knew she would need to know. Murray and Guhkta would help me teach and Malalai was a quick learner. To tell the truth, it was good to have a project other than normal rounds.

The conditional approval came with a caveat. I must supply a requisition document which included not only number of personnel to be used in what capacity, but what stores would be used and a cost for hiring native help.

To get this kind of data, I knew I had to travel to Dakka and get the advice of those currently running the native clinic. So in late April, I went to find Sturt and ask about convoys to Dakka. I had seen little of him since I had started the new project.

Finding Sturt's quarters empty, I found his orderly who informed me that he and two sepoys from the 27th had gone on a mission to gather information on the Mohmand tribe north of the Kabul River.

At the headquarters, Major Tucker informed me that Lieutenant Godard would be taking his company on convoy duty the following day to Dakka. I received permission to accompany the convoy. And so on the 19th, Murray, I and two doolie bearers found ourselves, once again at the tail end of a convoy ingesting huge quantities of dust.

Except for some intermittent and ineffective sniping from the hillsides, the company passed in relative calm. Telegraph wire had been strung the entire distance and we passed wire parties all along the way, repairing the breaks that were caused daily by the Afghans.

Arriving in Dakka late that evening, Murray saw to bedding down the mules and the bearers. I went in search of the hospital where I was well received by my fellow doctors.

Leaving a tour and discussion of the native clinic to the morrow, we retired to the mess and spent an hour or two. I'm afraid I don't recall the names of the doctors who were there. At any rate, the following day, Murray and I were treated to a tour of the hospital facility and the Afghan clinic. While I asked questions, Murray kept notes for me. The clinic was seeing upwards of 150 civilians a day now. Surely an impressive number and I only hoped our new clinic would not be quite so popular.

Our fact finding done, I found that the 5th would not be returning to Jamrud until the 23rd and so though other units would be headed back earlier, I decided to take the opportunity to spend a few days at the hospital. As it turned out, this was a most fortuitous decision.

Early the next day, I sent a wire to Jamrud asking if Sturt had returned. I had reason to be concerned. I knew that Sturt must have volunteered for his reconnaissance. It would give him the excuse he was looking for to penetrate deeper up the trail toward the treasure.

The Political Officer, Captain Trotter, had assured all that the Mohmands were not going to be a problem on the south side of the Kabul River, but the conventional thinking had been that they were massing on the north side for a foray. It was this information that Sturt had been sent to assess.

My concern had been raised that morning by Colonel Barnes' decision to take two guns of the Royal Artillery, a squadron of his own 10th Bengal Lancers and 3 companies of the Mhairwara Infantry on a reconnaissance in force toward Kam Dakka, about 7 miles distant, down by the Kabul River. Such a forcible recon meant Barnes was concerned about the Mohmands.

A reply to my wire came stating that Sturt had not returned and that he was twelve hours overdue. I went to find Godard.

"Nothing we can do, old man. We have our orders and besides, where would I look for him? If the Colonel wants to send us looking for him, fine. But you and I both know that won't happen. Too early anyway. He'll show up, rest assured." And with those words, Godard dismissed the thought of looking for my friend. He was right, of course. Three men stood a far better chance of going unseen and surviving than a whole company. The company would have been swallowed up and annihilated by thousands of tribesmen.

About three in the afternoon, my concerns were somewhat relieved with the return of Colonel Barnes. Having left his guns and cavalry after only four miles, he had gone on to Kam Dakka with his infantry. The guns were left behind because they were unable to traverse the goat trail that led through the hills of Kam Dakka Pass. The cavalry was left to support the guns as it was hard going for anything but infantry.

Arriving at Kam Dakka, a village that had proffered loyalty to the Crown, Barnes was welcomed by the village elders and asked by them to stay and help provide protection for the village. Unable to stay, Barnes returned to Dakka, but with the feeling of having abandoned his allies. That afternoon Barnes put together a mule train back at Dakka and by five o'clock, Captain Creagh of the 10th Mhairwara was leading a column of two companies with extra ammunition, rations and entrenching tools back to Kam Dakka. Colonel Barnes was fairly confident there would be little trouble but did not like the thought of leaving a friendly village unprotected. During the whole day's march, he had only been fired on a few times and then only from the north side of the river.

There was still no word from Sutter. Later that night, as Murray and I stood and talked outside the hospital, we watched a Jemadar and his platoon escorting a number of mules loaded with more ammunition boxes start toward Kam Dakka.

"You can never have enough ammunition, Sir," said Murray. "At least all those fellows use the same type."

"The same type?" I asked.

"Yes, all those short rifles they carry use .577 ammo. Our boys have Martinis. Different ammo. Can't share in a pinch, you see?"

"Hadn't really thought about it. It should all be the same, shouldn't it?" I mused.

"It's all left over from the mutiny, Sir. Always keep the native troops one piece of equipment behind. Keep the edge. Just in case, you see?"

"Yes, always that lurking fear, eh?"

"Yes, Sir. It's why the native artillery doesn't get anything but the little mountain cannon. Royal Artillery and Royal Horse keep the big stuff. We're all on the same side though, maybe!" Murray chuckled. "Night, Sir. See you in the morning."

Murray had given me much to think about that night.

We were at breakfast the following morning when a message arrived from Creagh for Colonel Barnes. Turning to the Political Officer, Barnes asked, "What the hell is going on with your tribesmen, Trotter?"

"Sir?"

"Message from Creagh. 'Elders refuse us entry into Kam Dakka Village. Want us to leave as we have no cannon. Have set up defensive position. Send instructions.' Well what now?"

"I don't understand, Sir. Perhaps if I went there and talked to the elders myself."

"Right, see the Major for an escort and tell Creagh to bring those two companies back if they don't want help."

Godard leaned over the table toward me. "That's the hell of this country. People always changing sides, never know who your friends are," he whispered.

The way Godard looked at me, I wasn't sure if he was talking about the natives or using it as a chance to suggest something else.

"Some of us know who our friends are," I replied.

Godard looked steadily at me. "I wonder, old boy. I wonder."

It was about an hour and half later that I saw a scramble going on in Godard's company. Water bottles being filled, packs strapped, weapons checked.

"Murray!" I called. "Go see what's happening over there."

He returned quickly. "Things have gone badly for Capt. Creagh, Sir. He's sent for help and LT Godard's company is going. Moving out in 30 minutes."

"Well if it's to be a fight, they'll need us. Grab four of the doolies and two of our mules. See if the commissary officer has any pack saddles, we can't take the ambulance. I'll get the supplies."

Thirty minutes later, we were on the road. A second runner had come in from Creagh. Mohmands were crossing the river. Falling back to Dakka was not an option for it would require his little force to fight in a running battle they could not win. He was looking for a defensible position and going to hold on awaiting help.

Hopefully, our little force would be able to extricate Creagh. We were but one company of the "Fighting 5th", one company of Mhairwara infantry and a squadron of the 10th Bengal Cavalry. Capt. Strong of the 10th was in command and Capt. Trotter, the Political Officer, accompanied us. He would be trying to figure out why the Mohmands had crossed the river and then trying to explain it to Colonel Barnes.

The goat path through the Kam Dakka Pass was indeed difficult and treacherous. It took hours of climbing and the mules, sure footed as they are, were having great difficulty. The infantry was being held up by the need to keep the column together.

The order finally came back to the cavalry and packs that the infantry was pressing on and they were to come up as soon as they could. We were getting near Kam Dakka.

"Murray," I called. "Grab a medical bag. We're going with the 5th. Have the doolies bring the mules on."

Murray and I, each loaded with bags of medical supplies scrambled after the infantry, trying to close the gap from where we were in the rear of the column to the front. We passed through the Mhairwara and as we caught the coat tails of the 5th, I could hear firing to our front.

We stopped, looking down toward the river. To our left was the river and next to it what appeared to be a small graveyard and in it about one hundred and fifty soldiers of the Mhairwara fighting for their lives. On the plain to the front and the hills surrounding were thousands of Mohmands. The firing from within the graveyard was intermittent. It was now three in the afternoon and surely their ammunition was running low.

The few soldiers in khaki in the graveyard, many with bandages visible, were in stark contrast to the turbaned natives in many colours with their red and white banners, pressing within a few yards of the miserable stone wall of protection.

Capt. Strong took all this in in a moment. "Godard, get your company ready to move. We're going in." Turning to the Mhairwara commander, he ordered them to cover the 5th from the hillside and protect their flanks as they advanced. Sending a runner back to LT. Pollack with the cavalry squadron, he ordered them up as quickly as possible. "Tell them to pitch in for the graveyard when he gets here," he told the runner.

Seeing me, Strong came over. "Doctor, best if you stay here with the Mhairwara Company."

"No, Sir, I'm with the 5th."

"Good for you, Doctor. Godard, you ready?"

"Yes, Sir. On your order."

"Right then, all those turbaned bastards are looking at the graveyard. We're going right down the trail. It's sunken and will keep us partially hidden. When we hit the plain, I want to break straight through. No stopping. Understand?"

"Yes, Sir," replied Godard.

I could see Godard was in his element.

"Doctor, I want you in the middle of the company. Stay with the pack, no matter what happens."

In a moment we were off. We moved as quickly as we could down through the rocky trail. I realized that even with all the noise of battle below that the noise of a company on the move was suddenly deafening. Even the click of rifle slings sounded like gunshots. Would the noise give us away before we reached our goal?

When we reached the bottom, the company reformed to charge. Murray and I stood to the rear. The word came and we were off. Bayonets fixed and a wild unexplained yell and we started to cut through the band of Mohmands. The unexpected charge from the rear instantly threw them into confusion. The Mohmands suddenly found themselves moving to the right, away from an unexpected enemy. A moment's hesitation on their part gave our little company its chance to run for the rock wall of the graveyard. But it was only a few seconds delay. We were but halfway and the bullets started coming our way. The Mohmands were not going to let us to our goal if they could.

As we closed to the graveyard we could hear a cheer from the defenders. That's when the terror struck. Murray was ahead of me when he went down in a heap. I nearly stumbled over him, reaching down I grabbed him by his braces with my left hand, trying to pull him up. In my right hand was my Webley.

Murray scrambled to his feet, we were already yards behind the company. I have an impression even today of a face, a turban and a sabre. I fired over Murray's left shoulder as I pulled him along. The face was now red. To our front, between us and the wall were two more warriors. I fired at the one on the right but both figures fell. Behind the one on my left stood Godard with pistol in hand. Murray and I scrambled over the wall.

"Thought we'd lost you, old boy" smiled Godard. "Do try to keep up next time, eh?"

"I'll leave no man behind, Godard."

"Hmm, as you like. Wounded are over there by the riverbank."

As Murray and I went to the riverbank, Murray walked in front. He turned to face me. "Thank you, Sir. Sorry I stumbled."

"Not a problem. You'd do the same."

We started tending to the wounded. A few minutes later, we heard another cheer from the defenders. The charge of the 5th had disorganized the attackers, now Lieutenant Pollack and his squadron of the 10th had arrived. Capt. Strong ran out from the defences and regaining the horse he'd left with them, led the 10th Bengal Cavalry in a charge that cleared the plain and drove the Mohmands into the hills.

The Mhairwara Company in the pass entrance continued to hold on. Both the old and new defenders of the graveyard gathered dead and wounded and headed to join them. Murray and I could do little until we could stop at the pass. Captain Strong's charge had given us the chance to evacuate the graveyard but his orders had been to hold the pass.

As we gathered at the entrance to the pass, Strong started to deploy his force to hold it. What ammunition that was available was shared but Murray had been right. The only unit with a full load of ammunition was now the 5th who Strong placed in the forward position. While I attended to the most severe cases, Murray helped the walking wounded.

We had hardly ensconced ourselves in the entrance to the pass when the Mohmands returned from the far hills. They swarmed into the graveyard and started climbing the hills to our right and left where they would be able to fire down into our position. Captain Strong was about to deploy his

Mhairwara company as skirmishers on the hillsides when the "Thunder of the Gods" erupted below us. It was artillery shells falling on the Mohmands in the graveyard! What a wonderful sight! A spontaneous cheer rose from the soldiers around me. Mohmands scattered in all directions. Anywhere they grouped, the shells sought them out. Once again, the Mohmands fled to the hills. Those in the graveyard tried to swim the river and I saw a dozen banners along with many turbans floating. Some drowned. Some made the crossing.

The two mountain guns we saw in the distance were supported by a company of infantry and advanced a few hundred yards at a time. It was soon clear that the Mohmand attackers were broken, at least for the moment.

Major Dyce of the Royal Artillery had arrived with two cannon and a company of the 12th Foot. As he joined us, he took quick evaluation of our circumstances. We were still receiving sporadic fire from the hillsides, we were low on ammunition, had no forage for the animals, no water for man or horse and Creagh's men had been fighting for 12 hours.

Taking command, as the senior officer present, Major Dyce ordered a withdrawal to Dakka. It was a most prudent decision.

The column, of necessity, moved slowly. The doolies could not move quickly with their human cargo and the mules and horses had a tough go of it. We were constantly under fire. We arrived back at the safety of Dakka with the setting sun. One of the mountain guns leading the way, the other to our rear. The gunners, with their cannon packed on mules, had saved us, surely.

But best of all, there, sitting at a table in my office, smoking a pipe and drinking a whiskey with the Surgeon Major sat Sutter.

Chapter 9
A Try for the Treasure

"Sutter" I cried! "I was worried about you! Glad you are alright!"

"Worried about me?" exclaimed Sutter. "Look at yourself. You're a mess. Tough go? Here, sit down, let me get you one of your Surgeon Major's whiskeys."

"Can't, we've wounded to look after. Just walked in to inform the Doctor here."

"Nonsense," said the Surgeon Major of the 10th, rising from his desk. "I'm on my way to the ward right now. Take a moment. You do look like hell, you know. Sit for 10 minutes, then, come over. One tends to make mistakes when overtired. Don't want any of that." And with that, he left the office.

"Now sit and have a drink, John. Been up at Kam Dakka?"

Taking the whiskey, I sat in a chair and looked at Sutter. Now that I took the time, he looked quite worn out also, even if the uniform had been cleaned up.

"Yes," I replied. "Bit of a go. We did alright though."

We sat for some minutes and I enjoyed the calm and the silence.

I finally broke the silence.

"Sutter, I killed a man today, maybe two. One I'm sure of, the other, well, he went down but I feel he's dead also. Had to be done, you see." I sighed and went on. "I mean, it was them or me as they say in those penny dreadfuls. But what I don't understand is I don't really feel bad about it. I think I should, but I don't."

"John, it's not like they were good people or your friends. They were trying to kill you for heaven's sake."

"But they may have been good people, really, in their own way. I guess I'm a bit confused right now."

"All I can tell you, John, is you did the right thing. You survived and you took care of the other survivors."

"But I haven't asked where you've been. You're days overdue and should be at Jamrud, not here. What happened?"

"Not much," he replied. There was another moment's silence while he leaned back and put his boots on the table. "We left Jamrud and headed north, crossed the river and then west, making what we thought was a large loop. What happened was that the Mohmands started spilling out of the hills behind us. We couldn't get back the way we'd come. It was obvious that they had to be gathering for a reason. I had to keep moving northwest to try and stay unseen and got around them. By the time we found an opening, we were well west of Kam Dakka. I was able to ford the river about six miles west of here and made straight for Dakka. We arrived about two hours after your relief column left. Wired my report to Jamrud, borrowed a fresh horse and went back out on a little scout of my own."

"Scout of your own? What for? You couldn't have been any help to us."

"No, but I could be of help to us!" he declared, pointing his finger to me and then himself.

"Ah! The treasure! I should have known," I smiled and shook my head.

Sutter took his boots down and leaned across the table. "I've found a second Roman cross further up the same trail! Now will you believe me?"

I pondered this new information for a few moments. "Well, it certainly is now possible. Surely worth a look. When do we go?"

"Don't you have wounded to look after?" he smirked.

"Yes," I said, suddenly coming back to the moment. I took my last swallow and stood to go.

"See you tomorrow, John. I'm to bed. We can lay our plans then."

Unfortunately, the following morning we were occupied in loading to depart with the convoy at seven. As we left the gates of Dakka on route back to Jamrud, Sturt rode up to me. The two of us spent time trying to plan a campaign of discovery, but once we arrived at Jamrud, the business of the army, and for me, the business of opening the clinic absorbed all of our time.

Within a week or two of our return to Jamrud, my little clinic was open. At first there were few takers among the local populace. That, I was sure would come in time as we built the trust of the locals.

Murray and Malalai were constant companions. Each day I would receive two or three hospital assistants and a writer from the infirmary to help at the clinic. They arrived after morning sick call and we would journey to our little clinic tucked under the walls of the fort. For six hours each day, we would treat all who came, few as they were. In the second week of our operation, the flood tide came. Word had spread that treatment could be had at the clinic by the English Doctor and for no cost. I finally had to close each night at sundown and still there would be a line. The next morning those same people would be in the same line, waiting our arrival.

Malalai was a God-send. Her English improved with each day and she appeared at my elbow whenever I needed her help, as if, by magic. I found myself relying on her more and more.

It was mid-May before we knew it and Sutter and I had not been able to plan a way to get to Dakka again when the news arrived. There might be a chance of peace.

Yakub Khan wanted to negotiate peace because the Russians had let him down. The Tsar had decided that relations with England were more important that supporting a petty despot. By the end of May, the "Treaty of

Gandamak" was signed. The treaty gave us control of the Khyber Pass and Kurram Valley, allowed a telegraph line to Kabul and put a British resident there to operate Afghanistan's foreign affairs. It also set a payment system to Yakub Khan by the Indian government.

On the first of June, Arty arrived in Jamrud, having taken a short furlough. Everyone was excited about peace. But what would happen to me and the treasure? Would we have time to find it before moving back to India? Sutter, Arty and I decided we must act now, and so, with a week's leave in our pockets, well mounted and well armed, we headed to Dakka. The Regimental Surgeon, Armistead, agreed to run the clinic in my absence and Commissary O'Rourke, as always, saw to it that the three of us were well supplied.

Much against the advice of Murray and Malalai, we left, without escort, for Dakka. Our journey to Dakka was amazingly uneventful. The road was well travelled by columns of soldiers in good humour, looking forward to a return to India and relief from the heat of the Afghan summer. Still, there was the occasional shot from the hillsides, from those who either didn't know or didn't care that the two enemies were at peace.

At Dakka, we spent the night and the next day made off for the trail where Sutter had found the crosses.

"It's a theory," said Sutter. "I think that because the crosses were in each corner of the map that it stands for an even distance between the crosses. The second cross was about 3 miles from the first, so perhaps the 3rd is 3 miles from the second."

"Or perhaps it's double the miles from the first," said Arty.

"Or maybe you missed the second and actually found the third," I chimed in.

"You bastards just won't let a man dream, will you?" Sutter replied.

It was a good six miles from the main Dakka-Jalalabad road that we turned off to the north; another 3 miles brought us to the first cross. We dismounted to inspect it.

"It's definitely a Roman cross and quite old. Look at how the weather has worn the edges smooth. If we only knew it was the right one," mused Arty.

"Oh, it's the right one. I know it!" said Sutter. "It has to be."

I could feel the adrenaline surge as I slapped Sutter on the back. "You're right. I'm convinced. Which way to the next one?"

"Now look. Gents. I've been up here before. We're in bad country and we're alone. No column to save us if we should get into a tight spot. Watch your surroundings all the time and don't get fixated on the trail. Watch the hillsides."

Sutter's warning brought me back to reality with a sudden thud. He was right. This was not just a ride in the park.

We continued our journey up the trail, and as promised, about 3 miles ahead, was another cross chiselled in the stone along the side of the road. We inspected it briefly and went on. About a mile further and we came to a fork in the trail.

"Now what?" said Arty.

"Hold on," whispered Sutter. "Listen, rider coming from behind us. Quick! Around behind those rocks. Watson, you're horse holder. Arty, with me."

As Arty and Sutter dismounted, I led their horses further back and they moved to where they could see the trail while laying on their stomachs. I cursed my luck for being horse holder and not where I could see.

I could now clearly hear horses from the trail. I saw Sutter and Arty whisper to each other and raise their carbines. Both carbines barked at once, and then both men slid down toward me. Arty ran left and Sutter right. Sutter held a hand up telling me to stay where I was, as the two both ran up to higher ground. No sooner did they reach it, they fired again. Once more they descended and running back to their original spot, fired a third time. Now they screamed some gibberish I couldn't understand and fired a fourth round, but this time in the air. They yelled again and stood up looking back down the trail. Laughing jovially they started back down to where I held their mounts.

"What the devil is the matter with you two and who were you shooting at?"

"Nothing the matter with us, old boy. But Godard is having a bad day," said Arty, laughing again.

"Godard? You didn't shoot him?"

"No," said Sutter. "But I don't think he'll be following us anymore today. We just shot over him and yelled so he'd think it was tribesman. He and his pack mule took off back down the trail as fast as they could go"

Sutter took a breath and thought a moment. "That damned Enderby sent him out here alone to follow us. Godard should know better. We probably did him a favour by sending him back to Dakka."

"What do we do now?" I asked. "We've a fork in the trail and we don't want to split up."

"I vote we go right," said Arty. "Sutter, what about you?"

"Right works for me. If we don't find anything in 3 miles, we'll come back."

And so we were off on the wrong trail. Three hours later, we were back at the spot where we had turned right and by now night was falling. Finding a spot off the trail we camped for the night. We did not allow ourselves a fire, afraid we would draw attention. We grained and watered our horses and spent a most uncomfortable night either trying to sleep on the rocks or standing watch in 3 hour shifts.

Next morning we continued up the left fork.

"I wonder if Godard will be back?" I asked Arty.

"Doubt it. He doesn't know exactly where we're going and for all he knows, those 'tribesmen' he ran into may have done us in."

"You can bet he's waiting at Dakka," chimed in Sutter.

Three miles further along we came to the third Roman cross. There was now no doubt. This was the trail taken by Demetrios over two hundred years ago.

We sat for a pipe and each tried to make believe he was not excited. We were close now. Would the treasure be there and would we find it?"

We re-mounted and started forward on the trail again. We had gone but half the expected distance when Arty reigned up and stopped.

"Smell it?" he queried.

"What?"

"Wood fire. Someone's nearby," he warned. "Stay here, I'm going up on that hill." With that he handed me his reigns and started scrambling up the hillside. I could see him pull out his binoculars and scan the distance for a moment. Then, keeping low, he hurried down and re-joined us.

"We're done for now, fellows," he panted. "Over this little rise in the trail, the ground falls off to a little valley, and in it must be a thousand Mohmands. Gathering of some sort. Must be 50 banners. All gathered around a single tent."

"We can't go back now," cried Sutter. "We're too close."

"And I say dying finding a treasure is not worth it," spat Arty. "That treasure has been there over 200 years, another few days or months, won't matter. You know the Mohmands won't care about Yakub Khan's peace treaty if they see us here. John, what do you say?"

"I say we come back again. Better alive and poor than dead and rich."

And so we started our journey back. Sutter was morose and would not say a word until late that night as we entered Dakka Fort.

"You Gentleman were right," he said as we left the horses to be stabled. "Let's get a drink and plan what to do next."

As we entered the officers' mess, who should we see but Godard, sitting alone in a corner, brooding over a glass.

"Godard, old man," bellowed Sutter. "How wonderful to see you. What brings you this way?"

Godard nearly knocked the table over, spilling his glass as he jumped to his feet.

"Sturt, I thought you were, uh, I thought you had gone to Peshawar or somewhere. What ever are you doing here?"

"That was quick," whispered Arty in my ear.

"Just doing the rounds, needed some time to ourselves, you know. Well let me replace that drink. Seen any excitement lately? No? Well, probably nothing going on right now. Have a seat, man."

Pulling chairs up to the table we sat down and ordered drinks. His face was starting to flush as the realization of what had happened set in. Initially he had thought we'd been overpowered by the force he had escaped. Now he realized his mistake. We were the force he'd escaped.

Sutter made light chatter while we drank. Arty and I said nothing. Finally, Godard got up to leave.

"Going already? Well good night then," said Sutter. Then, as Godard reached the door, Sutter called out. "Oh, and Godard, do tell Colonel Enderby we send our best, good lad."

Godard merely turned and left the room.

"You know Sutter; you don't poke a lion cub with a stick. He just might turn on you," I said.

"John. John. You worry too much. He now knows we're watching him. He even believes we tried to kill him. He can't be sure we missed on purpose. He's going to be very careful from now on."

"We'd best be the careful ones," said Arty. "I'm all in. See you in the morning."

Next morning we returned to Jamrud.

The moment I returned, I was overwhelmed by work. The heat of the summer was upon us and the sick list increased with the heat. I was forced to reduce the clinic hours to four a day or I and my assistants should have no rest whatsoever. Malalai had greeted me warmly on my return and without my seeming to even notice it was she with me all the time. She was running errands, cleaning, cooking, and helping at the clinic. I started to rely on her more and more.

Word came down on the 21st that the 5th Fusiliers were to march on the 23rd for India, back to Chuagi, but Sturt and I were not to go with the regiment. I was detailed to the hospital at Peshawar and Sturt to the General Staff. It was a mixed blessing. It kept us within range of the treasure but Enderby was at Peshawar as was Godard, who had been made an aide-de-camp. At least Arty would be there with is detachment of the 18th Bengal Cavalry. But what about the clinic? And Malalai?

I realized I didn't want to lose her. She was like my little sister, I thought, or was she more? I wasn't sure how I felt now that we would be separated. We never talked of anything more than work but somehow I knew there was more there. Was it love? I sat in my quarters that night and thought for a long time. By the time I'd finished my pipe, I knew what I had to do. It was indeed a kind of love, but not that special kind that makes you say, "This is the one."

The best thing for all would be to leave her in Jamrud. She now had skills and could be retained by the Army to assist in the infirmary. So it was that the morning of the 23rd we left for Peshawar with the 5th. Sturt, Murray and I to stay there and the 5th to move back to its garrison.

Early that morning, I had gone to see Malalai. She would not look at me nor say a word. I tried desperately to tell her how much I appreciated her and all her help and explain how important she was to the infirmary and the clinic. All I got were silent tears in return. Assembly sounded and as I left her hut, a sinking feeling overwhelmed me. Drawing a deep breath, I marched for the formation.

It was a very short march to Peshawar and I was soon at the hospital. It held well over 100 beds and was quite modern by Army standards. I was assigned a rounds schedule and all the first day found myself looking for Malalai at my elbow. It was a sad day.

Chapter 10
Back to Jamrud

The summer of 1879 was hot and long. Sickness among the troops kept the hospital near capacity but supplies reached us in good time and overall Peshawar was not a bad assignment.

Arty and Sutter and I met frequently. Arty seemed to have the most boring job. His assignment as escort detachment kept him busy but in an uninspiring way. Spit and Polish became his life.

Sutter was occupied with planning. "What if this happens? What if that happens? And what if nothing happens?" was what he called his job.

Enderby had stopped by the hospital several times over the course of the summer. He would always seek me out and make a little small talk. He did not have a winning personality and, of course, I didn't trust him at all.

Godard would never say a word to me. In fact, whenever he saw any of us, he would always turn and go another way. We three friends chaffed to find a way to get back to Dakka together.

Finally, in late August, we agreed that Sturt should go alone to Dakka. In his position as a planner, he had need of first hand information as to the status of all the tribes in the Khyber Pass area. Word had been reaching the headquarters of much discontent among the Afridis, Shinwaris and Mohmands. Evidently, Yakub Khan was receiving monies from the British government but not passing a fair share down to the tribes as agreed. Sturt would take a small detachment and test the water among the tribes. We agreed that if he had the opportunity to look for the fourth cross he should. So, the last week of August he started for Dakka.

Terrible news reached us on the 4th of September. Unpaid Afghan regiments had run amuck in Kabul the day before. They had murdered the British Consul, Major Cavagnari and all his party and were threatening Yakub Khan. The war had been reignited.

That afternoon, Sutter appeared at the hospital. He had just returned from his intelligence gathering mission.

"I can only stay a moment, John. I've got to get back to headquarters. Hopefully we'll be bringing a sizeable force from India. Including the 5th, I hope."

"I can be ready in an instant," I said.

Calm down, John. The Army never moves that quickly," laughed Sutter.

"Are we going straight to Kabul?"

"Doubt it. We're strongest in the Kurram Valley where your cousin is. They'll probably be the ones to take Kabul. Ours will be a supporting attack. I'll let you know more on that as I can." With that he was gone to report in to headquarters.

Late that evening, as I was about to turn in, a knock came on my door. It was Sutter and Arty.

"We came to drink your whiskey, John."

"On the table, Arty. What's going on that I'm honoured by such a nocturnal visit?"

"Treasure," sighed Arty, sitting on my bunk, glass in hand.

"Needed to fill you two in on what I found on my ride. Or more importantly, what I didn't find," said Sutter, sitting on the table. "I was able to get past the third cross and on down into the valley, I'm sure my detachment thought I was crazy. I took them up the trail allegedly looking for Mohmands to talk to. We found plenty, sitting on the rocks above us. But since we were nominally at peace, they watched but held their fire. We got down in the valley without incident but at around three miles, I could not find the marker." Sutter became frenzied. Standing up, he started pacing up and down the tiny room, clasping and unclasping his hands.

"I trooped that detachment up and down the road a dozen times. They thought I'd lost my mind. The Mohmands gathered in small groups and watched. I'm sure they were convinced we were plotting something. Finally I could do nothing but move on back toward the main road, the Mohmands starting moving along with us. They started taking pot shots from the hillsides. Fortunately, we made it back without any casualties."

"We need to all go back and try to find it. It's got to be there, my friend," said Arty.

"Not much chance of that now, I'm afraid, the whole frontier is on fire. We've got to wait for things to calm down again."

"All we can do now is our jobs and wait," I added. "But we don't do any lone reconnaissance like our friend Godard. Anyone shoots at us, it will be for real."

So each of us retuned to our respective jobs, setting aside the treasure and hoping our efforts would help bring peace to the area.

For me, the months of September, October and November dragged. The wounded, flowing back to Peshawar, were a constant reminder that the war was active and Lord Roberts was moving toward Kabul. Yakub Khan, as it turned out, was not involved in the murder of Major Cavagnari, but he was a weak ruler as well as corrupt. Yakub Khan had not realized that he had neither the leadership nor the charisma to hold his tribes together. Add to that his failure to pay his soldiers and giving Afghan territory to the British, which inflamed the tribes, and he was done. By the end of October, Roberts had taken Kabul and on the 28th day of October, Yakub Khan abdicated but that didn't stop the fighting. The lack of a strong Afghan leader left dozens of tribes each going their own way. Roberts executed 47 men accused of participating in the death of the British Consul and his men. While just, this action further inflamed the situation.

By December, confusion still was the order of the day in Afghanistan and the Indian government finally agreed to send a reserve division into the fight. The second division being needed in Afghanistan and off the supply line, the Reserve Division would take up the duty of securing the lines of communication.

Just before Christmas, Sutter and Arty came to see me in my quarters.

"The 5th has been ordered to Peshawar, John. Odds are it will move on from there."

"If the 5th is to see action, you and I need to be there, Sutter!"

"You're right there. Well, John, you're re-assigned to the 5th. They'll be passing through day after tomorrow so have your kit ready. We're headed to Jamrud first, then on to Jalalabad, is what I think. More convoy duty looks like. Good Night, John. Come along, Arty, your horses will be missing you."

As promised, the next morning I had my orders to re-join the 5th. It seems that in all the confusion associated with re-mobilizing the Army, Colonel Enderby had not paid attention to either me or Sturt and so lost us, at least for the moment.

Sturt and I re-joined the 5th as the convoy stopped at Peshawar overnight. It was good indeed to be back with the men I respected and trusted. I had learned so much so far. Even not to doubt Surgeon Major Bennett. He was truly a caring and gifted doctor, even if a little tipsy at times.

The march as far as Jamrud was uneventful. Once again, Murray and I were eating the trail dust and wondering if we would ever again be clean.

As we entered Jamrud, the regiment was tolled off to camp below the north wall of the fort. As soon as I was able, I found myself going in search of Malalai. Why I did so was plain to me. I cared for her very much and wanted to know that she was alright, that she had been treated well since I left. I found her in the native clinic. She looked wonderful and on seeing her, I felt wonderful.

She was talking to a local at the front desk as I entered. At first, she didn't notice me, so intent was she in the discussion.

"Miss Malalai, come here, I need you," I said in my sternest voice.

"Yes, Doctor," she responded and looking up, saw me. Her grin was a delight and she ran over to me. Suddenly catching herself, she stopped just as she reached me and looked at the ground.

"You wanted me, Doctor?"

"I've come to see my favourite assistant, Malalai. How are you?" I smiled and reached down to lift her chin so she would look at me. Her eyes were watery. She grinned and wiped them with a towel. "It is good to see you, doctor. You have come back to us?"

"No, just going on to Jalalabad. But I could not go past here and not stop to see how you were. You're doing well I see."

"Yes. The doctors are all good to me and Mr Moyer give me English teaching ever day, He is kind."

"Excellent. I'm glad you're doing so well. I must go now but when I come back through, I'd like to check on you again, if you would permit me?"

"Of course, Doctor. I would be very happy."

With that I left, pleased that Malalai was doing so well. The next day we left again for Jalalabad, where we were to spend a long, cold winter.

Chapter 11
Cattle Thieves

Jalalabad was a large fort by our standards, a major re-supply point. It was early January when I, Murray and Sturt and a quartering party arrived. For the first week we were occupied arranging for the arrival of the rest of the 5th. They had been delayed at Jamrud and there was talk of the battalion headquartering there instead. As it finally ended up, we had two companies at Jalalabad and the preponderance of the 5th at Jamrud, though on many occasions in the next few months, most of the 5th would be at Jalalabad due to escorting convoys.

The convoys were constantly under attack. Through the months of February, March and April, Lord Roberts was trying to settle the Afghan tribes, but without an Afghan leader who was both strong and friendly to us, his task was nigh impossible. The constant work kept me from any thought of the treasure, but I could tell that Sutter was constantly trying to devise a plan to once again search for it. Godard too, was ever present company. He had been reassigned to the regiment with duty at Jalalabad. This, I'm sure, was arranged by Colonel Enderby. Where I or Sutter went, there would appear our silent friend, watching.

In late April, things were still in quite an uproar everywhere. It seems that a Mulla Khalil was calling for a "holy war" and was assembling all the riff-raff of the frontier to his standard. Khalil had a large number of Safis, and with them he occupied Besud and Goshta. It was Sutter who let me know things were about to get worse.

"Colonel Rowland will be here tomorrow," he said, as we walked the parade ground. "He's on his way to Safed Sang. And with the Mulla making trouble we can expect some attacks on our communications lines. They say General Doran may move his headquarters here. We may be in for a small campaign to clean out this fellow. Better than just going back and forth up the road."

"How have your recommendations to protect the commissariat stores faired?" I asked.

"Fools won't bring up a proper security force for it or move it closer to the fort. They don't want to "smell the cattle". Tell me, Watson, what do you do with people like that?" Sutter's words were to prove prophetic.

On the following day, Colonel Rowland arrived with an additional 300 bayonets of the 5th. It was decided that they would rest here at Jalalabad before going on.

We had a jovial time that first night. Early May was a genial month. Warmer weather, snows melting, and what green the country had starting to show. Local villagers were starting to prepare the rice paddies for the planting season. But with the improved weather had come more raids on the lines of communication. It would soon be campaign time.

The next day was a busy one. I spent the morning attending to the usual complaints of soldiers on the march: blisters, corns and boils. I gave Murray some time off to visit with friends he hadn't seen in months and instead he spent his afternoon operating a cleaning station for the men of the 5th where they could have their leather braces and uniforms cleaned by the natives while they had hot water to bathe and shave.

It was late that evening, nigh onto three in the morning and most officers had long left the mess. Colonel Rowland, Sturt, I and two or three others remained at a table playing cards. We were discussing the coming campaign season and wondering if Ayub Khan could be brought under control quickly when the officer of the day rushed in.

"Is Colonel Rowland here?" he called from the doorway.

"Here, Lieutenant. What can I do for you?"

"Sir, the General's compliments and he wished you to fall out the battalion. The commissary stores and cattle yard are being attacked and need immediate assistance."

"Right. Go find Major Tucker, lieutenant, should be in quarters. Sturt, your men too." Turning to the table, he called to a young lieutenant, "Withers have the bugler sound assembly. Off now, quick!"

"Doctor," he said. "Gather your men and follow as quickly as you can. Hustle now. Can't let these locals have the cattle."

I ran from the mess and to the hospital calling for Murray, an ambulance and doolie-bearers. It took not more than twenty minutes for the mules to be harnessed, my horse saddled and supplies loaded. Yet we were still ten minutes behind the battalion.

I headed west on the road toward the cattle yard, it was just after four in the morning.

We caught up to the battalion at the cattle yard and fell in at the tail end of the column. As we did, a detachment of cavalry, maybe 20 sabres, passed us headed for the front of the column. I spurred forward with them and was soon up with Sturt's company. I reigned up here.

"Do we know what's happened? That cattle yard is awfully empty!"

"Looks like they've taken a thousand head, overwhelmed the guard detachment just like I feared. About 180 sheep taken as well. They can't move too fast, we'll catch them. Looks like they've headed toward Laghman. We can't be more than 30 minutes behind them."

I stayed with Sturt for the better part of the morning. About 8 we could hear firing to our front.

"Best get back to the ambulance, Doctor. Looks like the beggars are going to fight a holding action at Darunta gorge. They're liable to hold us up a bit."

From where we were in the rear, we watched the battalion form in line with a company in reserve along with the cavalry. (Cavalry being of no use in the gorge.) Even from where I was, the positions of the Ghilzais were easy to pick out. The black powder muskets sent large clouds of white smoke in the sky, revealing their positions in the rocks. I counted about 60. It would be hard work for the skirmisher to root them out. If we'd had mountain guns, we'd have made short work of it for the Ghilzais would not stand to artillery. As it was, each rock on the hillsides over the gorge would have to be fought for.

I determined to move forward with the ambulance. We had a 35 gallon water keg and there was a stream to our right rear. As the skirmishes inched forwards, I had the doolie-bearers supplement the bhisti's filling water bottles for the soldiers.

Finally, after almost 2 hours of fighting, the path through the gorge was taken and we moved forward. By now, however, we were far behind the cattle and moving further from any support. The soldiers were in light marching order; braces, haversacks, ammunition bag, water bottle, mess tin, blanket and glengarry, bayonet and rifle. We had not wagons save the ambulance, no food nor extra water. To continue after the Ghilzais would have been folly with so small and ill supported a force. We returned to Jalalabad.

The Ghilzais had made off with 800 cattle. We were able to collect 200 on the return and about 60 of the sheep. And the self-satisfied smirk on Sturt's face lasted a week.

I felt somewhat sorry for the villagers between Jalalabad and Daruta. Over the next few days, patrols exacted a fine of 4000 rupees from the villagers, for neither reporting Ghilzais in the area nor trying to delay their escape. Had they made the report they would have their villages threatened with destruction by the Ghilzais, but because they had not reported, we took their money. A sad predicament.

On the 9th, when Colonel Rowland thought he would continue to Safed Sang, he was ordered to remain at Jalalabad and await General Doran. There was to be a move to put down Mulla Khalil in Besud.

Chapter 12
Mulla Khalil

With the arrival of General Doran was the pleasant surprise of Arty and his detachment of the 18th Bengal Cavalry.

He caught up with me down by the stables, for while I had a native to take care of my horse, I had always enjoyed grooming and caring for Emmett myself, whenever time permitted. I've always believed in the bond between horse and rider. It's something special, more than once I've seen a fine mount stand guard over his fallen master or the tearful goodbye of horseman for his lost companion.

At any rate, that's where Arty found me, brushing Emmett and talking to him like he could understand.

"He has no idea what you're saying, old man. He's just waiting for a treat. Sorry job of grooming, afraid you'd never make it in the cavalry."

"Arty!" I exclaimed, shaking his hand. "Just popping in for a visit?"

"Escort again. The brass always likes the native horse along. Makes them feel more secure. Been on a ride?"

"Chasing some cattle thieves like this is the wild west of America or something. But come on, let's go find Sutter. He'll be delighted to see you."

"Want to talk to you about this bloody treasure no doubt. You know, John, if there is a treasure, it's probably been found a couple of centuries ago, and if it hasn't, it belongs to the church by rights. I've thought about that lately."

We left the stable and Arty insisted on checking on his picket line to see that his horses were being taken care of. I noticed he did not intrude on his sergeant's business but merely walked the line and kept going. "Good to let them know you trust them but you care enough to check," he said half nodding to himself. "Now where is Sutter's orderly room? Or perhaps he's already retired to the mess?"

"This time of day I'd say orderly room." And indeed, that is where we found him.

"Come in Arty, John, have a seat," grinned Sutter as we entered. "How good of you to stop by for out little foray. Cigars are in the box on the table, help yourself."

"With pleasure, old man," said Arty, opening the box and taking out two cigars. Handing one to me, he dropped into a chair by the table that served as Sturt's desk.

"What little foray are you talking about?" I asked.

"Seems the good General has decided to quash a Mulla named Khalil. This fellow has been gathering followers right across the river from here and causing problems, so we're going to stop him before he gets further along."

"Is it far?" asked Arty.

"No, look at this map."

The three of us stood to look at the map Sutter had on the wall.

"Here we are in Jalalabad," he tutored. "Just across the river is a triangle known as Basud. It sits between the Kabul and Kunar rivers. There are two paths that run north. One is along the Kunar River and goes past a place called Tokchi. The other goes over the Paikob Pass abut two miles to the west, and there is this long hill line that runs about 4 miles that separates them."

"The Tokchi Pass," he continued, sitting back down, "is pretty bad overall. Even infantry can only get through in single file, horses the same. Now Paikob is no problem."

"Well, this country out here," said Arty, pointing up at the flat area of Basud, "looks ideal for cavalry."

"Try it, my friend," laughed Sutter. "It's nothing but rice fields and this time of year they're flooded. Neither infantry nor cavalry cross them without getting shot to pieces. I surely don't want to try it."

"What kind of force are we facing?"

"Apparently, a sizable group of Safis. The General is holding onto the 5th and ordered the 4th Madras Infantry up. He's also ordered the locals to start building rafts for a crossing. The bridge has to be taken down before the spring flood waters arrive or they'll lose it. They'll put it back up when the waters go down."

Within a few days of our conversation, the 4th Madras arrived and on the 14th day of May, 200 of them were sent to the far side of the river to the fort of Pir Muhammad Khan, about ½ mile up from the bridgehead. This was done to assure the locals that we would protect them and to defend the north side for our crossing later.

The next few days were extremely busy. Fifty sabres of the Central India Horse, a unit my cousin had commanded in 1871, arrived and were sent to join Major Tyndall's force at Fort Pir Muhammad Khan. Then came the 9th Bengal Infantry to Jalalabad, along with the 12th Foot and four guns of I-A Royal Horse Artillery. We were becoming a sizable force.

On the 18th, Murray, I, three hospital assistants, a half dozen doolie-bearers and our little ambulance were ferried across the river with 200 rifles of the 5th, led by Colonel Rowland. The ambulance we would leave in Dabela by the bridgehead and use our four mules to pack in medical supplies.

The next morning at half four, we departed Dabela, leaving a small force to watch the stores. We were a force of over 500 bayonets, 80 sabres and two mountain guns. It always seemed to me odd and somewhat disconcerting, that mention was rarely made or record kept of the numerous commissary and medical department personnel that accompanied all the various expeditions during the war. And if little mention was made of these necessary auxiliaries to the force, none whatsoever was made of the bhistis or doolie-bearers and the like, although they all shared the hardships and the hazards. Perhaps someday the bhistis will get their due.

We were not long on the march, about an hour and a half, when a halt was called. We had travelled west up the right of the river and then turned north across the rice swamp.

I trotted Emmett up to the front of the column and on the hillside to our northeast I could make out General Doran and a small party. They appeared to be looking eastward. I sought out Sturt and asked if he knew what was happening.

"Seems there are about two thousand of those damned Safis to the east and they're headed to the south in small groups," he replied. "They're as close to Darunta and the bridgehead as we are! We've got to cut them off before they can get there. If they overrun the boys there, they can go on across the river all the way to Jalalabad and we'll be stuck over here."

"But aren't there sufficient men at Darunta?"

"Well. If they have improved their defences, they may be alright. Bradford said the Royal Artillery was putting two cannon at the bridgehead on our side of the river. Surely they can hold." But Sutter didn't sound convinced. Just then a rider could be seen racing down the hill. He rode straight to Colonel Dawson of the 1st Madras who was nearby in conference with Colonel Rowland.

The Lieutenant saluted as he reigned in his horse. "General's compliments, Colonel Dawson. The General says the Safis are headed straight towards us into the open ground. It doesn't appear they know we're here. He requests you form line of battle and prepare for an attack." With that, he was off again, riding for the hill to our front.

Dawson turned to the officers around him. "Rowland, take the left. Form three companies and refuse one to the left. The 12th will do the same on the right. I'll take the 1st and the 4th Madras in the centre. Lieutenant Bradford, I want your two cannon centred to the rear of the Madras. Colonel Martin, if you'll take the Central Horse to the left, that flank is very open, keep a lookout if the beggars try to come in that way. Use your own discretion if they fall back, you may be able to cut them off. Gentlemen, to your units please."

All saluted and rode post haste for their columns. I rode back to our little medical dctachment as fast as I could go. I quickly told my men what was going on and we moved forward behind the second company of the 5th. It is astonishing how quickly a well trained force of soldiers can form to line of battle. Ahead of us, 120 men, bayonets fixed; to our left, another 60 ready to reinforce the line or defend against attack from the left. To our right, mules and cannon unlimbering in an instant and ready to fire. And so we waited, but not for long, for no sooner had we deployed than the first dark figures came over the hillside. A few at first, then hundreds. But they seemed to be confused by the sight of our little Army and were gathering up. They stood a good 1200 yards away and static, neither wanting to advance nor retreat. We made the decision for them. The order was made to move forward. The entire formation advanced in unison; Infantry, Artillery, Cavalry. A wondrous sight to behold. We had closed about half the distance when the order to fire was given. Artillery and Infantry fire rained down on our enemy.

For a short while, the masses of turbaned men held their ground as the shells played back and forth across the front, the two gun crews working feverishly to support our soldiers across the entire area. But now it was the infantry fire that broke the Safis line.

The rifle fire from the 5th proved to be more than the Safis could stand and the enemy right began to flee. Like a house of cards, Mulla's army crumbled once their right collapsed, for the rest were in fear. Dawson seeing his chance, ordered the Central India Horse to overtake the enemy as they fled to the hills or to a small fort to their rear. The Horse swept down upon the fleeing throng with sabre and carbine. From where I sat on Emmett, I could see the Horse cut down our fleeing foe, creating havoc among their ranks.

We advanced again, and the Horse drew back to our lines. Those Safis in the hills melted away. The rest sought safety in the small fort. We stopped a few hundred yards from the fort while the cannon ripped holes in the walls and the towers. So far, I had had no work to do as we'd had but one soldier only slightly wounded. As the firing from the fort started to die off, the 5th advanced to storm the quadrangle and the artillery ceased its pounding. Colonel Rowland and the 5th swept through the fort, firing kept coming from the southeast tower. The guns were called on again to open a way in the wall of the tower and once breached, Rowland, Captain Kilgour, Colour Sergeant Wood and a few of the men stormed the tower, fighting hand to hand with bayonet and sabre.

Once the fighting died, I was busy indeed. Fortunately, we had no one killed, but Colonel Rowland and six soldiers had been wounded in taking the tower. The wounds were slight, most were made by sabres, and I had the privilege of seeing to Colonel Rowland.

The entire battle had lasted but an hour. And now, after destroying the remainder of the fort, we marched back to Dabela. It was only ten in the morning. The early afternoon found us back at Dabela and I left Murray to check supplies and see to the care of the men and mules while I went off to find Sturt. I came across McMullen first. His detachment had been left at Dabela and had spent the day acting as scouts, watching for the possible approach of Safis.

"Quite an adventuresome day you had, John. I hear you weren't kept busy though, professionally, that is."

"No, fortunately our injuries were few and none severe. Colonel Rowland and the 5th made an outstanding show of it. Very impressive. Have you seen Sturt?"

"Haven't, but we'll find him at sundown, never fear. He knows where the whiskey is kept," laughed Arty.

True to Arty's prediction, Sturt appeared later in the evening as we smoked cigars beneath the wall of the fort.

"Tomorrow is a day of rest evidently," said Sturt, walking up.

"Cigar?" I offered.

"Don't mind if I do."

"Do I take it from your remark that we've more to do afterwards?" Arty inquired.

"Two more forts to destroy to make sure the beggars get the idea. One called Azamulla Khan Kala and another at Danaras Khan, have to level them before we go back across the river."

"I hope the bridge is still standing by the time we have to re-cross," I observed. "The river is rising quickly."

"Engineer officers are afraid of the same thing. Let's hope there are plenty of rafts. Oh, and by the way John, the Colonel wants to see you. He's terribly grateful for your patching him up. Don't know why. Just a scratch after all."

"Quite a delicate operation, in fact," I said, striking a pose with my cigar. "Not one in a hundred surgeons could do so well."

We all laughed and enjoyed the evening. The next day, Colonel Rowland thanked me for being "Johnny on the spot" with the regiment and hoped we'd have a long affiliation. He was to be disappointed.

Chapter 13
Godard Explains

On the following two days, we made the two treks. One to Azimulla Khan Kala and the other to Danaras Khan. Both forts were destroyed with minimal interference from the locals.

It was now time to re-cross the river. In the time we had spent destroying the forts, the last bridge had been swept away. We would now have to cross the raging river on rafts or swim the horses and elephants. The effort to cross took two days and was not without loss.

A rope was tied down stream between the two shores which were about 400 yards apart. Those who could swim well were given unrolled turbans and posted along the rope to catch those who might be swept along. All day on the 23rd, troops and equipage crossed under the cover of the cannons on the right bank. The Central India Horse crossed both ways time and again to swim horses and mules packed with equipment. The cannon from the mule mountain battery were packed on elephants to keep them above the six foot deep waters and their mules swam across. As things will, with all the success, still, one artillery driver and a sowars horse were lost, swept past the catch line.

Our little ambulance had been loaded with cavalry saddles and rafted across to be reunified on the far side with our mules that were swum across by the Horse. This task I left to Murray. The 5th had been given the task of defending the re-crossing of the river and I had stayed with Sturt as our defensive perimeter had collapsed on itself, getting smaller and smaller as there were fewer and fewer soldiers to defend against attack. As night fell and operations had to cease, we were now but a single company of 65 men on the wrong side of the river. Sturt had now crossed also. Lt. Godard was the sole remaining officer and as much as I was uncomfortable with the situation, I also stayed. If an attack came, our little band would be sorely pressed and they'd have need of me.

Godard decided to make a show of things by stealing a well known tactic from history. Instead of refusing the use of campfires, which would give away our location and small strength, he instructed his sergeant to build a campfire for every two men and keep the fires burning all night. From a distance, in the dark, it appeared we had still a sizeable force on the left back of the river. I suppose I shall never know if the ruse worked or was necessary but we weren't abused except for the occasional pot shot out of the darkness and our picquets were quiet.

"Doctor, you really didn't have to stay here, you know. Nothing will happen and we'll cross in the morning."

"Perhaps, Godard, but one never knows what eventuality may occur."

We stood near the crossing site out of the firelight. Taking a hip flask out his haversack Godard offered me a drink.

"You know, doctor," he said as he took a pull from the flask. "You really would be better served by paying more attention to who your friends are and who you support. Colonel Enderby could be very useful to your career. He isn't such a bad fellow."

"Truly," was all I could say. I stood for a moment, puffing on my cigar while I thought. Finally, I came to a decision.

"Godard, why are you supporting Enderby in his attempt to steal Sturt's map?"

Godard laughed for a moment and walked over to sit on a nearby rock.

"Let me put it to you this way, Watson. Violet was my fiancé when McMullen and Sturt showed up. We were to be married in about 6 months time. It took only 3 months for them to interfere and destroy my life. I don't wish them dead, you understand. But I want something that means a great deal to them taken away. It's really quite that simple. Vengeance!" He spat the last word with a hatred I had seen in few men, as he rose from his seat.

"But, how did you know about the map?" I queried.

"Oh," he murmured, setting back down. "That rumour has been around forever. And when Sturt's had a few, he can't keep a secret."

With that, a bullet splashed in the water near us and I could hear the report to our left.

"Blighters are not going to let us rest tonight, are they?" remarked Godard. "I'd best assure myself that the good sergeant is making the rounds. Do try to get some sleep, Doctor." So saying, he rose from the rock and started for the campfires. A few paces out, he stopped and turned back toward me.

"Do remember my advice, Doctor. Choose your friends and your battles carefully. Your decisions can have rather far reaching effect." He turned again and I was left to my own thoughts once more. At least now I knew the origin of the enmity between the three men.

By first light, we saw the return of 20 elephants to our side of the river and we loaded on them to leave Besud.

On our return to Jalalabad, we rested a day or two and Colonel Rowland and most of the 5th headed once again toward Safed Sang. Jalalabad was now General Doran's headquarters.

On the second morning after our return, Sturt approached me out on the parade grounds.

"Watson, old man, our chance has come. Be ready to move tomorrow. We've got our chance to go after the treasure. "

"How can that be? We're stuck here at Jalalabad."

"There is a large convoy due to reach Dakkar on the 6th. It's going to need extra escort because of the large amount of ammunition and new screw guns coming up to support Kabul. My company is being sent down to bring them to Jalalabad. I've asked for you to go along as well as Arty's detachment."

"You Devil, they approved it? And we go a week early?"

"Old Doran doesn't much care. Doesn't pay much attention to the details you know. As long as he's plenty of soldiers here to play with, he's happy."

"I'll be ready to move in the morning." I grinned. Then I thought, "Tell me, what about Godard? Where will he be?"

"Oh, his company is staying here. Part of my overall suggestion to Doran's aide. Companionable fellow, Major Baskerville likes things presented in neat, little packages. Do that and he'll agree to almost anything."

"You Devil," I repeated. "I marvel at your sagacity. Always find a way, don't you?"

"Always, Doctor. We march at five. 'Til the morning, then." And with a wave of his hand, he was off across the parade.

Chapter 14
The Orthodox Cross

It was the 27th of May, 1880, and unbeknownst to me, the search for the treasure was about to take a marked turn. As planned, we departed Jalalabad before the sun had risen over the eastern hillside. Our caravan marched the well travelled military road with but a few incidents, the flankers provided by Arty's detachment doing good duty. We reached Dakka on the 29th. This play by Sturt would leave us nine days in which to search for the treasure, assuming of course, that the locals didn't make noise and cause us problems. That night, Arty, Sutter and I gathered at the mess to plan our strategy for the coming campaign.

"Just how do you intend to explain our absence from Dakka?" I asked Sutter.

He swirled his whiskey in his glass as he drew another puff on his cigar. "Splendid thing, reconnaissance," he finally said. "Any hint of a rumour about Mohmands re-organizing and people want to know more about it."

"Of course, having extra officers, with experience of course, laying about the fort, gives you someone to send on a mission." Smiling to himself, he leaned back and took another puff.

"What rumour?" I asked. "I haven't heard anything about it."

"Seems we picked up some information on the march down here. Don't you know, old man?"

"But Sutter, you never told me about it."

Sturt looked at me and shook his head. Turning to Arty, he said, "A true babe in the woods. How shall we ever be able to release him in the wild?"

The two of them had a hearty laugh and raised a toast to each other.

"John, old boy, he made it up for the brass, of course," whispered Arty in my ear.

The plan was suddenly clear. What a dolt I'd been. Of course Sturt would have had a plan to get us out of Dakka and into Mohmand territory.

We then discussed the make up of our little party. It was agreed that since we didn't know the exact location, nor did we know whether or if we would need tools to dig, we would need supplies and a pack mule.

"Do you think Murray is to be trusted?" asked Sturt.

"I'd trust him with my life," I replied.

"Good! We'll take him to take care of the mules. Two ought to do. Arty, do you have four men you can trust?"

"As the Doctor said, with my life."

"Good. We really don't know what the situation is with the Mohmands, so we'll bring a few along. Leave them at the second cross in case they're needed and take Murray with us into the valley. Six days rations ought to do. Your men ought to be safe at the hiding spot John used below the cross."

"If I'm going to risk a man's life, Sutter, I'm going to tell him why. I've got to explain this to Murray," I insisted.

Sutter thought for a moment, "You're right, John. If we find, no, when we find the treasure, we'll give him a small share. Agreed?"

Arty and I nodded. It was only fair.

We broke up late that evening, having discussed in detail what we would do for the next six days; eight would be the most that we could stretch our search out to. As we left the mess, I went in search of Murray. I found him doing his nightly check on the mules.

"Private Murray, I have something I want to discuss with you."

"Yes, Sir."

"Come over to the ambulance and have a seat on the tail board. I have something to discuss with you at length."

"Right, Sir. But I'll just stand here if that's alright."

Taking a deep breath, I launched into an explanation of the situations. Murray was incredulous at first; I could see it in his face. But as I laid out our series of adventures, I could see he was finally beginning to believe me. I explained everything, from the treasure to Godard to Enderby, to our search for the fourth cross.

"Well, Sir," he finally said. "I'm your man. I trust you and the other gentleman to give a fair amount. When do we go?"

"Tomorrow, early. Can you be ready? No more than two of our mules. Lieutenant McMullen will bring you a mount."

"I'll be ready, Sir."

I held out my hand to Murray. "Take it, Murray. We've an agreement among gentlemen."

"Aye, Sir," he said, taking my hand. "We're agreed."

As the morning sun rose, the eight of us departed Dakka Fort, in search of treasure.

We moved swiftly, for we knew our way and it was but a half day's journey to the second cross.

Arty had explained to his men that we were on a mission of importance that they would find rewarding but had not explained further. As we made our noon stop at the foot of the second cross, he explained to them that they were to wait there for our return but should they be discovered and threatened by Mohmands in force, not to await us but immediately return to Dakka.

Here we left also one of the mules with supplies for the four sowars and pressed on. By mid afternoon, we were at the third cross and looking down into the valley. We could see a good seven miles as the trail wandered through the valley and disappeared into the distant hills. This time there was no conclave of Mohmands.

We decided we would start by traveling the trail from one side to the other, searching both sides just as Sturt had done earlier. Perhaps because of the pressure of being watched by hostile tribesmen he had merely missed it. So we started down. By the time we reached the valley floor, we moved slowly, watching for the cross. The sun was starting to set and we decided to camp for the night. Dividing the watch up among the four of us, the first night passed uneventfully. Having watered and grained the animals, they were hobbled and allowed to graze for a short time. Once morning came, we allowed ourselves a small fire to cook and make tea. Then, having saddled and packed, we started on through the valley, crossing its whole length and back again. We could find no sign of the fourth cross. On returning to our original starting point in the late afternoon, we conferred on our next move.

"Perhaps the cross has been destroyed," ventured Arty.

"Or the trail is not where it used to be," I put in. "Though it seems the logical path through the valley."

"It must be here," stormed Sutter. "It must!"

"Well, I'll be damned if I know where," I jibed, and sitting upon some rocks, took to my pipe to try and think.

"We have to expand the search area." Sutter insisted and so, in an hour we were back out upon the trail. This time, Murray and I travelled about 200 yards to the right and Arty and Sutter 200 yards to the left. It was very slow going and we were only about halfway down the valley when darkness forced us to stop for the night.

The next morning found us continuing on our search. We could find nothing and by early evening we were back where we had camped the first night, no better for two wasted days of searching.

I now suggested we go back to the third cross and see if there was a clue there which would present itself. It turned out to be a fortuitous suggestion. We had been sitting on the hillside for about a half hour, having found no clue when Murray approached me.

"Sir, I was sitting here looking at the valley and I have an idea."

"All ideas are welcome, Murray," I said, reaching in my haversack for another cigar.

"Well Sir, you said we're looking for one of them Russian kind of crosses with those three bars on it, right?"

"Yes," I laughed, "but without much success." Striking a lucifer, I lighted my cigar while Murray appeared to be lost in thought. Finally he turned and pointed toward the valley which was below us.

"Well, the whole valley is one of them crosses, Sir. Ain't it?"

I sat stunned for a moment. Rising, I looked at the valley in the setting sun. He was right! The whole bloody valley was the cross. The trail that led straight from one end to the other was the upright and crossing it in three places were fingers of hills which formed the three cross members. The far and centre hills were almost perpendicular and the near crossed at an angle from left to right. That must be the solution!

"Arty! Sutter! Quickly before the light fades! Come here! Murray has solved it!"

Pointing to the valley, I outlined the orthodox cross for them. For a moment, we were ecstatic with joy. But then reality set in. A whole valley to search? And for a single casket of jewels? Where were we to start? Our depression quickly returned.

We each spent time that night trying to arrange in our minds how we could possibly search an entire valley. Was there an orthodox cross that also marked the spot? If so, where? We lay awake all night trying to come up with a solution to our problem. I was sitting with Arty as the sun was coming up, no closer to a solution than when the sun had gone down.

"You'd think these blasted priests would have made things a little easier for us laymen," fumed Arty.

"Well things that were obvious to them we may not even think of anymore," I ventured.

"Well it's not obvious to me."

I leaned back on the rocks and was watching the sun come up. I was suddenly tired. Trying too hard, I thought sun rise, or maybe son rise? I chuckled to myself. What did I know about a cross? Not much, surely. I was used to crucifixes more than crosses. Why were they different? I Know Miss Eileen had explained it to me. Let's see, upright and cross bar where Christ was nailed, of course. Then there is a small top cross where they nailed the notice INRI, Jesus, King of the Jews. The bottom crossbar was where they tied a person's feet. Most criminals were tied to the cross. The nailing of Christ was unusual. Tying a man to the cross, he actually drowned as fluids filled his lungs over the course of a day or so. Had to do with the position. Well, nothing in all that. I rose and started to walk around, looking out at the valley. Then it came to me. In a moment, I knew what it all meant.

"Arty! Sutter! Murray!" I called, half frantic with excitement. "I've got it! I know where to look!"

"Well don't just stand there, where do we look?" shouted Sutter.

"No fun if I just tell," I said strutting up and down, very proud of myself.

"John, I'll break your leg if you don't tell."

"Alright," I said, pointing to the valley. "What is the story of the foot bar on the cross?"

"It wasn't used. He was nailed on the upright," said Arty.

"Yes. Yes. But why is it crooked?"

All I received in reply were blank stares.

"Arty, I'm ashamed of you. You should know. The criminals of course!" More stares. "The criminals who were crucified with Christ." I looked at three blank faces.

"And.," said Arty.

"In the Orthodox Church the footboard is turned up on one side, pointing to the criminal who was saved and promised a place in Heaven. And what does the map say? A 'Sacred Trust'. A sacred promise by Christ to the criminal. That's where the treasure lies. At the point of the upward footboard!"

Chapter 15
Treasure

"You're joking, surely," grimaced Sutter.

"I'm not and get saddled," I ordered. "We've wasted three days already."

"Might as well, Sturt," shrugged Arty. "He may just be right."

In a few moments, I was back up on Emmett and we were headed back down into the valley. It seemed like only moments to reach the valley floor. Here I reigned up to await the others. It was only a few minutes and they were there with me. We started our search of the finger of hills turning to the northwest, in an orderly fashion. Forming a right oblique with our four horses, Murray still leading our mule, and spaced about 50 yards apart, we moved ahead at a walk, searching the hillsides for some sign of our goal.

We had gone about a mile and a half when our progress was stopped by the precipitate rock of the valley wall. My three companions were perceptibly disheartened. We followed the same system back to our starting point and found no cross or other marker.

"Well. Watson. So much for that theory. What else does your good catholic upbringing say we should try?" came the disheartened words of Sutter.

"She'd say try the other side of the hill. That's what she'd say," I retorted.

Sutter laughed and at least for the moment the tension was broken. So, riding around to the north face, we repeated our process. We had gone perhaps a mile when Arty called out for us to stop.

"Up there," he pointed. "By the large boulder, a cross!"

Rushing to his side, we looked where he pointed. There it was, an orthodox cross, perhaps 100 yards up the side of the rocky finger.

"Murray!" I shouted. "Watch the horses. Come on boys!"

But in the time it took me to say those words, Sutter and Arty were ten yards ahead of me, having leaped off their horses and scrambled forward.

When we reached the large rock with the cross chiselled into it, I started looking about the whole area as the other two began to grab up rocks at its base and look under them like they ere looking for prizes in a Christmas pudding.

"Stop, Gentleman. Stop," I called. The two of them looked at me quizzically. "Let's think this out for a moment. What do we see around the marker and where would you logically think a casket of jewels would be placed?"

The three of us studied the site. "Over here," said Sutter, pointing to a spot to the right of the marker. "The stones appear to be placed and not random. What do you think?"

"I say we move them," was Arty's reply. So pulling up rocks, we removed several layers when we came to a large, flat stone. This stone also had a cross chiselled into it.

"Murray!" I called. "Bring up the pick." In a moment he was with us, and using the pick for a pry bar, we moved the large, flat stone beneath which there was an opening to a cave. The opening was barely large enough for a man of medium build to slide though on his belly. It was but a moment and Sutter had entered the opening, Arty upon his heels, literally. As I prepared to enter, Sutter called back.

"Too dark in here, John. This cave opens up but goes back a considerable distance. We'll need a lantern."

Murray ran back down the hill and was back shortly with our lantern. Lighting the lantern, I passed it to Arty who had crawled back to receive it, and I then followed him in, leaving Murray with instructions to guard the opening.

In the cave, the lantern gave a feeble light, but enough to see by. The cavern extended but about 50 feet and barely tall enough to stand erect in. It was perhaps ten feet wide.

At first the cavern appeared completely empty and we started to search the walls and floors for any sign.

"It can't be gone," moaned Sutter.

"Keep looking," I encouraged.

We continued looking for a few moments when I heard a rush of outgoing air and softly Arty said, "I have it."

There in the far corner where Arty stood with the lantern, just below eye level, was a shelf of rock. We gathered around him and saw an icon, perhaps 4 inches wide by six inches tall, of whom I did not know. But below the icon and sitting directly on the shelf of rock was a small casket of wood, perhaps 8 inches long by 6 inches wide and 4 inches high.

We stood, without touching, and stared at the box. On the lid was some type of oriental scene which somehow seemed incongruous to a holy treasure. Around the edge of the box ran a ribbon of gold inlay and in what appeared to be the eyes of a dragon set two diamonds, each perhaps a carat in size.

"By God," whispered Sutter. "It is real." Reaching forward, he picked up the box and looked it over. "How does it open? I don't see a hinge."

"Try sliding the top," I suggested.

Pressing his thumb down on the lid, it slid easily to one side, exposing the contents. I had never seen so many rubies and diamonds in my life! It was an amazing sight! No settings. No gold. No semi-precious stones. Just diamonds and rubies. It was indeed a fortune.

"Let's get out of here," said Arty. "I want to see it in the daylight."

Picking up the icon, I placed it in my pocket and the three of us headed for the opening. Arty scrambled out first, Sutter behind and I trailed with the lantern.

Sutter had barely entered the opening when I heard Arty calling, "John! John! Get out here quick! Murray's been injured!"

Pushing the lantern in front of me, I scrambled out into the daylight. There, just down the hillside knelt Arty and Sutter looking at the prostrate form of Murray. Rushing over, I saw that I did not need a medical degree to know what happened. He had been struck in the head with something. Blood covered his red hair. Checking his pulse and eyes, I relaxed a bit. Murray would be alright. But surely he hadn't fallen? Then how…

"He has a bally hard head you know."

Turning my head from where I knelt next to Murray, I saw the grinning face of Lieutenant Godard, and in his right hand, was his service revolver, pointed at us.

"He really should have paid more attention to his surroundings, you know. But he was so intent looking in the hole, he never noticed me."

"You bastard!" I cried.

"Doctor. doctor. Really, such a temper. I had no idea! Is that my treasure Sturt?" he said, pointing at the box with his revolver.

"You do know you're outnumbered here Godard, don't you?" said Sutter.

"But I'm the one with the gun, old boy. Now just put the box down and all three of you back away."

Sutter hesitated. "Put it down," I said. "He does have the gun."

Sutter looked at me, then back at Godard.

"Follow the doctor's good advice, Sturt. That's a good man."

Sturt put the box on the ground next to Murray's prostrate form and took a step back.

"Keep going. Back up."

We took three or fours steps down the hill and Godard came forward and stood next to Murray. Keeping the revolver pointed toward us, he reached down and picked up the box.

"Nice of you to find this for me and the Colonel" he sneered. "We'll enjoy it. Maybe I'll even get Violet back. What say, Arty?" The smile was the kind of evil that makes the blood boil.

"Now if you Gentlemen will step over the hill, I'll take my leave." He flicked the revolver toward his left and we moved to our right, allowing him to pass us and go down the hill towards the horses.

Godard was watching us as he stepped forward. It was at that moment I saw Murray's arm shoot forward and seize Godard by the ankle and twist.

Godard fell forward and as he did the revolver fired and I heard Arty scream and go down. Godard scrambled to his feet, the box no longer his. Sturt had pulled his own revolver and fired at Godard, missing as Godard was scrambling, half rolling down the hillside, knowing his only purpose now was escape. Sutter was after him, firing in a fury, but each time he stopped to fire, Godard made progress in his escape, increasing the distance between them. I was busy with Arty. He had been hit in the right upper thigh and was in agony. The large calibre of the bullet had ripped a hole the size of a cricket ball out of his leg as it exited.

Murray was moving now. "Murray, help keep pressure on this. I've got to get my bag." Placing my kerchief on the wound, I placed Murray's hands front and back and ran for the horses. Godard and Sturt disappeared, along with their horses, but for now, I had no time to look for them.

Returning to Arty, I gave him a dose of laudanum and washed and packed the wound as best I could. In fact, he had been fortunate indeed. The bullet not only had passed through, it had hit no bone.

It was fully a half hour before Sturt returned. By then, I had cleaned and bandaged Murray's wound and I had been able to move Arty to the base of the hill. We were busy trying to construct a travois using the cargo tarp from the mule pack when Sturt rode back to us.

"How's Arty?" he asked, stepping down from his horse.

"I'm still alive if that's what you mean," replied Arty. "Where's the bastard?"

"Dead or dying, I think,"

"You think?"

"Brought down his horse about a mile back. He went down with it but got up and made it for the rocks. I followed him for a ways. Pretty sure I hit him at least twice. He made it over the top of the rocks. I decided not to follow our lion cub any further. If he doesn't die of his wounds, maybe the Mohmands will get him. Either way, he's not our problem. Our problem is getting out of here."

We relieved the mule of all the equipment, which we piled in the dust. We filled our water bottles and loaded grain and rations on Arty's horse. The mule would pull the travois with the sticks crossing the pack saddle.

It was now the early afternoon and we decided we would head for the second cross with the hope that Arty's four sowars were still there. We felt we would be able to make it by dark. As we were about to depart, I gave Arty another dose of laudanum. I knew the trip would constitute agony I would not like to suffer.

We progressed well but slowly. As we passed the spot where Godard's horse had gone down, I scanned the hillside for any sign of him. The flies were already gathering on the carcass of the horse. Murray and I continued on as Sturt stopped to search Godard's saddle bags. He re-joined us quickly having found nothing of import. We rode for a while before I spoke.

"What were you expecting to find?" I asked.

"Something to prove Enderby was behind this, but there was nothing there, just kit."

"How do we explain all this, Sutter?"

"We don't, old boy. Godard was just a babe lost in the woods for all we know."

"I had fairly assumed that," I replied. "But I was thinking of Arty."

"Oh, easy enough. Jizail bullet from the hillside. No one will even blink at that. It's Enderby who'll be the problem. When his boy fails to reappear, he will be all over us. He's going to have to come up with some story about Godard's disappearance. We'll just have to take it as it comes." We rode the rest of the way that evening in silence.

We reached the second cross as the last rays of the sun were setting over the western hills. Arty's four sowars were still there, faithfully awaiting their lieutenant's return. Upon seeing their officer on the litter, they rushed to his aid and it was only with the greatest difficulty that I was able to care for and redress his wound due to their constant "assistance".

That evening we took a calculated risk and made a small fire to enable us to make a decent meal for our invalid. Arty's daffadar or native sergeant, quickly organized the three sowars and assigned them to various duties of attending their lieutenant and standing guard on the hillsides. Murray had attended to our animals while I was occupied with my duties at Arty's side. Later, while the sowars stood guard and Arty slept, Sutter, Murray and I sat near the campfire.

"Excuse me, Sir," said Murray. "Hadn't we best put this out? I can fill it in."

"Yes, I suppose so," I agreed. "No use taking unnecessary risks."

"Before you do," chimed in Sturt, "I want to tell you both what I've done. While you both were occupied tonight, I reburied the box."

"You what?" I exclaimed.

"Yes, I know. We've gone through all this to find it but I have a bad feeling about it. It's where any of us can find it. It's covered by rock at the base of the cross up by the trail. I have no fear it will be found and we can come back for it now that we know where it is. We're going to have enough to explain at the moment and Enderby is going to be very curious about his missing dog."

I thought about this for a moment and, looking at Murray, nodded to him.

"It makes sense to me. At least we know where it is. What do you say, Murray?"

"Yes, Sir. As you say, we best come back later."

Having agreed to this, Murray started to cover the fire and I went in search of some sleep. Fortunately sleep came quickly and the next I was aware; Sutter was shaking me awake as the first rays of false dawn could be seen.

I rose and tended to Arty, who was now showing signs of a low grade fever. That was to be expected of course. In the meantime, Murray and the daffadar had been seeing to saddling and packing. I had just finished with Arty and was wanting my bit of dried beef and new potato when the sowar who had been posted on the hillside raced into camp. He reported straight to the daffadar. I knew something was wrong. The two came quickly to where Sturt stood by the cold fire pit, said something and then turned and went to gather their horses from the line.

"Doctor! Private Murray!" called Sturt. "Quick as you can now! Horses! There are a dozen or so Mohmands trying to circle us from the north! We've got to move now! Quick as you can!"

Fortunately we were prepared to move except that we hadn't set Arty on the travois yet. Murray brought up our mule and with the help of one of the sowars, I placed him on it. We tied a lead strap under his arms, attaching it to the travois lest he should slide down and off. We had no time for the slow movement of the day before. Speed was essential if we were to escape.

Our preparations took but moments and we were up on the trail moving at a brisk walk. The daffadar and one sowar took the lead, then I leading one mule and Murray the second, which transported Arty. Sturt and the other two sowars brought up the rear of our little column.

Within minutes I could see the turbans on hillsides as they raced to try and get ahead of us. I knew it was at least six miles to the main Dakka-Jalalabad road. The entire trail could now turn into a deadly gauntlet from which we might not reappear.

I could hear firing to our rear. We were keeping a good pace and I knew that the men moving along the hilltops could not keep up. If we could keep the Mohmands from overtaking us by the trail, we should prove to be alright. My one worry was that "lucky" shot from a hillside.

By the time we reached the first cross, we had outstripped those on the hills but now Sutter and his sowars were no longer even occasionally in sight and the sounds of firing increased.

We had halved the distance to the road again when one of the sowars rushed past me up to the daffadar. The daffadar and both sowars turned their horses about and as they rushed past, the daffadar reigned up for a moment.

"Sir. Please to continue. We shall return."

With that, he was gone after his men. I continued and for a few moments I could hear a great increase in rifle fire.

Within 15 minutes, we were out upon the road and I slackened the pace. Another mile and I stopped to check on Arty. His wound had reopened and I could see the agony in his face.

"Don't worry about it, John" he smiled. "I'm going to be fine. Let's keep moving. We're not safe yet."

"Two hours and we'll be in Dakka," I told him. "but first, I'm going to re-bind your wound. Then we'll move on."

I quickly rebound the wound and we moved off again. It now seemed that our luck had changed for we met a patrol of Bengal Cavalry led by a Jemadar.

I quickly explained that Lieutenant Sturt and four men had been holding off the attack of the Mohmands to allow our escape. Leaving four men to escort us to Dakka, he galloped off with the rest of his patrol to extricate our little force. So it was that about two hours later, with great relief, we entered the fort at Dakka.

The next hour was busy. I installed Arty in the hospital and was now able to properly treat him. The Surgeon Major agreed that after a day's rest, Arty would be sent to the hospital at Peshawar.

Having taken care of the animals, Murray came to find me. We had had no word about Sturt nor of the patrol which had gone to his aid. It was not until the late afternoon that the patrol returned. It was the Jemadar who had led the patrol who came to find me at the hospital. Two of his men had been wounded slightly and were being brought in. But the worst news was yet to come. There had been one fatality, Lieutenant Sutter Sturt, of the 5th Regiment of Foot.

Chapter 16
The Partial Truth

I was stunned. This could not be! Sturt, dead? I had to go somewhere and think. Other people died, not my friends. And his treasure, for I thought of it as his, he'd had such plans. Plans weren't much use now. The sadness overwhelmed me.

I decided not to talk to Arty about it until the next evening. By then, he would be wondering at not having seen our friend, but for now, he needed rest.

In the meantime, I was called to the headquarters and asked to report what had happened. I kept to the story that Suttor had proposed. No sightings of gatherings of Mohmands until McMullen had been hit by a surprise sniper. The rest was easy, I merely made no mention of treasure or Lieutenant Godard and gave the details of our escape the day following Arty's wounding. It was all taken at face value and I was allowed to return to the hospital.

That night, I broke the news to Arty. He appeared to have no reaction. He stared off into the ceiling for a while.

"I think I need some rest, John. Do you mind?"

"No, but if you decide to, we can talk tomorrow before your convoy leaves for Peshawar."

"Yes, we'll talk then. Good Night, John." With that, he closed his eyes and I left.

I didn't sleep that night. All our adventures kept flooding my thoughts. One gets very hardened to death and suffering of others in the Army. But when it's your own, well, that's different. I never have gotten over Sturt's death. Come the morning, I went to see Arty prior to the convoy's departure.

"Sorry you won't be here for the funeral," I said. "But you need to get to Peshawar as soon as possible. Best hospital we have you know."

"Oh, I'll be fine, John. Be back in the saddle in no time. As for funerals, well, I've seen plenty of them. Sutter wouldn't want us moping about. He did his job, what else needs to be said? I'll surely miss him though. I do have something else to say," he looked about to make sure we were alone. "I don't want my share of the treasure, John. Do what you want with it. You already know my feelings."

"Arty, surely you need to give this time, think it over."

"I have John, all night. Don't worry about me regretting it. I won't. Understand?"

As they loaded Arty into the ambulance, I said goodbye and shook his hand. We would meet again, sooner than I expected.

That afternoon we buried Sturt in the cemetery under the walls of the fort. Reverence for the dead and the conduct of the funeral is something the Army does well.

We paraded for funeral at half one and all were in dress uniform. The garrison paraded at the slow march, rifles reversed, to the cemetery. It was indeed a solemn procession. Sturt would have appreciated it. I couldn't help smiling thinking that somewhere, Sturt was also smiling. I resisted the temptation to bless myself at the end of the chaplain's words and as the soldiers marched off the band, played a cheery little dance hall ditty. How odd, I thought.

As I walked back to the hospital, I wondered what to do next. It was now the 5th of June. The convoy of cannon was due tomorrow. I reasoned the best thing to do would be move on with the convoy on the 7th,. Go on back to Jalalabad. So we did.

Murray and I arrived at Jalalabad on the 9th. Colour Sergeant Wood had commanded the company on the return trip. Arty's havaldar had taken his detachment to Peshawar in concert with the convoy moving their Lieutenant. I don't know that they had orders to do so but no one thought to question them.

I was in a sad mood at Jalalabad. The line officers seemed to deal with losses differently than I did. Among them there was a much more fatalistic attitude. It was not that they did not care about their fellow officer. In fact, he would be remembered on the role of "honoured dead". It was more than that; this was the business they were in. Death was common enough in peace, in active service, it was an expectation. So while the officer's mess that night had a certain sombreness to it, (there were many questions) there was also a light heartedness. Hurrah for Sturt, may his soul stand guard in the streets of heaven.

I went about my duties that first day back with little to say to anyone. I was able to wire through to Peshawar and found that Arty was doing well and should be returned to duty in a month or two. He also had kept with our arranged story, a sniper from the hills.

It was on our first day back in Jalalabad that I was sent for by Major Tucker. I reported at the headquarters.

"Doctor. Good of you to come so quickly. I've been instructed to ask you some questions about the incident in which Lieutenant Sturt was killed."

"Gladly, Sir, but I don't know what I can really tell you since I did not actually see what happened. I and my orderly were taking Lieutenant McMullen to safety. Perhaps the Jemadar from the 12th Bengal saw something."

"I understand that McMullen was wounded in the incident. Not seriously, I hope."

"Serious enough. Should be back to duty in a month or so. But to answer your questions, no. He was wounded the day before." At this point I detailed the story as Murray and I had rehearsed it. Everything was exactly as it happened except there was no treasure and Godard was never mentioned.

When I had finished, Tucker leaned back in his chair behind the desk and looked at me for a moment. "You know, Doctor, that almost word for word, what your orderly told me. I wonder why?"

"Perhaps because it was what happened. And of course, we have discussed it at great length, trying to decide what we might have done differently."

"Well, that does seem to make a certain amount of sense." He now leaned forward over the desk and looked at me intently. "I've received a wire from Colonel Enderby of the General Staff. He's asking about Lieutenant Godard and seems to think you might know where he is."

I furrowed my brow and thought a moment. Did I know where Godard was? In truth, I didn't. Sturt had said he'd wounded him, but where he went in his run from Sturt or where he was now, I had no idea.

"No, Sir. I cannot say that I know. Is he on leave?"

"Yes, he took a week but why should Colonel Enderby think you would know?"

"I'm sure I can't say, Sir. Is that all?" I rose from my chair.

"That's all, Doctor," he said, rising also. Coming around the desk, he patted my shoulder. "Sorry about Sturt. I know you and he were great friends. Well, carry on."

I left with a feeling of dread. I was now in a position I had never imagined I would be in. And I had placed Murray in a like position. We had found the treasure, yes, but we were now lying about the whole incident. If only Godard hadn't tried to steal the treasure, if he hadn't shot Arty, if Sturt hadn't shot Godard. What a mess had become of such a great adventure. I sought Murray out and asked him about his interview with Major Tucker. True to Tucker's statement, the stories had been consistent. But our troubles were not yet over.

That evening, I received orders to report to the hospital at Peshawar and Murray was ordered with me. We started the following morning. I knew who had arranged this, for who would want to talk to me at Peshawar? Only Enderby.

It was the 12th of June before we arrived at Peshawar and my first act was to go see Arty. He was still assigned to the hospital but the wound was healing well and as long as he didn't overextend, he could get about. I met him outside where he sat in a gazebo, shaded from the afternoon sun.

"Watson!" he cried as I entered and started to stand.

"Sit down you fool or I'll be in trouble for re-opening your wound," I grinned.

"Excellent to see you!" He settled back in his wicker chair. "But let me guess what brings you here." He grinned from ear to ear. "You've been ordered to Peshawar and you're going to get a call to visit our friend the Colonel, eh?"

"That about has it." I said, sitting in the chair next to him.

"Yes, well, old boy tried to bully me about it, didn't do him any good. Didn't see Godard, don't know anything about a treasure. Held his little palaver in private so he didn't have to say the word 'treasure' in front of anyone else. Poor soul is beside himself with rage. He doesn't know if we did something to Godard or if Godard has double-crossed him. He's in quite a tizzy.

"Tell me, Arty. What do we do about the treasure?"

He took a long breath and sighed. "I've told you, John. I don't want any of it. I just want to get back to the 18th and get on with it. It's all yours and Murray's for all I care. Queen's regulations say if we find a treasure, we're supposed to turn it to the crown. We would be entitled to a 10 per cent share."

"Sturt never told me that."

"Lots of things Sturt didn't tell." Arty was quiet a moment. "I really miss him."

We sat quietly for a while.

"I'd best report in." I finally said, getting to my feet. "I'll check back in on you soon."

That evening I was summoned to General Headquarters to report to Colonel Enderby. My loathing of the man was reaching no bounds. I entered the headquarters and found it almost deserted. A sergeant at the front desk asked if he might help me.

"I'm to report to Colonel Enderby."

"Ah, yes, Sir. Second door right, Sir."

"Thank you, Sergeant." I answered. Turning, I went to the door indicated and finding it closed, I knocked.

"Enter." It was Enderby's voice.

Entering, I took the scene in quickly. Enderby was alone in the small room. There was only a small table and two chairs and behind where the colonel sat, a window, closed even though the heat was oppressive. This was to be a private discussion indeed.

Enderby was watching me intently as I closed the door. I then reported and stood at attention waiting. For a moment, he said nothing. He looked me up and down as if considering his course of action. Finally, he made a decision.

"Have a chair, doctor. We know each other fairly well, no standing on formality.

"Well, Sir, I do have a number of patients to attend to. Is there something I can do for you?" I stood where I was, not moving toward the chair as proffered.

"First, doctor, I want you to know that whatever our differences, I'm still sorry about your friends."

"Thank you, sir. But what is it I can do for you?"

"Alright, Watson, have it your way. What were you and Sturt doing out near Dakka and where is Godard? That's what I want to know." He leaned forward over the table, his face was tinged with red and his breathing was coming quickly.

"It was a reconnaissance patrol and I don't know where Godard is," I replied.

"Bull!" he yelled, slamming his fist on the table. "You were looking for the treasure! Do you think I'm a fool?"

I stood my ground and looked at him with a smile.

"Do you really believe you can fight me, doctor?" His control was returning. "What have you done to Godard?"

"Sir, I assure you that I have done nothing to Godard. Is he lost?"

"You know damn well he is missing. If I can prove you or the other two have done him in, even the treasure won't save you. Do I make myself clear?"

"Quite, sir. Anything else?"

"Yes, I believe your services are going to be needed around Kandahar. I've arranged with the medical department to have you reassigned down there. You'll be taking Private Murray with you. The two of you can perhaps remember better what happened last week."

Saluting, I turned about and left the room. Kandahar was as far away in Afghanistan as he could send me. Perhaps it would be a good thing.

Chapter 17
I Meet the 66th Regiment of Foot

It was Friday, the 12th of June when Murray and I left for Kandahar. We were being sent to the 66th Regiment of Foot. It was an outstanding regiment with a great history and just recently arrived in Afghanistan.

In my writings over the years, I had mentioned that I was "removed" from my regiment. Those not truly familiar with the Army system assumed I meant seconded. They were wrong for two reasons. Firstly, at that time, medical officers were not properly part of a regiment. They belonged to the Medical Department and assigned as needed. Secondly, I felt "removed". I was disposed of by a loathsome creature, to better his own position, but the result of these actions would lead me to a wonderful place in the end. It would lead me to Baker Street. Miss Eileen had always been right. God, indeed, has plans.

It took about a week on the military road to travel the distance from Peshawar to Jhelum. Before we left, I had visited Arty one last time. We wished each other well and I never saw him again. I did keep up with his career and saw he was mentioned in dispatch from the Kurram Valley. We have corresponded over the years.

On arriving at Jhelum, I was fortunate to get room on the transport train for Emmett as I was loath to part with such a good horse. I felt in a way fortunate to be on my way to the 66th. Things had been relatively quiet in the Khyber and the fighting appeared to be moving south. Ayub Khan had not been installed by the British government but instead Abdul Rahman was to be given the throne. Ayub Khan was gathering forces outside Herat and I would be needed. The treasure and other troubles were pushed from my mind.

Four days later, Murray and I arrived at Sibi, the northern terminus of rail leading toward Kandahar. It had not existed the last time I had passed the area. Colonel Lindsay, R.E. had been given the task to complete the line from Ruk junction to Sibi, a distance of 133 miles, in order to eliminate the requirement to walk across a horrible desert. He accomplished this at the rate of one mile a day with almost no injury to the men. It was a truly remarkable effort. The survey was now in hand to extend the line to Quetta.

At Sibi, I was able once again to secure a mount for Murray. We were traveling with few impediments as most our kit was still in Jalalabad. Even so, it would take 10 days to reach Kandahar and during our journey, there were forces moving of which we, nor the British, had any knowledge.

Much is known now about what was happening, but at the time, British intelligence had completely failed. Spies were caught, reconnaissance was poor and deciphering of what intelligence there was, was left to political officers. The countryside from Sibi to Kandahar was deceptively quite, but as

Murray and I moved toward the 66th, Sadar Mohammed Ayub Khan was also moving toward Kandahar, along with 20,000 soldiers and 30 cannon. His location and exact strength were completely unknown to General Primrose and the British Army.

As Murray and I proceeded in the false calm, Ayub Khan was moving his cavalry from Herat. As we had ridden the train, the Wali of Kandahar was at Girishk asking for British troops to support his soldiers, who were wavering and on the verge of going over to Ayub Khan. As Ayub Khan approached Girishk, he was gathering tribes along the way and moved slowly in order for the gathering to occur. He had even succeeded in quelling some of the squabbling between the Kabuli and Herati. Ayub had succeeded in getting to Farah before Primrose had even received permission to support the Wali. Massive troop movements from India would be required to support Primrose. None of this did two lowly soldiers know, as we walked our horses towards Kandahar.

It was late on the 3rd of July when we arrived at Kandahar cantonment. Unbeknownst to me, I had only 4 weeks left to my active Army career.

Having reported in at the 66th to Major Oliver, I was given into the care of their Surgeon Major, A.F. Preston, with an admonition to return later to meet Colonel Galbraith.

"Well, Doctor, we're very pleased to have you along. We've just learned this morning that we march in two days for Girishk. Much to do, much to do."

We talked as we went from the headquarters building toward the hospital area.

"We can much use some more help, hard pressed for help. At least anyone that knows anything. Come from Peshawar, have you?"

I wondered if he knew why I was there but decided not to raise the subject. He was a fine gentleman from his looks and speech. He was probably 5 foot 8 or 9, greying hair and moustache and a pleasant smile. His skin was tanned and wrinkled from many years in the orient and I knew he had a reputation as a good doctor and caring soldier.

"Yes, Surgeon Major. Been here a while now, but what is it that you would like me to do?"

"We'll get you properly started tomorrow first thing, but what I need most right now is for you to meet our staff and then get some rest. Had anything to eat?"

"I must admit not since early this morning."

"Excellent. Excellent. So, first to the mess, I'm sure your man can take care of your kit. I'll have my man see that he's well taken care of."

"And the duty tomorrow?" I asked.

"Need you to start going through the people the Commissary boys are sending us." He stopped walking for a moment and clasping his hands behind his back and looked me straight in the eyes. "As you know, we don't hire our own men. Damnable shame I call it! Commissary Department goes about the streets hiring riff raff and fools to be dressers or compounders or ward servants or doolie bearers or whatever. We in the medical department must be allowed to train and hire our own! Damnable, that's what I say!" With that he grinned and took a deep breath. "Right then. Excellent. Excellent. How about something to eat?"

I laughed and we went off to meet and eat.

The next morning was a frantic scene. The cavalry brigade under Brigadier General Nuttall left Kandahar with the 3rd Sind Horse and 3rd Bombay Light Cavalry. The Infantry Brigade with the 66th Foot, 1st Grenadiers, Bombay Infantry and Jacob's Rifles along with E-B of the Royal Horse Artillery, No. 2 Company Sappers and Miners, Commissariat, Hospital and ordnance stores would follow the next day.

I watched with great interest as the months of supply, rations and equipment to support 2800 men was loaded on wagons, camels and mules. For while, there were over 2400 soldiers to be fed and cared for, there were the muleteers, camel drivers, doolie bearers, etc., who also must eat. Add to this, grain and bhusa for the 3000 animals and the convoy would stretch for miles. But against what appeared to be a sizable force were to be arrayed perhaps 15,000 Afghanis, as many as four regiments of regulars from Kabul plus more from Herat. Much would depend on the allegiance of the Wali's 4,000 men.

It was barely light on the 5th when we marched out. Once again, my position gave me great freedom of movement. While Murray stayed with the hospital near the front of the baggage column, I roved from place to place, asking questions of our situation. It was at this point I met Captain Slade of the Royal Horse Artillery.

Captain Slade had been detailed to General Burrow's staff as an orderly officer. This really was a position of trust as his duty was to gallop orders to different parts of the field of battle. It takes someone knowledgeable of military affairs to properly communicate oral orders and have them understood. In later years, he would be British Commander in Egypt.

I had ridden up alongside him as he was keeping just to the rear of the staff. "Good morning, Captain." I said and saluted.

Looking over his shoulder, he returned the salute. "Good Morning, Surgeon. Hope there's no problem."

"No Sir. Just inquisitive. Like to know what's happening so I can be prepared."

He looked me up and down for a moment as if considering if I were serious or a fool. He finally nodded as though he made a decision and smiled through his moustache. "Good idea to know what's happening. Lets one plan for contingencies. What regiment are you with, Doctor? I don't remember seeing you before."

I introduced myself and explained I had just arrived from the Khyber Field Force.

"Well, you should have seen a bit then. Our job is going to be to keep old Ayub Khan from trying to take Kandahar. We've support coming from India but he'll be here before they will. Or so we think. The Wali has just been installed and we're none too sure of his followers. Our job is to make his men stand and fight with us if Ayub Khan actually comes."

"I must admit, I've no faith in the Afghans ever taking one side or the other. It seems to be expediency of the moment with them."

He looked at me for another moment and then came a great guffaw. "By God, Doctor, you do understand these people!"

We continued to ride together and spoke at length of our situation. If the Wali's men stood fast, a good defensive position could be established and even at a disadvantage of two to one or three to one, we were sure of holding.

We had been talking the better part of an hour when I decided that I had been gone long enough from my position and took my leave. The Captain had impressed me. He appeared to have an excellent understanding of our situation and capabilities. He was also a superb horseman, as were most horse artillerymen.

That night, having travelled but seven miles, we camped at Kohkaran and I went about the normal business of blisters and boils. Each day, for seven days, we made camp where the cavalry brigade had camped the night before. This system was necessitated by the large number of animals each brigade had and the limited grazing available.

I saw Captain Slade a few times over the following week but spent some of my time getting to know the officers of the 66th. Colonel Galbraith and all his officers were excellent men. Most of my time, however, we spent at the end of the day's march trying to explain the duties required of the newly hired natives to them with the help of those who had been there. We made adequate progress under trying conditions. For after a day's march, camp must be set, animals cared for, defences built and men fed. There was little time for instruction. Through it all, Surgeon Major Preston was a steady friend, helping to guide me through my additional duties.

During the march itself, I made it a point to get about and meet each of the officers of the 66th. Captains Cullen and Roberts were especially friendly and made it a point to seek me out each night as did Lieutenant

Faunce. All of whom were great horse fanciers and we spent a bit of time talking about the merits of different horses and jockeys.

On the fourth night, we reached Kushk-i-Nakhud. (We would return here sooner than we had expected.) And by the 11th of July we arrived at the Helmand River directly across from the Wali's fort at Girishk.

Chapter 18
To the Helmand and Back

On the day of our arrival at the Helmand River, we were still unaware of Ayub Khan's nearness. His cavalry was already at Washir. We were not in a good location nor was luck with us at the moment. General Burrows had been ordered by General Primrose not to cross the Helmand but the Wali's fort of Girishk was on the opposite bank, forcing us to form a defensive position separate from the Wali.

The last leg of our journey had only been six miles and as the infantry worked on establishing our defensive perimeter Surgeon Major Preston, Surgeon Collins and I strove to establish a working hospital in concert with the Surgeons of the other regiments.

Late that evening, I ventured over to where the 66th had established its headquarters to see what information I could glean from the officers. I wanted to know how long we would be in place and if there was word of our enemy for our camp was an open plain with little cover. I found Major Oliver standing by a campfire, smoking a pipe and looking very introspective.

"Good Evening, Sir. Mind some company?"

He looked at me a second as if gathering his thoughts. "No, doctor. By all means. All going well at hospital? No list of illness to report, I hope."

"No, Sir. The soldiers are in quite good shape. Normal problems." I took out my pipe and as I started to charge the bowl, the Major turned back toward the fire.

"Any idea how long we'll be in this position, Sir?" I asked. "Just want to know for planning purposes. How much to get off the wagons, etc. You know the issues."

The Major thought for a moment as if deciding what to say. He looked around and seeing we were alone, moved closer to me.

"Look, doctor" he said sotto voce. "This place we're in is a great parade ground but it can't be defended. We're not allowed to cross the river, which would be the best thing. It's easily fordable this time of year. We either need to move across the river or find another spot. See that wooded area just across the river?" He pointed and I turned and looked. "Put a few cannon in there and some good riflemen and they would give us a beating out here in the open." He turned back and smoked for a moment more. "No, doctor, don't put too much on the ground. We will need to move."

We smoked for a few more moments and then I took my leave. Major Oliver was still studying the fire as I left.

The next few days were spent quietly while the troops tried to improve our position. I talked with Captain Slade the following morning and learned that most of the Wali's troops were in a mutinous mood. A number that reached 6000. One of the Wali's sardars had already deserted with the Alizais but for the moment, the rest of the soldiers remained.

We had been four days on our "parade field" and were finally given the order to move further up the river to a more defensible position when the worst news possible came. The Wali's soldiers had deserted en-masse and were headed to join Ayub Khan who was now reported only 55 miles away at Eklang, or at least his cavalry was there. The Wali's force deserted well armed, taking 6 cannon and massive amounts of small arms and ammunition.

Oddly, the Wali's cavalry took it upon themselves to deliver the Wali and his treasure to our political officer, Lieutenant Colonel St. John, before deserting themselves. What was even more unusual was that instead of going toward Ayub's cavalry, they headed towards Kandahar as if to wait for Ayub Khan to catch up.

Murray ran into the hospital area as we were tearing down to load the wagons.

"Sir, General Burrows has ordered a column to chase the Wali's forces and disperse them and reclaim the cannon. The 66th is sending 4 companies. Do we go?"

"I say yes, but we'll have to get permission from the Surgeon Major. Start packing two mules and I'll be right back." So saying, I went in search of permission. It was easily obtained. By the time I returned, Murray had two mules packed, a handful of doolie bearers and Emmett saddled. As the 66th moved off in pursuit, we trailed the column.

Besides the 66th Foot, there were three companies of Jacob's Rifles and the No. 2 Company of Sappers and Miners. In the distance, I could see the elements of the 3rd Sind Horse and 3rd Bombay Cavalry, along with our battery of Horse Artillery. The mounted units quickly outdistanced us and by the time we reached the ford of the Helmand, two miles distant, they were but a dust cloud. It was now mid-morning.

As we struggled on in the heat, it was the duty of the infantry to clear a number of villages and nalas to the right of our line of march. The mounted units were little impeded by the few Afghans who sniped at them along the way. The infantry, moving more slowly, came under more constant fire. More importantly, we did not know their strength and therefore, whether they posed a clear threat. Each village and gully had to be cleared as we marched. By noon, I had two wounded and before the day was over, two more. One would die in August of the wounds he suffered, Private John Holmes.

By 11 o'clock, we could hear distant small arms fire. The cavalry under General Nuttall was trying to hold the enemy in place while they awaited the cannons and Infantry. In a few moments, we could hear the cannon fire. But it was not the crack of rifled guns; it was the ring of smooth bores. The rebels had opened up with their cannon on our cavalry. The officers started pushing our soldiers to move more quickly. I bandaged an arm as I walked beside our mules, pressing forward.

Now came the crack-thump of the rifled guns. The Royal Horse was in the fight. As we marched, the cannons played point and counter-point. Gradually, the ringing of smooth bores came less and less frequently. Major Blackwood's battery was winning through! The cannons had been duelling for more than half an hour.

As we crested a hill, I could see the bulk of the cavalry riding to the left. They were going to take the battery which the mutineers had abandoned. There were, however, enough of the enemy infantry to cause the cavalry to dismount and fight as skirmishers. The Royal Horse was moving forward also and in a few moments they were in action again, throwing shell among the Afghans and causing them to flee once more.

Our cavalry mounted and gave chase until the hillsides prevented further pursuit. We were now in possession of their artillery, their ammunition and their supplies. By 4 pm., we had returned to camp, the 66th Foot escorting the captured battery with drivers supplied by the Royal Horse.

That night, as I sat on the tail board of the ambulance, cleaning my Webley, Murray approached.

"Excuse me, Sir, but I thought you might want to know there's a big palaver going on at the headquarters."

"I'm sure they'll let us know what's going on, Murray," I said, putting away my rags and oil. "But I haven't had a pipe all day, think I'll see what the Surgeon Major knows.

"Yes, Sir," smiled Murray. "Excellent idea. I believe I'll check water barrels. Evening, Sir." With a knowing nod, he saluted and left.

Re-holstering my revolver, I secured my pipe and helmet and went in search of Dr Preston. He was with Major Oliver at the Major's tent.

"Ah, Doctor Watson. Excellent. Excellent. It looks like we'll be leaving in the morning," grinned Preston.

"No official word yet," interrupted Oliver. "Be the best plan though."

"Why is that, Sir? Is there word of Ayub Khan?" I asked.

"We know his cavalry is at Eklang, about 55 miles from here, and according to Lieutenant Colonel St. John, he's probably got 15,000 men assembled at this point. Let me show you what the problem is." Oliver got up and going to his table, unrolled a map.

"Look, Doctor. We're here, at Girishk on the Kandahar side of the Helmand. Now, our orders are to keep Ayub Khan from marching on Kandahar by making him stay on his side of the river."

"I understand, Sir."

"Well, there are just a few problems with that, good fellow." He pointed at the map again. "The Wali's soldiers, who we were supposed to fight with, have deserted and taken their Snider rifles. His cavalry has just dispersed but his infantry is joining Ayub Khan. That may bring his strength to 20, 000. Now, the river is falling and within a day or two, he won't have to come through here." He stabbed at the paper. "He can cross anywhere. He can cross above or below us. We also have no supplies. We have water and grazing for the moment, but we'd need grain for the animals and food for the men. I believe, we'll be moving back to a more defensible position closer to Kandahar. Right now, we're outnumbered almost ten to one. If I were you, doctor," he looked me in the eyes, "I'd be checking my bandages."

The next morning, the decision was made to move back to Kushk-i-Nakhud where supplies could be had. There was an old fort there and it sat upon the Girishk-Kandahar road by the Maiwand Pass.

The ponderous task of an Army packing for the move took most of the day and the march didn't start until 7 that night. Before we left, I could see a huge fire down by the river and went to investigate. There, I met Captain Slade. He was in a fury.

"What's going on, Captain?"

"I live among fools, doctor." He looked at me, hands on his hips and shaking his head. "That heap of charcoal you're looking at is ammunition wagons for the battery we captured yesterday. And those fools," he pointed at the soldiers "are throwing ammunition in the river!"

"But why?" I exclaimed.

"Because there aren't enough horses to go around for cannons and baggage. We've already sent a dispatch to Kandahar asking for more horses but instead of leaving tents and cots, we are leaving ammunition. I tell you, doctor, they may well regret this." He shook his head again.

Inwardly, I grinned a bit and thought, "An artilleryman's love of his sport". Outwardly, I asked, "What of the guns?"

"Oh, we'll move them, and each gun has 52 rounds with it. I've even convinced Blackwood to haul some of the ammunition for these guns. He believes it's a mistake also." Once again, he shook his head and with a parting look at the burning wagons, turned on his heel and left.

The march the first night was about 26 miles. We arrived at Mis Karez about mid-morning the following day. Men and beasts were exhausted, having been on the march for 14 hours and without sleep for 27. We rested here the rest of the day and started the march again the following day. It was a short march of about 8 miles. We were now 84 miles from Girishk and 46 miles from Kandahar. On this day, Ayub Khan's cavalry entered Girishk. Heliograph messages and dispatch riders were now flowing between Kusk-i-Nakhud and Kandahar. We camped on the Kandahar side of the old fort in what appeared to be a good spot.

Loading and unloading our little hospital had become fairly routine. Our training of the commissary hires had gone well and as a consequence, there was little for me to supervise. I decided to walk through the 66th's camp and talk with the men.

On the whole, all to whom I spoke were in good spirits, but the constant marching was beginning to show. They were willing, but tired, and I made a note to myself to talk to Major Oliver about what we could do to help the situation. As things happen, I was able to speak to him that evening and he assured me that, at least for the moment, General Burrows intended to stay at Kushk-i-Nakhud. As I left the Major's tent, I could see more dispatch riders coming and going from the General's staff tent and wondered what new orders they brought.

Late the next evening, I sat smoking my pipe and found myself wondering how Arty was fairing and where he was. My thoughts were broken by Murray, who came to tell me that we were moving again in the morning. The move was only a distance of three miles to the right bank of the Kushk-i-Nakhud stream. I had come to the point of admitting I did not understand military tactics, for we were moving from what appeared to me a good position from which to fight and 5500 men and over 3000 animals were moving to an open valley. Perhaps it was to position to better intercept Ayub Khan. I just didn't know.

As we unloaded again at our new position, a detachment of 3rd Sind Horse arrived from Kandahar, bringing more horses and more dispatches. As had become my norm, I went in search of information. I could see the men of the 66th digging breastworks, but an officer was walking the ranks, calling out the occasional soldier, who dropped his tools and taking up his rifle and equipment was falling into formation. Thinking that perhaps there was another large patrol, I hurried over to see if my assistance would be required. I found Lieutenant Faunce giving the formation over to a Sergeant to march off.

"Lieutenant Faunce, is there a patrol?"

"Ah, Doctor. No. It seems that Captain Slade has convinced the General to form a provisional battery with the Wali's cannons. I was told to find 42 men who had some knowledge and toll them off to the good Captain. I go also."

"You don't seem displeased," I remarked, for surely he was grinning under the skin.

"Well, chance to do something different, always liked the cannons. He's also pulled Lieutenant Fowle from the Ordnance and Lieutenant Jones from Transport. They're both Royal Artillery. We'll each take two guns and see what we can do. Major Blackwood is sending men to command each piece."

His demeanour changed and looking somewhat more serious, he looked to the hills that surrounded us. "Doctor, if we're attacked here, we'll need every cannon we've got. We're surrounded by high ground. I hope they have adequate reconnaissance out."

I gazed around me in a complete circle, while Faunce watched me. He was right, this was a bad location. At no point could you see beyond a mile.

"Well, I saw more cavalry coming in, surely that will help."

"Let's hope, Doctor. They brought more horses for the Wali's battery too. At least we'll have enough artillery horses to move the guns. The Lieutenant who came with them seems a decent fellow, name of Dragon I think, lost an eye in Africa last year. Anyway, must be off to drill the men. See you later, Doctor."

Over the next few days, except in front of the 66th, little improvement was made to our position. The Jacob's Rifles and the 1st built breast works out of the kit bags and camel saddles. Day after day brought no news of Ayub Khan and his horde. The cavalry patrolled constantly but nothing was seen.

I spent a considerable amount of time over at the Wali's battery, watching the 66th's new gunners train. They were quick studies and Captain Slade kept them working until every crew was precise in its drill.

Murray came to me one afternoon to discuss some concerns of the day's orders. Once we had disposed of business, he hesitated.

"What is it, Murray? You've something to say?"

"Well, Sir. All this time since our little incident back at Dakka, you see. And well, I've been thinking. What do we do about the treasure?"

"I've thought about that too, Murray." I put down my pipe and looked at the camp before us. "Doesn't seem too important at the moment."

"No, Sir. That's what I was thinking. Doesn't mean much. At least not out here. I keep thinking about Lieutenant Sturt. He might be here if we hadn't gone looking for it."

"It's what he wanted to do. He'd also be here if Colonel Enderby hadn't sent Godard after us. Godard would be here too."

I turned back to my pipe and started to recharge it. "I believe, Murray, it's better left where it is."

"Thank you, Sir. I'd much the same idea. I'll be getting back now, Sir." He saluted and was off.

That night, Surgeon Major Preston and I decided to visit Major Oliver and try to determine what the forces status was. We had heard that the Bombay Cavalry had a short fight that morning and we wanted to know if a fight was expected. We found him at his tent.

"I'm happy to tell you what I know," Oliver stated, leaning back on his camp stool. "Colonel St. John can only give us the merest estimates. We know the Wali's men, with our rifles mind you, have joined Ayub Khan. St.

John thinks we're facing about 5000 infantry, 3000 cavalry, about half regular and half irregulars and 30 cannon. Plus there will be 5 or 6 thousand ghazis armed with who knows what.

"We know they're close, but we don't know where. And our job is still to keep them from attacking Kandahar until it can be reinforced. That little skirmish the cavalry had this morning was against about 500 horse according to Major Leach. They've increased patrols, but unless we can find them, we don't have a plan of attack."

The afternoon of the 25th, Lieutenant Smith of the 3rd Sind Horse, finally brought some positive news. He'd been to Maiwand and found that Ayub's patrols were almost to Sangbar and that Ayub himself would be in Maiwand by Tuesday the 27th. Ghazis were already starting to assemble in Maiwand, awaiting their leader. General Burrows decided to beat Ayub Khan to Maiwand and stop his advance on Kandahar in compliance with his orders. It was a decision that would change my life forever.

Chapter 19
Maiwand

Much has been said and written about the battle of Maiwand. I can only describe it as I knew it. What I saw was not the big picture of tactics and strategies. What I saw was the close in fight of desperate men against overwhelming odds. Did Ayub Khan outnumber our force by 10 to one or only 8 to one? I don't know. Neither does anyone else, not even Ayub Khan himself. That we were to lose 1000 men and Ayub Khan 5000, was hours in the future. We would suffer a severe tactical defeat and yet achieve a strategic victory.

We had started packing at 10:30 on the night of the 26th and the force paraded at 4:30 in the morning. It would be seven before the advance party would leave and in the intervening lull, I tried to eat some dried beef and drink some water. In the Army, at that time, the practice was to have the last meal of the day at four in the afternoon so it had already been a long time since we had eaten and there was to be no morning meal. I was sitting astride Emmett near the hospital wagons as the sun rose, smoking my first pipe of the day, when Captain Slade rode by.

"Morning, Doctor. Ready to march?" he said, reigning up.

"Any time you are, Captain. There will be some action today, I expect."

"Yes, I think there will be. Would you like to ride along with the smooth bore battery? Your men are manning the guns. We may need you."

"I'll have duties with the hospital but I'll see what I can do. I'll try to catch up."

"Good show. Well, have to find which wagons have our little bit of extra ammunition." He emitted a great sigh and shook his head, "I told them to dump tents instead of gunpowder." And giving his horse a nudge, he rode off.

I went in search of Surgeon Major Preston and found him sitting on the seat of one of the wagons. On explaining my desire to march with the men of the 66th who were manning the smoothbore battery, he just grinned.

"Enjoy yourself, Watson. Carter and I will send for you if you're needed."

After gathering some additional medical supplies to my rather overstuffed saddle bags, I gave Murray instructions as to where I would be and for him to stay close to the Surgeon Major so we could find each other. I then went in search of Captain Slade and the smoothbores.

The column was now on the march and I decided to sit on a small swell of ground and have the battery come to me. I watched as Lieutenant Geoghegan and his men left at a trot. His half company of the 3rd Bombay

Light Cavalry were evidently to conduct the reconnaissance ahead of the main body. About five minutes elapsed before the next unit came by. It was Captain Mayes squadron of the 3rd Bombay and two guns of Major Blackwood's battery of rifled guns under Lieutenant Maclaine. I had met Maclaine in passing and he appeared a bright fellow but had a reputation as a glory hound.

Now there was a short gap and then came General Nuttall, his staff, more cavalry and two more of Major Blackwood's guns under Lieutenant Fowell. As they passed me, troops of the 3rd Sind Horse took off to left and right of the column to act as flanking guards.

About 100 yards behind was the main column of infantry. The 66th and Jacob's Rifles were on the right, Bombay Grenadiers on the left, in the centre, the sappers and miners and the smoothbore battery. The rear guard was made up of the last two cannons of Blackwood's E/B Royal Horse Artillery and some 3rd Sind Horse.

As the main column came abreast of my position, I left my little hillside and trotted over to where Captain Slade rode in advance of this battery of infantry and artillery soldiers. To the right of the main column, moved the baggage trains.

The baggage trains, I knew, were a constant thorn in the side of the line officers. While it had to exist to support our soldiers, it also drained manpower that was needed on the firing line. Each of the three infantry regiments had had to supply a company of soldiers to defend the baggage plus a treasure guard and a commissariat guard. I could see Major Ready of the 66th who commanded this small guard, riding to the left of his columns.

Captain Slade welcomed my salute as I approached the moving guns. "Fit yourself in anywhere, Doctor. You can ride with me for a while if you like."

"Do we know exactly where we're headed?" I inquired.

"Toward the village of Maiwand, Doctor. The Maiwand Pass would give Ayub Khan easy access to Kandahar and we need to plug the bottle, if you will, before Khan can get there. General Burrows believes we should arrive about a day before the old Khan does. We set up a good defence and we'll be able to hold him off… I think."

We rode for a time in silence. The slow pace of the infantry with which we travelled was especially hard on the horses. The natural gait of an artillery horse is a trot. Simple inertia is the problem. Once rolling, it's easier on the horses to keep the 2000 pounds they're pulling moving than have the constant start and stop behind the walking of the infantry. The horses I knew would be tired before the morning had gone.

Matters were made worse by the need for the infantry to stay aligned with the baggage train which moved even more slowly.

As the sun rose higher in the sky, the temperatures rose. By nine in the morning, it was already approaching 100 degrees and we had stopped for the second time to allow the baggage train to close up. While we waited, the artillery drivers watered the horses in a little stream.

I had dismounted and taken Emmett to the stream for a drink when I saw an officer ride up on the far right of the battery and report to Captain Slade. They spoke for a moment, but before I had remounted and returned, he was gone.

"Any news?" I asked, as I returned to Slade's side.

"Oh, no. That was just Lieutenant Dragon. Major Ready has placed him with the few extra rounds of ammunition we have and he wanted to tell me where it was in the column. Good to know. Ah, looks like we're moving again, doctor. Not covering much ground, are we?"

"Horrible pace. Hurts the horses and the men." I replied.

For the next twenty minutes we walked on until cresting a small knoll. I could see two small villages to our front and another, larger, to our right, some miles off.

"What's the larger village, Captain?"

"That's Maiwand, doctor. Those two little ones are Mandabad and Khig."

"Seems deserted."

"No, Doctor, they aren't, I assure you. See those dust clouds off to the north? Cavalry. They'll have scouts in the villages. I hope we do."

We continued down the knoll and lost sight of the villages again. By 10 o'clock, we had stopped again when Captain Slade was called forward. I took the time to go among the men and check on their welfare. They were hungry and tired, but the moral was high.

I was talking with Lieutenant Faunce when he suddenly held up his hand and stood in his stirrups, looking to the front. Officers, including Captain Slade, were galloping back to their units. Slade reigned up next to us and called for Lieutenants Jones and Fowle to join us, which they did at the double.

"Well, Gentleman. Looks like we've lost the race. Evidently Ayub Khan is already in Maiwand. We're going to have to attack him immediately if we're to keep him from securing the pass. There is Afghan cavalry about two and a half miles to the front and infantry probably five miles out."

Just then, the advance was sounded and our column started to move again. The four of us stayed together as the Captain continued. "We'll be moving up the Kushk-i-Nakhud ravine. I can't tell you what's going to happen because I don't know. I do know the old man will pitch into anything he finds. All right then, back to your men. And Doctor, stay close to me. Lieutenant Faunce, send Sergeant Cacy to find Lieutenant Dragon and tell him I want that little bit of ammunition moved to the front of the baggage train."

"Yes, Sir" responded Faunce and saluting, rode back to his division.

As Faunce rode off, I could see the flanking cavalry closing in on the column.

"Why are the flankers closing in?" I asked.

"Keep the column moving faster and keep in closer touch, doctor. It's a risk, of course. They can't give as early a warning if something happens."

We moved on in silences for a brief while, covered in dust and perspiring in the awful heat. The infantry was suffering greatly with no food and little water, at least their valises were in the baggage. They carried their weapons, water bottles, ammunitions pouches and haversacks. Their khaki uniforms blended with the dust but the black equipment and dark brown puttees made each man of the 66th a target. I suddenly looked down at myself and realized my dark brown Sam Browne belt and boots made the same of me. Captain Slade's voice brought me out of my reverie.

"Something's happening!" he exclaimed, pointing to the left front. "We're moving toward Mandabad, toward that dust cloud."

As I looked up, a rider from Major Blackwood's battery was running pall mall at us and barely checked his horse in time to avoid colliding with me. He snapped a salute at Slade.

"Major's compliments, Sir, and would you advance your battery at a trot? The Major will be on the far side of Mandabad across the nala. You're going to come into action on his left, Sir."

"Very good, Corporal. Tell Major Blackwood I understand." With that, the Corporal saluted and was gone.

The air was split by the crack of Blackwood's rifled cannon as we moved at a trot between the engineers and the Bombay infantry. The infantry was now moving at double time and the baggage and hospital were being directed into the nala to provide some protection.

As we crossed the nala, I could see four of Blackwood's guns firing on the Afghan cavalry who were falling back, and in the distance, what seemed to be a forest, truly odd for this area.

As we moved to the left of Blackwood, Slade called "action front" and the battery came into line. Guns were dropped and limbers moved to the rear of the guns. As the men prepared to fire, I could see Lieutenant Osborne's guns coming into action to the right, completing Major Blackwood's battery. Our twelve little guns seemed alone on a vast plain, without cover for man or beast.

The first rounds of cannon fire from the smoothbores were sent at a range of about 1800 yards. It was now, when I saw the trees move, that I realized it wasn't a forest on the distant hills, it was thousands of men! I'm ashamed to say that for a moment, a sense of panic set in. I looked behind and saw our infantry in line, lying on the ground to the rear of the guns. The enemy was well out of rifle shot and lying down afforded our infantry some protection from the enemy cannon. To our right, left and immediate rear, stood the cavalry as flankers for the guns. I could also see Major Ready and Lieutenant Dragon behind the infantry, with our supply of ammunition.

The horde of Afghan infantry was moving to our right as our guns played on them and their cavalry was feeling to our left. A shell burst within a few hundred yards of me. I was no longer a spectator on a great stage. I was a target and the 30 cannons of Ayub's artillery were coming into action.

Emmett, the fine horse he was, stayed steady under my hand and I rode him to the rear of Faunce's division. Here I dismounted, and holding the lead strap, started walking up and down the line looking for who might need assistance.

Captain Slade rode up and down the line, giving each division orders as to how to direct their fire. We were in a fight, cannon against cannon, and we appeared to be outnumbered, probably three to one. While we stood on a barren, flat plain, the Afghans were in what was actually rolling hills, ravines and nalas, which provided cover. It was an uneven match but we were holding our own for the moment. I now had no time to think of the fight, as we were now taking casualties. Handing Emmett's lead strap to a driver, I gathered my saddlebags and ran for Jones' division where the first casualties had occurred.

Lieutenant Jones was between his two guns, giving direction to their aim points. Two of his men were already down and as I ran to them, I could see the drivers cutting a dying horse out of the traces. Fortunately, the plain that made us and the cavalry such a visible target, made us a difficult one also, as the flatness and haze of battle made range prediction difficult.

I was now going man to man, a quick patch and those that could be, were back on the guns. These men of the 66th and Royal Horse were amazing. One would think they were firing on a parade ground. Each round was a smooth load, steady aim, fire.

The artillery battle continued as I moved from gun to gun and wished I'd brought Murray with me. I completely lost track of the overall battle as I worked to bandage and stitch.

It seemed like only moments, but I knew we had been battling for some time when I heard a new sound. It was shell, moving faster and with a heavier explosion than ever before. Slade was nearby and I called to him from the spot where I was bandaging a leg.

"What the Devil is that, Captain?"

Slade walked his horse over and grinned down at me. "Fourteen pounder, breech loading, Armstrong guns, old boy. Bigger and faster than anything we've got. Five rounds a minute, even with an untrained crew. Wish we had them."

"Look, Slade, infantry moving up." I pointed to where our men had risen and were moving forward and establishing themselves to our left and right. To our left came 2 companies of Jacob's Rifles and to our right, the 1st Bombay. I couldn't see the 66th, so I assumed they were somewhere to my right. I went back to my business and now understood the calm of the 66th and Royal Horse. I didn't control the battle, just my part of the battle.

The enemy artillery seemed to increase in intensity. Many horses were going down, the cavalry suffered horribly, unprotected and without the ability to respond to their attackers. At least the artillery could respond with shell.

We had been in the artillery fight for over an hour, when Slade approached me again.

"Doctor, I need you to stay with Lieutenant Faunce. Jones is taking guns to the far right, the 66th is being pressed over there by Ghazis. Fowle is taking his guns to the left of those two companies of the 30th. The 3rd Sind is going to reinforce also, the beggars are trying to flank us with their cavalry. I'm told the baggage guard is being hard pressed too. I'm leaving the seriously wounded here with you and Faunce." With that explanation, he was off, not even waiting for a response. I went back to the wounded. The lack of water was becoming critical. Few could make it across the open plain the mile back to the baggage where water and supplies were plentiful. With them under attack, re-supply was out of the question.

I inspected my watch, 12:45. We'd been at this for two hours now. The Afghans had moved their artillery closer and our casualties continued to mount.

"Does it matter what time it is, Doctor?"

I looked up and there, mounted on a fine bay, was the one-eyed Lieutenant known as Dragon.

"Godard! But I thought.."

"I know what you thought, Doctor! Or more to the point, what you bastards hoped for!" He leaped down from his horse and stood an inch in front of me.

"Left me to die, didn't you! But I didn't, did I?"

I placed my right foot back to gain balance in case of an attack.

"You were ready enough to kill us," I countered.

"I didn't want your life, Doctor, just your treasure. You boys could have shared but you were too good for that! Well, Doctor, you're going to tell me where it is and maybe I won't kill you." He placed his hand on his holster. "In this mess, who's going to notice another body more or less?"

Never before had I seen a man's eye actually glow with hate.

‘I should care about what happened to you after you shot Arty? You’re lucky I didn’t shoot you. You would be dead.”

“Arty was an accident. You know that! Leaving me half blinded and at the mercy of the Mohmands, that was no accident!” he spat at me. His body was shaking with rage.

“You’re a fool, Godard. And I’ll expose your little charade when this is over. Let the pieces fall where they may.”

“Doctor Watson, over here, quickly! Sergeant Ryan, if you please, legs gone.” It was Lieutenant Faunce.

Godard and I continued to stare at each other.

“Doctor!”

“Coming,” I said, taking a step away.

“I’ll be back, Doctor!” snorted Godard and turning, mounted his horse and galloped toward the baggage train. I hurried over to Ryan, but it was too late.

The temperature in the afternoon was increasing. Some accounts say the temperature by one o’clock was 120° Fahrenheit, though who had the time to take a reading, I can’t imagine. The 1st Bombay on our right and the Jacob’s rifles on our left, had been lying on the ground all this time with little to shoot at, but taking horrible casualties from the artillery fire which missed our battery but fell among them.

Fowle and Jones were ordered to re-join with Faunce as their ammunition ran low. It was as they re-joined us, I was called to Lieutenant Fowle who had been wounded severely in the leg. I was able to stop the bleeding and one of the soldiers helped me to get him back on his horse. He wanted to stay but Captain Slade ordered him off the field. I gave his horse’s lead strap to a driver who no longer had a team and saw him off. I was now down to almost no medical supplies. By now, half the horses were dead and a good fourth of the men, dead or wounded. One by one, our six guns fell silent. Slade had been right at the Helmand. The officers had tents, but we had no ammunition!

Captain Slade called Osborne and Faunce to the centre of the battery.

“We’ve no ammunition wagons to supply us, Osborne. Take the battery to the rear, find Lieutenant Dragon, he has a few rounds in the supply wagons, get them and return as quickly as you can. I’m going to Major Blackwood to see where he wants us next.” The three saluted and dispersed.

Having empty saddlebags, I mounted Emmett, who, up to now had been untouched by the chaos around us. As the battery limbered up the guns, I could see the faces of the men of Jacob’s Rifles to our left. It was a look of dismay. You didn’t have to hear the voices, the question was plain. “Where are the guns going?” “Why are they leaving us?” The enemy was now in rifle range and the guns were pulling out. You could smell the fear.

The ground rumbled as we rode for the baggage train. The dust was so thick I could hardly see. The wounded occupied every spare inch of the limbers and guns.

Suddenly, I found myself on the ground, laying face down. I was dazed. As I tried to pick myself up from the ground, I felt a weakness in my left shoulder. I couldn't get it to respond. Rolling to my right, I tucked my legs up and got off the ground. There was blood pouring down my left arm and all I could seem to do was look at it.

"Bloody shame you were wounded, old boy. Could have been killed, you know. How does it feel? It'll hurt much more when they try to fix it. The doctors are such butchers here. Maybe they'll just take it off."

It was Godard, on his bay, with his pistol in his right hand, pointing at me and grinning like a madman.

"Damn you, Godard! We're fighting for our lives here!"

"Doesn't bother me, Doctor. I'm already dead." He grinned again and a strange laugh emanated from his throat. "Now, tell me, where did you put the treasure?"

"Damned if I'll tell you after you shot me!"

"Makes no difference to me, John. If you don't tell me and die, 'en combat', shall we say, there's always your boy Murray. Probably give it up quite easily when he learns of your demise, facing the enemy and all, what?"

Shells were landing closer and closer as the Afghans pressed around us but neither of us paid any attention.

"I'm asking one last time, doctor." He cocked the hammer of his revolver.

Again, I found myself on the ground. The concussion from a shell had thrown me to the ground. It had landed behind Godard and he and his horse were down. The animal, screaming in pain, was trying to rise but could not. His right foreleg was gone and his hind legs were tangled in his entrails. Shell fragments had ripped open his belly and spilled his insides out.

Godard was trying to pull his right leg from under the horse, trying to get away from the flailing hooves. Without thinking, I picked myself up and ran forward. Putting my one good arm under his shoulder, pulled him free. We fell back in a heap and I scrambled back to my feet. Godard bounded up, pistol still in his hand.

"Thanks, John. But that changes nothing." Taking his pistol, he turned to his horse and putting it to the animal's head ended its pain. Turning back to me, he re-cocked it and pointed it at my head.

"Now, John, for the last time. Where is the treasure?"

But in the time it took him to turn from his horse I was on him. It seemed to be a bizarre struggle. A one armed man against a man with one eye. I grabbed the barrel of his revolver and twisted it away from me but he still held tight to the grip. I pushed into him and the two of us went down falling over his horse. We were covered in blood and entrails yet we still rolled about the dirt each struggling for survival. Godard was using his free hand to try and get at my eyes, tucking my head down I smashed into his nose and he released the pistol, but I couldn't hold onto it. The slime of the dead horse had made everything slick. Godard pushed me away and scrambled to his feet searching for the weapon. It was only a yard or two away, dropping on one knee he picked up the pistol and turned to me with that insane grin.

I fired three times in rapid succession. Godard went down in a heap. So intent had he been on finding his weapon he never saw me draw my revolver when he was turned away.

I stood up and went over to where Godard lay. There was no doubt, this time he was dead. "It didn't have to end this was, Godard. It was only jewels. Now you've lost the only real treasure."

I looked for Emmett but could not find him, so I trotted as best I could for the baggage train. It seemed like forever but I finally reached the comparative safety of the nala. The three companies with the baggage trains had been engaged for some time as the enemy pressed down the nala from direction of Maiwand.

As I stumbled into the hospital, I called out for Murray. It was only a moment until he found me and was taking me to Surgeon Major Preston. As he helped me forward, I was surrounded by other wounded. Murray sat me on a stool and removed my tunic. Preston obviously tired and worn from treating the wounded looked at my shoulder.

"Not too bad, Watson. No exit wound and there is not time to get it out now. We'll stop the bleeding and get you some rest."

As he dressed the wound, I could still hear the crack of Blackwood's guns and the musket fire had become general. Men from the 66th baggage guard were holding the Ghazis back in the nala and the other two companies tried to keep the cavalry off our left and ghazis off our right.

As Preston bandaged my wound, my mind was racing. What would I do about Godard? Surely it would never come back to me, and I had only defended myself, but the whole tragedy of the treasure seemed to be suffocating me.

"Watson. Watson! Answer me!"

It was Preston. "Are you alright? I thought we were losing you for a minute. You seemed to stop breathing."

"I'm fine, really." I sputtered out. "Just thirsty and tired."

Murray gave me a water bottle and I drank copiously.

"Now, give me my blouse and belt."

Murray hesitated and looked at Preston. Preston nodded and Murray helped me.

"Stay with me, Murray, and you can help be my hands. Lots of wounded here." My shoulder ached but movement was better than sitting and we started making the rounds. I saw the smoothbore battery to our left and went to check on our men. They had fired the only two rounds they had at the Afghan rifles to try to protect their guns. We passed through the ranks doing what we could and returned to the hospital to find Surgeon Major Preston being bandaged by Surgeon Carter. Preston had taken a bullet in the hip and was unable to walk. Murray helped place him on a doolie when I realized something – The artillery. It was still firing but the rate had slackened. Were the Afghans running out of ammunition? Climbing the bank of the nala, I looked toward the plain and the fighting beyond. To my horror, I could see Blackwood's battery moving toward us, then stopping at the ammunition wagons to re-supply. None of our guns were firing. Herati Infantry and Ghazis were pouring through our lines! The Jacob's Rifles that had been on our left and the Bombay Infantry on our right were no longer there. What appeared to be a wave of running infantry was rolling to the right toward the 66th with little ripples of waves heading straight toward us. Our lines had completely broken! I could see our cavalry to the left form in a loose knot and charge toward the centre, then swing right and toward us. In a moment, they were forming to the left of the nala as Blackwood's battery came in sans two guns. Blackwood wasn't with them and Slade was commanding. Slade unlimbered and started firing into the Afghan cavalry and infantry and ghazis. Men of all units ran into the hospital and baggage train and formed up where they could. Colonel Griffith gathered a small force of the 1st Bombay and they formed up with the company of the 66th and men of Jacob's rifles in a mud-walled enclosure. General Burrows now came in riding double with the Wordi Major of the 3rd Sind Horse, having given his horse to a wounded officer. Burrows ordered us to fall back and Captain Slade formed the rear guard with his cannon. The doolie bearers and the like deserted in a wholesale manner.

Murray and I frantically helped the wounded onto every conveyance we could find. Every limber and gun of the 66th's smoothbore battery carried the wounded out. Preston's doolie bearers left him on the ground, but we were able to get him on a gun limber. A thousand men were gone and we were fleeing for our lives.

The artillerymen and a portion of Major Ready's baggage guard were the only units who appeared to maintain their formation and discipline. The retreat to Kandahar was on in earnest

Chapter 20
Retreat

There was no stemming the flood of the rout. Mixed groups of followers and sepoys, dismounted sowars and soldiers streamed away from Mandabad. Lieutenant E. Monteith had formed a handful of his sowars on the left bank while Slade, whose artillery had kept their formation and nerve, continued to fire. The two groups covered our work to get the wounded loaded on pony or horse, camel or bullock, anything we could find. In the meantime, General Burrows had ordered the few men of the 66th, along with a few of Jacob's Rifles and 1st Bombay to retire from their enclosure so as not to be left behind.

At the time, neither Burrows nor any of the rest of us knew of the desperate fight of the 66th going on a mile distant at Khig, where they had fallen back. It would be days before anyone knew what happened.

It was now, as we tried to load the wounded, that I was felled by the second bullet. For the third time that day, I found myself on the ground. My left leg, just above the knee, had taken a bullet. As it turned out, it was from a Snider. Whether a misdirected round from our own men, from a deserter of the Wali's Army or a weapon taken from a dead sepoy, I'm sure I will never know.

It was Murray who was standing by me when it happened. He was holding the lead of a cart pony. Reaching down, he grabbed me by the belt as I had once grabbed him, he helped me rise on my one good leg. I grabbed at the pony's harness to steady myself.

The last gun of Slade's battery was limbering to move. The infantry was gone and Monteith's few troopers were surrounding Slade's gun. If we didn't move with them, we would be at the mercy of the Ghazis. With a super-human effort, Murray half lifted, half pushed me upon the pony's back. Pain screamed through my leg and up my spine, light blinded my eyes and I almost passed out. It was the terror of falling into the hands of the Ghazis that kept me going and able to hold the harness saddle to stay on the pony.

"Hold on Sir! Hold on! We're staying with the guns no matter what! Don't worry, Sir! Don't you worry, Sir! I got you!"

I looked in Murray's worried eyes but all I could do was nod as we moved off.

We weaved through the mass of moving men and animals, toward our last camp at Kushk-i-Nakhud. As Murray led us along, we sought out the guns, whatever safety there might be, would be with them. In a short time we were able to find Lieutenant Faunce and the men of the 66th with the smoothbores. Every inch of his limbers and guns were covered with wounded. Having no ammunition, he was doing all he could to use his ordnance and horses to transport those who could not walk. Just behind us came the guns of Blackwood's battery commanded by Captain Slade. What had become of Blackwood, I didn't know. Slade, seeing me, rode over and stopped momentarily.

"Doctor, how bad is it?"

"I'll be all right, bleeding is stopped. When we halt somewhere Carter will patch it up. Where's Blackwood?"

"He was wounded and couldn't ride. Last I saw, he was with Colonel Galbraith on the right with the 66th." He looked at the ground, then back at me and smiled. "Perhaps he'll be in yet. Too much of a mess to know who's where." Pulling back on the reigns and watching as we walked on, he called out. "Stay with the guns, old man. Stay with the guns." Turning his horse to the rear, he trotted back to the battery. We pressed on towards the old camp ground.

Here, I will comment on the contradictions which I saw in General Burrows. I will never understand the man. A man who had given his own horse to a wounded fellow officer but who now abandoned us. Colonel St. John had been to our old camp and back. There was plenty of water and the men had been without water or food for 24 hours. True, some had already passed the old camp but a few minutes stop to water horses and men was much needed. The next water was 15 miles distant at Hauz-i-Madat on the Kandahar road. Burrows however ordered our column on, past the camp and to keep moving. He, in the meanwhile, took the remnants of Nuttall's cavalry on a 7 mile ride to Ata Karez where they watered and rested, leaving Captain Slade and Major Leach to drive on exhausted men and animals, and taking away manpower and carbines needed to defend the rear of the column. Major Leach was right on his later criticisms of the retreat.

More infantry now gathered around the guns as we continued on to Hauz-i-Madat. Night came on and had it not been for Major Leach's knowledge of the area, we may well have never found the tanks there and died on the Afghan plain. As it turned out, General Burrows and the cavalry had been ahead of us, but had not sent anyone out to guide us to the wells in the late darkness. It was nigh on 11 p.m. before we found the water.

For the next two hours, men and animals shared the small tanks of water. It was here that Surgeon Carter was able to clean and dress my wounds. I will be forever grateful.

All that two hours, men and animals came in. The tanks were a good quarter mile from Hauz-i-Madat and General Burrows now ordered the cavalry to continue the march toward Kandahar. It was Major Leach who took five sowars and rode back to the tanks to gather the men there so they wouldn't be left behind.

We were not being pressed by any organized enemy at this point. The occasional local with a Jizail or matchlock was all that occurred. It would be days before we would find out that Ayub Khan had won a tactical, but not strategic, victory. While we had been driven from the field with the loss of almost 1,000 men, he had suffered almost 5,000 casualties, killed and wounded. His Ghazis would leave by the thousands to take their wounded and dead home to their villages. It would be days before he could move on Kandahar. But the fear of an organized pursuit was all too real to us. As the hours wore on, we realized we had only to fear each village as we passed.

The cannons at Hauz-i-Madat were joined by Lieutenant Goeghegan and his men of the 3rd Bombay Light Horse. They were to stay with the guns as we waited for the last of the men to come back from water. The gun horses were giving out and before we left Hauz-i-Madat, one gun was spiked and left along with a spare carriage and the store limber wagon.

As we moved out of Hauz-i-Madat, the cavalry, less Geoghegan's men, moved to the front travelling at a pace neither the men nor the worn out artillery horses could keep. The gap between us kept getting wider and grew to three miles or more. It was five in the morning when we reached Ashikan. The cavalry had long been there and were well watered and rested. I was barely able to ride and had taken more than one does of laudanum. Murray was footsore and tired and I begged him to ride a limber for awhile. He refused.

At Ashikan, two more guns were spiked and abandoned and General Burrows ordered the cavalry to give up horses to the artillery so that the limbers of wounded could move on. Burrows was full of conflicting messages!

We marched on through the early morning light and still we received the occasional shot here and there. At Sinjiri, we reached the river Arghandab. While the river was low, it was still a dangerous crossing for men and animals that had fought a battle and been on the move for over a day. Again, a gun had to be spiked and abandoned when it became bogged down in the river bed. It was here too, that we were met by Lieutenant Anderson and sowars of the Poona Horse. They had been sent from Kandahar for our relief and to escort us through the hostile villages. A few miles on, we met the infantry and artillery of the relief column. They gathered the wounded and helped us on. Poor Slade would have to abandon one more smoothbore to save horses and the cargo of wounded carried by the limbers before we reached the citadel of Kandahar.

It was 2:30 in the afternoon when we reached the cantonment, about a half hour behind the cavalry. We had been on the move for over 33 hours and had gone 45 miles with wounded men who had little water and no food for more than two days. It was a miracle!

My time at Kandahar is somewhat of a blank. I was taken within the citadel to the hospital, along with Surgeon Major Preston and about 173 other soldiers and followers. The hospital was well supplied and in good order. I have only the best to say of the surgeons, warders, writers and others of the medical department. Murray stayed with me every moment. Another surgeon, I'm afraid I don't know his name, was able to remove both bullets on the evening of the 28th. I thought I was out of danger. I was wrong. During the next few days, I lay in a bed next to Preston. He was excellent company, with never a discouraging comment or unpleasant word to anyone. I was vaguely aware of the bustle around us as we lay there. The garrison was preparing for the inevitable arrival of Ayub Khan and his army.

Chapter 21
Kandahar and Home

On the day following our arrival at Kandahar, I awoke to find Murray sitting on a stool next to my bed.

"Feeling better, Sir?" he asked with a grin.

"Yes." I replied. "Just weak. But what are you doing here? You're the one who should be resting; after all, I rode all the way."

Murray chuckled. "I'll get you something to eat, Sir. You need it."

"Wait a moment. Murray, give me your hand." I reached up from the bed. He looked at me a bit quizzically, but extended his own.

"Murray, I owe you my life. I'll never forget that. Someday, I hope to repay the debt."

Murray looked like he felt, a bit overwhelmed, as he shook my hand. "You did the same for me, Sir. Guess that makes us even." We clasped hands for a moment more then he stepped back. "Well, sir, about those victuals. I'll see to it right off, sir." And he turned and left.

"Afraid you have a friend for life there," came a voice from the next bed. I turned and looked at the smiling face of Surgeon Major Preston.

"Yes," I replied. "Murray is a good man. We need a few million more like him in this Army."

"We'll certainly need them. The powers that be have sent every Durani out of the citadel for fear of having to fight enemies inside and outside at the same time. Afraid it's just us and the Indian Army now."

"Surely there will be a relief column from India."

"Oh, I'm sure, Watson. But will they arrive in a timely manner? That will be the question."

"I have faith."

"So do I, Doctor," he said, leaning back in the bed and looking to the ceiling. "And I'll pray every day," and he turned and winked at me.

I'm afraid that day was my last clear recollection for the next four weeks. It is a terrible thing in a way to be a doctor. You know what's wrong with you when it happens and yet you can't prevent it. By the second day, I knew I was in the first stages of enteric fever. How did I contract it? The better question was how could I not? Horses, camels, bullocks and men had been forced to drink from a single source of water. And while I knew that the death rate was only about sixty-five in 100,000, that was in a fairly healthy population. I was not a healthy population. Weakened as I was from my two wounds and lack of food and water, mine was a risky case. The possibility of infection of the wounds combined with the enteric fever gave me pause to think hard of my own mortality.

As the garrison built additional defences, Surgeon Major Preston and Murray tried to cheer me. I'm afraid that I remember no more for the next four weeks. In my fever and delusions, I fought with Ghazis and Heratis, cannons manned by the 66th blazed and I killed Godard time and time again. In my few lucid moments, I felt sure of my own demise. While the men of the 66th and the Kandahar garrison fought for all our lives, I fought for my own. The month of August, 1880, is literally unknown to me.

It was the 29th of August when, having survived the fever, I next have a clear recollection. Doctor Preston was no longer my roommate, having returned to partial duty, but Murray was there, sitting on the same stool beside my bed, when my mind finally cleared.

"Murray," I croaked, holding out a hand. "Have I been sick long?"

"Why no, Sir. It wasn't even a month until tomorrow."

"A month?" I couldn't even recognize my own voice. It sounded dry and parched. "Water, please."

"Here, sir" and he held my head off the pillow. "Missed quite a bit, you have, sir. Been a regular donnybrook, it has."

He gave me a drink and put my head back down. "Almost over now, sir. Relief column is at Robat. Been getting regular heliograph messages now. Must be ten thousand men coming to help is what I hear."

"We've held out then."

"Yes, sir. Fight here and there, of course. Nothing to worry about. You get some more rest now."

The next morning, the 30th of August, I was feeling very weak but knew I was going to be all right. My wounds had mended well considering my debilitated state. I continued to have periods of shaking and both my leg and arm would spasm, but I knew I would live. Murray supplied me with the most welcome of all news; General Roberts was only twelve miles from Kandahar and would arrive the next day. Much cheered by this news, I insisted on trying to get up, and with a good crutch and Murray, I made a slow round of the hospital. I was greeted well by the other doctors and everyone appeared in good cheer with relief so close. In less than an hour, I was back abed, thoroughly worn out.

It was early the next morning when I was awakened by the news of General Robert's arrival and I insisted that Murray help me to the citadel walls. As we took the steps to the parapet by the Shikarpur gate, I could hear the skirl of the pipes of the 92nd Highlanders. Never a more beautiful sound had I ever heard. I sat for the better part of the morning on the parapet wall watching the arrival of even more troops and lost in my own thoughts. It was only Murray's kind voice that finally broke the spell as the heat intensified and we returned to hospital about noon.

Evening was coming when Surgeon Major Preston limped into my room. The hospital had been busy all day, for while the relief column was overall in good spirit and health, they had marched some 230 miles in 20 days and had a sizable sick list.

"Watson, good to see you've been up and about. Brought you something," and from a pocket, he pulled a flask and two small cups. Sitting on Murray's stool, he poured out two measures and handed one to me.

"Thought you might want to know what's going on. At least know what I know, that is." He took a drink, as did I, and he started to tell me of the size of Robert's force and the plans for battle on the morrow. Our four remaining companies of the 66th would be used as a holding force out on Picquet Hill while Robert's men, along with a strong force from Kandahar, enveloped Ayub Khan's force and tried to cut off any retreat.

"Oh, I don't pretend to understand tactics, my boy," smiled the old man. "I just patch them up so they can go back to doing what they're doing."

"What are we doing?" I asked. "I mean, here, in Afghanistan. What have we accomplished?"

"Now don't go getting queer on me, Watson." He patted my shoulder and poured us each another whiskey. "If we keep Afghanistan from the Russians, we keep India intact. Simple as that."

"I suppose," I replied and thanked him for all his kindness during my illness. Murray had told me how Preston had checked on me day and night.

"Watson, you're not making this easy for me." He looked down at the tin cup in his hands. "There has been a board of the medical officers here and it's been decided that you need to return to England. I'm afraid active campaigning is out of the question for you now. It's really for the best, my boy. After General Roberts rids us of Ayub Khan, you'll be going home. I envy you in a way. Been a long time since I've seen home."

I was stunned. I never imagined this would happen. But in my heart, I knew he was right. My leg, especially, would never be the same. I was filled with an unimaginable sadness. I said not another word and finally Preston sighed and promising to return in the morning, he left me to my thoughts.

That next morning, Murray appeared early as usual and I convinced him to take me back up on the parapet wall. From here, we could watch as our forces deployed against Ayub Khan and his minions. The destruction of Ayub Khan's army took less than four hours. The artillery opened the assault at 9:30 and by 1 o'clock, Major General Ross was in possession of the Sardar's camp and ordnance, to include the two guns of Blackwood's battery that had been lost at Maiwand. As I returned to my bed there was general rejoicing in all of Kandahar. Ayub Khan's army of 15,000 was scattered to the wind and he was on the run. As Murray helped me back to the hospital I decided to ask his help one more time.

"Murray, I've got to get to Dakka. Will you help me?"

Without a moment's hesitation he responded, "Yes, sir, of course. Soon as you're able to travel, sir."

"I'm able to go now."

Murray looked askance at me. "Yes, Sir. If you say so. We'll have to find a convoy, Get some passage south."

"You leave that to me, Murray." And smiling to myself, I went to bed and took a nap.

Later that night Preston appeared again. His smiling face trying to hide his concern for my welfare. "Great things today, Watson. Great things. We'll be able to get you home soon. Afghanistan will be a safe place, you know."

"Yes, doctor," I smiled, putting on my best face. "I'd like to be on the first transport out. Murray can help me to Karachi and then return to the 5th. I suppose they're still in Jalalabad."

Preston was a little taken aback by my enthusiasm but agreed to find out what he could about any movement going south. I had not long to wait.

The morning brought mixed news. General Robert's victory had indeed been decisive, over 600 dead ghazis were buried between Kandahar and Pir Paimal and no remnants of an army could be found. This was great news. But in the abandoned camp of Ayub Khan was found the body of Lieutenant Maclaine of Blackwood's battery. He had been captured during our retreat and foully murdered in the last moments of the battle the day prior.

It was Preston who brought me the news I really wanted. Major Evan Smith, a political officer, was taking elements of the 3rd Bombay Cavalry and 19th Bombay Infantry to open communications with General Phayre whose column was coming up from the south. I would leave tomorrow.

By the 5th of September, Murray and I were well on our way to Quetta and then Sibi and the train. It would take 14 days on native ponies moving with small detachments from place to place to complete the journey. We were more than half way one night and I was feeling none too well when Murray queried me about my intentions when we got to Dakka.

"Sir. If you don't mind, I'd like to know what we do when we get the treasure."

"I guess it's pretty obvious why we're going there," I replied. "I've not made up my mind entirely though. I just know I can't leave it there. Too many lives have been spent on it. It has to do some good."

Murray looked somewhat relieved. "Yes, sir. Hoping you were going to say that." He was quiet for a moment, staring into the fire at our little camp. "Sir," he finally said. "I know about Lieutenant Godard." The hair went up on my neck and my muscles stiffened. I said nothing. "It was while you had the fever, sir. You talked about it over and over."

I looked into the fire, not daring to speak for a moment. "Does anyone else know?"

"Yes, sir. Surgeon Major Preston. He told me to be quiet about it, but I wouldn't have said nothing anyway. He said he knew a way to get you out of here and back to England. I never told him about the treasure. He knew that Lieutenant Godard tried to kill you and you was just defending yourself, but he thought it'd be best for you to get away from here."

I tried to stretch my tensed up muscles. So, that was the reason for the short work on the medical board. Preston was looking out for me!

"Murray, I've decided what to do with the treasure."

"Well, that's fine, sir. If you don't need anything, I'll be calling it a night."

"Goodnight, Murray." I lay back with my pipe and thought way into the night.

From Sibi, we were able to entrain as if going to Karachi but we left the train at the junction in Ruk and got on another headed to Jhelum. I had thought that might be a problem since our orders didn't take us that way, but it was simplicity itself. No one even questioned a wounded surgeon and his orderly but accepted what I said. Once in Jhelum, it was again simple to get with a column leaving for Peshawar. We had been on the road for 28 days when we finally arrived in Peshawar back with the Khyber Field Force.

The 25th of October was a horribly busy day. I had acquired ponies at Jhelum but I now needed a reason to get to Dakka. I still had kit in Jalalabad, not much of a reason, but it would have to do..

"Well, sir," advised Murray, as we sat pondering our strategy. "Don't the native clinic need extra supplies maybe and we're going to bring them afore you leave?"

So with Murray's brilliant suggestion and my grovelling in the hospital at Peshawar, the next morning we left with a patrol of the 13th Bengal Cavalry and three pack mules full of medical supplies.

The countryside was now extremely peaceful. Since the defeat of Ayub Khan and his retreat to Herat, it seems the fight had gone out of the Afghans. That, with the infusion of money from the Indian government brought quiet, if not peace, to the area.

We spent the first night at Jamrud where four companies of the 5th were and had a fine reunion with Surgeon Major Bennett, Colonel Rowland and the rest. They kept me up long into the night wanting all the details of Maiwand and Kandahar and the great battles. It was here that I first came up with the falsehood of the Jizail Ballet. It was perfectly believable and readily accepted, and so, it became "the truth".

We pressed on, all the way to Dakka the next day, riding in at early evening. Here too was a company of the 5th and numerous companies of the

27th Punjab. But our first stop was the clinic outside the gates. We hoped there would still be someone there and I found myself moving more and more quickly in hopes of finding Malalai.

And there she was. An assistant surgeon of the 27th by the name of Banks had taken over the operation. As Murray and I dismounted, I could see him and Malalai, inside conversing and two ward men were loading a mule with supplies to be taken back to the fort for the night.

I handed my pony's reigns to Murray. "Wait here a moment, Murray. We probably just need to hand these mules off. No need to unpack."

I walked into the little clinic. "Malalai." I said sternly, "Come here, I need you." Both Banks and Malalai turned to look at me and before I could breathe, she was in my arms and crushing me with an embrace. Poor Banks looked stunned as it took me a moment to dislodge myself from the crushing embrace and saw the flow of tears on her face.

"Here, here." I said soothingly. "Sit down on the bench. I'm afraid I gave you a fright." She sat on the bench but would not release my hand and continued to sob. I looked at Banks. "The name is John Watson," I smiled, "and I usually don't have this effect on women!"

"Ah, now I understand. She talks about you all the time. Seems you're her hero." He smiled down at the girl as she tried to compose herself. "But, you see, we thought you were dead, killed at Maiwand, you know."

"Well," I said, touching Malalai's shoulder with my good hand, "I don't believe I was. Wounded, yes. Killed, no!" As Malalai gained control of herself, I gave an uncomfortable laugh.

"How have you been Malalai?"

"I've been wonderful, doctor. More now. I told you killed. Many killed."

"Yes, but thanks to Murray not me. We've brought you supplies for the clinic," I said, addressing myself to Banks. "They're outside with my orderly."

"Ah, well, I'll have my men take them back in the fort. We can always use more, back in a moment." So saying, he stepped outside.

Malalai had controlled her tears for now and smiled up at me, still holding my hand. She was indeed lovely, and intelligent, and kind and all the rest.

She looked at the ground as she said, "You must come and see my husband tonight."

Suddenly, there was a heavy weight in my chest. "Your husband?"

"Yes, Guhkta. He and I marry last week. He is a good man."

I regret that I let out an audible sigh, but catching myself, I picked her up by the shoulders and looking down into her dark eyes, I told her how lucky she and Guhkta were and how proud I was to have been able to play a part in their lives.

"Ready, Sir. Hello, Miss." It was Murray at the door. "Handed off the mules, Sir. We'd best get on to the fort. Doctor Banks wants you to meet him at the officer's mess."

"Yes, coming Murray. Malalai, I will see you again before I leave. Congratulations on your marriage. I wish you only the best."

That night was spent much as the previous one and it was all I could do to answer the plethora of questions about Maiwand. Many of the questions, I simply did not know the answers to: Why the line broke? Why the cavalry was so ineffective? Why the lack of reconnaissance? I could only answer as to what I saw. Toward the end of the evening, I approached Banks and asked for the loan of his hospital warder, Guhkta for a day. To this request, he was only too happy to oblige.

So, armed with the carbines and mounted on 3 good ponies, Murray, Guhkta and I left Dakka Fort in the pre-dawn light headed for the second cross. Murray and I never told Guhkta where we were going or why. The listener to this story will be greatly disappointed that the trip was completely uneventful. Within six hours, we had travelled to the cross and returned. In the saddlebag of my pony rested the small coffer of jewels and the icon that had stood on the shelf with it. Having sent Guhkta to the stables with Murray, I went to the small room I'd been given as temporary quarters and spread the contents of the saddlebag on the bunk. I looked again, amazed, at the enormous wealth of rubies and diamonds.

I separated about 10 per-cent of the jewels as best I could estimate and put them in a chamois bag for Murray. Then I did the same for Guhkta and Malalai and once more deposited the 10 per-cent in a chamois bag. The rest I put back in the coffer. I knew what Arty wanted done with his share and I knew what I would do with mine and Sturt's. The only thing left was to get to Bombay and home, well, at least to England. I was wearing down and I knew it. The gruelling pace of the last month and the debilitated condition of my health had taken its toll. I just wanted to be somewhere and rest.

Outside the walls that afternoon, I bought a small decorative box. Its designs meant nothing to me but the local said it was for weddings so I paid my rupees and took it back to the fort where I placed the chamois bag for Guhkta and Malalai inside. I sent Murray to find Guhkta. He returned quickly with Guhkta at his side. I presented Guhkta with the box and had him promise not to open it for six months.

"If the Surgeon sahib does not wish it, I will not."

"Guhkta, you are the luckiest of men and this will only add to your good fortune." I smirked as I said the words. "You will do me the greatest of considerations by doing as I ask."

"Of course, sir." We shook hands.

"Tell your wife that you and she will forever be my friends and I wish you many children and a long life."

"Of course, sahib, and for you, our house is always open."

Taking the box, Guhkta left.

Murray and I departed the following morning with the 13th on its return patrol to Peshawar, arriving on the 11th and were able to form up with a column leaving for Jhelum on the 13th. But during our two days at Peshawar, my curiosity got the better of me. Where was Colonel Enderby? I had fully expected he would hear of my return and would somehow interfere with my plans by attempting to waylay me. To my delight, my enquiry as to his whereabouts resulted in the knowledge that he had been transferred to the Kurram Valley. To this day, I do not know if he was behind Godard going to Kandahar but I find it hard to believe he was not.

By the night of the 26th of October, 1880, Murray and I were in Karachi and boarded ship for Bombay. He would only be with me a few more days and so on our last night before reaching Bombay, I asked him to come to my cabin as I wanted to speak to him privately.

"What can I do for you, sir?"

"Ah, it's what I can do for you, Murray." I went to my kit and extracted the chamois bag with his share of the treasure and handed it to him.

"This is little enough, Murray. Especially as I owe you my life."

"Why you don't owe me nothing, sir. You took care of me, I took care of you. That's all."

"Well here."

"No, Sir, I can't. I suspect I know what you're going to do with that and my share goes too."

"No, Murray, you can't."

"Why, sir? What do I need that for? Don't I get fed and a place to sleep and clothes? Oh, and a little excitement now and then? Don't need the bother, sir. Put it with the rest."

I had mixed emotion of frustration and pride in my fellow man.

"Well, here." I reached in the bag and pulling out a large ruby, placed it in his hand. "I'll do what you ask, but on the condition that you take this. Let's say for in case of emergency."

Murray looked at the stone in his hand, gave a little nod and said, "All right, sir. In case of emergency. But you must do the likewise."

I laughed and reaching in the bag, took out another ruby and placing it in my pocket, said "In case of emergency."

So we shook hands and said goodnight.

On arriving in Bombay, I found my luck was holding as the Orontes was to sail for England in two days and I, having been wounded at Maiwand

and medically released, had priority on sailing. There was only one more task to accomplish. So I set off in search of my final goal.

The Catholic community in Bombay was exceedingly small, compared to the native religions. For almost 100 years the British Government had continuously inserted itself as an obstacle to the growth of the church for fear of Papal influence on the natives. It was a poor community of Capuchin Fathers who oversaw the Bombay Vicariate which extended from Bombay to Kabul and the Punjab. It was quite an impossible task.

So it was to the complete consternation of one Father O'Callahan that a British Army Surgeon handed over a coffer of jewels worth a King's Ransom, a 17th century icon and an assurance that both were church property.

The flabbergasted Padre wanted to know everything, but I was tired and for the first time in a long time, felt relieved of a tremendous burden. So despite his protestations and with the briefest of explanations and the further gift of Sturt's map, I left Father O'Callahan and spent my last night in India at Watson's Hotel. The next morning I boarded the Orontes. The passage home was indeed tedious and more than once I wondered what I was to do next? England? Australia? The United States and my only family? Where should I end up?

Murray and I had said farewell on the docks and I have only seen him two or three times over the years. I shall be sad never to see him again.

Chapter 22
With Holmes

"The rest, Holmes, you know."

"Amazing, Watson! You've had more than a lifetime of adventure!" Holmes rose from his chair by the fire and placed his pipe on the mantel. Crossing to the window he drew back the drapes, the sun shown brightly into the room.

"Oh, Holmes. I've kept you up all night with my silly talking!"

"On the contrary, my friend. It has been an amazing tale of a very courageous man. You're a kind man and a great friend"

"If you say so." I blustered. "Perhaps we'd best try for some sleep."

"No, I for one am not tired at all; perhaps you'll ring Mrs Hudson for some breakfast."

"Yes, I think that would do." As I pulled the bell rope, I saw Holmes looking out the window.

"And the medal? How did Murray come in possession of it? I presume it was given to you for the kind 'donation', shall we say?"

"Oh, It was given to me here, back when we had first taken rooms together. We had not yet become friends. In fact, at the time, I wasn't sure we would. You seemed the oddest of characters and I had no idea of your business. Most of all, it brought back sad memories so I sent it on to Murray with a note saying he deserved it as much as I."

"Since the ruby was in Murray's box to you, I assume no emergency ever arose for its use. And yours?"

I turned to the desk and removed from the top left drawer a small Bakelite box with a Celtic Cross engraved on the lid. I handed it to Holmes. Opening it, he found another ruby similar to the first. "Ah, again, no emergency." He returned the box to me and putting it with Murray's, I placed them in the drawer as a tapping came on our door. It opened and Mrs Hudson asked if we were ready for breakfast. I was about to answer when Holmes interrupted.

"Not yet, Mrs Hudson, but be good enough to bring up some tea for four if you would."

"Certainly, sir," replied Mrs Hudson and departed.

"Holmes?"

"Growler outside, Watson. Man and a woman talking. He's not sure about coming up but she'll convince him. Banker I should say. She's a governess. Yes, she's convinced him. Be good enough to get the door for Mrs Hudson, would you, Watson?"

"Holmes."

"Yes, Watson?"

“I’m glad my Afghan adventure led me here.”
Holmes grinned. “As am I Watson, as am I!”

SHERLOCK HOLMES
AND THE
MYSTERY
OF THE
BOER WAGON
KIERAN MCMULLEN

Foreword

The adventure I relate here came to me in a most unexpected manner. I had thought that I had seen the last of my days of active campaigning with the forces of the crown when I was invalided out of Afghanistan during the Second Afghan War as I described in *Watson's Afghan Adventure*. This assumption on my part proved to be a particular error, for twice more I would be called back to the flag; as I relate here in the Boer War and again during the Great War. (See *Sherlock Holmes and the Irish Rebels*.)

This was a dramatic time in the history of the empire. The old century was about to close and a new one open. A new century of discontent that would see revolution and attempted revolution across the globe. Not only were there the Boers to deal with but the Boxers in China. The Matebele had only recently been quieted after the Zulu. In the first 18 years of the new century there would be revolution in Russia, China, Indo-China, Mexico and a "War to End All Wars". It was both a terrible and fascinating time.

This story is about both a success and a failure. Holmes was indeed at his best, but like the problems that related to the round-up of the Moriarty's forces there would be issues that would plague Holmes through no fault of his own. His was work to be well proud of. I can honestly say that but for his great effort the war in South Africa might not have gone as well as it did, at least, to the taking of Pretoria. The remainder of the war and the work of Lord Kitchener are for another time.

John H. Watson
Captain, RAMC

Sherlock Holmes and the Mystery of the Boer Wagon

By
Kieran McMullen

Chapter 1
AN INVITATION

It was the winter before I was to turn forty eight years of age and eight years since the death of my second wife, Mary. I was once again sharing lodgings at Baker Street with my friend, Sherlock Holmes, and spent more of my days writing than practicing medicine.

I had found that my scribblings about Holmes and his unique faculties left me with both time and money to pursue other interests (and the racing season was not far off). It was a good life. I enjoyed the writing and Holmes, though he fussed about my turning a "serious study" in criminalistics into penny dreadfuls or schilling shockers, was conscious that my writings brought him new cases and allowed me a living.

It was Saturday, the third of February 1900. It was a rather cold and dreary afternoon. My friend Thurston and I had been playing billiards for the better part of it at his club. Thurston was a nationally known champion. Why he should play with me I have never understood, for rare was the occasion when I beat him. None the less, we were good friends and an afternoon at sport was well spent.

It was during our third game that I noticed my literary agent, Dr Conan Doyle, enter the room. He, like I, had been a trained surgeon who found more fulfilment in writing than in medicine. I had gone into medicine largely due to the circumstances of my stepmother's death in Australia.[1] Why Doyle had entered medicine I was not sure, though I suspected a similar tragedy of some kind in his own family. It was not the type of question one asked.

"Ah, there you are, Watson," said the big man, extending his hand. Doyle was hard to overlook in a crowd. He was tall, athletic, had a great moustache and a booming voice. He drew attention by his mere presence.

"Doyle," I replied, taking his hand, "what brings you here? I don't owe you the final on the blackmail case until next week, do I?"

Doyle chuckled and shook his sizable head. "No, Doctor, I was wondering if I might impose on your time tonight? I'm meeting with a few friends about this dreadful war we are in."

Suddenly remembering Thurston's presence, I introduced the two men.

"Thurston?" said the big man. "Champion billiard player and table maker? Indeed this is a privilege, sir."

---

[1] See Watson's Afghan Adventure

"No more than mine, Doctor. I am delighted to meet you. I greatly enjoyed 'The White Company', marvellous novel."

Though Doyle tried to hide it, his delight at the praise was evident.

"You have a brother-in-law named Hornung, don't you?" continued Thurston.

Doyle nodded.

"I thought so. He's trying to make a run at Watson's clientele with his new stories about Raffles, the Gentleman Thief. Don't say as I get the concept, but the story is good enough."

"I'll be sure to tell Willie you like his work."

Doyle turned back to me as Thurston started circling the table for his next shot. Stories were fine, but billiards was serious business.

"So may I count on your presence tonight, Watson?"

"I suppose," I replied, "but can't you say what it is all about?"

"Time enough for that. Until tonight then, say about eight. We'll be meeting in a private dining room at the Cecil Hotel. Now, if you gentlemen will excuse me, I have some other important business I must take care of." With a nod Doyle turned and was gone.

"Well, your friend Dr Doyle is a bit mysterious," sighed Thurston.

I picked up the chalk and wandered to his side of the table.

"I cannot imagine what all that is about unless he's made a committee to raise funds for the soldiers or something."

"You'll find out tonight. Now if you don't mind, it's your turn, so hurry up and miss so I can run the table." I laughed and for the moment forgot about Doyle and his mysterious invitation – long enough to lose two more games to Thurston.

It was later that evening as I was preparing to meet Doyle that Holmes interrupted my thoughts. "You're right of course, Watson; they always say it will be a short war."

"Holmes, how did…. Ah, never mind. You won't trick me again."

I picked up my hat and gloves as I made for the door to our sitting room.

"I was looking at the picture of Gordon, then at the photograph of my reunion with the 5th and finally at the calendar. Simplicity itself! The government always says it will be a short little war, and it never is. Am I right?"

"Watson," said Holmes putting down his paper and rising, "you have it exactly." I was grinning like a Cheshire Cat as Holmes went to charge his pipe from the Persian Slipper.

"So will you go to South Africa with Doyle?"

"What? Nobody has said anything about going to fight the Boers. Doyle would be the biggest target on the battlefield. No, here you're wrong Holmes. I'm sure this dinner will be about some committee to get pledges. Though I admit with the Northumberland Fusilier (my old regiment) going, I have an urge myself."

"Good old Watson. You'd do well by them too." Holmes lighted his pipe. "Have it your own way. I'll tell Mrs Hudson you'll be back in a year or two."

With that Holmes seated himself by the fire and picking up the paper proceeded to fill the air with clouds of smoke.

"Really, Holmes," I muttered as I closed the door behind me.

Chapter 2
AT THE CECIL HOTEL

The Cecil Hotel is only a few blocks from Charing Cross Station. It occupies about three and a half acres of land along the Thames and fronts on the Strand. It is a wonderful hotel. At the time it had been newly rebuilt and was reported to be the largest hotel in the world. The main restaurant of the hotel faces the Thames and the gardens. The orchestra sits on a raised platform across from an enormous fireplace. Everywhere one looks there is polished marble and granite, tapestries and fine American walnut.

Passing the billiard room with its four full sized tables, I regretted that Doyle hadn't extended his invitation to Thurston. I was to meet with Doyle in a small dining room off the main restaurant. Even here all was elegance. At one end of the room stood an open balcony looking out on the river.

"Right on time, Doctor," bellowed Doyle from across the room. "Come meet your fellow invitees."

Crossing the room, I found myself in the company of four other gentlemen besides Doyle. "We are all here, old boy, to convince you to join us on a great adventure and to serve your fellow man."

"I hope I do that already. At least I try," I responded. I was already getting an uneasy feeling that Holmes was right. Just what type of committee was this?

"Let me present my fellow adventurers," Doyle continued. "Mr Archie Langman, Dr O'Callaghan, Dr Gibbs and Dr Scharlieb. Gentlemen, this is my friend Dr John Watson, formerly of the 5th Northumberland Fusiliers and a man I hope you will help me convince to come along on our great adventure."

Hands were shaken all around and smiles passed. I was offered a whisky on a tray by a sour-looking waiter and considered taking two. "Just what is it that you gentlemen look for me to do?" I asked, taking a sip from my glass.

"Oh," replied Doyle, "plenty of time for that after dinner, but first gentlemen, let us repast!"

Dinner was filled with small talk of local events. Cricket occupied most of Doyle's conversation. Though an enthusiast, my knowledge of the sport and its folk heroes was miniscule in comparison. Gibbs and Scharlieb were both young and enthusiastic about their profession as surgeons so for a while talk drifted into medicine. O'Callaghan, it appeared was a gynaecologist with an extensive practice. If O'Callaghan is involved, I thought, this surely can have nothing to do with going to war as Holmes believed. My confusion was growing.

At last our seven courses were done and I was hoping to retire to the billiard room. Instead, brandy and cigars were passed, the door to the kitchen closed, and the one to the balcony opened. "Shall we bring our colleague on board?" smiled Doyle, looking around at the faces at the table.

"By all means," replied O'Callaghan.

Doyle leaned forward, elbows on the table and looked straight at me. "It's this way, John. We need you to come with us to South Africa as a member of the Langman Volunteer Hospital."

He leaned back and looked around the table as heads nodded. "You see," he continued with glass in hand, "the army has need of doctors and hospital equipment. You are surely already familiar with the sorry state of our medical corps. Oh, don't protest, the army already admits it.

"Archie's' father, John," he pointed to Langman, "is footing the bill for a 50-man hospital with all necessary equipment to go assist as soon as we can get men and supplies put together. Archie will be Chief Administrator of the hospital. He has been given a Lieutenants Commission in the Yeomanry.

"Dr O'Callaghan is Chief of surgery, and Drs Gibbs and Scharlieb his assistants. I, myself, am going as an extra surgeon. We'd like you to come."

"I'm honoured, gentlemen," I replied, "as you can imagine. But I must be honest. My skills, I'm sure, do not compare with Dr Gibbs or Dr Scharlieb here. Why, I spend most of my time writing these days."

"John, John, don't deprecate yourself. We know you are a skilful surgeon, plus," Doyle looked about for nods of re-enforcement, "we have another motive in asking you."

I leaned toward Doyle as he put both palms on the table cloth. "Yes?"

"It's like this," injected O'Callaghan. "We need your military experience. For two reasons really...."

"Quite," interrupted Doyle. "John, we have a problem. We've been required by the War Office to have a military liaison officer with us."

"And you want me? But I've been out of uniform for the past, oh, almost twenty years."

Doyle held up his big hand. "No John, you don't understand. The problem is that they have given us a liaison officer."

"What?"

"Unfortunately, they've given us a Major Drury, an Irishman. Oh, he's pleasant enough, but a bit of a martinet when he's crossed. Let me just say he has the failings of his race.

"Don't look at me like that, O'Callaghan; you know that Drury drinks too much. Why Drury has even told me that the height of his ambition is to leave the service and to 'marry a rich widow with a cough'.

"I'm afraid he does not like to be crossed and, John, we need you, your ability to handle people, your knowledge of military matters and surgical skill. Will you help us?"

I must say, it was rather an awkward moment for me. Fine professional men were asking for my help in a noble cause. Was I up to the task? "So you need me to be the liaison to the liaison is that the idea?"

"You might say that a large part of your duties will be to keep us on the straight and narrow and on good terms with the army," responded Gibbs.

I sat back and thought for a moment, all eyes looking at me. "Well, I've no big practice to keep me here, but I do have a task master for a literary agent. Someone will have to do something about him. I'll never get that blackmail story done in time."

Doyle almost leaped over the table to shake my hand, crushing it in his large paw. "Watson! Watson! Stout fellow, I knew we could count on you!"

"When do we leave?" I asked. "I still have much to do."

"We leave by the end of the month, old boy, but for tonight, billiards and brandy, eh?"

Doyle and I retired to the billiards room, but the others made their excuses and departed.

"What compelled you to take this journey on?" I queried as I circled the table looking for a shot.

"Actually, my mother," replied the big man.

"Your mother? Why if I know her, she would be dead set against you going."

"Exactly!" Doyle missed another shot. "You see, she and I have very opposing ideas about this war with the Boers." He leaned heavily on his stick. "The Boers have refused to give the franchise to Englishmen just because they were late in coming to the interior. Outrageous! And they started the shooting you know."

I was half listening as I looked for a shot.

"Mother believes that it is all about gold. She believes that Cecil Rhodes is to blame and that the Boers are in the right. Why, she even claims that the Cape Colony Minister, Milner, has caused the war." I was now paying attention. "To quote her 'we are doing to the Boers what Rome did to Britain' and 'Gold is the root of the matter'. Well, we are past any discussion of that now."

"We are in it good now, I'll admit," I said. The Boers are not to be trifled with. They are not savages against Enfield rifles and Maxim machineguns. 'Black Week', as the papers call it, was a considerable set back. Four major defeats for British forces in a week shows that we are in for a fight."

"And," sputtered Doyle in reply, "the Boers are taking in French, Italian, German, and American volunteers. What kind of countries let their citizens fight for a foreign government?"

"Yes, well, I'm afraid it is getting late." I put down my stick and took Doyle's hand. "It will be an adventure, I can see that. I'll be in touch tomorrow." With that, I started for the door.

"And oh," I remarked over my shoulder, "that Milverton Story - after the war!" Smiling, I waved and left.

Chapter 3
A CALL FROM MYCROFT

As I walked up the stairs at Baker Street, the hall clock was just chiming midnight. I had much to think about. Physically I had no question as to my abilities and I felt myself an adequate surgeon. My ability to mediate between a civilian hospital and an army Major, that might not be as easy as it first sounded.

"Watson, turn around and try for a cab. We have an appointment with Mycroft."

"Holmes, at this hour? Whatever for?"

"It seems, Watson, that the crown is in need of our services. I told the messenger to inform Mycroft that we would be available whenever you returned. Come, man, or you'll get no sleep at all tonight and you know how you get!"

Holmes rushed by me on the staircase and was out the door. I had to fairly run to keep up. He continued his blistering pace for the better part of three blocks before we found a hansom at such a late hour.

The horse was moving almost before I was in the seat as Holmes gave the driver instructions for the Diogenes Club. The Diogenes Club, of which Sherlock's brother Mycroft was a founder, was a gentlemen's club for the "most un-clubbable men in London". It was a club where no member was allowed to take notice of any other member and talking was allowed only in the "Strangers Room", where non-members might be brought on rare occasions.

"Now, Holmes, really, what is this all about?" I stammered.

"There is no sense in speculating before we arrive and are given information. Here is Mycroft's note."

Taking the paper, I read Mycroft's almost indecipherable scribble: "Sherlock, come. Bring Watson. Mycroft."

"It surely does not tell one anything, does it?"

"No, but it is an affair of state which would require one to go somewhere, I'm sure. So that eliminates Mycroft."

I spent the next few minutes trying to come to a conclusion on what the note could possibly mean, but such an exercise was completely meaningless.

Few were the lights in the windows when we arrived at the Diogenes Club. The club was the third leg of a triangle that encompassed Mycroft Holmes's world. His government office and his flat were the other two legs of his stool. It seemed like such a small world, and yet Sherlock's older brother moved entire pieces of a global empire from that little triangle. Mycroft had proven before that, as Sherlock claimed, at times, he WAS the British government. Before we reached the door of the club it was opened by a commissionaire who stood silently as we entered. Without a word, he closed the door and started down the hall to the 'Stranger's Room'. It was here that we met Mycroft.

"Ah, thank you Fritz," said Mycroft rising from the Queen Anne chair by the fire. "You may go now. There will be no need for your services for the rest of the night."

Fritz did not reply, but clicking his heels and giving a Prussian bow, withdrew, closing the door behind him. "New man, Franco-Prussian war veteran, wounded left arm," stated Holmes.

"Yes, we took him on about a month ago. His English is horrid, but that doesn't matter so much here," replied Mycroft.

"Good of you to come and bring the doctor. Whiskey and syphon are on the table if you like. I, for one, am going to return to the fire." Mycroft seated himself while I made busy making whisky and sodas for myself and Holmes. Sherlock dropped into the chair across from Mycroft.

"Tell me, good brother, why have you dragged two middle aged men out in the dead of night? What great state secret has been purloined?"

Mycroft looked more exasperated than riled by Holmes's remark.

"In a way you are correct of course Sherlock, but it's not so much state secret as secrets, plural. There is also a question of materials gone missing. These are things I need you to look into for me at some great distance from here. With the current state of affairs I dare not leave London myself."

"Nor would you," smirked Holmes.

"Well, alright, nor would I." Mycroft rose from his chair as I handed Holmes his whiskey.

"In case you are unaware, I know affairs of nations don't interest you, just crime in the streets, we are at war in South Africa with the Boer Republics: the Orange Free State and the Transvaal, or South African Republic as they like to call themselves."

"I've heard something of it, yes." My, how Holmes liked to bait his brother!

"Well, you may not know that things are also about to explode in China as well."

"Now that, I was unaware of."

"The short version of that is that I expect the lid to blow off over there any time now. A group called the Boxers or Righteous First is about to try and throw the major powers out of China by revolution and they have the secret backing of the Chinese government. They will not succeed, of course but when it happens, it won't be pretty."

"Well, if you know about the plot, you can stop it, surely," I imposed.

"Doctor, if there is one thing you should have learned by now, it is that governments never act to avert a crisis until it is upon them. Besides the Chinese, the Boers are in touch with the Irish Republican Brotherhood trying to make trouble there. And some woman with the preposterous name of Maud Gonne is trying to plot the blowing up of British troop ships with dynamite made to look like coal."

"Surely not, nothing so heinous!"

"Oh yes, Doctor. And a volunteer unit of Irish and Irish-Americans captured our cannons at Colenso. Some former American Colonel, an Indian fighter named Blake and an Irishman named MacBride are leading them under a green flag."

Mycroft turned back to Holmes. "But China and Ireland are not why I asked you here, Sherlock. I just mention it so you understand that our resources are stretched and I have more that South Africa to worry about."

"Mycroft, would it not be best to sit down and come to the point?"

Mycroft gave that same exasperated look and re-seated himself.

"Sherlock, someone is passing our war plans in South Africa to the Boers and I need you to find that person."

"Good, Lord," I exclaimed. "How can such a thing happen?"

"Oh, the usual, Doctor. Money, promise of reward or fame, or perhaps a threat of some sort, you know, to one's reputation or physical harm to a loved one. There are a million variations.

"But surely Milner would be on top of such a situation!"

Mycroft looked disgusted.

"Milner is the fool who got us in this mess. He and Rhodes! They and their gold and Cairo-to-Cape Town railroad."

"But I thought this was about the treatment of Englishmen in the Boer Republics."

"Doctor, do you think Jameson's raid a few years ago to try and overthrow the Boer Republics was about the franchise? Of course not. Rhodes paid Jameson to try and start a revolution because the largest deposits of gold and diamonds lie in the Boer territory between the Cape Colony and Rhodesia."

"So Doyle's mother was right." I murmured, sitting beside Holmes.

"If she said that, she is a very insightful woman. But to get on with this," he sighed. "Things have not gone as well as they should. Early on we sent ten thousand soldiers to Natal. This action precipitated the war. I know the Boers attacked first, but I can't say I blame them.

"The Boers are well armed. Over the years they have bought modern Mauser rifles and French cannon. Every Burgher is trained to shoot and ride, and they can live off the land."

Mycroft pulled out a map, and spreading it on the table, started to point out places I had only heard of.

"Our forces are invested at Ladysmith, Kimberly, and Mafeking. We greatly underestimated the Boer's fighting ability. Methuen and Buller are good generals, but they've been fought almost to a standstill by an amateur army. Lord Roberts has been sent to save the situation but what is really going to save it is a massive influx of troops. Not only do we have to fight an enemy in front, the distances are so great that we have to leave thousands of soldiers to protect the railroads behind our advance."

"So, brother," chimed in Holmes, "you still haven't stated your need for us."

"Sherlock, someone is providing our troop movements on the ground to the Boers. They know our next move before we make it. I need you to go to Cape Town and wherever else you need to, to find and stop this leak of information.

"You will be going as a correspondent of the Times of London named Escott. One of your favourite aliases, I believe. The doctor will go as a medical correspondent. His knowledge of military matters should help immensely. Your reason for being there is allegedly to report on all the war material that has gone missing from the docks. And the doctor is looking into the failure of the Army Medical Corps."

"I'm afraid I can't, Mycroft. Just tonight I gave my word that I would go to South Africa with Mr Langman's Hospital," I responded.

"That is very inconvenient," said Mycroft. "Can't you get out of it?"

"Heavens no," I blustered. "I gave my word."

"Bother!"

“That may work out just as well,” declared Holmes. “Mycroft, can you see to it that this Langman’s Hospital is sent forward to wherever Lord Robert’s headquarters will be?”

“Easiest thing in the world.”

“Good, then I will have Watson where the information may be being passed. What say you, Watson? Up for a two-sided game?”

“Of course, Holmes, whatever I can do.”

“Good, then that is settled.

“Mycroft, I will want full particulars tomorrow. In the meantime, I will start my investigation here. Is it possible that known information here is going by a circuitous route to the Boers?”

“Oh that is possible surely. Portuguese East Africa is a hot bed of spies and supplies for the Boers. The rail line runs from the Port of Laurenco Marques in Delagoa Bay straight to Pretoria. In fact, there are hotels there that cater to the spies of the world.”

“Secrets passed that way, though, would be more strategic than tactical. The Boers know the timing and that means a leak in South Africa.”

“Good night, then, Mycroft.” said Holmes standing. “Come Watson, we need to get you your rest. You have much to do.”

Chapter 4
ON TO CAPE COLONY

The next three weeks were busy, to say the least. I saw little of Holmes, since when I was not with Doyle interviewing men to support the hospital, Holmes was down at the docks and warehouses looking into how, where, and when supplies or information might be moved.

It was near the end of our third week of preparation that I finally ran into Holmes in our rooms.

"News of the war goes well, Holmes," I said, putting up my stick and hat.

"It is truly a wonder, Watson, truly a wonder."

Holmes was clipping the end off of one of his cigars.

"I assure you, Watson, there is almost no reason to have a secret service if you are a power opposed to England."

"Whatever are you talking about?"

"Just read the newspapers, my dear fellow. That's all one need to do, just read the newspapers." Holmes threw the *Times* on the table. "Every ship we send out to the Cape Colony is listed In the *Times* and every other paper. Not just the ship, but the unit going, the number of men, and the officers by name.

"It tells one when they leave, where they are going, and when they have arrived. Why, with the telegraph it takes less than twenty-four hours to know they've disembarked and only a fool would not know their route depending on where they land; Cape Town, East London, wherever.

"Defeats, victories, unit strength, all reported openly in the press."

"Yes," I replied, "in a way it is disconcerting."

"There's much more going on than Mycroft would have us believe."

"How is that?"

"Watson, I already know there have been a number of plots to blow up the docks in Cape Town. The Cape Boers are not all friendly and there is one by name of Duquesne, a Fritz Duquesne who appears to be the ring leader of the sabotage plots. I've also found out that there are more than supplies missing - in fact, the missing supplies are minimal. What is missing is gold. About 260,000 ounces of gold so far. Quite a considerable sum."

"My God, Holmes! That is a king's ransom!"

"Quite a bit more than that, Watson." Holmes shrugged and started for his favourite chair. He sat and was quiet for a moment. "But tell me, how go your plans with the hospital?"

"Well enough. Major Drury isn't as bad as Doyle seems to think. He just has a more rigid attitude about things. I'll be able to handle him.

"Other than that, we are about ready. We have all fifty men and our equipment. We sail on the 28th on the P & O ship the Oriental. Poor Doyle is having fits though."

"Too long delayed, eh!"

"Yes, he's convinced it will all be over and done before we get there. I try to assure him that wars are never short, but with Kimberly relieved, he's quite positive he'll miss everything."

"Men can be such fools," declared Holmes and picked up his paper."

"You do know that Doyle will have to be brought in on your masquerade, don't you?" I inquired. "After all he knows you."

"Yes, hopefully he can be quiet about the matter."

"Once I tell him it's a matter of national importance, he will be quiet as the sphinx. He'll be thrilled to be 'playing a part', as it were."

"Quite. I should thank your friend Paget, too."

"Why is that Holmes?"

"Ever since he drew my likeness in that silly hat, no one recognizes me without it."

Holmes chortled at his own joke and picked up his paper.

"Now Holmes, you can't tell me there is so much gold missing and drop it there!"

"Nothing to tell you. Milner says it's accounted for, but my sources say it went missing on the way to Cape Town and is in the Orange Free state. Mycroft agrees that Milner is hiding the loss." With that he put his nose back in the paper. "Oh, one more thing Watson. I will be sailing with you on the 28th, so be good enough to go ahead and talk to Doyle."

On the 27th of February, I found myself, along with Doyle and the rest, watching the loading of our equipment on the *Oriental*. I had already spoken to the “Big Man” about “playing the game” - when he met Mr Escott of the *Times*. He was excited that he was to be involved and assured me he would not open the bag.

The following morning, we found ourselves loading aboard our last-minute provisions and ourselves. I admit I was excited to be off. Thoughts of my time in Afghanistan, things I hadn’t thought of for years, came rushing back. Mycroft had arranged that I should hold the rank of Captain in the RAMC, allowing me to deal more easily with Major Drury, for which I was grateful.

We were quite a conglomeration on our little ship: Officers of Engineers, Light Infantry, Borderers, Yeomanry and Quartermasters, men of the Royal Engineers, Warwickshire Regt and the Essex regiment along with five surgeons, five dressers, and forty men of the Langman Hospital.

Our first stop was to be Queenstown for five hundred officers and men of the Royal Scots and our first incident.

Holmes had joined us in the early hours and was introduced all around as an outbound correspondent. He was well met and hit it off immediately with Major Drury. It was probably the early sharing of a whisky flask that brought the two together. I felt that my best course was to stay away from Holmes as much as possible lest I give away his disguise.

Another traveller on our ship was a man by the name of Conway. He was a munitions merchant who had been known to sell to the Boer Republics before the war. He was treated with courtesy, but not much more by everyone except Holmes and Drury. The three would play American poker well into the nights with Holmes constantly winning and then forgiving Drury’s debt. Only Conway would be the loser.

The trip overall was of no great consequence. We had no foul weather and only a few incidents come to mind. The first though set a disquieting tone upon us. As the lighters ferried soldiers and equipment to the ship at Queenstown, an Irishwoman aboard one of the craft threw a white towel on board and shouted out, “You may be after finding it useful.” Before anyone could respond, the lighter pulled away. I would learn more of what lay under the surface in Ireland years later.[2]

The rest of our three-week journey brings only a few memories. Doyle organized a cricket match in Cape de Verdes. He also gave a lecture on the war to all hands one night. The toughest part was the illness brought on by the Enteric Fever inoculations. Unfortunately, the inoculations were not mandatory and the illness brought on by it caused men to refuse to take it.

---

[2] See Sherlock Holmes and the Irish Rebels, MX Publishing, 2011

This would have devastating consequences, for we would lose more men to disease than to bullets in South Africa.

Holmes, Conway and Drury were fast friends before we were half done with our cruise. Though Doyle knew Holmes was not really a correspondent for the *Times*, he insisted on explaining to him at length, his theory of having 20,000 soldiers stand shoulder to shoulder, and by pointing their rifles in the air at the fixed elevation, bringing a rain of bullets onto the opposite side of a hill. It seems that neither the *Times* nor the War Office were interested in his theories.

On the night before we reached Cape Town, Holmes asked me to visit him on the fantail. He would be getting off the *Oriental* and going to start his investigation in earnest. I was now feeling a bit guilty about abandoning my old friend.

"Perhaps I should stay here with you, Holmes. After all Langman, is an excellent administrator and Drury will get the hospital forward. You may need me here."

"No, Watson. I need you up near the headquarters with Roberts. If it is as I believe, the gold has every possibility of being in Bloemfontein. We'll get war news here. Unless I'm much mistaken, Roberts will have pressed forward by now. Mycroft will see to it that the hospital is where I need you to be."

"But why would the gold be in Bloemfontein?"

"No gold has been shipped to England since the start of the war, Watson. Milner says that the last gold shipment out before the war is safely in hand." Holmes paused to light another cigar. "However, if that is true, why hasn't it been shipped? Neither the mine owners nor the government have been given a good answer." He looked out into the night as the glow of his cigar lit his face.

"You remember the armoured train that Cronje destroyed?"

I nodded.

"I believe Milner lost the gold that day and is hoping to regain it before he is discredited. Keep your ears open, Watson. A shipment that large cannot have gone unnoticed. Someone in the army knows something. And keep on good terms with Drury. If he learns anything everyone will know it, I assure you. He is most congenial and talkative, especially after a few whiskeys."

"What about this fellow Conway, Holmes? Has he anything to do with the missing supplies?"

"Oh, easy enough, Watson. I've known for quite some time what he is doing. He delivers goods here to the dock in Cape Town. The supplies are signed for and then a few Boer stevedores re-mark the boxes as something else and send them on to Portuguese East Africa."

"The cads!"

"Yes, I'll hand Conway over to Milner tomorrow and we'll put an end to that. But what I want are his confederates on the dock. Someone must know Duquesne and about the plot against our facilities. If I can solve that and find the gold, we'll have done good service. There is still the question of information to the Boers. It could be that the information is passed here, but more likely it will be forward."

"I've no doubt of that, but what shall I do while I'm waiting for you to contact me?"

"Listen and watch, Watson. Look for unusual relationships or people who appear to have problems which distract them from their duties. Someone in need of funds or who seems to hold a grudge of some sort."

Late the next afternoon, we arrived at Cape Town. By evening Doyle, Langman, Drury and I had gone ashore to get information, while Holmes was off to the Times office to report in and would collect his box on the morrow.

The news at Cape Town was both good and bad. The good was that not only had Kimberly been relieved, but so had Ladysmith,. Cronje had surrendered, and Bloemfontein, the capitol of the Orange Free State, had fallen to Lord Roberts. The bad news was that we were to stay in Cape Town until a final determination was made about the use of the hospital. I had to smile to myself, for I had no doubt Mycroft would win out.

On the 26th of March, we would leave Cape Town for East London on the East coast to unload and make our way to Bloemfontein.

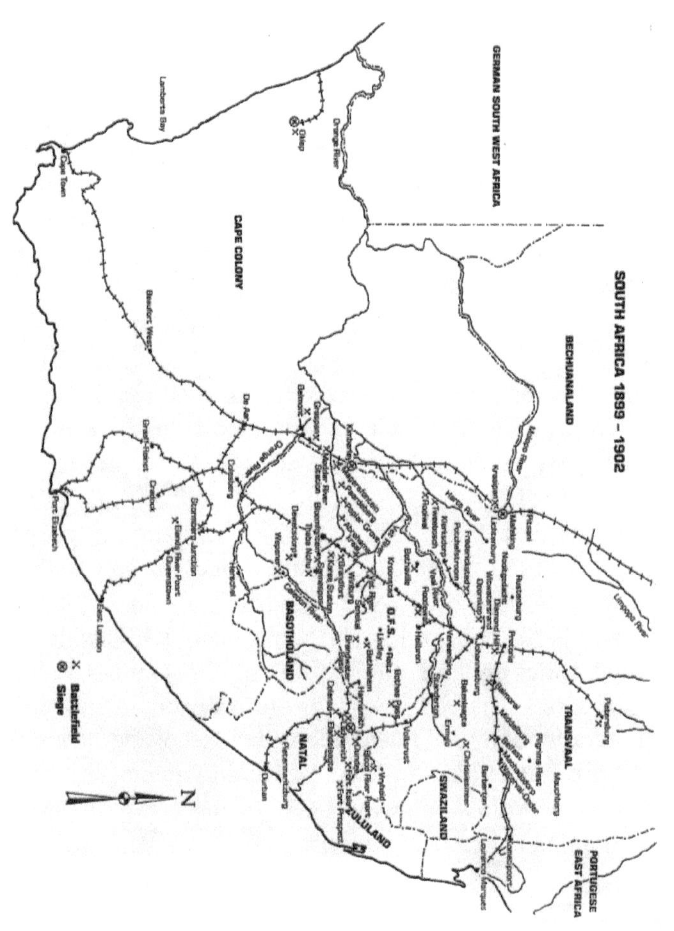
SOUTH AFRICA 1899 – 1902
GERMAN SOUTH WEST AFRICA
BECHUANALAND
CAPE COLONY
TRANSVAAL
O.F.S.
BASOTHOLAND
NATAL
SWAZILAND
ZULULAND
PORTUGESE EAST AFRICA
Cape Town
Port Elizabeth
East London
Durban
Orange River
Battlefield
Siege
N

Chapter 5
BY RAIL TO BLOEMFONTEIN

Before our departure from Cape Town, Holmes came to the Mount Nelson Hotel, where Doyle and I had put up until news should come of our assignment. Doyle was fascinated by the conglomeration of wounded officers, ne'er-do-wells, adventurers, and adventuresses to be found in a capital at war. To me it seemed much as I remembered Bombay and Watson's Hotel in the early '80's. Human character had not changed. I suspect that adventuresses were present with the armies of Alexander the Great as much as they were with the Army of General Hooker in the American Civil War and would always be with us.

As Doyle had gone off to view the imprisoned Boers where they were held at the cities race track, I met Holmes alone on the veranda of the hotel.

"About ready to leave, Watson?"

"Yes, Holmes, we're off to East London with the tide. Hopefully we'll be in Bloemfontein in a few days."

"Oh, you will be Watson. But here comes the man I really came here to see."

Coming up the walk was a gentleman who appeared to be in his mid-thirties. He was quite tall and angular and dressed as a professional man. Tripping along next to him was a boy that I would venture was about eight years old. The boy held tightly to his father's hand with his own left. In his right he held a wooden sword with which he occasionally parried the assaults of an imaginary foe.

"Excuse me," said Holmes, stepping toward the pair. The gentleman stopped. "I believe you are Mr Rathbone, are you not?"

"Mr Escott is it?" replied the man. He released his grip on the boy and the two men shook hands.

"Yes, I'm glad you could come. Let me present my friend, Dr Watson. He is recently arrived like me. Who might this young soldier be with you?"

"This is Basil. Say 'good day' to the gentlemen, Basil."

The boy stood straight as an arrow, and saluted with his wooden sword in the best military manner. He smiled from ear to ear when I returned the salute. "Good morning, sirs."

"Shall we have a seat?" Holmes indicated some chairs on the far side out of the sun.

"I'm afraid I had to bring Basil along. His mother has the other children and is packing for our return to England tonight." He looked down at the boy and sighed. "I'm afraid this one spends all his time fencing and playing with a magnifying glass that he has taken from my office in Johannesburg. I'm sure I don't know what is to become of him."

"He is a fine lad," I said. "I suspect he will do well."

The boy smiled at me again and moved over closer to his father. When we had seated ourselves Holmes looked about a moment and, seeing we were quite alone, continued.

"Watson, Mr Rathbone was, until recently, a mining engineer in Johannesburg and one of brother Mycroft's best men." Holmes turned back to our visitor. "Can you give us any word on the gold shipment?"

"I thank you for the kind words, sir. But, truth be told, it was touch and go getting out of the Transvaal. The old boys are pretty smart up there. They suspected I was not just a mining engineer but they had no solid proof. It was suggested that it was time for me to go somewhere else by some men I knew well. I couldn't risk things with the family as I would have alone." He looked at his son and patted the boy's shoulder.

"As to the gold," he went on. "There is no doubt it left Johannesburg. My sources here assure me that it never made it here to Cape Town or to Durban or East London or Port Elizabeth or anywhere. I am convinced the Boers have it. I also think that Lord Roberts has moved so swiftly that it may have been overtaken and it has been hidden. That, sir, is all I know."

Rathbone rose from his chair, as did Holmes and I. We made our farewells and Rathbone and little Basil departed. Basil had to present his sword salute. I very solemnly returned it. The last I saw of the boy he was fencing his way down the street vanquishing who knows what enemy.

"Well there is confirmation, Watson. Milner is lying through his teeth. When you get to Bloemfontein I want you to contact a Lieutenant Murtry of the Dragoon Guard. He is a junior aide to Lord Roberts. He will be your contact with me. I believe I can clear up this business at the docks fairly quickly. Conway has given me all I need about the supply shipments. My problem is Duquesne. He has not showed among those we have rounded up so far. I don't believe he is here. I think he has acted through intermediaries everywhere. We don't even have his description."

"But surely," I replied, "he had to talk to someone. Someone has seen him."

"Oh, they have Watson, they have." We walked out onto the lawn.

"The trouble is," continued Holmes, "that none of the descriptions match. He's tall, he's medium height; he's stout, he's slim; he's got brown hair, his hair is blond; he has a Boer accent, he sounds like an American." Holmes sighed.

"He's been quite elusive and done very well at presenting himself not only in different disguises, but in different guises - as lumberman, banker, and gentry. I look forward to meeting the gentleman." We walked toward the veranda steps.

"Remember, Murtry will know me as Escott and will pass information between us."

"I'll remember, Holmes." We shook hands and Holmes started to leave.

"One last thing, Watson. There is a young man up there named Churchill. Keep away from him if you can. He's attached himself to a colonial unit and is acting as an independent correspondent."

"Lord Churchill's son? Glad you warned me. He's got quite the reputation for getting in and out of scrapes. Already escaped a Boer P. O. W. camp hasn't he?"

"Yes and caused all sorts of problems inside and outside the government. Just keep clear. We don't need to advertise our presence."

We bade each other farewell and good hunting. I watched Holmes disappear into the crowd on the street.

Later that day, the *Oriental* started the short journey to East London, where we arrived two days later on the 28th of March.

Our landing went well; men, equipment, supplies of every kind were quickly off-loaded onto the docks. But here was all the chaos of an army in motion. Trains came and went all times of the day and night carrying food, clothing, ammunition, men, horses, cannon and wagons. Somehow a fifty man volunteer hospital was to be found a place on one of these trains.

Here I must give praise to Major Drury who was able to make us a priority for space and to the transport officer, Leo Trevor, whom Doyle apparently knew from amateur theatricals. We were given a choice of moving in two trains or waiting a week to go together. We pressed forward. Doyle appeared to be everywhere, lending both his mind and his physical abilities in loading the hospital.

Though the distance was merely about three hundred and fifty miles, the trip would take days as we travelled through the beauty of the Veldt and the stench of dead flesh. Dr O'Callaghan approached me in the twilight of our first day out as we sat at a siding. (All the senior members of the staff had chosen the first train out, leaving the dressers to come on with the second part of our equipment.)

"Whatever is that stench, Dr Watson? It's been going on for miles."

"Death, Dr O'Callaghan."

"Death?"

"Yes, it's the hundreds of unburied horses, mules, and oxen that an army uses up in a campaign. Even as we speak, there are men in Australia, Canada, and the States buying up tens of thousands of replacement animals."

O'Callaghan looked out the window into the gathering darkness. Doyle approached and sat next to him.

"But, Watson, surely the animals are taken care of."

I had to laugh a bit inside. How little these gentlemen knew about where they were going.

"Yes, yes of course." I responded searching my pockets for my pipe. "You must remember, Doctor, that most supplies and equipment move by animal power. The men depend on them to keep them alive, to bring them food, water, and ammunitions, to move them about so they can chase the Boer who are well horsed.

"But every time you move a horse, he also needs food, water and sleep. So now you have more horses, moving supplies for the first horses. And if the first horses moving through an area have grazed it off, what do the second horses eat?" Having found my pipe, I charged and lit it.

"I see, and there are casualties of course." continued O'Callaghan.

"Certainly. Which is the bigger target, the horse or the man? Bring down the horse, you bring down the man. If you want to capture your enemies' artillery or supplies, how can you best do that? Kill the horses in the traces, of course."

O'Callaghan looked shocked.

"Doctor," I went on, "without the animals the artillery can't escape. Then all you have to do is kill or capture the men."

The two doctors looked back out the window.

"That smell, Doctor is war. You might as well get used to it or light a pipe."

I got up and leaned out the window. The train lurched into motion as a southbound ambled past and once again we were on the main track. The camp-fires of the thousands of men left to guard the supply lines glowed in the darkness as we slowly rumbled past. It seemed like every few minutes we stopped to let other trains depart south. At Sturmberg we waited half a day as repairs were being made on the temporary bridge ahead that crossed the Orange River.

It was while we were stopped at Sturmberg that I received my first communication from Holmes. It was a telegram that simply read, BEWARE THE TWO HEADS STOP ESCOTT.

“What the devil does that mean?” I thought. Two heads? Two heads of what? Holmes was infuriating. Somehow I was just supposed to know the meaning. I would file that information away in my mental “lumber room” and ponder on it.

Once we crossed the Orange River, the sites of war were more evident - farms without livestock, burned off pasture, and fresh graves could be seen along the railway.

We did not reach Bloemfontein until five o’clock in the morning on the second of April.

Chapter 6

TWO GOOD MEN

The Scots, who had been with us and occupied most of the space, were off the train, formed up and marching away from the rail yard almost before the train had stopped.

As Langman and Drury started to organize the offloading and consolidation of our equipment, I went in search of information. No one seemed to know where the second train with the rest of the hospital equipment was, so I left the rail yard in search of Lord Roberts' headquarters.

"Where the devil has Doyle gone?" shouted Drury, as I went bye.

"I'm sure I don't know," replied Langman.

"I'm off to the headquarters," I called. "I'll see if I can find him." And without looking back waved my hand and headed for town. It was not fifteen minutes later when who should pass me but Doyle, well mounted on a borrowed horse, with two other men riding along.

"Off to see the Boers, Watson. Supposed to be some shooting up ahead. Get a horse and come along."

"No, I have things that must come first." I replied. "And keep your head down," I shouted as he and his two new friends charged off to the North.

Lord Roberts' headquarters was in a large hotel in the middle of town and easily found.

Getting to see Lieutenant Murtry was also fairly easy. Clerks are much easier to get along with when a subordinate is asked for rather than the Commander. The clerks always assume you are, like them, a cog in the wheel, with business and not there to make a problem for them or others.

Murtry greeted me in a small anti-chamber off the side of Lord Roberts' offices. "Welcome Dr Watson. Mr Escott told me of your coming and asked me to look out for you. May I show you where the hospital is to go? Wonderful cricket pavilion really. Come this way."

We walked back out of the hotel. As we started down the street, Murtry leaned close.

“Things are not all peaches and cream here, Doctor. I’ve been instructed to help you by a message from White Hall and told not to inform my superiors. Puts me in a bit of a bad spot, you know.

“Mr Escott has me looking for evidence of any unusual shipments out of Bloemfontein, anything really unusual or particularly heavy. But that doesn’t really tell me anything. It would help if I knew what he really wanted.”

“He is a frustrating man, I admit,” I whispered. I thought for a moment of how often Holmes had kept me in the dark and how much more valuable I felt I could have been if he had informed me what the problem was. I made a decision.

“Lieutenant, we are looking for two things. First, we are looking for a large shipment of gold that has gone missing. Second, we are looking for a man named Duquesne. We think he is running a band of spies and smugglers and is responsible for the missing gold.” I decided not to mention that we knew plans had gone missing.

“Alright, sir. Is there a description of the man?”

“No, unfortunately, there is not.”

Murtry frowned as we walked a distance in silence. The sun was almost half to the top of the sky as we approached the cricket field.

“You know sir, with all the freight coming and going every day, it would be almost impossible to open every crate to search for gold. Do you know if it’s in bars or coin?”

“Bars, at least it was. It could be in any form by now.”

“Yes, here’s the area for your hospital, sir. You’ll have to make arrangements at the rail yard for transport of your equipment up here. As soon as we get back to the hotel, I’ll give you a note to the coordinator that Lord Roberts considers you priority.”

It was a good two hours before I returned to the rail yard. By then Doyle had also returned, having found that a soldier must get use to alarms and that no battle was in the offing. It was only a short time later that the second half of our equipment was located. We were soon moving up the hill and to the cricket pavilion in a combination of local and army transport wagons.

“Expecting lots of wounded, are you?” The remark came from a large-boned Irishman atop a Boer wagon pulled by four mules. His brown slouch hat had the brim turned up in front with a green cockade. He hadn’t had a shave in about a week and his dark blue waistcoat and trousers were patched in a number of places. His boots showed a new sole on one and a hole in the bottom of the other. He smiled down from the driver’s box, a pipe in one side of his mouth. I liked him already.

"It's like this, my friend; best to have what we hope we don't need."

"Aye, I'm for that sure."

"Have you been in Africa long?" I asked. It might be good to have a friend among the teamsters. Especially one who knew the area.

"Six years and some." he replied

"Gold fields?" I asked with a grin.

"Sure, it seemed a good idea at the time, your excellency. It's just Rhodes and his kind already had it all. So here I make my fortune, me and my four ladies." He flicked the reins and called, "Step up, Victoria, pull your share now, step up."

"What's your name?"

"Cacy, sir. Step up, Victoria! Walk on, now. Walk on." The wheels of the wagon groaned under the weight of the boxes.

The wagon was a small freighter with Archibald wheels and a canvas cover across the bows. On the canvas was painted a yellow harp about a foot and a half high. The box and wheels had been painted not long ago.

"You take good care of your wagon." I ventured.

"Only way to make me living, sir. Best keep it in order. You're making me tired now, ya are. Get up on the box, sir; we've still a bit to the cricket field."

Cacy pulled up while I climbed on and we sat in silence the rest of the way.

Doyle, the first back, was busy directing the arrangement of beds and equipment. Langman, Drury, and I soon decided to keep out of the way of our Scottish friend and let him arrange whatever he wanted. He was an unstoppable force. By nightfall tents were up next to the pavilion and enough room was available for about fifty patients. I dreaded the thought of so many, but it was best to be ready. That night we showered for the first time in days and went to sleep under the stars on cots we had placed on the roof of the pavilion. We were ready for patients, but my thoughts were not there.

I was watching the moon as it moved slowly across the sky and wondered where Holmes was, and what had he meant by his curt telegram, "two heads"? What the devil was he talking about? I pondered this until I drifted off to sleep.

Chapter 7
WATER

As the sun rose and the Army started to stir, I wandered over to the edge of the roof putting together the first pipe of the day. Below I could see my new friend Cacy and his four mules moving slowly down the street toward the edge of town. He saw me and waved a hand. Snapping the reins, he called out "Victoria, step up I say, step up." Victoria leaned into the collar for a moment and the mules started into a trot. Victoria would get the rest going then back off herself. Smart mule.

"Hello, Doctor Watson." It was one of the dressers.

"Good morning, Moyer. Beautiful day, is it not?"

"No sir, it's not. We've no water. Have you seen Major Drury?"

"No water? Ah, no, Major Drury is staying in town. It seems one of the senior aides, a Major Pelham is a friend and he has put up with him. Not sure where. Let me get Doyle, you look for Mr Langman. We'll get this solved." But we were not to 'get it solved'.

Having awakened Doyle and informed him of the situation, we went below and started checking pipes. There appeared to be no breaks nor any sabotage. Moyer came back to tell us that the water was off everywhere. Clean water was critical, so Doyle and I decided to go to Army Headquarters to find out what we could. Here we found Drury in conference with both Major Pelham and Lieutenant Murtry.

"Ah, Doctors, glad you're here. I'm afraid we have bad news." Pelham had been the first to notice us and speak. Pelham was a fairly small man, not taller than five-foot-four, I would say. He had brown hair, brown eyes and a moustache that drooped just below the corners of his mouth. His grin seemed somehow artificial, but I noticed that the droop of the moustache was used to try and cover a scar on his left side that extended from the corner of his lip. It was perhaps a sabre or lance wound that had been not well treated and in healing had caused this facial distortion.

Murtry greeted us with a smile and a "good morning", while Major Drury sat shaking his head and muttering at a map.

"Where the devil is the water?" burst out Doyle. It was a remark not like him at all.

"Doctor," replied Pelham, taken a bit back by the outburst, "we are well aware of the problem, but you see, this is a war and our enemy will use all at his disposal to defeat us.

"You may not be aware that just a few days ago, we lost control of the waterworks which supplies Bloemfontein."

"It is here," he continued while pointing at a spot on the map. "It is about twenty miles East out by the mountains. Broadwood had a devil of a time trying to get back. He lost a considerable force and a number of cannon at Sanna's Post, a river ford between here and there."

"Makes sense they would cut off the water," said Drury. "I wonder why they didn't burn the town before they left."

Everyone looked at the map for a moment.

"Where does all this leave us, Major Pelham?" I asked. "Is there to be a relief force to retake the works?"

"No, not right now. There are wells about the town and these will be reopened. That should suffice for now. There won't be any excess of water, but we should have enough."

"When was the last time any of these wells were tested or treated?" Doyle was already beside himself.

"I have no idea, Doctor, but the engineers are working with the few city workers left in town to get some pumps up and running. Most of the units will have to rely on the water wagons. Major Drury will keep you informed. Now, if you'll excuse me, I will need to get back to my other duties." Pelham had obviously dismissed us.

Drury, Doyle and I left for the hospital as Murtry and Pelham went back to their papers.

"This could be catastrophic," commented Doyle, taking the outside steps three at a time. "Has Pelham no sense of what this may mean?"

"No," I replied, "he does not. And doesn't much care either. He has no concept of what is going to happen. His army may be wiped out by disease, but he doesn't see disease as his concern. Battles are his problem, sickness ours."

The rest of the day was spent trying to assemble a system by which water could be treated before we used it. Doyle gave strict orders that water was not to be used unless boiled first. We took all the precautions we could, yet we knew only too well what was coming.

Later that evening, I went in search of Lieutenant Murtry. He was to be found at his desk, but upon my arrival, he recommended we take a walk to the stables so he could check on his horse.

He said nothing as we walked, but once beside his horse, a bay gelding of about 15 and a half hands named Boy-O, he began to update me.

"No patients yet, Doctor?"

"No, not yet. We should be getting some wounded in tomorrow, but for now all is quiet." I paused a moment, looking about. Only the stable guard was present and he was out by the corrals. "Any word from your men?"

"No, sir, it's hard when they don't really know what they are looking for. And as far as unusual activity, well, what is unusual in a war? I've a couple of sergeants who are watching to see if more supplies move to any unit than should reasonably be needed, and we're keeping an eye on the locals, but I honestly don't know what else to do."

"Nor do I," I admitted.

Murtry picked up a brush and idly rubbed Boy-o's back.

"It hasn't been a good day, Doctor. Besides the water being cut off, we've word that two companies of the Northumberland and three of the Royal Irish have surrendered at Redderburg. Lord Roberts is not happy."

"No, I imagine not. Any word on a force to retake the water works?"

"Sorry, Doctor. Lord Roberts won't move until he thinks the men are rested and ready. Can't afford another loss like Sanna's Post. Bad for morale and bad in the papers. Not that he really cares about the papers, but when he leaves here he wants a straight push to Pretoria. He wants to end this thing."

"Sad about his son being killed in Natal."

"Yes. He doesn't show it much, but we can tell it has really saddened him. Well, sir," Murtry threw the brush in a grooming box, "I've got to get back, got to brief our new chief scout about a job for tonight."

"Why a new chief scouts? Where is the old one?"

"Burnham? Been missing since Sanna's Post." We started walking back toward the hotel. "Don't know if he was killed or captured. American chap. He did exceptional service in the Matabele Wars. In fact, I understand he was in Alaska when Lord Roberts sent for him to come here and help. Came as fast as the ships would bring him. Best scout and tracker in Africa. Good fellow too, for an American."

"Who's the new man?"

"Named Frederick Fredericks. How is that for lack of imagination? He's a Cape Boer, but trustworthy, I suppose. Seems to know the area, speaks Dutch and a few native dialects. Hope he measures up. Anything else, Doctor? I must get back."

"Yes, one other thing. Does the phrase 'the two heads' mean anything to you?"

Murtry thought for a moment. "No, can't say as it does. Only thing it brings to mind is drama. You know, the two faces, comedy and tragedy."

"Hum, yes. Well thank you, Lieutenant. Be sure to let me know if anything comes up."

I started my walk back to the hospital lost in thought. As I walked around the back of the hotel, I nearly walked into the side of a wagon.

"Easy there, your Lordship, you'll dent your helmet."

It was Cacy, looking down from the wagon box.

"Ah, Mr Cacy. Sorry I was lost in thought. What are you doing here?"

"Back from my rounds, sir."

"Rounds?"

"Aye, I go each morning and make the rounds of local farms and get what I can fresh for the hotel and the boarding houses. Farmers are afraid to come in. They're afraid they'll be arrested or shot for just living here."

"Rediculous!"

"Not to them, sir."

"Aren't you afraid of the Boers?"

"Not at all, at all. I carry no gun so each side knows I'm not fighting. And I'd as soon sell to Boers or Brits. That is, if they have gold."

"Seems to be a chance you're taking," I replied. "Must be off, wagon's a bit dirty isn't it?"

"Aye, clean her up tonight. Take care, Doctor."

I continued back to the hospital to report what little I had found out. I was consideralby disheartened by the news of two compaines of my old regiment having surrendered. Not finding any sign of gold or the man Duguesne just compounded my ill mood.

As I passed the boarding house where Pelham and Drury stayed, I noticed Drury through the window in apparent deep conversation with Mrs Foster the landlady. She was a widow of about forty, and while I had not noticed a cough, she at least had assets of two kinds so perhaps she would meet the major's requirements.

On arriving at the hospital, I relayed my news about the lack of a force to retake the water works. Doyle spent the rest of the night blustering about the incompetence of the military. Something he would never say to Roberts himself.

In my absence, we had received about five cases from one of the other hospitals. None were severe, but it had buoyed the men up to now actually have something to do that they felt was worthwhile.

The rest of the night passed uneventfully.

Chapter 8
THE SCOUTS

The next two mornings passed as the first. As dawn came up, I smoked my first pipe and watched Mr Cacy and his four mules come past on the way to their rounds. I had added an A-frame tent to the roof so that I might avoid the coming rains and remain at the pavilion if needed. Doyle was searching accommodations in town.

By now we had about twenty patients who were split up among the five of us. But in all truth, the dressers and orderlies had things well in hand at this point. A week later this would not be true.

This morning I was the first doctor to appear in the ward. I was met by a small flurry of activity. A man in somewhat rough clothing was being attended to by Moyer. He gave every appearance of being a Boer, but by his accent, he was obviously an American. He was about the height of Major Pelham, but with bronzed skin and grey-blue eyes. He was exceedingly muscular and seemed uninjured. He wore a moustache, but no beard.

"Doctor Watson," called Moyer, looking up at me. "Sir, I'd like you to meet Captain Burnham. He just escaped from the Boers."

"Captain, I've heard about you," I said extending my hand. "They were afraid you might have been killed."

"Just captured. Bad bit of luck. But I'm here now." He took my extended hand in a vice like grip.

"What seems to be the problem?" I asked.

"Nothing," replied Moyer. "But Major Pelham sent him down here to get checked out. He's been traveling alone on the Veldt about five days since his escape. Just needs some rest and good food, I'd say."

I turned to Burnham. "And what do you say, Captain?"

"I say it's time to find a place to sleep, a good horse, and get back to work." His smile filled the room.

"Then that is what the doctor prescribes," I grinned. We shook hands again and he left with a nod to Moyer.

"Well," said Moyer, replacing his instruments. "I shall remember this."

"Why?"

"You don't really know who that is, do you?"

"Burnham, an American and Chief of Scouts."

"Yes, sir, used to be a scout for the American Army. He fought Apaches and Cheyenne, scouted for us in the first Matabele War, and fought with Baden-Powell in the second Matabele War. They say he ended the war single-handed when he killed their medicine man M'Limo. He has also been put in charge of training the long range sharpshooters. Quite the fellow."

Moyer finished putting his things up. "They also say he never says a word about any of his life. Just goes about his business."

This was a man Holmes and I could use. If there were unusual movements, this is the man who would know it.

I finished my minimal rounds and decided to find Major Drury. He had not been seen for the last two days. Though he really wasn't needed, his appearance here and there might help with assuring a constant flow of supplies. After trying the boarding-house, I went to army headquarters, where he was also absent. However, to my surprise, Lieutenant Murtry was anxious to talk to me.

"Oh, Dr Watson. I may have some good news for you this afternoon. Close the door, will you? Right."

Murtry came from behind his desk as I shut the office door.

"I've a sergeant named Weaver," he continued in a hushed conspiratorial tone. "He has noticed something odd. There are boxes of canned goods missing. Not a lot, but a few. The problem is that none of the units have noticed any shortages in their requisitions. The food seems to be getting where it's supposed to be, but the count is off at the depot." He looked at the door again.

"Interesting. But if the units are getting the goods, where is the problem? Is it a simple miscount, is it being sold on the black market out of the depot, or perhaps the unit cooks are trading it off for local food or favours?" I pondered out loud.

"Could mean nothing, of course, Doctor. But you said to watch for the odd event and that is what we've found so far." Murtry walked back around his desk as a knock came at the door.

"Enter. Yes, Fredericks, come in won't you? Let me introduce you to Dr Watson. He's assigned to Langman's Hospital down at the cricket pavilion. Dr Watson, Frederick Fredericks. He's a scout that Lord Roberts has just put on to assist. What can I do for you Fredericks?"

Fredericks was a young man. He stood about five-foot-ten and was in his early twenties by my guess. He was clean shaven with short brown hair and brown eyes. He was in shirt sleeves and breeches with high riding boots. His slouch hat was pinned on one side in the Boer manner and pushed to the back of his head. He was an impressive figure with a giant smile.

"Glad to meet you, Doctor. Lieutenant, Major Parker would like to talk to you. He said to bring your file on someone called the 'Black Panther'."

"I'll be leaving you, then," I said getting up to go. Murtry was pulling open drawers looking for his file. "I suppose Fredericks that you'll be staying on even though Captain Burnham is back."

"Yes, Doctor. Seems Lord Roberts wants me to concentrate on finding this 'Black Panther' fellow. Burnham is pretty lucky you know."

"Why is that?" I asked.

"Boers must not have known who they had. They have put a price on his head dead or alive. They'd have watched him closer if they'd known."

"Alright, Fredericks, tell the Major I'll be there in a minute, will you? Hold on, Doctor, I've one more thing for you." Murtry had evidently found his file.

"Right, see you later, Doctor."

When Fredericks had closed the door, Murtry came back around the desk. "See, Doctor, this is part of what puts me in a bad position."

"What does?"

"The 'Black Panther', of course."

"I'm afraid I don't understand."

"Duquesne is the 'Black Panther'. Now I'm caught between two parties, both looking for the same man and I'm not supposed to tell either what the other is doing."

I admit I was somewhat at a loss to help the young man. "Lieutenant, do what you believe is in the best interest of the command." I started through the door my hand on the door knob. "I do not envy your position."

By noon I was back at the hospital and, to my surprise, so was Major Drury. He and Archie Langman were deep in conversation over the number of cots and linen required at the hospital.

"You were supposed to come here fully equipped, sir, and not require extra materials from the army. Sustenance and replacement of equipment as needed." It was Drury and he seemed in a foul mood.

"We did not come prepared for so many, Major. We came prepared to hold fifty patients, but Dr O'Callaghan and Dr Doyle say the men we took in this morning is only the start of the problem. In a week our numbers will double and we'll need more tents, cots, linen and men to help. We must be prepared!"

Langman looked away from Drury and saw me.

"Captain Watson! Perhaps you can make the Major here understand that with all the extra cases we need help from the Army Medical Corps."

"Afraid I've come in in the middle of the conversation Archie. What's going on?"

"We've thirty beds of our fifty filled now with wounded and regular sick call, and we just added five with enteric fever. Dr Doyle and Dr O'Callaghan say that it is just the start because of the water being cut off and we need to double our size for what's to come." He turned back to Drury, glaring at him. "And we need the army to help!"

"Enteric already?" I walked over to Drury. "Major, if the water works are not retaken we'll be losing men in the hundreds, if not thousands to fever. Mr Langman is not exaggerating. You are a doctor, you've seen it before."

Drury stared at me a moment and I could almost see him thinking. "Alright, Dr Watson, you're right, we've been through this kind of thing before. Not like these civilians." He slid his eyes toward Langman. "I'll get with the depot and get all I can. Mr Langman, give me a list and one man to help in case I need a runner. Good day gentlemen."

"Thank you, Doctor," said Langman as we watched the Major depart. "He's a bit hard to deal with these days. Spends his time either with that Mrs Foster or drinking with Major Pelham and that's fine, but right now we have use of him."

I excused myself and went to the ward. If we were about to start a bout with enteric fever, this is where I needed to be. I had made it a special interest of mine since it had caused the death of my step-mother. Now I would put that knowledge to use far beyond what I had ever imagined.

Chapter 9
MURTRY HAS AN IDEA

Within three days, the ward was full to over-flowing and men were dying at an appalling rate. All the hospitals were beyond capacity and we, who had planned for fifty had three times that number. Men would soon be dying at the rate of fifty a day. If Roberts didn't move his army, he would have no army, and yet he still made no move to take the water works.

On the 10th of April, Doyle was invited to dine with Lord Roberts. I considered myself fortunate to not be included in the invitation, for I was afraid of what my frank friend might do or say to Lord Roberts. The retaking of the water works was most prominent in his mind.

I had now developed something of a routine. Every morning I would wave to friend Cacy from the roof, work the day in the wards, and at night meet Lieutenant Murtry by the stable so he could brush his horse and we could share what little information there was.

It was the night that Doyle was dining with Lord Roberts that a number of curious things occurred. I had made my usual visit to the stables. Murtry had little to impart. Each day Sergeant Weaver had reported four or five cases of canned goods missing, but had not been able to find the culprit. I had now come to regard this as a petty theft issue, but I did not want to dampen Murtry's enthusiasm, so I let him continue to speak of it. Fredericks had been out among the Boers trying to identify the location of the 'Black Panther', so far, to no avail. Burnham had been on a number of scouts and provided some good information on the placement of some of the Boer commandos. Among them was the Irish Brigade under the American, Blake.

"Seems Colonel Blake rides a horse he calls DG," mentioned Murtry. "Captured it from the Dragoon Guard. His Brigade is armed with Krags and some Lee-Metfords that they took at Dundee."

"I'm sorry, Doctor. We don't seem to be making much progress. We know that every time we move a troop or company, they move to counter it.

But the question is, is it because they see us or because they are told? I just don't know."

"What does Major Parker say?"

"Our Intelligence Chief?"

Murtry thought a moment.

"I think he believes there is a leak inside the headquarters, but for now he is checking up on the lower echelons - you know, clerks, telegraphers, people like that - who have to be used to transfer orders."

Murtry brushed Boy-O for a few minutes in silence. "I've got a theory, Doctor, but I need to check it out."

"What is the theory?"

"No, I might be accusing an innocent man and I wouldn't want to do that."

"Come, come, it's just we two. Surely you can tell me."

"No, doctor. I'll let you know tomorrow or maybe the next day if it proves out!"

"Suit yourself, but keeping things secret is unwise," I sighed. "I'll see you tomorrow."

"Good night, Doctor."

"Good night, Lieutenant. And don't take any chances."

"I will." He grinned.

I started my walk back toward the hospital lost in thought when I heard laughter coming from a barn to my right. It was actually the barn behind and belonging to Mrs Foster's boarding house. The laughter was easy to recognize. I knew it was Cacy before he walked out of the barn. With him were two other men. All seemed to be in the best of spirits and that is what I attributed it to.

Seeing me, the laughter stopped abruptly, but Cacy's head leaned over as if to squint through the coming darkness. Recognizing me, he laughed again and waved.

"Evening, Doctor. How are you this fine evening?"

"Well, Mr Cacy and you?"

"Fine, fine, sir. My mates and I have finished for the day and are about to go to the Yager's Hotel where a man may get a drink. Will you joint us?

"I appreciate the offer, but I must get back to the hospital. Perhaps another time."

"Suit yourself, doctor."

"Been shoeing mules tonight?" I asked.

Cacy stopped abruptly. He was like a crow as his head twitched side to side. "Why do you ask, Doctor?"

"I could see the glow of a forge inside the barn." I replied. He looked back at the barn and when he turned back, he was his jovial self. "Ah, sure. Me and Seanan and Keenan here were shoeing their horses."

"So you are a man of many skills."

"More than people know," he said putting a finger to the side of his nose. "More than people know. Good night, Doctor." With that, he and his two companions turned on down the road.

I did not know what was to be made of his odd actions, but I had more important things to do. I had a ward of patients to look after.

Chapter 10
ENTERIC

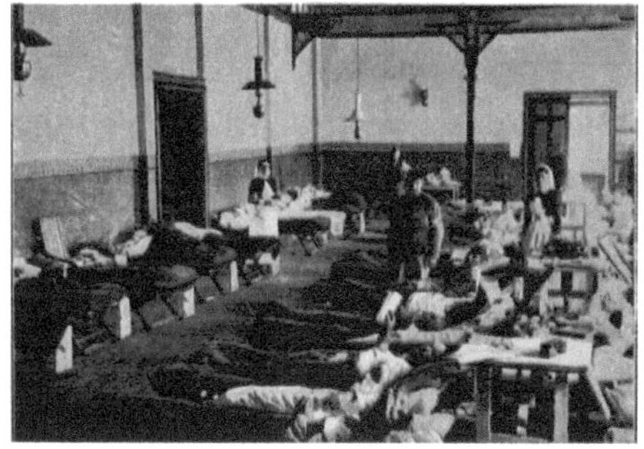

Conditions in the hospital were worse the next day. All fifty beds were filled and more were on the floor. Drury, to his credit, had done what he could. That morning, as I watched Cacy drive his team up the road, a detail of soldiers were erecting additional tents and offloading supplies to augment our hospital.

Doyle had come back from the night before in a better mood with Lord Roberts' assurance that the water works would be re-taken 'as soon as practical'."

I smiled up my sleeve at Doyle's announcement. He did not understand the secret code of the military. What Lord Roberts was telling him was that he would move when he was damn good and ready. Sometimes one has to learn slowly and the hard way.

Lord Roberts had agreed to visit the hospital on Doyle's insistence. That afternoon, true to his word, Roberts appeared.

The effect of the visit was greater on the men than on Roberts. They were impressed that the Commander-in-Chief should take time to visit them and morale was much bolstered.

Murtry and Parker had accompanied Lord Roberts, but it was Doyle who made all the introductions.

On being introduced to Lord Roberts, I saluted and then shook his proffered hand.

"I want to thank you, Lord Roberts, for having saved my life in Afghanistan," I said.

"I?" he puzzled.

"Yes, sir. I was among the wounded at Kandahar. Your relief force saved us."

"Ah, Kandahar. Great march that. Gave them a good thrashing! We'll do the same here, sir. We'll have it over soon!"

"Not if we don't get fresh water," interjected Doyle.

Roberts looked daggers at Doyle. "I've told you, Doctor, as soon as we can. Now, I must be back to headquarters. Major Parker, the horses. We've got to meet some reporter for the *Times*, Mr Langman or I'd be glad to stay a while. Always busy, you know." With a further sideways look at Doyle, he left the pavilion with Parker and Drury bringing up the rear trying to smooth things over.

Murtry pulled on my sleeve as the others left the room. "I was going to let you know about Escott. He arrived about four this morning. He said to tell you he would be on an official tour of the hospital this afternoon."

"Does Lord Roberts know his true identity?"

"No, I don't believe so. He refers to him as 'another damned reporter', but he's received word from the war office to talk to him. I'll try to let you know what else I find out."

"How comes your theory?" I asked. "Any new thoughts?"

"I'll tell you this much, sir. I think I'm getting closer. It involves canned goods, Sarvins, and two kinds of potato diggers." He grinned.

"What?" I exclaimed.

Murtry didn't wait to explain, but hurried off to join Lord Roberts' party, as we could hear the horses departing.

"And two kinds of potato diggers? Whatever does he mean?" I muttered out loud.

"Whatever are you talking about?" Came a voice.

"Nothing, just talking to myself."

Doyle had re-entered the pavilion.

"Looks like we're to be extra shorthanded now that the real work has started. O'Callaghan has decided to go home. He leaves tomorrow. He isn't one for roughing it, I suppose. We'll at least give him credit for trying."

"He couldn't have picked a worse time to leave. We're already over full. How many more cots have we?"

"We'll be able to hold a hundred by tonight. Best make rounds now."

The rest of the day was the real start of the horror for us at the hospital.

Enteric fever, or typhoid as it should properly be called, is a disease for which, as I write this, there is no cure other than time, a strong constitution and good care. Perhaps in the future science will solve this problem. We know it's cause - unsanitary conditions and contaminated water.

Within a week, our hospital was overflowing. One hundred and sixty men were on the cots and on the ground.

The fever runs a course that lasts about four weeks if one is to survive, less if not. It starts with headaches, thirst, lethargy, and aching in the limbs. Many is the man who believes he's just "not feeling well". Then comes the coughing, spitting, thick tongue and fever.

The fever increases each day until it peaks and stays at 104 degrees for a number of days. Along with this will be a rapid pulse of 110 or more. By the end of the second week, the disease is usually at its' worst. There is diarrhoea; bloating and the muscles have uncontrollable shaking. By the end of the fourth week the patient should be getting better. That is, if he is to recover.

I had been fortunate in Afghanistan and survived my bout with enteric fever. As I said, one of the keys is good care. For in many cases, the lower intestines will tear and once blood is seen, there is not much hope. Men must be kept quiet and not allowed to move about. Everything must be constantly disinfected, or not only will the patients die, so will the staff. For the diarrhoea we would give five to ten drops of aromatic sulphuric acid in water. If men were allowed out of bed, they would surely tear their thin intestines. All we could do was use hot water bottles to keep in body heat and give a pint of normal salt solution under the skin. At no time could we give the men any form of solid food. The best things were tea, coffee, boiled rice water, and best of all, milk. We tried to get fresh milk, but that seemed impossible and condensed milk had to be shipped all the way from England. All we could do was our best with what we had. By the end of the week, the hospitals would be losing fifty men a day. In all we would lose thousands to fever. More men than would be lost than to any Boer Commando.

Chapter 11
TWO HEADS

Holmes came to the hospital late in the afternoon that day. He had been invited to dine that night with Lord Roberts and had little time to spend with me.

Having greeted him as Escott, I took him on a quick tour of the hospital. Doyle played, or should I say over-played, his part, welcoming Holmes as Escott in a voice loud enough for the world to hear.

When we were able to get back outside, I started to fill Holmes in about all that had happened. He listened attentively until I had finished then took his pipe from his pocket and I did the same. We sat upon one of the benches outside the pavilion. Neither of us spoke for some time as we filled our pipes and puffed slowly.

"All you have told me is very interesting, Watson. I must spend some time pondering on it."

"But you, Holmes, what has happened? You've said nothing. And what the devil did your telegram mean, 'Beware the Two Heads' or some such nonsense?"

"No nonsense, old boy. You've not run across the two heads or you'd know what I had referred to." Holmes leaned back and puffed. "As to the first part of your question, I can say that it is done for now. Duquesne's minions, like Moriarty's were easily gathered. The head man eluded us, however. In fact, I believe he was gone about the time that we arrived. The ports are safe for the moment. I'm also convinced that while Cape Town is filled with spies, thieves and charlatans, the loss of information is from up here, not down there."

"And the gold?"

"No sign of it. Milner has been, shall we say, less than candid and forthcoming." Holmes stopped to re-light his pipe.

"However," he continued, "I feel certain the gold is here In the Orange Free State. It may have already made it to Pretoria, but I don't think so."

“And the two heads?” It was like trying to draw teeth.

“Secret identity folderol. Duquesne has kept segments of his organization separate, but given them half pond gold coins with Kruger’s head on both sides to identify each other. Quite melodramatic.” He took another puff.

“Ponds?”

“The ZAR equivalent of our pound.”

We sat quietly for a few moments each with our own thoughts.

“Any description of Duquesne, yet?”

“No Watson, quite the elusive creature. But fear not.” He stood to go. “We shall have him yet. I’ve no doubt that he is the brains behind both the loss of information and the gold.” He turned to walk off and called over his shoulder, “Interesting, Doctor. I shall inform my readers. Stay in touch.” Off he went down the road.

The rest of the day was spent in preparing for more patients. Evidently the enteric had first been contracted at Paardeberg before the soldiers arrived in Bloemfontein. The bad water here only made things worse. Our problems were compounded by incessant rain. Before we left, one in five soldiers had enteric, and there were 1800 more shallow graves. It was so bad that no wood could be found to construct coffins and the men were buried in their brown blankets.

Early in the evening, I went in search of Mr Cacy. If he was making the rounds of the farms for hotels and boarding houses, he might be able to get milk for the hospital. I found him behind Mrs Foster’s boarding house. He was alone and washing down his wagon.

“Mr Cacy,” I started, “good evening. I’ve a question to ask you.”

“Evening, doctor. I don’t know if I’ll have an answer, but you may ask.” He threw his horse brush in the water bucket.

“Since you make the round of farms, do you know if there is milk to be had?”

“Milk, is it? Well, some I’m sure, but not much. And if it’s to be had, it won’t be cheap, but for you I’m sure I can find a bit.”

“It’s not ‘a bit’ that I want, I’m afraid.” I went on to explain to him the critical nature of the need, probably at more length than he needed or wanted to know.

When I finally stopped, Cacy assured me he understood the what and why of my request.

“Sure, sir. You may need to come about with me and explain yourself to the farmers and use your silver tongue. I’m sure you’ll convince them. But the price may be not to your liking.”

I agreed to his proposal and he said he would let me know if he failed and take me around if necessary. This was at a time when the Boer farmers or their families were still on the land. A few months later, when Lord Kitchener had taken over from Lord Roberts, the situation would be wholly different. The farms would be burned to the ground and the families in concentration camps. The earth would be scorched. But for now, I would be able to make some agreement with the farmers.

Chapter 12
A MURDER

Come the morning, Holmes had returned to the hospital and was standing with me as we watched Cacy pass the Rambler's Club grounds on his rounds. He waved and I returned it.

"I'll do what I can, doctor." He called. I smiled and waved again.

"Tell me about your friend down there, Watson."

"Not much to tell," I replied. I expressed what I knew about the man, even to his habit of washing his wagon daily.

"Most interesting," replied my companion when I had finished. "And what are your thoughts on Lieutenant Murtry?"

"Seems to be a good man. Dragoon Guards, good family. He is in a bit of a bad spot. Two masters you see." I went on to explain the awkward situation in which he found himself. "He also has a personal theory about what is going on."

"Has he shared it with you?"

"No, all he would tell me is that it involves canned goods, two kinds of potato diggers, and Sarvins. Whatever that all means."

"Hmm," sighed Holmes looking down the road after the disappearing wagon.

Holmes started to the stairs which went below. "The hospital is short-handed now, I hear."

"Yes, O'Callaghan has left, but I understand a Dr Schwartz is coming in and we will be getting two Sisters of Mercy, nursing sisters, to help. They're quite wonderful."

"Our friend Churchill seems to be everywhere nosing into things," Holmes continued as we exited the pavilion. "Not only attached himself to a colonial unit, but sending some blistering reports to his newspaper. I believe I've met him on two occasions, so I need to keep out of his way. If he sees you he'll undoubtedly ask about me. He has a suspicious nature."

"I assure you, Mr Holmes is home!" I grinned.

I took a cigarette from my case and tapped it on the lid. "I met a most fascinating man the other day, an American named Burnham. Scout, it seems. Well thought of too. We might think about using him, Holmes. If something is out of the ordinary, I believe he'll spot it."

"Yes. I've met him and Fredericks who, they have recently hired."

"Saw Fredericks in passing." I replied. "Don't know much about him."

"Aside from the fact that he is a Boer, educated in England, an excellent shot, been wounded at least twice, once in the left shoulder, once in the left foot, spent time in East London and Paris, neither a cricket nor a rugby fan, is partial to Turkish cigarettes, and quite the ladies' man, I know nothing."

"And his shoe size?" I muttered.

"Nine and a half," said Holmes taking a drag on his cigarette.

"Never mind," I chortled. "Sorry I asked."

A young private of mounted rifles thundered up to where we stood and reigned in his sorrel mare.

"Sir," he saluted, "where can I find Dr Doyle?"

"Inside private, may I help you? Are you injured?"

"No sir. Been a murder, sir, and I'm to get the Doctor straight away."

"Murder? Where?"

"At the headquarters, sir. The hotel, that is, upstairs.

"Alright Private, I'll inform Dr Doyle that he is wanted."

"Thank you, sir," responded the private and saluted again. As he was about to depart, Holmes called out, "Who was murdered, soldier?"

The private looked back. "Lord Roberts' aide, sir, Lieutenant Murtry." With those words he put spur to horse and rode off.

"Quickly, Watson! We must go to Lord Roberts and explain who I am. I must see this room before it is disturbed."

"I'll get Doyle. Lord Roberts sent for him" I looked about. "Moyer," I bellowed, "get me that ambulance." I pointed to a wagon being hitched by two of our St. John's men. "I'll be right back, Holmes."

In a few moments, Doyle, Holmes and I were on board the ambulance moving at a brisk pace toward the headquarters.

"Doyle," instructed Holmes, "you must go straight to Lieutenant Murtry's room. Under no circumstances let anyone touch anything. Do you understand?"

"Quite, Holmes. Fear not, I'll see to everything."

We had barely reached the hotel when the three of us bounded down from the ambulance and rushed for the door.

"Where is Lieutenant Murtry's room?" demanded Doyle of a sentry at the bottom of the stairs as Holmes and I turned right toward Lord Robert's Office.

Major Pelham was outside Lord Roberts' door as we approached.

"Lord Roberts is too busy to see the press this morning, Mr Escott. You know we had an accident here this morning and he is far too busy to see anyone."

Holmes pushed me forward toward Pelham which moved him to the side. I nearly fell into the door when it opened. "Pelham, get me Dickworth in here!" shouted Roberts.

"Yes, sir." replied Pelham.

"Your Lordship, I have come with Dr Doyle and Dr Watson. May I speak to you in private for a moment?" Holmes piped up and at the same time forcing his way through the door.

"I've no time for you Escott. There is too much going on. Pelham get this man out of here." With that Roberts tried to shut the door.

"Sir, I would suggest you look at this." Holmes held a paper before Roberts' face.

"What is this nonsense?" Roberts looked a moment then took the paper from Holmes. "Come in, sir," he said more calmly. As he closed the door he looked back at Pelham. "And get me Dickworth!" he shouted.

It seemed like forever, but in all probability was not more than five minutes, before the door reopened and Holmes came out.

"Where's Dickworth?" the voice inside bellowed as Holmes closed the door.

"His Lordship is not happy," whispered Holmes. "Not with me, not with you and definitely not with Whitehall! He does not appreciate being kept in the dark in his own command."

We were exiting Pelham's outer offices as I asked, "Are you to investigate?"

"Yes," replied Holmes, "but not exactly with his blessing."

We turned to the stairs and headed for Murtry's room.

Chapter 13
THE MURDER ROOM

Holmes and I found Doyle in the room above in quiet discussion with Major Parker, Lord Roberts' Intelligence Officer. On seeing us, Doyle advised that with the Major's help he had convinced everyone to leave the room.

"Should we go in?" Doyle asked.

"In a moment," replied Holmes, looking up and down the hallway. Half a dozen soldiers stood by waiting the Major's directions.

The hallway consisted of a dozen rooms on each side with windows facing the main road or the street behind. Lieutenant Murtry's room was second from the end on the right once one came up the stairs and turned left. His room would face the back street.

"Right," said Holmes, "lets' take a look inside."

We entered the room behind Holmes like a line of ducks. Holmes, myself, Doyle and Parker. Holmes stopped mid-way into the room. "Lestrade's men could not have done worse." He remarked. "Everyone stand still for a moment please."

We all watched as Holmes circled the room. He leaned over the body lying on the bed for only a moment, then stepped back to scan the area around it. Slowly he studied the carpet and walked to the window looking out on the back street, came back to the left side and rattled the connecting door to the next room. It was locked.

"Who is in the next room?"

"Why, that's my room, Mr Holmes." replied Parker.

"You heard nothing in the night, Major?"

"Hardly, sir, I wasn't here. I was out on a scout with Captain Burnham. I just got back an hour ago. No sooner walked in than I heard all this commotion. An orderly had been sent to find the Lieutenant. When he couldn't get an answer at the door, he opened it. Thought the Lieutenant was sleeping, but when he went to wake him, he saw the blood and gave the alarm."

"I see." Holmes pondered a moment. "Major, would you be good enough to go around and open this door, while Dr Watson inspects the body? Thank you, sir."

I came forward and looked closely at the Lieutenant. "Why didn't you tell me what you were up to?" I muttered to the corpse.

"Don't blame yourself, Watson. You cannot control the actions of others." Holmes patted my shoulder. "What can you tell me about the wound?"

"Single deep thrust to the heart. Death was quick, but not instantaneous as they say in the novels. He had time to know he'd been murdered."

"And the weapon?"

"Ah, as to that, I'd say it was a bayonet. Not a usual kitchen knife or something. See how the top of the wound is wide and has a flat look to it and the bottom is thin and angular."

"Could it have been a hunting knife?" Doyle asked.

"Yes, possibly, but I'm more inclined to think bayonet. A hunting knife would probably give a taller wound."

"I see," said Holmes.

Parker had re-joined us by this time and the connecting door stood open. Holmes turned, and, studying the carpet, strode into the major's room and over to the windows.

There were two windows in the room. One looked out on the back street behind the building and the other to the alleyway to the East. Holmes then looked about the rest of the room. It was appointed much like Murtry's - bed, nightstand, chest of drawers and a small writing table with a single chair.

"Major, can you send for whatever sentries were on duty last night at the bottom of the stairs and have them come here?" inquired Holmes.

"Certainly, sir. I'll be right back." With that reply, Parker left.

Doyle walked over to the windows and looked out.

"Can't say as I see anything, Holmes. What are you looking for in here?" asked the big man.

"Exactly what I knew I would find," smiled my friend. "But we'll wait for the major to get back; he'll have to report to Lord Roberts." Holmes walked back into Murtry's room and lighted a cigarette. A few minutes later, Major Parker returned with a young private who looked both sheepish and tired, and not at all sure what was about to happen to him.

"This is Private Morris, Mr Holmes," introduced the major. "He was on duty from midnight to four. I have another man looking for his replacement."

The private had stood to attention on entering the room. Holmes, always able to put people at their ease if he felt the situation required it, came up and put his hand on the boy's shoulder.

"My good sir, all I need to know is who went up the stairs last night during your watch. You're a good soldier; you can remember that, can you not?"

Private Morris seemed to relax a bit.

"Why, yes, sir. Just the usual people. By the time I come on most of the officers are already upstairs, so I only see a few."

"Well, then," Holmes took his hand down, "who were our late arrivals?"

"About one o'clock, there was General Kitchener, sir. But about ten minutes later comes Major Pelham and Captain Dunn." Morris leaned toward Holmes and in his best stage whisper said, "They was a bit done-up, if you know what I mean, sir." He looked sideways at Parker, who just stared back. Morris came back to attention. "That was it, sir. Didn't see nobody else until my relief came."

"Fine, thank you private," replied Holmes. "Would you be good enough to relay that I do not need to see your replacement after all? Excellent. Good day, private."

Morris saluted and left the room.

"Watson, can you give me a time of death?"

I looked at my watch. "Based on the body, I'd say it was between one and two in the morning, but you could stretch it an hour one way or the other."

Holmes walked over and sat on the bed with the body while he lighted another cigarette. We all stood quietly for a few moments and then Major Parker could take it no longer.

"Well, Mr Escott, what shall I tell Lord Roberts you have found?"

"First," started Holmes, "that the lieutenant was not murdered in this room."

"What? Where was he murdered?"

"Why in your room, of course."

"My room?"

"Quite. He was murdered in your room and then carried back in here and placed in his bed."

"But how do you know that?"

"It was obvious when we entered this room, Major. Look around. What is out of place?"

We all three looked about us until Holmes sighed and shook his head.

"What side of the bed is the body?"

"The left."

"And where are his book and the lamp?"

"On the right!"

"Murtry was right handed, if I remember correctly. So it does not make sense he would put himself to bed on the side away from his book and light. Therefore, someone else must have placed him there." Holmes strode to the centre of the room. "And here, sir, see how these foot marks are so deep in the carpet? And they come from where?"

"Through the connecting door," shouted Doyle, pointing at the next room.

"But why should he be in my room?" asked Parker.

"What does your room have that his does not?" replied Holmes. Parker shrugged.

"A fire escape onto the alley, Major." Holmes pointed to the second window, the one that emptied out onto the alleyway. "Lieutenant Murtry needed to use your room to secretly meet with someone. Someone he hoped would give him information, but instead gave him a knife in the heart."

"But there should have been some sign of blood," I protested.

"There is Watson. There are brown stains on the window sill and outside on the fire escape landing. I'll warrant the maid is short some towels when she does the rooms today."

"All you say makes complete sense, Holmes. I just wish we knew who did it."

"But we do, Watson."

"Holmes? I thought your name was Escott, sir?" It was Parker. I had spilled the beans, as they say. I was mortified.

"Don't worry Watson. Too many people were getting to know our little secret anyway." Holmes turned to the Major. "Yes Major, my name is Sherlock Holmes. Lord Roberts knows of my identity, but we are trying to keep as few people in the know about that as possible. I'm sure I can rely on your discretion."

"Certainly, sir. Now I understand why Lord Roberts sent you up here."

"Can we get back to your knowing who the murderer is, Holmes?" I blustered trying to change the subject.

"We know by this." Holmes held up a short length of watch chain. On the chain was what appeared to be a ZAR half-pond coin with two heads.

Holmes slipped it back in his pocket before I could look at it closely. "Found it by the window. Evidently pulled off going in or out."

"But why move the body, Holmes?"

"Just to give the murderer more time to get away and establish an alibi. What if the major had come back early? No, the body had to be moved."

"What do we do now?"

"I, Watson, am going to ask the major here to allow me to go through the Lieutenant's papers. Perhaps he wrote something down. As for you and Dr Doyle, I suggest the hospital has need of you both."

Once again, Holmes was correct.

Chapter 14
MILK RUN

Around mid-afternoon, Mr Cacy arrived at the hospital with his wagon. On it were a few cans of milk, for which I was very grateful. It did not, however, nearly meet our requirements.

"Is there more milk out there to be had, Mr Cacy, or is this all that we can hope for?"

"Ah, doctor. There's more sure, but for a price. It's a war-time economy and like I told you, the farmers are not trusting. I had to leave extra money on a promise to bring back these cans. Now, if you could give me the cans, it might help."

"I'll find what I can," I assured him. "May I come with you tomorrow? Perhaps I can convince these good people how critical all this is, not only to the army, but to the civilians."

"You could get us both killed wearing that uniform of yours, Doctor. I'll get you some clothes that won't stand out." He looked me up and down and shook his head. "But if you get me killed, me mother will never forgive you." Cacy flicked the reins and called for his mules to 'walk on'. "I'll get you those clothes this evening, Doctor," he called over his shoulder.

I did not see Holmes that night. I'm sure he was busy tracking Lieutenant Murtry's movements of the day before.

Holmes had come by to see me off on my adventure that next morning. We had drunk coffee while waiting for Cacy to appear. We watched as Cacy stopped at the hospital to retrieve his empty milk cans.

"Watson, I am going to ask you to be on your best behaviour today."

"What are you talking about?"

I want you to get as much information as you can from your new friend. One never knows what tit-bit of information may be of use and he travels everywhere."

I took leave of Holmes and descended to greet Cacy and climbed up on the seat beside him.

"Why you clean up real nice you do, doctor," he exclaimed, with a smile. "You look quite the proper Boer."

True to his word, he had provided me with 'less offensive clothing' - slouch hat, waistcoat, trousers and a sack coat large enough to hide an elephant. I'm sure I looked quite ridiculous.

Holmes waved from my spot on the roof and called down. "Remember."

"Why, what does your friend mean, doctor?"

"Oh, just to look for some fresh fruit if it's to be found."

Cacy nodded. "Not much likely there, sir."

We rode on in silence.

We were not more than twenty minutes beyond the picket lines when Cacy made his first stop. It was a small, pleasant-looking farm with a fair sized house, barns, outbuildings and corrals. Among the livestock were only four or five milk cows. This was our first stop. Cacy called out in a loud voice for someone to come meet us. An old man and a boy appeared from the barn and a woman of middle age came to the door of the cottage.

The boy ran forward and held the bridle of the offside lead mule (I think that was Anna) as we climbed down.

"Mr Van der Loot, this here is a doctor from town. He'd like to talk to you. I've got your cans in the wagon. I'll get them for you." Cacy turned to go to the back of the wagon.

"Aye, no one sick here, sir. We've no need." The old man looked at me with the inherent mistrust of a Boer for an outlander.

"No, sir, I know that, but you were kind enough to supply some milk to us and I see you have four or five fine milk cows, so I want to make an offer to buy all your milk if I can. I'll supply the cans if that would help."

"I don't know," replied the farmer. "Our own people have need of the milk, too."

"Mr Van der Loot, I have hundreds of men who are very ill. Many will die and there is nothing I can do about that. But some I can save. Some you can save. Men that you can send home to their families alive instead of leaving here dead."

"They'll be sent home, will they?"

"Yes." I agreed.

"I'll sell you all the milk I can, sir. If it will get these damned British out of here." The old man turned on his heels and headed for the barn.

"Gustaf, come help me," he called to the boy. "That Englishman can hold the mules."

This scene replayed itself in one form or another for eight more farms. We had half the wagon full of cans before we started back. We also had to find room for Cacy's usual load of produce.

It was at the third farm that I was surprised to find the two young men that I had seen before with Cacy, Seanan and Keenan. They helped us load a small amount of milk and corn when I heard Keenan ask Cacy if he had any canned goods to trade for the fresh corn and milk.

"Not today, boy," came the reply, "maybe tomorrow. Today you'll have to settle for silver." Keenan shrugged and looked at me with a curious resentment, or so I supposed.

As Cacy and I were returning that afternoon, Keenan's look kept coming back to me.

"I'm surprised," I remarked, "that those two Irish lads are not off on commando."

"Seanan and Keenan? No, not them. They work at the freight yard when trains come in and at night they make wagon parts in the barn behind Mrs Foster's. I don't know when they sleep. Wish I was that young again. Their sister Molly is Mrs Foster's maid."

We continued in silence until we got back to the hospital. Here Cacy saw to the unloading of the milk before going on to his usual rounds. Langman was there to pay him. I explained the arrangements I had made with the local farmers. Langman agreed to give Cacy funds each morning for the day's milk since the farmers would not agree to any other system.

I spent the rest of the day with our patients. In every soldier I looked at I saw myself lying in Kandahar sick with the same disease and delirium. It was the most horrible experience of my life.

It was well past nine o'clock that night that Holmes appeared. Doyle and I were sitting on one of the benches outside the pavilion trying to remove the stench of disease with the smell of shag tobacco. Holmes sat with us for a moment. We were all quiet.

"So, Mr Holmes, for I believe I may call you that now, what of the murder?" Doyle bit down on his pipe stem.

"Do not worry Dr Doyle, we shall prevail. But as you should know, there are other matters which need our attention more."

"More? More than the murder of that poor boy?"

"I assure you, Dr Doyle, the boy will be avenged. It is all part of a single plot, a plot that he got too close to. He should have confided in others. Instead, we will spend valuable time trying to find out what he knew."

We sat again for a moment.

"Where is Major Drury?" asked Holmes.

"I'd like to know the same thing, Holmes," responded Doyle. "Not doing his job as far as I can see. We see the man twice a day, morning and night, and never between. Were it not for Langman and Watson, no telling what state we'd be in."

"Yes, well, Watson would you care to accompany me? I've a few stops to make."

"Of course Holmes, if you need me."

"Go on," said Doyle. "I've got things here."

Holmes and I walked toward the main part of town.

"Where are we going, Holmes, or does it matter?"

"We are going to find your errant major and see what he knows. If I do not miss my guess, he is with Mrs Foster and should be quite in his cups by now. A perfect time for a discussion, is it not?"

"Where does he spend his days, Holmes?"

"He spends them with Major Pelham and trying to hob-nob with the general staff. I'm afraid he has reached the summit of his career, but he keeps trying to progress. It will not happen."

True to Holmes' prediction, Major Drury was both 'in his cups' and with the lady of the house. I could see them through the parlour window as we approached. I could also hear the ring of hammers on iron coming from the barn out back.

"It seems Mr Cacy's friends are busy making wagon parts," I advised.

"Really?" Holmes stopped for a moment and listened. "Yes, perhaps. Shall we knock?"

Taking the steps two at a time, Holmes rapped on the door. It was Mrs Foster who let us in.

"We are here to speak with Major Drury," stated Holmes as he brushed by the woman and walked into the parlour. I nodded, smiled and followed my friend. I did have time to notice how lovely the raven-haired mistress of the house was.

"Ah, Mr Escott, how are you. Haven't seen you since the trip over. Come in, come in."

Drury was definitely in a light mood.

"How is your reporting going, old boy? You'll get lots of copy soon. Lots of copy." His words were slurred and his tongue thick.

"Actually, major, we have been traveling under somewhat false pretences. Although I am reporting for the *Times*, my name is Sherlock Holmes, not Escott."

"Sherlock Holmes! Well what about that. And you, Doctor," he looked at me with a smile and wagged his finger, "I should have known. Where one goes, so goes the other.

"But I'm forgetting myself. A drink gentlemen?"

Holmes winked toward me. "Not for me thank you, but the doctor will have one."

Drury poured two whiskeys and handed me one. "Cheers."

"Well, what can I do for the famous Mr Holmes?" Drury leaned heavily on a settee.

"It seems," said Holmes, who had now seated himself, "that there is to be movement soon. As a reporter, I would be greatly helped if there is any information that you could share."

"With a reporter? No, sir. With a friend I might, but no, sir." He put a finger beside his nose. "I do have things I know you know." He laughed at some personal thought; the drink definitely had the better of him. And then he continued, "I won't tell just anybody."

"I can see that, sir and I will not press you." Holmes stood and turned to go. "Watson, if you've finished your drink, it's time we were off. Good night, Major."

I had to rush to keep up with Holmes passing Mrs Foster in the foyer and getting up with my friend only as he reached the bottom of the porch steps. Instead of turning down the road toward the hospital, Holmes went around the house, past the garden and toward the barn. Just as we approached it, Seanan and Keenan came out, each leading a saddled horse. Cacy was behind them.

"Shoeing tonight or making wagon parts?" I asked smiling and waving.

The two boys said nothing but mounted their horses and rode off toward the freight yard.

"Not very talkative tonight," I remarked to Cacy.

"Those two never are, Doctor. But they're good lads. They've got to go supervise the kaffirs unloading at the yard. Be a long night for them."

"You use keg shoes Mr Cacy?" Holmes spoke for the first time.

"Not me, but the boys there do. It's quicker, but not as good as far as I'm concerned. Are you a friend of the Doctor? I know I've seen you about."

"Yes, the name is Holmes. I'm reporting for the *Times*. Well, good night sir. Watson, we go in opposite directions I believe, but may I have a moment? Good night, Mr Cacy."

I wished Cacy a good night and Holmes and I walked to the road.

"Tell me, have we learned anything tonight?" I was feeling as though nothing had occurred.

"Watson, we have learned a great deal."

"We have?"

"We've learned that Major Drury will tell people whatever he knows. Which, of course, we already knew. He would have told us everything that occurred at the headquarters today with but the slightest help on our part. And we know that your Irish friends, whatever they were doing, were not shoeing horses."

"How do you know?"

"Watson, the only two horses in the barn were theirs and when they left it was easy to see that both horses had well-worn shoes. Cacy's mules were in the corral and had been since we went into the boarding house. So, whose horses were they shoeing?"

"But what was your question about keg shoes?"

"Cacy does not use keg shoes - you know, pre-made shoes that come in twenty five pound kegs. If he were shoeing, his hammer would make a dull thud as it hit hot iron. Keg shoes need not be heated and so make a ringing sound when shaped. They also require no forge be lit. If they were fabricating wagon parts the same would be true. Heated metal does not ring."

"So," I pondered, "if the boys were shoeing horses there would be a ringing sound. But they weren't shoeing because there were no new shoes. And the forge was burning, but didn't need to be. Do you understand all this Holmes?"

"Not yet, Watson. But I will. I have a meeting with Parker in the morning. Meet me there, eight o'clock."

Holmes hurried down the street toward the headquarters.

Chapter 15
THE INTELLIGENCE OFFICER

The following morning, I waved to Cacy as usual. Now, however, he was stopping to pick up empty milk cans and get funds from Lieutenant Langman. Our Boer friends had agreed to supply what milk they could, but only at a price paid daily.

I worked my rounds and by half seven, I started my walk to meet Holmes. I found him just going in to meet Major Parker when I arrived. The major took us straight away into his office and closed the door.

"Please, gentlemen, have a seat. Lord Roberts has already explained that you have full authority in the matter of Lieutenant Murtry's death, Mr Holmes. What can I do for you?"

"Major," started Holmes, "people who work closely together in trying circumstances get a feeling about their fellows. I would like your opinion on a few things."

"Of course, Mr Holmes, whatever I can do."

"Give me your opinion of Lieutenant Murtry."

"That's easy enough. Good man, fine family, well educated, loyal, hard worker. In short, Mr Holmes, I wish we had a lot more officers like him. Never a shirker. Kept his mouth closed, too."

"I see, and Major Pelham?"

"Yes, different sort there. He works hard, intelligent; don't really know anything about his family. He's very efficient, but, well, he somehow rubs people the wrong way."

"Does he have any particular associates?"

"Let's see, I believe he and Captain Dunn spend a close bit of time together, but since your chap Drury showed up," he nodded toward me, "he spends considerable time with him. I think he used to be sweet on his landlady, but she dropped him for Drury, so Pelham moved over here to the hotel. That's really about all I know."

Holmes sat quietly a moment then removed the coin and watch chain he had found in Murtry's room from his pocket.

"Tell me," he said handing the coin to Parker, "have you any ideas on this?"

Parker took the coin and examined it closely.

"Crudely made. Kruger's head on both sides. Copied from a '92 I'd say."

"Are you a numismatist, Major?"

"Oh, bit of an amateur, I guess. This coin was never made properly. They've taken a flan, that is, a blank, and stamped it without turning it into a planchet first."

The major saw my blank stare and smiling continued.

"You see, Doctor, first you make the blank or flan, then the blank is put in a collar to form an edge, then it is stamped. This coin was made by someone in a rush, or who doesn't understand the process." Parker handed the coin back to Holmes. I'm afraid that's all I can tell you about the coin. I've never seen another like it."

"Another thing, Major. What can you tell me about the 'Black Panther'?"

"I suppose it's no secret that we are looking for him. Everyone is. He's a man named Fritz Duquesne and he's a bad lot. Hates us with a passion. We believe he has a ring of spies that report through him to the Boer commandos. We've put £10,000 price on his head, but so far we've had no luck."

"Was Murtry doing something for you on Duquesne?"

"Mostly just keeping his eyes open. I wish he'd told me if he was really getting into something."

"Do you have any thoughts on who might have killed the boy?"

"No, Mr Holmes. I've thought a great deal about it, but I've no idea. I don't know anyone who disliked him." Parker thought a moment. "Mr Holmes, whoever killed Lieutenant Murtry did it because of what he had uncovered. I just don't know what that is."

"Another thing occurs to me, Major. Who is responsible for clearing the hiring of local men to work for the army?"

"There really is no clearing process, Mr Holmes. The units hire natives or white men as they see fit. In the headquarters, the junior aide would keep a record of names for those who worked here." Holmes' next question took me back a bit.

"What do you know about a man named Clint Cacy who brings produce to this hotel?"

"Yes, I know whom you mean. Good man. He spent six years in the Irish Rifles before coming to Africa to make his fortune, mustered out as a sergeant. Why? Have you anything I should know?"

"No, nothing at the moment, but I will keep you posted." Holmes rose from his chair. "Thank you, Major, you have been most helpful.

"Before I go, let me share this with you. I have reason to believe there is a leak in information coming from this headquarters. I don't know who yet, but Lieutenant Murtry found out something and didn‘t share it. Don't make the same mistake."

"I won't, Mr Holmes. But I also won't give testimony unless I'm sure of my suspicions."

Holmes and Parker shook hands. I followed suit and spoke for the first time.

"Major, I know how much Lieutenant Murtry thought of his gelding, Boy-O. I'd like to buy him so you can send the money to his family."

"Of course, Doctor. We normally auction off such things. We just send personal items home. I'll see what I can do; we might be able to arrange the sale. You'll pay premium for such a good horse, you know."

"That would be fine, sir. I'll take good care of him."

"Watson," said Holmes once we had taken our leave of the major, "I want to speak with Captain Burnham. Let us see if he is in his room."

Chapter 16
BOY-O GETS NEW SHOES

Burnham's room was on the same floor as Lieutenant Murtry's, but down the opposite end of the hallway. On Holmes' knock came that deep American voice calling us to enter. Burnham was standing by the window.

"Ah, Doctor, how are you? What can I do for you this morning? I was just about to head downstairs." He came forward and shook my hand.

"Captain, let me present my friend, Mr Sherlock Holmes."

"Sherlock Holmes!" exclaimed Burnham, shaking hands enthusiastically, "A pleasure, I assure you. Why you're quite famous in the States. Thanks to the doctor here."

"I know much of you also, Captain." replied Holmes.

"Not many places to sit down gentlemen, but grab a seat. What can I do for you?"

Holmes sat on a corner of the small table and I seated myself on the bed.

"Captain Burnham," started Holmes, "I have come to you, a man of impeccable reputation, because I need some insight which you may have."

"I'll help you in whatever way I can, of course, but what exactly do you need to know?"

"You have been here some time with the headquarters. What is your opinion of Major Parker?"

"Why, as far as I know he's a good man. I don't have any reason to distrust him. Just what are you getting at Mr Holmes? What is all this about?"

"Captain, I believe I can trust you and I need an ally within the headquarters. It is my job to stop the transfer of secret information that is occurring. The Boers are finding out our movements almost before the orders go out."

Holmes went on to explain all that had occurred. Burnham stood in rapt attention. When he had finished, he showed the two-headed coin and asked if Burnham had ever seen another like it.

"No, Mr Holmes, I have not. But what can I do to help?"

"Answer a few questions, if you would. Besides Major Parker, what are your thoughts on Majors Pelham and Drury, Captain Dunn and your new scout, Fredericks?"

"Pelham seems to be alright I guess. Bit stuck up, I think, but he backs Rhodes well enough. He drinks too much for me, as does the doctor's friend, Drury. He's a bit of a waster, but honest I'd say. Dunn I don't know very well. He's an operations officer, so he'd know plans ahead of time, and he drinks with Major Pelham, never to excess that I've ever seen. I don't drink myself."

Burnham stopped for a moment, obviously thinking.

"And Fredericks," prompted Holmes.

"Yes, I was just thinking about him. He's new, of course. I hunted and fought in this area for years. I've never heard of the man. But he's young; maybe 22 or 23, and I've been gone for some time. He's a first-class hunter and scout I've seen that. He was raised a Boer, but he speaks with an English accent. He went to school in England. If you want to know anything about him, just ask. He is definitely not shy about telling you about himself. Some of it is made, shall we say, bigger than life. But I've nothing against him and he never talks shop, just about himself."

"I believe we've taken up enough of your time, Captain. I know that I may rely on your discretion."

"I'm going on a scout with Fredericks tonight, Mr Holmes. Should anything untoward occur, I will let you know."

Shaking hands all around, Holmes and I left. It was now noon. I told Holmes I must get back to the hospital. For his part, Holmes wished to send off some telegrams and so we parted. To my good fortune, Cacy was delivering milk to the hospital as I arrived.

"Looks like you have the gift, Doctor. I've half a wagon of milk. If this keeps up, I'll have to get a second wagon just for you."

"I believe the convincing argument was the silver coins and not my silver tongue," I laughed.

I was about to walk on when I remembered something.

"Mr Cacy, I may have a new gelding this afternoon. Do you think you might be able to shoe him tonight?"

"I'm not like the boys, sir. I need some daylight, not lanterns. Bring him over before seven and we'll see what we can do."

I agreed and went back into the hospital while Cacy and a half dozen soldiers unloaded the wagon.

Later that afternoon came word from Major Parker that Boy-O would be mine. I must say a princely sum was asked, but I felt the gelding worth it. The bay was what I would call a "parade horse". He was sound, with four white stockings and a blaze. I judged him to be about ten years of age and of an even temperament. It was close on to half six when I finally got away to the stables. Fortunately Boy-O was taken daily care of by the headquarters stable detail, so my chores would be few.

As part of my agreement with Parker, he had included the tack in the price of the horse. Though a groom could have saddled Boy-O, I preferred to do it. There is a bond that must be forged between a man and his horse. That bond can be stronger than any human one. In Afghanistan I had seen more than one steed stand by the body of his fallen rider while confusion and battle raged around them.

Having saddled, I rode to the barn behind Mrs Foster's boarding house. Cacy was already there, as were his two friends, Seanan and Keenan.

"Ah, Doctor, right on time I see. You can give the horse to Seanan to hold. Keenan," he called, "get on that bellows for me like a good lad."

I dismounted. Handing the reins to Seanan, I followed them into the barn.

"Have a seat, Doctor. This won't take too long. We'll have you out of here within the hour." Cacy was pulling bar stock from off a shelf. He looked back at Boy-O and with a practiced eye decided on the size of the bars to bend.

Little was the discussion over the next hour as Cacy forged and hammered. I did notice what Holmes had mentioned, but I had never really thought of it before. Hot Iron does not ring. Instead it makes a dull sound as the almost-molten steel is formed.

I took the time to look around the inside of the barn. It looked the same as any other I had ever seen. Barrels, boxes, hay, harness and wheels were hung or laid about. By the forge itself were stocks of steel and some iron pots. There were all the usual tools of a blacksmith: forge tongues, vice, anvil, hardy tools. There were also piles of canvas and a complete repair kit for tents and tarpaulins. Along the wall were boxes of grommets and dies for the canvas and numerous coils of rope.

Cacy was an excellent farrier. In less than the promised hour, Boy-O had shiny new shoes.

"What is the bill, Mr Cacy? That is a fine job."

"Don't worry, Doctor, I'm happy to do it. There's no charge. But I'll tell you, next time the boys and I are at Yager's Hotel, we'll put a pint on your bill."

Laughing, I could only agree. Keenan came up to Boy-O and rubbed his neck.

"Doctor," said the young man, "you won't be here forever. When you leave, I'd sure like to have this fine animal."

His remark, though innocent enough, made me nervous. "Should you still be about when I leave, we may make an arrangement, but for now I think that such is premature."

"Just remember, Doctor. I'd take good care of him."

"Yes, well, good night. And Cacy, I'll tell the barman you're owed a few." So stating, I rode off.

It was just turning dark as I got to the stables. Holmes was there, along with Burnham and Fredericks. The two scouts were saddled and about to depart. As I dismounted, Burnham and Fredericks both wished me a good evening and departed.

"Anything new, Holmes?" I inquired.

"No. But I believe we are making progress. And you, Watson, I see you've had your horse shod."

"Yes, Cacy is quite the excellent blacksmith. But, I must say that his two fellows make me nervous. I cannot but feel they are up to something. Could they be involved in your leak of information? They do work at the rail yard, after all. They see quite a bit."

"The answer, Watson is both yes and no. They could, of course, pass on information about stores and troop strength, but they would have no access to plans. No, if they are involved, they are merely couriers, not the spies we seek."

"Let me give Boy-O a quick brush, and I will buy us some refreshment. I need to put some money on the tab for Cacy. It was all he'd take."

"Excellent, Watson, we shall socialize and listen."

Chapter 17
THE SECOND MURDER

We may have listened at Yager's Hotel that night, but as far as I could tell, we heard nothing of any import.

The next morning, I was in the wards early making rounds, long before Cacy came for the milk cans. To my surprise, I found Burnham and Fredericks in the tent beside the entrance to the pavilion. This particular tent was used as a triage station to sort the critical from the ordinary. The two scouts seemed both the worse for their night of travel. Fredericks was sitting on a camp stool while Moyer stitched a long jagged wound in his left calf. Burnham was just watching the process. Both were dirty and obviously tired. Regardless of wound or lack of sleep, Fredericks was still cheerful.

"Good morning, Dr Watson," he cheerfully called as I entered.

"Some bad luck last night?" I queried. "Well, you could not be in better hands than Moyer here. What happened?"

"I think they were trying to kill us, Doctor. That's my opinion. What do you think Burnham?" Fredericks laughed as if he had made an exceptional jest.

Burnham stared at his fellow scout and, turning, left the tent without a word. There was something between these two men. Was it jealousy, envy, or just competition for favour in the eyes of Lord Roberts?

"Well, I must get back to work," I said. "You must tell me later what has happened. I'd be greatly interested."

"It's of no consequence, sir. We didn't get done what we wanted, but there's always tonight."

I left the tent to find Burnham outside. He was standing alone deep in thought when I approached.

"May I offer you a cigarette, Captain?"

He looked up at me and shook his head.

"No thank you, Doctor. I don't smoke. It's bad for your sense of smell."

With that I had to agree. Later I would find that besides not smoking and drinking, he ate very little and drank very little water. He asserted that he had learned this in his days fighting Indians. He trained his body to do without and therefore survived where others could not.

"What happened last night, Captain? Where are your horses?"

"Lost, sir, both of them. I hated to lose that little mare. She was a good one, Basuto pony you know." He shook his head again. "You know it is a truism that the English don't know how to take care of horses. The animals here should be in good shape by now. They're not."

"Some Englishmen do know how to take care of their horses, you know."

"Sorry, Doctor. Present company excluded of course." He took a deep breath. "We did exceedingly poorly last night."

"Sometimes one just doesn't have the right luck, you know."

"That wasn't it. We were moving too quickly. I wanted to slow our pace, but Fredericks insisted we hurry. He was afraid we would not make the kopjes we went to scout and return before sunrise. I admit it was going to be a close run thing, but you still must be cautious.

"At any rate, we were about five miles out when we came upon fresh tracks. Probably six or seven riders. They were going in the same direction as we were. By the stride I'd say there were at least two thoroughbreds. The rest were native ponies. It had to be Boers. I made Fredericks slow a bit, but about two more miles on we decided to cross the saddle between two kopjes. I guess there was a donga on the other side or a dry wash. At any rate, we were caught in it. The Boers jumped us and the shootin' was pretty fast.

"My mare went down almost immediately. We'd only been able to retreat a few hundred yards. I'll hand it to Fredericks; he came back, caught me up behind him and made a run for it. We'd gone down a steep slope when the horse lost his feet and we tumbled over into another dry wash. The drop must have been twenty feet. The horse, then Fredericks, then me. Poor beast had two broken legs. Nothing we could do but put him down. Fredericks had that gash on his leg, but I just had the wind knocked out. Landed on all that padding, I guess. But one thing I still don't understand."

"What's that?"

"Why didn't they come after us?"

"Perhaps they didn't want to fall in the dry wash." I laughed.

Burnham looked at me as if he was thinking deeply. Finally he threw up his hands.

"And perhaps you are correct, Doctor perhaps."

"How did you get back?"

"We walked. We'd have been back sooner except for Fredericks's wound. When we got to the line of pickets, we were able to find a wagon coming in.

"And now I really need to report in. I hate to report a failed scout. I take it very personally. Ah, Mr Holmes, good morning, sir."

I looked around to find my friend approaching up the walkway.

"Good morning, gentlemen. Captain Burnham, I believe that the headquarters has need of you. There is a bit of a crisis at the moment."

"What is going on, Holmes?" I asked.

"It seems that Major Parker has disappeared. No one has seen him since late yesterday."

"I had best be off, gentlemen," put in Burnham. "Doctor, will you tell Fredericks where I've gone?"

"Of course, sir, of course."

Burnham literally trotted down the road.

"Holmes, surely Parker has learned from Murtry's death. He hasn't done anything precipitous!"

"Watson, if there is one thing on which you may always count it is the folly of men. I fear he has done just what he was asked not to do. But come, let us go to the headquarters and see what progress has been made."

I sent a St John's man to Fredericks with Burnham's message then accompanied Holmes.

As we walked up the dusty road toward the centre of town, a spring wagon passed us. Whatever was in the back was covered with a pauline. Beside the wagon rode two men, both in colonial uniform. As they came abreast of us, one, a lieutenant, looked down at us then drew rein.

"Mr Sherlock Holmes, is it not, sir." It was a statement, not a question.

"And you, sir, are Winston Churchill. I don't believe we have ever been formally introduced, but allow me to present Captain Watson, Doctor, RAMC."

I nodded my head and proffered my hand. "Delighted, Lieutenant. I've read some of your works, very enlightening."

"And I yours, Doctor, very, ah, entertaining. I'd heard rumours that you were about, Mr Holmes. Whatever you are here for I'd appreciate being made part of. Still reporting, you know."

"Who is in the back of the wagon?" asked Holmes, ignoring Churchill's request.

My head snapped around to Holmes. "I saw the outline of a boot, Watson."

"I'm sad to say that it is Major Parker from the headquarters. My lads found him in a donga this morning out on the road to the Modder. Horse and equipment were gone." Churchill looked down the road where the spring wagon and his sergeant were disappearing into the distance. "I'd best catch up. Until later, gentlemen." He spun his horse around and with a nudge of the knees trotted after his men.

"Once again we are denied access to a crime scene, Watson."

"Now, Holmes, it wasn't really a crime scene. This is a war."

"No, Watson, I assure you, this was a murder. A cold, calculated murder. Let us get to the headquarters and see what we can find.

By the time we arrived, Churchill and his men had already departed and Parker's body had been placed in a shed behind the hotel.

Going to what had been Lieutenant Murtry's office, we met the lieutenant's replacement. He was older than Murtry had been. Lieutenant Barthelme had been a sergeant in the Royal Horse Artillery and received an offer of a commission because of his actions at Colenso, where Lord Roberts's son had met his death. To say the man looked uncomfortable would be an understatement. The change from file closer to lieutenant would take time.

On introduction, Barthelme shook our hands vigorously. It seemed he was a fan of my small works about Holmes.

"Lieutenant," started Holmes. "We have been engaged by Lord Roberts to investigate the death of your predecessor, Lieutenant Murtry. I believe that Major Parker's death may be related and I desire to inspect his body. Can you arrange that?"

"Oh, certainly, Mr Holmes. I was just about to go back there. I must account for his personal effects. Would you and the doctor like to come along?"

We entered a small shed behind the hotel. It was empty except for a single table in the middle of the room where Parker had been laid out.

"Take a look, Watson, and give me your medical opinion."

I approached the table and inspected the man's body finding nothing save four bullet wounds. One was in the neck, two in the chest and one in the abdomen.

"I'd say the neck wound would have been survivable. The other three were all mortal. The abdominal wound would have been a lingering death. In a sad way, it's fortunate the other two took him quickly."

"Can you tell what weapons may have caused the injuries?"

"No, Holmes, all of them exited the body. But I'd venture that they were of about thirty calibre." I could hear my own sigh. "Either side could have imposed these wounds. They were all fired from a distance. You can see there are no powder burns on the clothes or flesh. The only other thing I can say for certain is that he was facing his executioners at the time."

"If you are finished I must collect his things now, gentlemen." The lieutenant started to turn out the major's pockets as Holmes watched attentively. There was not much - a pencil, a few coins, a watch, around his neck a miraculous medal. But in one pocket there was a piece of paper. Barthelme looked at it then held it out to me. "It's for you, sir."

"Me?" I asked as I approached and took the missive. On the outside of the folded paper were the words, "Dr Watson". I unfolded the paper, read it and then handed it to Holmes.

"Supply wagons. Meeting scout. Will explain," was the entire note. It was signed, "Parker".

"What can this mean, Holmes?"

"I'm sure I don't know, Watson. Not yet. 'Supply wagons'- he used the plural not the singular."

"How is that significant?"

"Had it been singular, I believe it would confirm a hypothesis. But as it is, it seems to add a cloud of fog to our problem." Holmes handed back the note.

We thanked the new lieutenant and walked out into the sunlight. From where we stood, I could see the dust of the rail yard as scores of supply wagons made their way from the trains to the units carrying everything needed to keep an army in the field. Which wagons had Parker meant?

"Holmes he said 'meeting scout'. Burnham didn't mention anything about Major Parker. What scout was he meeting? It couldn't be Fredericks, he and Burnham were together all night."

"Yes, Watson, but Burnham has a whole section of scouts. I'll make inquiries, but I do not hold out much hope."

I spent the rest of my day at the hospital. The dead were being carried out constantly and grave digging had become a full time job for some.

Chapter 18
MRS FOSTER GETS A SHOCK

The next morning I hoped for two things: Relief from the new cases of enteric fever and some solution to our mysteries. The sun had barely risen when I heard Holmes's familiar tread coming up the steps to our roof. He drew out his pipe and joined me at what had become my 'thinking spot' at the roof's edge. Neither of us spoke for quite a long time as we watched the army awake to another day.

There were regular army men, colonials, yeomanry, Scots with their plaid kilts and khaki aprons, all going somewhere, all performing the functions of everyday life and the serious business of an army at war.

As we stood watching the road, a battery of the new Pom-Pom guns trotted by below.

"What type of weapon is that, Watson? It seems to be a very large machine gun."

"You've fairly well described it, Holmes. It's a 37mm automatic cannon. Fires a one-pound shell from a belt of, I think, twenty-six. It's kind of an oversize Maxim gun. It's new to us, but the Boers have been using them all along. To great effect too, I might add. Doesn't do a lot of damage, but the effect of all that fire coming in on one makes one slow down and re-think whether or not one wants to charge into it. Very effective. I'm glad we finally have some." I started to tap out my pipe on the wall. "I'm afraid Mr Milner underestimated our Boer friends and their preparations."

Holmes was busy re-lighting his pipe. "What type wheels are on the carriages of those guns?" He asked between puffs.

"Wheels?" I looked at the last of the guns moving rapidly away from us. "Sarvins, I believe."

"And what had Murtry said? He referred to Sarvins, did he not?"

"Yes, he did, Holmes, but most wheels these days are either Sarvins or Archibalds. That's pretty standard."

"Interesting. Spoke to your Major Drury last evening at some length. He is really a pretty good fellow when not in his cups."

"Yes, he's not a bad sort. He has really pitched in here during the day of late. But the nights are his, I assure you."

"It seems, Watson, that he much resents this particular duty as liaison with a civilian hospital. He feels very keenly he should have been assigned to a forward unit."

"I can understand that. You always want to be where there is action."

"He is also quite smitten with Mrs Foster. It is not just a casual thing with him. I believe he actually thinks he's in love with her."

"Ah, Holmes. One does not 'think' they are in love. It is a feeling; it is an emotion, not a thought process."

Holmes puffed a moment.

"No doubt you are right, Watson. But in any event, he spends each night drinking and telling his life story to the woman. I fear, however, he is to be disappointed in his affair de coeur. She is in love with Pelham."

"Holmes, how could you possibly know that?"

"Oh, it's just a feeling, Watson." Holmes smirked and looked down as Cacy pulled his wagon to a halt beside the pavilion to load empty cans.

"And those wheels, Watson, they are which?" Holmes pointed at the wagon.

"Archibalds, no, they are Sarvins. But, as I said, they are so common I don't know how that information will help us."

"I don't know yet, Watson, but we shall see, we shall see." Holmes tapped out his pipe and started for the stairs.

"Four o'clock Watson, at the hotel. Be there, my boy. I've things to do in the meantime and so have you."

This day was as bad as the rest. We now had one hundred and sixty men in our little hospital for fifty. The excess made our sanitary conditions as bad as any I had seen in Afghanistan twenty years before. So, I shamefully admit, it was almost with relief that at half three I started my walk to meet Holmes. It was as I was leaving that Cacy and his mates arrived.

"Stand now, Victoria, Anna! Stand now." He called out.

"And what are the names of the other two?" I called up to Cacy.

"Oh, they'd be Polly and Pattie, but they're good wheelers. They'd much rather stand, you know. It's the lead that always wants to do something." He jumped down from the box and patted Polly as men came to unload the milk. "Of course, if all I ever saw was blinkers and a mule's ass, I wouldn't want to walk on either." He and I both laughed.

Cacy looked toward the pavilion. "It's sad, these men, you know. If they'd never come here, they wouldn't die here." He took a deep sigh. "Right, then. They've unloaded, can I take you somewhere?"

"No, Mr Cacy. Thank you, but I'd like to walk."

Cacy tipped his hat, and, climbing back up on the box, flicked his reins and called "Walk on" as I started my way to the headquarters.

As I came up on the headquarters, I saw Captain Burnham approaching from the opposite direction. We met at the walkway to the veranda.

"Another scout last night, Captain?"

"Hello, doctor. Yes, every night right now."

"How is Fredericks?"

"He's fine. That scratch won't slow down a good scout. Hello, Mr Holmes."

Holmes had come out on the veranda to join us.

"Captain, anything of interest last night?"

"Well, I can't really discuss exactly what I find, Mr Holmes, let me say I saw the same men as the night before, but this time I could skirt them no problem. One man can move much better than two. Don't get me wrong. Fredericks knows what he's doing, it's just easier."

"Do you think we'll ever move on the water works?" I inquired.

"I hope so, Doctor. From what I can see they aren't putting much effort into holding onto it. I think we should move now. But I guess Lord Roberts knows what he's doing."

Holmes approached the captain to ask his next question.

"Would it be possible for me to accompany you on a scout, Captain?"

"Depends, Mr Holmes. I wouldn't want to jeopardize the scout or you. Maybe if it's nothing too serious. You have a good horse?"

"No, but I have a friend with one." Holmes looked straight at me.

"Yes, Holmes. You may borrow Boy-O, but nothing better happen to him, or you."

"All right, Mr Holmes, be ready by eight. I'll let you know then if I can take you. But what are you looking for?"

"Information. Come, Watson, we must hurry down to Mrs Foster's. Good day, Captain. Until eight then, at the stables."

I wished the captain a good day and, as usual, hurried to catch up with Holmes.

"Why Mrs Foster's?" I puffed out as we hurried down the street.

"The barn behind, actually. I want to inspect it before Cacy finishes his deliveries or Major Drury comes back from the hospital."

Reaching the barn in question, Holmes called out in a loud voice for anyone there to come out, we wanted to talk to them. There was no reply, so we entered.

"Watson, stay at the door and let me know if anyone is coming."

"Right, Holmes. But what are you looking for?"

"As I told the good Captain, I seek information."

I admit that I was half watching the roadway and half watching Holmes. He held his hand over the forge, which still retained heat from its use the night before, then he started in a clockwise direction around the inside of the building. He checked the iron pots, the blacksmith tools, the empty wooden crates, the empty stalls and the spare canvas. He took out the canvas repair kit, looked at the dies and rawhide hammer and rummaged through the grommet boxes. Finally he started an inspection of the harness hanging along the north wall.

After what seemed an eternity, he came out of the barn.

"Curious."

"What is curious, Holmes?"

"There must be four sets of team harness and another three saddles and bridles in that barn, but only one bridle has polished rosettes. Why would a man only polish one set of rosettes?"

"Perhaps he only had time to polish one. Or perhaps that bridle has a special meaning." I offered.

"Of course it has a special meaning, Watson. The question is - what is that special meaning?"

"Is there something I can do for you gentlemen?"

I nearly jumped. The voice belonged to Mrs Foster. She had approached as Holmes and I were lost in thought.

"Ah, Mrs Foster. Dr Watson and I were just looking for Mr Cacy."

"He should be back any time now, Mr Holmes. Would you like to come in and wait for him?"

"No, thank you, my dear lady. I know you are quite busy with your duties. We will come back later. Come, Watson, I promised to help Major Pelham pick out a gift to send his wife for their anniversary and I don't want to disappoint the man."

Mrs Foster touched Holmes's arm. There was an anxious look in her face. "Mr Holmes, I'm afraid you are much mistaken. Major Pelham is not married."

"No, my good woman, I'm afraid he is. She lives in Sussex with their son, Timothy."

"But that can't be, sir. Why he said…" The woman was now completely distraught. With visible effort she gathered herself. "Excuse me, gentlemen. I have things I must do." Mrs Foster turned and went up toward the house.

"Holmes," I admonished once the woman was out of ear shot. "That was cruel. Is it even true?"

"Yes, Watson, it was the response to one of the telegrams I had sent."

"But why be so cruel and tell her in such a callous way?"

"I am stirring the pot, Watson. It may produce nothing, but I think it may bring us some good yet."

"I hope you are correct."

"Watson, I wish to send some additional telegrams. Would you inform Captain Burnham that I will not be going with him tonight? Good fellow. I will see you later tonight."

I did not see Holmes later that night as promised, but did receive a note from him. "We have been invited to meet with Mrs Foster at nine tomorrow morning. Holmes"

His assumption I had nothing else to do was always irritating, but I knew I would attend.

Chapter 19
THE THIRD MURDER

I awoke late that morning. I had been up until almost dawn working in the wards. It was the clanging of the milk cans that awakened me. It was fortunate they had, for Holmes was already present and sitting quietly on a box near my bunk, smoking.

"Good morning, Watson. It's time you were up and about, is it not?"

"I've just gone to bed, thank you." I turned over onto my back and sat up rubbing my eyes. I could see Doyle just coming up the stairs.

"Holmes," bellowed the big man. "I understand we use your correct name these days."

"Yes, Doctor. No need for subterfuge except to my true mission. How is the hospital?"

"This is disastrous, Holmes. About one in six soldiers is ill and I can't get Roberts to make a move. It's a disgrace." Doyle drew in a deep breath. "You can smell our problem." He exhaled. "But how goes your investigation?"

"Not well either, I'm afraid. We are making progress. I hope it will not be too late when we find an answer." Holmes looked to me as he continued. "Get your boots on, Watson; we shall get you something to eat before we make our appointment."

"I really cannot go. There is too much to be done here. You'll have to get on without me, I'm afraid."

"As you wish, Watson. I can see you are needed. I will keep you posted. Gentlemen, good day."

He was gone as I pulled my boots from under my bunk. I and two or three others were the only ones still living on the roof. Doyle had gotten a room shortly after our arrival.

"I'll be down in a minute, Doctor. Was there anything you needed?"

"No, I saw Holmes coming up and thought I'd find out how things were. See you below." Doyle left as I gathered my things.

Despite my best intentions, I was not destined to spend my morning with patients. To our great good fortune, our little hospital was bolstered that very morning by the arrival of two Catholic Nursing Sisters. These women were true angels of mercy and I can never express how much they meant to us or how hard they worked. In the coming weeks, there seemed never to be a time when I was in the hospital, that they were not there tending to the sick and wounded. But I go off on a tangent.

Hardly had I reached the ward when Major Drury accosted me. The man was shaking and tears were running down his face. He leaned heavily on the door frame of the entryway.

I rushed to the man's aide when I saw him. His legs were wobbly and I pulled over a stool and sat him upon it.

"Take a breath, man. What has happened?"

"Mr Holmes needs you, Doctor! He needs you now." Drury gripped my arm with his trembling hand.

"Drury, get a hold of yourself." I said sternly. "Then tell me what has happened."

The major took a gulp of air. "She's dead! Murdered! The bastards have blown her head off." He fell to weeping again.

"Who, Drury, who has been killed? Is it Mrs Foster?"

"Yes, Watson. We couldn't find her this morning. But when Mr Holmes arrived," he sobbed, "when Mr Holmes arrived, we found her in the garden, dead. The side of her face was gone. It was horrible." Drury dropped his head in his hands.

Leaving Drury to Moyer, I hurried on to the boarding house where I found Holmes, the Bloemfontein Constabulary and Lieutenant Barthelme.

"I know we are under Martial Law here Lieutenant, but this is a civilian and a matter for the Constabulary to deal with. Don't you agree, Mr Holmes?"

"Normally I would, Inspector. But as the lieutenant says, this murder may have other aspects. I'm afraid I must agree with him. Perhaps you should discuss this with major Pelham at headquarters."

"I assure you I will sir," replied the inspector in a heavy Boer accent. "We are not an English Colony, yet!" The inspector stormed off down the road.

"I do not believe you've made a friend there, Holmes." I chided.

"Watson, good. Come tell me what you can of this wound."

The body lay in the middle of a small garden. The woman was in a nightgown and a brown robe. No wonder she had been overlooked in the dim morning light. Kneeling down I examined her head.

"Why, she's been bludgeoned to death, Holmes. This is not a gunshot wound as Drury supposed."

"No, Watson. I believe that blacksmith's hammer behind you will prove to be the instrument of death. Can you say how long ago?"

"Well, the body is in complete rigor, so not less than eight hours."

"That would put it between midnight and one, you would say?"

"Yes, but it's never an exact science." A shadow fell across the body and I looked up. It was Drury. He seemed to have gathered himself together.

"I'm sorry I hadn't control of myself, Watson." He started. "It seemed so fiendish. And to leave her out here in the open… Who does such a thing?"

"We intend to find out, Major, but I need you to answer some questions."

Holmes had come forward, and taking Drury by the arm, led him to the barn. I asked Lieutenant Barthelme to have his men remove the body, then joined Holmes.

"When did you last see Mrs Foster?" Holmes asked the man.

"Let's see, it would be about eleven, I think. She was most distracted all evening. Something was preying on her, but she would not tell me what it was."

"Yes, I see." Holmes gave me a knowing look.

"Did anyone come to see the lady?"

"Not from eight o'clock on. We were together until I went upstairs."

"Anyone unusual about the place?"

"Not that I noticed. There was the usual working going on in the barn, but those men left about ten or so. They usually leave about then and go to one of the hotels. They're the only establishments allowed to sell drinks."

"Alright. Thank you, Major. I think it would be best if you went up to the house."

"I think I'll go to the hospital, if you don't mind. I've some things I should be taking care of." With a look to where the lieutenant's men were loading the body on a spring wagon, Drury shuffled out toward the road.

"Is there anything else you can tell me, Watson?"

"Didn't want to say it in front of Drury, but I believe she was attacked from the rear with that hammer. The blow came to the right side, in the temple area. But the heavy crushing is toward the back. She was hit from behind, Holmes."

"So, we have a right handed man whom she knew and did not fear or was surprised by."

"In the quiet of the night with the foliage and dead grass? She could not have been surprised surely."

"You are correct, of course, Watson. But one should look to all possibilities before discarding any out of hand."

"Of course. Did you find anything before I got here?"

"Nothing much. The poor lady was allowed to fall where she was attacked. The body was not moved from somewhere else."

"Any footprints?"

"Far too many, Watson. Besides her own, there were none that I could say were directly associated. And those that were there were all plain leather. Not so much as a sole with a hole in it like Mr Cacy's."

"You noticed that?"

"Oh, yes."

"So you've no clue as to who did this?"

"I have one, my friend. I have this." Holmes held up a woman's fob watch, the kind worn by nurses, nuns and housekeepers. It was the kind that pins to an apron with the watch face showing 12 at the bottom, so a woman might look down and tell the time.

"It was on Mrs Foster's robe. I took it off. Do you notice anything curious about it?"

Holmes handed me the watch. It was a good, sturdy watch. Heavy for its size and nickel plated. The fob pin had an inscription, *"Facilis est Descensus Averni."*

"The decent to hell is an easy one," I mumbled. "What an odd inscription for a watch."

"It is not so odd, really. But look at the back."

I turned the watch over. On the back was the head of Kruger, the same as on the coin we had seen. "Holmes!"

"Open it, Watson. On the inside is the second head." And it was.

"So Mrs Foster was part of the spy ring?"

"Certainly, but I believe she was only a messenger and provided a safe place for men to stay."

"So is Drury involved? I can't believe it. Why would he be? He came with us. How would that explain the gold or the spying before we got here?" I handed the watch back to Holmes.

"I really don't know, Watson. But we must make progress and soon. But come, you must get back to the hospital and I must think. I will walk with you."

We walked quietly as my mind raced. Who had killed the poor lady? She was our enemy, but loyal to her Boer roots. "Holmes, surely Pelham would not do such a thing. I mean, Mrs Foster was quite upset, but even if she confronted him he would not stoop to murder."

"Who knows what one would do when faced with the threat of destruction to one's career? So we must not rule him out - or Drury for that matter."

"Have you found out who Parker was going to meet on the road to the Modder?"

"Neither Burnham nor Fredericks nor any other of the scouts claim the honour I'm afraid."

I was about to ask whether Holmes believed Cacy and his friends were involved, but our progress was suddenly halted by a young sergeant. He had come up alongside us on the road and was quite out of breath.

"Captain Watson, sir." The young man waited for me to return his salute. "Sir, I'm Sergeant Weaver. I work for Lieutenant Barthelme now, but I know you and this gentleman here are trying to come up with the bloke what killed Lieutenant Murtry. He was a good officer, sir. Treated the men right. It weren't right what happened." He stopped to gulp some air and raced on. "I wanted to let you know what the lieutenant asked me to find out afore he was killed."

"Yes, Sergeant," said Holmes "We'd be very interested to know what you've discovered."

"Yes, sir." Weaver now addressed himself to Holmes. "It was like I told the lieutenant. Those Canadian blokes is missing two colt machine guns. They haven't reported it official like. They're trying to find them and not get laced into by the brass."

"Very interesting. Thank you, Sergeant. Should you find out any more, will you please let Dr Watson know? Your information may well help us find the lieutenant's murderer."

Sergeant Weaver was well pleased with Holmes' words and after a "You're welcome, sir" and a salute in my direction, he departed back toward the rail yard.

"My god, Holmes. We can't let those machine guns fall into the hands of the Boers. We must end this!"

"We will, old fellow, we will. The end is in sight."

"For you maybe. Where are you going?" Holmes had done an about turn and was headed back the way we had come.

"You, Watson, are going to the hospital. I am going to speak to a few people and find out where they were last night."

"Who?" I called.

"All the usual suspects!"

By now he was a hundred yards off.

CHAPTER 20
THE FOREIGN VOLUNTEERS

It was later than usual that afternoon when Cacy returned with the milk for the hospital. I had just walked outside when he arrived and called out for men to help unload.

"A horrible thing last night, doctor."

"That it was, Mr Cacy."

Cacy jumped down from the box as men pulled off the cans. Here was an opportunity for me to perhaps gain some information for Holmes.

"Did you see anything odd going on last night, Cacy?"

"Odd?"

"You know, man, unusual. Anyone there you hadn't seen before or someone perhaps arguing with Mrs Foster."

"Ah, no, I can't say as I did, Doctor. The boys and I left about ten as usual and went to Yagel's Hotel for a drink."

"Is anyone staying at the boarding house besides Major Drury?"

"Oh, yes, three or four officers. Mrs Foster's girl Molly could tell you who they are."

"What about Mrs Foster? Did she seem like she was upset or anything?"

"You've hit that right, Doctor. She was the shrew herself last night. I don't know what had happened, but she was all tears and meanness. Rest her soul." He crossed himself and looked to see if the cans were all off.

"I'm running late, doctor. Good day to you."

Cacy climbed back up in the box and called his mules to 'walk on'.

It was an hour or more later, near time to get something to eat, when Holmes finally re-appeared. He had spent the day verifying the location of everyone remotely involved in our drama. I suggested looking into the officers staying with Mrs Foster other than Drury.

"There are two lieutenants of artillery and a captain of engineers. All three were at their units late into the night. None returned before two this morning and their alibies are sound."

Holmes gave me a sly sideways glance and continued. "It seems that our friends Burnham and Fredericks were familiar with our late boarding house mistress also."

"Romantic or business?" I asked.

"Captain Burnham and his wife and child stayed with Mrs Foster in years back. He informed me of this when I told him of her death. He seemed to be truly saddened.

"Fredericks confessed he had met her numerous times when bringing hunting parties through. He also seemed to be genuinely upset by her demise."

"Holmes, this is too confusing. Everyone knows everyone. Half the people we know are involved with spying, and somewhere there is a person who does not mind solving all his problems with murder. How much worse can it get?"

"Never fear, Watson, we shall solve all. I see the clouds disappearing even now. You need a pipe and a meal, for we have a busy night before us."

"What are we to do?"

"I have left a message for your friend Mr Cacy. Unless I am very much mistaken, he will feel the need to tell some friends that Roberts will move tomorrow to re-take the water works. And when he goes, we shall follow him."

"You can't give away secret plans."

"Oh, Roberts isn't ready to move. If he were, Doyle would be dancing on your roof top. No, it is false information, but it should get the response we want."

"So Cacy is a spy." I sat on one of the benches fishing for my pipe in my pocket. "I must say I am disappointed. How long have you known?"

"Just about from the beginning," he replied, sitting with me. "Who better to move information than one who can move freely about the landscape? I suspect not only is he a loyal burgher, but a Fenian as well. Many are the Fenians who have been trained by the British army."

It was just getting dark when we arrived at the stables. I saddled Boy-O and Holmes had a Basuto pony he had borrowed. I felt ill-suited or ready for the task ahead. I neither knew the territory nor was I was much of a tracker. Hopefully Holmes was.

It was a short ride to a place down from which we could watch the barn behind the boarding house and not be seen. It was now nearly dark and I could see the lantern glow in the barn.

"Holmes, shouldn't we have someone with us? Like Burnham or Fredericks maybe? After all, this isn't like following a man through London. There won't be any cabs to catch or alleys to hide in or doorways for concealment. What was that?" I looked quickly around.

"Just a noise, Watson, just a noise. We shall do admirably, I'm sure. Ah, there they go. Quickly, Watson, to horse. We must not lose them in the darkness."

Cacy and the two other men had come out of the barn. Each led a horse and mounted once the barn door was closed. They walked their horses in the direction of Yagel's Hotel, but did not stop. We followed at a considerable distance. They slowly left the town. About a mile out they were stopped by the line of pickets. The pickets seemed well acquainted with the three horsemen and passed some banter before letting them go on their way. Of course, Cacy knew the day's password, so no suspicions were raised.

We followed once our quarry had moved on, gave the password and hurried into the darkness, trying not to lose the three men.

The moon was only at the half, but with no cloud cover the veldt was fairly lighted. We were able to keep the three men in view. As they would cross a small hill top, we would hurry to catch up, then drop to the military crest just below the skyline to search for the men. It seemed odd to me that they moved at a walk now that they had crossed the picket with valuable information such as they possessed. Why did they not rush pall mall for the Boer lines? Every hour would count if the Boers were to prepare a proper defence. I was soon to find out the reason.

They had just crossed a rather large Kopje and we hurried to catch up. As we crossed the hill top, we could see the three men in a donga not forty feet below. They had stopped their horses and sat with pistols pointed directly at us. I cursed our luck. "Holmes," I called, "run!" I started to turn Boy-O just as a man stepped from the darkness and grabbed his bridle. Another man had grabbed Holmes' horse and each held a Colt revolver.

"Now, boss. I wouldn't be trying to do nothin' dumb. You're caught and that's it." The man holding Boy-O's bridle grinned up at me. He wore a slouch hat, a waistcoat with brass buttons and canvas breeches. His face had the full beard of a Boer burgher, but the accent was definitely American.

"Off the horse now, Doctor, you too, Mr Holmes. Major MacBride will you be kind enough to bring Mr Holmes over here?"

Cacy, Seanan and Keenan had all ridden up to our little group. Cacy was shaking his head. "Doctor, it's sorry I am, but you've done this to yourself."

"Mr Cacy, how could you, a former soldier, become a traitor?"

"Sir, I'm no traitor. I'm a burgher. Sworn in at the start of the war we were. Besides, I enjoy fighting for the little guy. Be nice to him, Colonel, he's a good man." The last remark had been addressed to the man who had held Boy-O's bridle.

"Colonel Blake of the Boer Irish Brigade is it not?" asked Holmes.

"You've heard of me?"

"Yes, Colonel. Indian fighter, West Point graduate, now a soldier of fortune."

"No, Mr Holmes, there you are wrong. Just a little payback to England for what she's done to Ireland is all. Whenever we can, wherever we can." Cacy and his men chuckled at the remark.

"Tell me, Colonel, now that we are your prisoners, may I ask a few question of you and Mr Cacy?"

"I see no real harm. You'll be on your way to Pretoria before daylight as guests of the ZAR. What would you like to know?"

"Mr Cacy, is this where you came each night?"

"Yes. Mrs Foster always gave us some extra for the boys here. Food, whiskey, clothes and, as you've guessed, we brought information."

"Who was the source of the information you received?"

"Ah, now, that I don't know, sir. And wouldn't tell you if I did."

"Now is that all, Mr Holmes?" spoke up Blake. "We've much to do yet tonight."

"Just a couple more questions please." Holmes re-addressed Cacy. "I had, of course, noticed that the tracks made by your wagon were just as deep going out in the morning as coming back at night, which meant you were smuggling something. In addition, you actually had two wagons. One with Sarvin wheels, one with Archibald wheels. You switched them each day. Of course the wagon canvas with the painted harp was to keep everyone from looking too closely. What were you smuggling? "

"You are good Mr, Holmes. No use saying you're not. Yes, people see what they expect to see. The two wagons were similar, not identical, but with the harp painted on the canvas, well people just say, 'oh, that's Cacy coming' and don't look twice. It worked real well, it did."

"And the cargo?"

"False bottom, ya see. The McMullen boys here stole ammunition at the yard and put it in boxes of canned goods. The canned goods go in the ammunition boxes and get nailed back up. Some of these Tommy Atkins is going to be real surprised one day when they need some cartridges."

"The boys load the false bottom of the wagon at night. I take it out to that third farm we went to, doctor, and swap wagons so the boys can unload. And we do that every day."

"One last question," continued Holmes. "What about the stolen gold?"

"Mr Holmes, I swear I don't know anything about any stolen gold."

Colonel Blake held up his pistol hand.

"This is enough, Mr Holmes. It's time we were leaving. Keenan, bring up Fenian Boy and DG for the major and me."

Keenan was about to turn his horse in response to the Colonel's request when a voice sounded from behind me.

"Gentlemen, if you would be good enough to place your weapons on the ground." Churchill stepped out of the darkness with two men of the Mounted Yeomanry. In each hand he held a Mauser pistol with a 10 shot box magazine. The Yeoman had their Carbines pointed at the mounted men.

"Well, well. Mr Churchill isn't it? I've seen you in the papers I have." Cacy, Keenan and Seanan all still held their pistols in their right hands.

Complete silence reigned for a moment. Blake and MacBride had continued to hold their Colt single actions on myself and Holmes.

"It seems to me, boys, that what we have here is what we call in the States a 'Mexican standoff'! You can't shoot us 'cause we'll kill your boys here and you'll have a hell of a time explaining it. You may get us, but we'll get you. So how do you think we should work this?" Blake had pretty well summed it all up.

"I say," MacBride said breaking his silence, "that we all back off. Mr Cacy, you and the boys go on. Mr Churchill won't shoot. Will you Mr Churchill? That's a good lad."

Cacy and the boys backed their horses into the darkness until all we could see was a faint outline. "We're covering them, Major," called Cacy. "Come on."

Blake swept off his hat in an elaborate bow. Then he and MacBride backed into the donga where their horses were hidden. No sooner had they dropped from sight that Churchill started firing wildly pouring twenty rounds into the darkness. As the firing ended, I could hear Cacy's laugh. "I'm afraid you'll have to get another man to deliver the milk, Doctor. I'll leave word your to get it. Goodnight, Doctor." I heard their horses trot off.

"After them," cried Churchill to his men.

"No!" the order came from Holmes. "Who knows how many others there are out there? It is best we retire for now. But first I want to thank you, Lieutenant. Your help was indispensable as you saw."

The two men shook hands.

"I'm glad you let me in on it, Mr Holmes, though a couple of times I thought we'd lost you."

"You mean that Lieutenant Churchill was following us all the time?" I asked.

"Of course, Watson. That was the noise you heard earlier in town. I thought it advisable to have some extra protection, shall we say."

"Really, Holmes." I was quite agitated. "Someday you must learn to trust me." I mounted Boy-O in a huff and headed in the direction I believed I would find Bloemfontein.

CHAPTER 21
HOLMES PONDERS

Churchill and his men had reclaimed their horses in a moment and caught up with us.

"Sherlock Homes uncovers Boer Spy Ring," Churchill waved his arm across the sky. "'Report by special correspondent who aids great detective.' Yes, I can see the banner headline. If you gentlemen will excuse me, I must get to the telegraph office. I've a story to send."

Churchill put spurs to his horse. In a moment he and his two men were gone into the night.

"Alright, Holmes, we now know that Mrs Foster supplied information to Cacy, but where did she get the information? She has no real contact with headquarters or any of the men assigned there. And who killed her? Was it related or a lover's quarrel?"

"Watson, we have all but a few of the answers. Let us reason this out."

"Certainly, what do we know?"

"To start, we know that Cacy was moving information and ammunition to the burghers. For another, we know that Lieutenant Murtry was killed in Major Parker's room. Why? He knew something he hadn't told us, but his enemy was aware of the discovery. Probably that Cacy had two wagons.

"Why was he in the room? To meet someone at the window or use the window as a method of egress.

"Who was free to move at night and meet him? Who also had access?"

"So you think Cacy....?"

"No, Cacy was out here on the veldt reporting. He most likely never even knew of the discovery."

"And Major Parker's murder?"

"Oh, the same reason, Watson. He discovered something or it was feared he was about to discover something. He trusted that knowledge to someone who he should not have. I believe he was following someone when he was killed. Someone who knew he was following."

"Alright, but why kill Mrs Foster? She was only a courier."

"Her death, as you said, could be related to the spy ring or personal, or both."

"And where did she get her information from?"

"I suspect that, of late, she had gotten all the information she needed from your friend Major Drury."

"Drury!" I exclaimed. "Never! He may be a lot of things Holmes, but I can't believe he's a traitor. He would never do such a thing."

"Oh, it is not intentional, Watson. It is an old story, though. Man wants to impress woman, woman feeds his ego and his whiskey glass. Man responds with a puffed up chest and tells her things he shouldn't to show how important he is - as I say, an old story."

"But where would Drury get any information? He's merely a liaison for a civilian hospital."

"Where does he spend his days, Watson?"

"At the headquarters." The wind now left my sail.

"And would anyone doubt his loyalty? Or, like you, would they take him to be the honest soldier he really is? They would have no reason to doubt him. His failing is not disloyalty, but drink and women."

We rode on in silence. It was just as we were coming to the pickets that I heard Holmes mutter, "Not the best of them, not the best of them" and shake his head. I know he was thinking about *'the woman'*, the one who had bested him, Irene Adler.

We gave the counter-sign and passed through the pickets before Holmes spoke again.

"I want to go back to the barn at Mrs Foster's, Watson. We haven't learned all of it's secrets yet."

"Secrets? What are you talking about? It's a barn."

"Oh no, Watson. Did you not ever wonder about the forge being used so constantly?"

"Well, yes but…"

"I believe I've just time for one pipe if we take our horses to the stables first. It is time to think, Watson."

In other words, he was saying, 'Watson, it is time to be quiet'. We rode on in silence.

Chapter 22
SECRET GOLD

By the time we had stabled the horses and walked back to Mrs Foster's barn, it was well past midnight. We opened the doors wide to let in what light there was. I was able to find a number of lanterns and lighted three or four.

"What are you looking for, Holmes? We have already been through here."

"I have missed something, Watson. I know I have. The keys are here, I must only find the lock." Holmes seemed to wander aimlessly around the interior of the barn. But I knew his movements were not aimless. There was great purpose. I seated myself on a keg and watched. Had I known what he was looking for, I would have helped.

Holmes went to the forge, now cold, and picked up various tools: hoof trimmers, pritchels, and tongs. He ran his hand around the inside of one of the iron pots and stared at his hand when he took it out. He put down the pot and started a tour around the exterior walls looking at boxes and bags and sheets of steel. Some sheets had holes, some not.

When Holmes came to the pile of canvas he reached into a wooden box and removed a set of grommet dies.

"Watson, do you notice something odd about these dies?"

I rose and went to his side, taking the dies from his hand.

"They seem to have been used quite a bit recently, Holmes. The surfaces are shiny, especially the head where you hit it with the hammer."

"Should there not be a stud on the upper half that centres the grommet while it is hammered firm on the canvas?"

I turned over the top die.

"Yes, Holmes. This die would be useless."

"No, not useless Watson. Hand me the bridle with the polished rosettes."

I went to the other side of the barn and returned with the requested item. Holmes immediately began to take the bridle apart. Removing the rosettes, he went over them carefully. Finally, placing one in his left hand, with his right he used the staple on the back and unscrewed the brass cover. Holmes smiled and lifted his right hand to show me that the brass decoration, when removed, revealed a steel stamp. The face of which showed the face of Paul Kruger. It was the size of a half-pond piece.

"Holmes, they were making money!"

"Yes, Watson, that is why you heard the ring of steel, but saw few shoed horses and no new wagon parts here." He pointed to the forge. "They would melt the gold in those pots, pour the molten gold into those iron sheets to rough the coins and then, while still hot, place the flans in the grommet dies, and using the stamps from these rosettes, make coin of the realm. The ringing you heard was a steel hammer hitting a steel die to impress the coin."

He smiled, almost to himself, and placed the rosettes in his pocket.

"Then Cacy lied about the gold."

"No, I don't think so. You asked him, Watson, about stolen gold. He did not consider it stolen."

"I guess there is that," I laughed. "And I suppose they carried the coins out in the wagon also. But why not leave it as bars?"

"Elementary! Coins are much, much easier to hide and distribute. Gold coins to be used for goods, services, and ammunition."

"So that is the end of it."

"No, Watson. They did not expect us tonight. We were poor at following our quarry. We should have done better. I don't believe Cacy saw us, but they were meeting Blake and either he or MacBride saw us and set the ambush. That means there should be more here. Had you noticed that the horseshoe kegs show no dust? Help me move them Watson."

In a moment, we had moved half a dozen quarter kegs of shoes and below was a trap door to what may have at one time been a root cellar. Each of us took a lantern. While I stayed above, Holmes descended a small ladder into the damp earth.

"Watson, I have something that may interest you," came Holmes' muffled voice. "Wait there." In an instant the barrel of a Colt machine gun appeared above the trap door. I grabbed it and placed the weapon on the forge. Holmes followed, coming up from the hole.

"Is the second one down there, Holmes?"

"No, Watson. I'm afraid that it is not. It, I fear, has already been delivered to our Boer friends. But there is something else."

"And that is?"

Holmes held out a gold bar. "I believe there to be about 5,000 ounces of gold down there. Surely something our friends won't want to leave. How maddening it must be for them. You recognize the weapon, of course."

I patted the side of the machine gun. "Yes Holmes, a Model 1895 Colt." It was then that Murtry's remark came back to me.

"Holmes, the potato digger!"

"Watson?"

“It was what Lieutenant Murtry was telling us. He said the plot involved two kinds of potato diggers.”

For once Holmes looked at me blankly. It was a proud moment. I would be the fountain of knowledge.

“This Colt machine gun is called a ‘potato digger’. It has an armature that comes out of the bottom of the receiver when it fires. If it is set too close to the ground, it digs furrows, hence the name.” I took a breath. “The other type of potato digger was…”

“Yes, yes - Cacy and his men. A slur for an Irishmen. Well, you have cleared that up let us put the gun back and we shall be on our way.”

“Put it back?”

“Of course. Otherwise they shall know we’ve found their secret hiding place. We do want them to come back. This game is not yet finished.”

“No, Holmes, we can’t take a chance on them getting away with this weapon.”

“Watson, if you do not return the machine gun, it is probable that the real leak of information at the headquarters will find out. Once they know we have found the gold, they may decide to disappear. You must return it.”

“Wait a moment. I thought you said Drury supplied the information to Mrs Foster.”

“Of late, yes. But who supplied it to him? Who knew him well enough to know he would tell all to impress the woman?”

“I don’t know.” I was crestfallen.

“That, Watson, is what we’ve yet to find out. Now be good enough to give me the gun.”

“In a moment.”

It was much more than a moment before I gave the machine gun back to Holmes. He agreed to sit quietly while I struggled and strained and after many an error, finally determined how to remove the mechanism’s firing pin. Then, with the light of false dawn, Holmes and I blew out the lanterns, replaced the kegs and departed.

CHAPTER 23
ONE LESS TRAITER

I did what I could at the hospital for the next few hours. By noon the lack of sleep had caught up with me and I went to a small copse of trees on the far side of the field. Here I rested and quickly fell asleep.

It was Moyer who found me what seemed like only moments later, but was actually three hours.

"I hated to wake you, Doctor, but Dr Doyle said to tell you that you and he are requested at the headquarters."

I rubbed my eyes and looked about. "What time is it?"

"Just four. Doyle says he'll wait for you at the pavilion."

I gathered myself together and walked with Moyer back to the hospital. Doyle was standing on the pavilion steps waiting.

"It seems we have been summoned to the headquarters where Holmes will 'reveal all', as they say in the detective novels."

"Yes, well, he'll have to wait a moment while I wash and get a clean shirt."

Grabbing one of the few dozen natives we employed, I pulled off my boots and gave the man instructions to give them a quick brush. In all, it was a delay of no more that fifteen minutes, but all the while Doyle was chewing his bit and anxious to go. One thing the army would never be able to teach the big man would be patience.

Having washed, put on a new shirt and pulled my boots back on, I re-joined Doyle and we walked toward the headquarters. I felt like I was being pulled along by a giant puppy on a leash, anxious to see the world.

We stopped at Barthelme's office and were taken on into Lord Roberts.

Roberts was sitting behind a large mahogany desk, looking rather sour of disposition. Disposed in chairs about the room were Churchill, Pelham, Burnham, Fredericks and Drury. Holmes stood by the French doors looking out into the tiny garden behind the hotel.

As we entered, Holmes greeted us. "Watson, Doyle, good. I thought it best we all be here."

"Can we begin now, man?" half-roared Roberts.

"Will Lord Kitchener not be joining us?" replied Holmes.

"No, now get to this; I've no time to dilly-dally."

Lieutenant Barthelme had entered with us, followed by an orderly carrying tea.

"Lord Kitchener is inspecting the Scots Brigade, Mr Holmes. He is not available." He turned to Roberts. "The tea, sir."

"Have him leave it on the table and get out. Not you Lieutenant, the corporal."

The corporal departed post haste and Barthelme tried to absorb himself into the wall by the door.

"Allow me, sir." Holmes poured tea and started handing it around, Lord Roberts first. Holmes was having too much fun. It showed on his face.

"I'll not say it again, begin, Mr Holmes. My time is precious." Roberts pushed his full tea cup away.

"Certainly, sir. Let me begin at the beginning, if I may. Of course you know all those present. Each has shared in our little investigation in some manner, so I felt they would want to be present. Some have had no part except to give aide. However, let me start at the beginning."

Holmes started by laying out the entire case at it had transpired. He spoke of his entire assignment from Mycroft, his stopping of the plot to damage the ports in Cape Town and his belief that both the gold and the information were reaching the Boers from this headquarters. Roberts snorted derision.

Holmes went on to explain our discovery of the system Cacy had used to move ammunition, gold and information provided by Mrs Foster to his compatriots in Blake's Irish Brigade. He finished by describing our search of the barn and his discovery of the dies and gold residue in the iron pots.

"And here, sir, are the dies that were being used." Holmes placed the two bridle rosettes on Roberts' desk. The general took up the two items presented and examined them. Then, placing them at the edge of the desk, he asked Holmes if he had found the gold also.

"Not yet, sir, it may have all been coined and moved. I do not yet know."

It was all I could do to sit still. Holmes must have his reason to lie to Roberts. I hoped all would turn out well. But that was only to be the first shock. I decided I could use some of that tea, but decided not to move.

"I understand, Mr Holmes." Roberts looked about the room a moment.

"Barthelme."

"Yes, sir.

"Go tell Mr Hatchett I want every ammunition box opened and checked."

"Yes sir."

Barthelme opened the door to go. As he went through, Roberts yelled after him.

"And don't tell him he's looking for canned vegetables!"

"No, sir."

"Now, Mr Holmes, let's get to the serious work. Who supplied Mrs Foster with the information she gave to this Cacy fellow?"

"Well, sir, it happened in two parts." Holmes walked about the room, moving from chair to chair, then back toward the French doors. He turned back to face the whole room. God he enjoyed being at the centre of the stage!

"The first part is rather sad, in a way. For Mrs Foster was a loyal Boer. She had lived almost her entire life in the Free State. She was widowed here and her children are buried here. So it was an easy task when our spy came to her and asked for her help.

"At first she was a bit hesitant. She was now surrounded by her enemy and she must learn to adapt. But her new friend quickly played on the woman's loneliness and became her lover. He had moved into the boarding house. So it was simple to bring information to her and let her pass it on to Cacy. It gave our man a degree of separation from the next level. Cacy only knew that Mrs Foster gave him information, not from whom it came."

Holmes paused as people started to look at Drury. After all, he lived there. Everyone knew he was sweet on the woman.

"I didn't!" Protested Drury in a state of anxiety.

Holmes went on. "We shall get to Major Drury in a moment." Holmes started walking about again as the door opened and Barthelme re-entered.

"No, in the first instance, our spy pre-dated Major Drury. I refer to Major Pelham."

"You're mad!" spit Pelham leaping from his chair. "Why would I pass information? What cause could I have? I've been loyal for twenty five-years. This is crazy."

"Oh, protest if you must, Major, but you promised the good woman marriage to make sure she co-operated. When I told Mrs Foster you were already married it all became clear. She was upset more than any casual acquaintance would be.

"You moved out of the boarding house when Major Drury arrived. You thought 'here is a man I can use'. He is sweet on Mrs Foster and he likes to bray. If I tell something to him, he will tell her when he drinks and I can separate myself even more'. In fact, you hoped that she would turn her affection to him and you could stop playing the lover."

"This is madness! Lord Roberts, surely you don't believe any of this," cried Pelham.

"Of course not. Holmes, this man has been with me for years, why since the Second Afghan War. You've no proof," stated Roberts.

Holmes stood nose to nose with Pelham. "Let me see your watch fob, Major."

Pelham didn't move. We were all now standing. Holmes reached forward and pulled the fob from Pelham's watch chain and without looking said, "Two headed coin of Ohm Paul," and threw it on the table.

Pelham stepped around Holmes. As he did so his pistol came out. Before anyone could react he had it pointed at Lord Roberts who had been the only one to remain seated.

"You, bastard! For twenty years I worked for you. Never a reward! Never a decent assignment! Who picked you up when you were injured at Kandahar? Who made sure you ate and drank and had paper to send out your snivelling little orders? I did! And now you wanted me to help kill my own people? I'll see you in hell!"

Pelham pushed the muzzle of the Webley into his own mouth and pulled the trigger. The room was soaked in blood and brains. Doyle ran to the body. I'd seen enough violent death; I felt no need to attend.

A moment later guards were flooding the room and Roberts was yelling at Barthelme. "Get it out of here! Now, Lieutenant."

Barthelme had the men carry the body out while two orderlies tried to soak up the blood with towels and wipe off the furniture. Roberts had re-seated himself after having jumped up at the gunshot. He pointed at Drury.

"I shall deal with you, sir. It's prison for you."

Drury was beside himself and protesting as best he could when Holmes intervened.

"Lord Roberts, you do not understand. While Major Drury was indeed passing information to Mrs Foster," -- Drury collapsed in a chair, head in hands, --"he was passing false information provided by me. He cooperated with me fully in rooting out this nest of spies."

I have never seen anyone more surprised than Drury was at that moment.

"The good, Major," continued Holmes, "agreed to my plan early on and has been of great benefit. This was the second part I spoke of." Holmes extended his hand to Drury. The major took it without rising and shook it limply. Drury was in as much shock as I was. "And now, Lord Roberts, I should like to stay a bit with my friend Dr Watson and shall trouble you no more. I will, of course, with your consent continue to look for the Boer gold, though I fear it may well be gone."

"Of course Mr Holmes. I have a good deal to thank you for." Roberts seemed a bit shaken. But his handshake was firm as, for some reason, he shook hands with all of us as we left the room.

"Well, so much for the spy ring Mr Holmes," grinned Churchill. "Well done, this will be quite a coup for me."

"What would that be?" asked Holmes.

"Why, a spy in the very centre of Lord Roberts' staff. 'Villain Takes Own Life'." He waved his arm in the air again.

"Why, whatever are you talking about, sir? Major Pelham died of enteric fever in Langman's Hospital. Isn't that so, Watson? Doyle?"

"Mr Holmes," laughed Churchill. "You can't hide this, it's too big. Everyone knows what happened."

"And what good does your story do, Lieutenant? Who does it help? Does it make anything better? Does it help at home or improve morale here?"

"But Holmes, you are a hero!"

"We are just doing what we can, Lieutenant. And there is more to do. We must find the 'Black Panther'."

"But I thought…"

"Oh no, Pelham was not the brains. He may have been a knight or bishop, but we must find the king. Good evening, Lieutenant."

Holmes, Doyle and I started our walk back to the cricket field.

"I don't know if you've stopped that story, Holmes," commented Doyle.

"Oh, I believe that if the story is written it might not be sent."

When we arrived at the pavilion, I stayed outside to talk to Holmes.

"What you did for Drury was a fine thing Holmes. He's not much, but he didn't mean harm."

"I know, Watson. This war has enough casualties. It does not need more."

I started laughing out loud. "The look on Drury's face when you bailed him out was priceless. I believe you have a friend for life."

"Perhaps, Watson. But sometimes doing a good deed breeds resentment. We shall see. And now I think it is time for a pipe."

Chapter 24
MEDICAL INSPECTION

On the morning of the 20th of April Holmes sent word to me that he was to have a private interview with Roberts in the morning. Come the afternoon, he would have need of me. To our good fortune, the hospital had received our additional volunteer. Dr Schwartz had arrived by the early up train and was hardly introduced when put to work.

Doyle was in a gleeful mood this morning, for word had come to us to assist in giving the mandatory medical inspection for the soldiers who would move against the water works. It would be good to see an end to the constant procession of dead. It seemed the dead march sounded constantly as soldiers moved down the roads with arms reversed.

Reveille had sounded at 5:30 as usual and by 6:15 five companies of yeomanry were in parade order in front of the tents outside the pavilion. I will admit it is a somewhat cursory inspection, but it is quite easy to identify those men who will have trouble on the march.

We had them remove boots and stockings and inspected each man's feet, hands, lungs, and ears and had a look in their eyes. This quick look would allow us to remove those that will fall out of the march early due to a defect. An army going to meet the enemy cannot afford the extra burden of men who are unfit, no matter how much those men want to help their mates.

By 9:15 the men were being marched off to the musketry range. There would be one more firing of all the weapons to check their serviceability. Once firing had been completed, each man would clean his weapon and then himself. It had always struck me as foolish to make the men use their mess tins to wash in, and then eat their meals from the same tin. But to have them carry even more equipment seemed just as bad.

Once the men had marched off to the musketry range, I returned to the pavilion and our rounds of the sick. Doyle decided to accompany the yeomen to the range. He was always appalled at the poor marksmanship of our men, especially when compared to the Boer foe. Once back in England, both he and his friend, Kipling, would be driving forces in establishing shooting clubs throughout Great Britain. There would be over 1,000 clubs just before the Great War. It was a service neither he nor Kipling was ever properly thanked for. But that is a different story.

It was noon before I was able to take a break and sit with my pipe trying to collect my thoughts. Somewhere I must find another source of milk. I wondered if, without Cacy, the farmers would still sell to us. But Cacy had said that he would make it happen and for some reason I believed he would. It was then that I saw Drury for the first time that day.

"Captain, do you know where Mr Holmes might be? I would like to thank him. He saved my career yesterday. I have much to be grateful to him for."

For once Drury, appearing quiet and somewhat contrite, was sober and exuded no odour of alcohol. The shock of his actions and their possible consequences had evidently come home to him. It was one good thing that had happened so far.

"He was at the headquarters this morning, Major. I'm not really sure where he is now."

Drury sat on the bench next to me, his uniform clean and his boots shined in the sun. This man, I knew, would have to find additional work. Idleness would put him back where he had been, feeling his life and work had little purpose.

"Major, as you know, we have lost our man who was able to get us milk for the hospital. The milk makes a wondrous difference in the men and their recovery."

"Say no more, Watson, it shall be done. Do you know what farms were supplying the milk?"

"Well, yes. I've been there. I might draw a map for whoever goes."

"Good. You draw a map and I'll get a couple of men. I know that Mr Cacy's mules and wagon are still at the boarding house. If no one else has commandeered them for their own purposes, they will suit ours quite nicely. I'll be back."

Drury sprang from his seat. I could hear him calling names as he entered the pavilion. It was exactly what the man needed.

I had expected to see Holmes by now, but he was not to re-appear until much later in the day. In fact it, was while Doyle and I were taking some tea on the roof top that early evening when Holmes finally appeared.

"Welcome to the 'Café Enterique'," called Doyle as Holmes appeared on the stairs. "Would you care for some tea with your microbes?"

One had to forgive Doyle his odd sense of humour. Fatigue had set in. The long hours, the constant deaths, the dust and poor diet all made one a bit balmy.

"Most pleasant, Doctor. I could use some refreshment." Holmes seated himself on one of the boxes and accepted a tin cup from Doyle.

"How goes the search, Mr Holmes? Have you found your man?"

"I have devised a plan and I shall have it carried out tonight."

"What is our part?" Doyle said in a stage whisper leaning forward on his box.

"We - that is - the three of us, have no part in the plan except to wait."

"No!" cried Doyle. "We are not to be in on the kill?"

"What is your plan, Holmes?" I wanted to know as well and would also be disappointed not to be part of the final moment.

Holmes looked seriously at Doyle. "If I inform you, doctor, you must keep absolutely silent about all I say. Is that understood?"

"Yes, yes, of course."

"Well, I see no harm. Lord Roberts has agreed to it and given me a company of men." Holmes extended his cup and waited for Doyle to re-fill it.

"It is to be this way. Both Burnham and Fredericks have been given a mission tonight. Each has been briefed on an attack plan for the water works. But each has received a different plan. Neither is correct."

"Burnham and Fredericks?" interjected Doyle. "What have they to do with anything?"

"Who, Doctor, moves about constantly, is never noticed except in passing, and yet must be trusted with all the army's plans in order to properly do his job? Who did Pelham, Parker and Murtry have constant contact with? Who goes out into the night, unwatched, and unseen, to possibly not only spy on the Boers but contact them?"

"Well, then why weren't they doing that all along instead of using Cacy and his men?"

"For the simple reason that they weren't here. They are both fairly new arrivals."

"True." Doyle sat back and was pondering the fact.

"But surely not Burnham," I said. "He's loyal, a veteran of the Matabele Wars and all."

"He is also an American," responded Holmes. "Fighting natives might be one thing. Fighting what he may see as an independent nation like his own may be quite another."

"And Fredericks?"

"He is a Cape Boer. His family is now in the Free State somewhere. And you remember he was in Cape Town about the time I was dealing with Conway."

"You think he's Duquesne?"

"Either he or Burnham. How do we know Burnham was in Alaska? Right now we have only his word."

"Not a very trusting man, are you, Holmes?" Doyle was grinning from ear to ear. "So what is the rest of your plan?"

"As to that, each man goes on his scout tonight. Our friend, Churchill, has been detailed to take a couple of men and follow Burnham. I believe the easiest way to control our reporter is to keep him involved. He can put all this in his memoires when he's Prime Minister."

I laughed out loud at this.

"Oh, he will be, Watson, he will be. As to Fredericks, I've been given a Captain Saxon of Colonial Light Horse to follow him. Each man has the same instructions: follow, watch, report. We shall know if either man makes contact with the Boers to pass on the plan they have been given."

Holmes stayed a bit more and we finished our tea. Doyle and I finally gathered ourselves together to return below. I felt like I was descending into the bowels of hell. I think that when I die I shall stand before St Peter and behind him will be two gates - one marked Heaven, and the other, above the arch of the gate, will be the word "Bloemfontein".

Chapter 25
SCOUTING

It proved that the night's watch by Churchill and Saxon was futile. Neither Burnham nor Fredericks had made contact with anyone. Having completed their assigned tasks, both returned without incident to the headquarters. Holmes appeared upset that morning, but not completely disheartened. He had arrived as the men whom Major Drury had assembled for wagon duty were loading empty cans on what had been Cacy's wagon. It was the one with Sarvin wheels. I assumed his other was somewhere on the veldt. Drury had my map. Deciding it was safer to move in force, he had a half dozen extra mounted men with the wagon.

Today the soldiers who were destined to take Pretoria would be moving to staging areas for tomorrow's start toward the water works twenty miles distant. I watched as men of the Scots Brigade started loading kits, blankets and great coats into wagons. For now it looked like it was to be light marching order.

Light marching order meant that they might move more quickly, but they would also have no extra creature comfort. Sergeants were going down the lines checking each man. One blanket, 150 rounds of ammunition, water bottle (full of course), one day's ration in the haversack and a clean rifle. Off they marched to the East, pipes playing. I prayed they would all come out unharmed.

"What now, Holmes?" I asked as we watched the Gordons disappear down the dirt road.

"We continue the same plan as last night. Burnham and Fredericks will both be given scouts and Churchill and Saxon will follow."

"You're running out of time Holmes. Can't you just have Roberts arrest both men and hold them for now?"

"On what charge, Watson? I am convinced one of these two men is Duquesne. The problem is which? If we take out Duquesne we not only eliminate our current problem, but hopefully a future one.

"And what of the innocent man? Are we to destroy him for no other reason than to stop the first? Surely, the mere act of his arrest or detention would forever be remembered against him. No, Watson, we must be able to stop Duquesne without injury to others."

I handed Holmes a note I had received by messenger that morning.

"I'm thinking of doing this Holmes. After this I may be too old for active service."

Holmes read the letter which offered me a position on General Ian Hamilton's staff for the push to Pretoria.

"Well then, we must hurry and end our little puzzle so that you may join the advance. What does Doyle say of this?"

"Oh, he only wished it was he who had been offered the position."

"I understand that Rundle has already made contact with the enemy. There appears to be quite a bit of long range sniping, but Barthelme tells me they don't believe there are but about 3,000 Boers in the way."

"Only takes one to kill you," I said, taking out my pipe.

"Yes, remember, that old boy, I'd hate to lose you. When will you join Hamilton?"

"I've told them I'd be there on the 23rd. The day after tomorrow."

"Oh, we shall have finished by then, Watson."

I spent a few minutes that afternoon making sure my own kit was in order and arranging for a few boxes of medical supplies and equipment to be packed for me to take on the march. Most of the day was spent back in the pavilion and the tents full of sick men. I saw no more of Holmes that day, but he re-appeared just after midnight. I was unable to sleep and welcomed Holmes' company when he came to see me.

"I've asked Churchill and Saxon to report to me here if you do not mind, Watson. I knew you would want to be in on things at the last."

"I appreciate the company Holmes. Have a seat. Sorry I've no brandy to entertain with. You'll have to settle for a pipe."

"Exactly what I should like, my friend."

Holmes and I sat in silence for the better part of an hour before we were interrupted by the sound of horses below. This was followed by the sound of foot-falls on the steps. Holmes continued to sit and smoke while I rose to see who our visitors might be.

Churchill and Saxon followed each other onto the roof.

"Good evening, Doctor, Mr Holmes." It was Churchill who spoke first. "I'm afraid we both have bad news for you Mr Holmes." He threw himself down on a box.

"Neither man made contact with anyone that we could see." He looked to Saxon, who shook his head in confirmation. "You may be on a completely wrong trail here, sir."

"There was nothing either man did?" Drop something perhaps, or mark a rock or tree?"

Both men shook their heads again, but then Saxon looked thoughtful for a moment.

"What is it, Saxon?" pressed Holmes. "The smallest thing may be of the greatest importance."

"Well, sir - It probably means nothing at all, but, well, both tonight and last night Fredericks got down and checked his horse's right front hoof. Like he was checking for a stone or maybe he felt the animal was going lame. I never saw the horse limp, but sometimes you can feel it, you know, that the animal is stepping just a little lightly on one foot."

Holmes stood up and went over to where Saxon stood.

"Now think carefully, man. Where did he do this? Was it at the same place each time?"

"Now that you mention it, Mr Holmes, it was. I remember thinking it odd at the time that the animal should go lame at the same spot."

Holmes clapped the Captain on the back. "Excellent, my good man, excellent. We shall have him."

"Then Fredericks is our spy!" I exclaimed.

"Perhaps, Watson."

"But you just said..."

"Watson, Watson. Can you charge a man with spying or treason for checking a hoof?"

"But you believe it is he, don't you, Mr Holmes?" said Churchill.

"Yes, I believe he spotted Captain Saxon here and used that method to warn off his contact. Tomorrow he shall not be followed."

"Captain, can you find that same spot in the daylight?"

"Yes, sir, I'm sure of it. That will not be a problem."

"Good. I will need you and about twenty men. Oh, yes you may come along also, Mr Churchill. Meet me here at about seven tomorrow night." He looked at his watch, it was now past 2 am "Or maybe I should say tonight. And now Watson, I will leave you. I have much to coordinate. Goodnight."

Saxon and Churchill said their good nights also. I was left to finish my pipe and get what sleep I could.

Chapter 26
THE AMBUSH

It was only two hours later that I heard, at 4 a.m., reveille sounding throughout the town. I was anxious to go but would wait this one more day for Holmes.

I rolled back over on my cot, but sleep was not to come. The noise from below kept me from sleep. Most of the army was already eight or ten miles to the north or east of Bloemfontein in their assembly areas. Those moving now were support elements and their escorts.

I finally decided to get up and light a pipe. Below, lines of wagons stretched as far as the eye could see in both directions. Wagons pulled by ten span of oxen and guided by natives with huge whips, mule wagons, and horse drawn wagons, wagons filled with the supplies of war.

Their escorts of marching men and mounted infantry walked or rode to each side and opened their distance to the flanks for protection as the line of supply disgorged itself from the town, giving the appearance of a huge inverted funnel.

There was the creaking harness, the rumble of wheels, the sound of drivers yelling at their teams. If I closed my eyes I was back in Afghanistan. How little things had changed.

Having finished my pipe, I went below to start my rounds in the pavilion. I had a biscuit and some tea at some point in the morning, but it was Holmes' arrival at about noon that finally caused me to take a break.

We went to our mess area and, taking a cup of tea went out under one of the trees which covered some benches.

"Holmes, I've been meaning to ask, has anything happened at Mrs Foster's barn? Anyone come to get the gold?"

"No, Watson, though I've had the barn watched constantly. It is a little hard to accept that they would make no attempt to recover such a sum."

"They'll have to reclaim the gold soon or give it up for lost. If what Rundle reports is correct, they will be pushed beyond reach of it in short order."

"Or, perhaps, they are content to leave it there and decide what to do about it when their cause is lost."

"You mean, keep it for themselves?"

"Let us say, as an insurance policy. If Fredericks is in fact Duquesne as we believe, he may decide he needs a certain amount of treasure to escape. No, Watson, I do not believe that we are watching that cache in vain. If nothing happens by the time we leave here tonight, Barthelme has orders to remove the gold and return the machine gun to the Canadians." Holmes finished his tea. "It was not a sure thing anyway."

Our conversation was now interrupted by a detachment from General Hamilton's staff. They had been ordered to collect my kit and I took leave of Holmes, who promised to return by seven. I spent the afternoon working with Dr Schwartz and thanking the many members of Langman's Hospital with whom I had become so familiar. It was especially hard to part with Moyer, Gibbs and Scharlieb. There would be time later that night to say adieu to Langman and Doyle, who had made the decision to accompany the troops on the assault of the water works. Doyle desperately wanted in on the fighting. Langman, however, was more curious than wanting to fight. Both, I knew, would find Pole-Carew's staff to see the fight. They would be off before sundown to catch up.

By five o'clock I was over at the stable where I found Boy-O almost alone. There were but half a dozen horses left in this one area, all of which belonged to members of Lord Robert's staff.

Having groomed and saddled my fine bay, I walked him back to the hospital and checked my equipment one more time. I was one who believed that British cavalry and mounted troops were overloaded with equipment. But my thoughts, though I'm sure shared by others, I kept to myself. Since I was to be on staff, I could do certain things which a soldier could not. I had stripped down all my equipment to the barest few things. I carried my Webley-Pryse pistol and left the sabre. My saddle bags carried but ammunition, a metal mirror for signalling, a day's rations, and spare horseshoes. My great coat was packed on the saddle along with oats for Boy-O. Besides my revolver I wore my double brace Sam Browne belt, water bottle and haversack. I had discarded my helmet for a slouch hat which I turned up on the left side. I had taken special care to double blanket Boy-O. I had learned to do that on campaign in Afghanistan. It was easier on the animal and I was always able to swap the blankets, keeping a dry one near his back. It helped to prevent galling. My haversack was filled with medical supplies. On the saddle's near side, where normally hung the sabre, was a second haversack with additional bandages and medications. The pommel bags held only cigars, matches, and a pint of brandy. A small set of binoculars hung from my neck.

It was now near seven and I had not long to wait until Holmes came up on his Basuto pony. We had but said hello when the rest of our party gathered. There was still a good hour and an half of daylight to be had, but Holmes wasted no time. As soon as Captain Saxon arrived with his twenty men, we started toward the Veldt. Saxon and Holmes were in the lead. Behind them came myself and Churchill, followed by Saxon's men. We moved in silence as we passed first supply, then infantry and cavalry units bivouacked for the night. From ahead came the roar of artillery. Pole-Carew was trying to weaken the Boer defences before tomorrow's battle. After a fast-paced ninety minutes, we passed some of the artillery on our left. Twilight was upon us. The flashes of the muzzles lit the sky and gave the gunners an unreal appearance as they moved calmly about their duties, their blue leather gaiters reflecting the muzzle flash of the cannons.

Now we were ahead of the guns and moved down into a donga which ran to the northwest and below the trajectory of the artillery firing over our heads. We finally stopped near a saddle between two Kopjes and dismounted. Horse holders took our mounts back around into a deep part of the donga as the rest of us made our way up the west side of the saddle. About half way to the top, Saxon split his men. Half he placed in extended order along the south side, the other half on the west, setting up an L-shaped ambush. Many are the men who have been killed by their own comrades in a cross fire. This would not happen here.

Holmes, Churchill, Saxon and I placed ourselves in the angle of the L and settled down to wait. As darkness completed its' shroud the artillery fire started to die off. Until, unable to see their target any longer, the cannons fell silent. The Boers knew we were coming. The only question was where would be the main attack. Fredericks believed he knew the answer to that question.

Hour upon hour we waited. The occasional cough or sneeze of a soldier down the line sounded like an explosion in the stillness of the night.

"Are you sure we are in the right place?" whispered Churchill to Saxon.

"Yes, this is it. He'll be along."

"It's almost midnight already."

Holmes held up his hand. "Quiet" was the inaudible command. I tensed. The last three hours had been excruciating. No talking or movement, no smoking for fear that the glow or the smell would give us away. My bones ached, but if I moved the creak of my leather seemed to have the loudness of church bells.

Holmes pointed silently to the right. Entering our trap was a man on horseback. He moved slowly and searched all about him as he rode. Surely, I thought, he must see the men to my right. He looked to be almost upon them. But it is true that, at least in the night, it is difficult to see an object plainly, unless it moves. Our attention is always drawn to an object in motion. Something that does not move is easily overlooked.

On rode our quarry. I could see him plainly now. I could not make out his face, but by the hat, and his movements, it was Fredericks. He rode to a place not more than twenty yards from us and stopped his horse. Taking a final look around at the rocks and boulders which surrounded him, he stepped out of the saddle and raised his mount's left front hoof. I looked to Holmes who smiled, acknowledging my thought. The left hoof meant all was clear.

Suddenly, like apparitions from a ghostly world, half a dozen men appeared out of the darkness.

"What news, Fitz?" said the man in the lead.

"You know the attack is at first light," responded Fredericks.

A couple of the men laughed. One spoke to another, but I did not understand Dutch and so did not know what was said.

"Yes, Paul. The cannons were a clue. But they won't attack from there." Fredericks had knelt in the dust and was drawing a map in the dirt with a stick. "They come from here, from the south-east. They think the guns will make you move your men to the north-west, but Rundle is there and will hold you in place while they roll up a flank that they hope is lightly held."

"It is a good plan," said the Boer. "I'm not sure if we have enough men to hold in any case. I will report this to the general. Will you come away with us?"

"No, Hans. I go back. As far as I know you are moving all your men from this area. That's what I'll report. I'll report where and when I can. Back here tomorrow if you hold."

"As I said," replied Hans, "that is for the generals. God go with you."

The two men shook hands and Hans turned to go.

Fredericks pointed at the man whom he had called Paul. "And keep Paul out of trouble and away from the women!" The group laughed and disappeared into the darkness.

I looked to Holmes. Churchill and Saxon did the same. Were we to let them get away? What were we doing out here if not to capture Fredericks and his men. The adrenalin was pouring through my veins. We must move before he got away.

Holmes just smiled at us and stood up. Duquesne, as I shall call him now, had watched his Boer companions leave and had not yet mounted. We were on him in an instant, before he could draw a weapon or put a foot in a stirrup. Saxon reached in Duquesne's holster and retrieved the spy's pistol.

"Well played, Mr Holmes, well played." Duquesne was smiling in spite of his plight. He looked into the darkness where his comrades had disappeared.

"Oh, they are within earshot, sir. But their duty is to get the information you gave them back to their general. They will not be back." Holmes was, of course, correct.

"We must stop them! They have important information." Churchill had both of his pistols out and was frantic.

"No need, sir. The information was quite incorrect. Rundle will hold, but the attack from the south-east is but a feint and the main attack is where it should be, under the protection of the guns. Let them go."

"It might be best if we chased them a bit, Mr Holmes." Saxon had spoken up for the first time. "They may think it odd if we did not."

"Excellent point, Captain. But please, do not catch them. Watson, Churchill and I will await your return with Mr Duquesne."

"That's, Captain Duquesne," stated our prisoner.

In a moment horse holders had been called up, the men mounted and with much noise and to-do "gave chase" to the Boers. Churchill seemed quite put out, and taking his horse, which had been brought up with ours, he walked to a distant rock to pout.

"You didn't let him go on purpose, Holmes."

"Something about that man irritates me, Watson. I'm afraid he will make his way stirringly in the government. It will do him good to have to wait for things now and then. Ah, but Captain Duquesne, we are neglecting you."

While Holmes was busy talking, I had taken to watching Duquesne. One man who had been left with us was tying our guest's hands behind his back. He'd be able to ride, but his horse would be led.

"While we are waiting for our friends to return, would you mind answering a few questions, Mr Duquesne?" asked Holmes.

"Not at all, Mr Holmes, although I think you probably know all there is to know, with one exception." The man looked about then seated himself on a large rock. Churchill came back to where we stood.

"If you are wondering why I did this, the reason is simplicity itself. I hate you bastards." Duquesne smiled as he said the last sentence, not angrily, but in a voice as calm as if he had been sitting at the dinner table.

"You push my people off their land and when they move and re-establish themselves, you decide you want that, too. You murder and plunder and steal and then you ask why we fight you. You're well aware it is about the gold and the diamonds."

"You abuse our citizens," interjected Churchill.

"They were treated well. Why would we give them the vote? They were not citizens! You may tell lies to yourself, but the world knows what this is about."

"If I may interrupt your political discussion," said Holmes. "You ran the sabotage organization at the port in Cape Town?"

"Yes."

"And you had men in place to move the stolen gold. They were yours, of course."

"There was stolen gold. Stolen from the Boer people and retaken by them."

"Of course," Holmes bowed, "and Pelham was the reason you came to Lord Roberts' headquarters."

"Yes, he was weakening. He could see things were starting to go against us. So he was becoming afraid of his position. Maybe he would have to give his whole thing up. Like most British, he needed to have his back stiffened."

"And yet we win, don't we," snarled Churchill. "The Empire not only stands, it grows."

"For now, perhaps."

"Enough," said Holmes. "I've no time for this. Is there anything else you would care to tell us, Captain Duquesne?"

"Just one thing, Mr Holmes. Don't expect to find any gold when you get back to Mrs Foster's."

"It'll be there," I said. "It's being watched."

"Yes, Doctor, by my men. Well, they're technically MacBride's men. They relieved your guard mount just after dark. Fine looking lot of Royal Irish they were. The gold, machine gun and ammunition were loaded and are now within the Boer lines." A smile ran across the scoundrel's face from ear to ear.

"As you said earlier, sir. Well played. Well played" replied Holmes. "Mr Cacy, I suppose?"

"Yes, he and the McMullen boys."

"And the uniforms were taken from the Irish Rifles who surrendered last month."

"Yes, again, Mr Holmes."

"And the deaths of Lieutenant Murtry, Major Parker and Mrs Foster?"

"Hated to do Murtry, he was a nice lad. Wanted me to take him to watch Cacy, I couldn't allow that. Parker I sent out to be taken care of by the boys. Told him where to find Cacy, poor man didn't know when to surrender. As to Mrs Foster," he thought for a moment. "Never rely on a woman Mr Holmes, they are too emotional." Holmes glanced at me with a smirk. "She," continued Fredericks, "would have given us up for spite just to get at Major Pelham. I had to remove her."

Saxon and his men had now returned. The private who had remained with us helped Duquesne up on his horse and passed the bridle reins to another man.

"I'll take those reins," said Churchill. "I owe a Boer a ride into captivity."

Looking to his captain, who nodded, the man passed the reins to Churchill who led off without waiting for the rest of us. I was tempted to depart from my friend here and try to find Pole-Carew and his men, but I realized I would be far better off returning to Bloemfontein and getting the best location they could give me and a few hours of sleep.

Holmes and I stopped at Mrs Foster's barn to find the cellar empty except for a lone coin which had been laid on the top of the trap door. It was a coin with two heads.

Chapter 27
THE WATER WORKS

"I'm sorry, Holmes. You couldn't have known that they would come back in uniform." I felt sorry for my friend's failure. Even though he had captured the spy, Duquesne, any part of his plan going astray always bothered him.

"Watson, do you really think I would leave the gold here when just such an eventuality was possible? I'm afraid the boys will find that they not only have a non-functioning 'potato digger', but also a number of boxes of horseshoes instead of gold." Holmes flipped the coin over to me. "A souvenir for your collection, Watson. You may put it in the box with your ruby.[3]

"I also gave a note to the boys' sister Molly. She was to give it to Cacy if she saw them loading the wagon."

"What did the note say?"

"Well done!"

Holmes and I rode on to the headquarters. The sun was rising and I needed to rest and feed Boy-O. He would be no good if he were over worked. The morning's battle would have to wait.

Lieutenant Barthelme greeted us as we arrived with word that Roberts was in an exceptionally good mood. It was expected that the day's battle would go well. Burnham had returned before dawn with critical information. The Boers had been drawn to exactly where he wanted them. Their centre had been weakened when they sent re-enforcements to the south-east. Now Roberts' forces would attack the weakened centre under the protection of the guns.

"Then everything has gone as planned." Churchill had entered the room. "I will wait until the end of the day and wire the good news to the world. But first I must write up last night's adventure."

---

[3] See *Watson's Afghan Adventure,* MX Publishing

"Where is your charge, Mr Churchill?" Holmes looked concerned.

"In Major Parker's old office, I put a man on the door. Not to worry. He'll be off on the next train to prison in Cape Town."

"I think I have one more thing I would like to discuss with Captain Duquesne. If you gentlemen will excuse me." Holmes went off down the hall.

I agreed to some tea offered by Barthelme. Churchill sat at an empty table with notebook and pencil scribbling furiously.

"Have you seen Lieutenant Langman and Doctor Doyle, Captain?" I was curious if they had gone out to the Water Works.

"Yes, Doctor, they left early last evening. I imagine they slept under some wagon or other. They wanted to be in on the battle."

"Well, I think we are done here, Watson." Holmes had returned and stood in the doorway. "Shall we take care of the horses? Then I know you want some sleep and I must arrange to go to Cape Town. And Lieutenant Churchill, I should like to ask a question. Did you leave the Captain alone in Major Parker's office?"

Churchill had a startled look. "Yes, why? Is he not alone now?"

"He is not there now, my good fellow. You really should not leave a prisoner alone. You, of all men, should know that."

Except for Holmes, we pushed from the room. Parker's office had been on the first floor. We raced up the stairs, past the guard, and through the door. The room was empty and the window was open.

"He's gone," yelled Churchill. "After him."

I grabbed the fellow by the sleeve as he tried to rush past. "After him, where? By now he probably has a half-hour start. And which way did he go? East? I wouldn't. I'd go North or West. You've lost him old boy, calm down."

Churchill ripped himself free and ran down the stairs and out the front door, Barthelme was in close pursuit.

I descended and met Holmes in the hallway.

"Watson, I don't think we shall read of this adventure in the papers." It was as close to a laugh as I'd seen on Holmes in quite a while.

"Now you have to start all over, Holmes."

"No, Watson. Duquesne may be back, but for now his spy ring is broken and at least we have recovered some of the gold. I think it is time for me to return to Baker Street. Let us put up the horses and have some refreshment."

Come the afternoon I took leave of Holmes to go in search of Langman and Doyle, with a promise to return the next day to bid farewell.

Holmes had agreed to stay one additional day to give some recommendations to Parker's replacement, who was to arrive that evening.

On finding Doyle, near the Modder, he was all news and excitement. He and Langman had indeed slept under some wagons and seen Hamilton consolidate his forces for his day's battle - a battle that Doyle thought "magnificent".

"I admit, Watson, I was a bit concerned when we came through Sanna's Post, where we had that disaster a few weeks ago. Dead artillery horses lying about everywhere, the place covered with the litter of war – puttees, broken helmets, haversacks, belts. It was depressing. But you should have seen the men this morning."

"Quite the show, eh?"

"Hamilton was already there, of course, but Smith-Dorrien brought up his brigade this morning. Straight up the middle, extended order, and when the Boers moved men from their left to help the centre, our mounted infantry swept round and rolled them up."

"And the casualties?" I asked.

"Oh, very light, considering."

I was a little put out by Doyle. I know I should not have been, but while the war was being fought, I could not think of casualties without sadness.

"Going to move with the army or is the hospital staying here?" I asked.

"We'll be moving when Roberts does," replied Langman. "Probably in a week or so, in the meantime we shall finally get clean water."

"Yes, you know the battle may be "magnificent" as you say, Doyle, but to the soldier it is a minor thing. To him it's the need for clean water, firewood, enough biscuits for the march and how to get away with a chicken and not get punished. It's trying to stay dry or cool or warm and keeping his feet from blisters. Those are the real important things in life."

"You cannot bring me down, Watson; they did a glorious job today. But tell me, what of you and Holmes? Has he solved his mystery?"

I explained the events of the last few days to my two companions as we rode back toward Bloemfontein and the Langman Hospital. It was almost a four-hour ride and pitch black by the time we got there. The rest of the staff was overjoyed with the news that fresh water would soon be flowing again.

I left Doyle regaling the crowd with tales of the great battle, gave Boy-O to a groom and lay out on my old cot on the roof. I was asleep in an instant.

DENOUEMENT

The next day I tarried a bit longer than I should have. I was already a day late reporting in to Hamilton's headquarters, but I felt my reasons would be acceptable. I took my leave of the staff at Langman's. Finding Holmes, I went with him to the railroad station to see him off.

"You've done well, Holmes. You've succeeded in everything that Mycroft asked of you."

"True, Watson. It is unfortunate that Lestrade let Duquesne escape."

"Churchill, you mean."

"Yes, Churchill, just a slip of the tongue. We shall see more of both of them I'm afraid. How soon will you return?"

"If Lord Roberts is to be believed we'll be done in three months. He's going to push straight to Pretoria. But I don't know, I'm not sure just taking the South African capital will end it. They may fight on."

"Take care of yourself, old boy. I shall tell Mrs Hudson to expect you in August."

I had to laugh at this precise prediction and we shook hands as he entered the train. I stayed on the platform until the train had disappeared from sight. Having mounted Boy-O, I started a long ride to catch up with Hamilton.

On the 5th of June we marched into Pretoria. Roberts would consider his work done, having annexed the two Boer Republics as new British Colonies. Before the end of July he and I were on our way home to England.

I saw Langman and Doyle occasionally and by mid-July Doyle, was also on the way home wanting to be the first to turn out a precise history of the Boer War.

Churchill returned about the same time with his usual criticisms of whatever was done.

Kitchener took over from Lord Roberts and became involved in a terrible guerrilla war that lasted two years.

As for Duquesne, he escaped to England, joined the British army and received a commission as a lieutenant and returned to Cape Town. He states that his sister was murdered and his family farm burned by Kitchener's army. His mother was raped and she and the baby died in one of Kitchener's concentration camps. Duquesne used his new position in Cape Town to organize another ring of saboteurs, who were only caught because one man did not want his own property destroyed. Of the twenty men who were captured, only Duquesne was not executed, upon his giving to the army the secret to a Boer code. He was sent to prison in Bermuda, from where he escaped. In the Great War he would spy for the Germans, sink British ships with bombs and claimed to direct the submarine that killed Lord Kitchener. He had his revenge.

I saw a good bit of work accomplished by MacBride, Cacy and the McMullen brothers. They had become the 'wrecking crew' of the Boer army. Not a bridge was taken on the way to Pretoria. The Irish Brigade's men, always the final guard, blew them apart.

Burnham was wounded in early June but had accomplished incredible things. I hope he someday writes his memoires. He was offered the Victoria Cross, but refused as it would have required the giving up of his American citizenship. He and Churchill returned to England aboard the same ship.

Boy-O I hated to part with. He served me well and was a good companion on the veldt. I left him in the care of Lieutenant Barthelme and the last I knew Boy-O was serving out his retirement on pasture near Cork City.

As for myself, I have had the second, no third, adventure of a lifetime. The first two being: Afghanistan and the friendship of Sherlock Holmes.

As Holmes had predicted, I was back in Baker Street in August, just in time to assist in the story I have decided to call "The Adventure of the Six Napoleons".

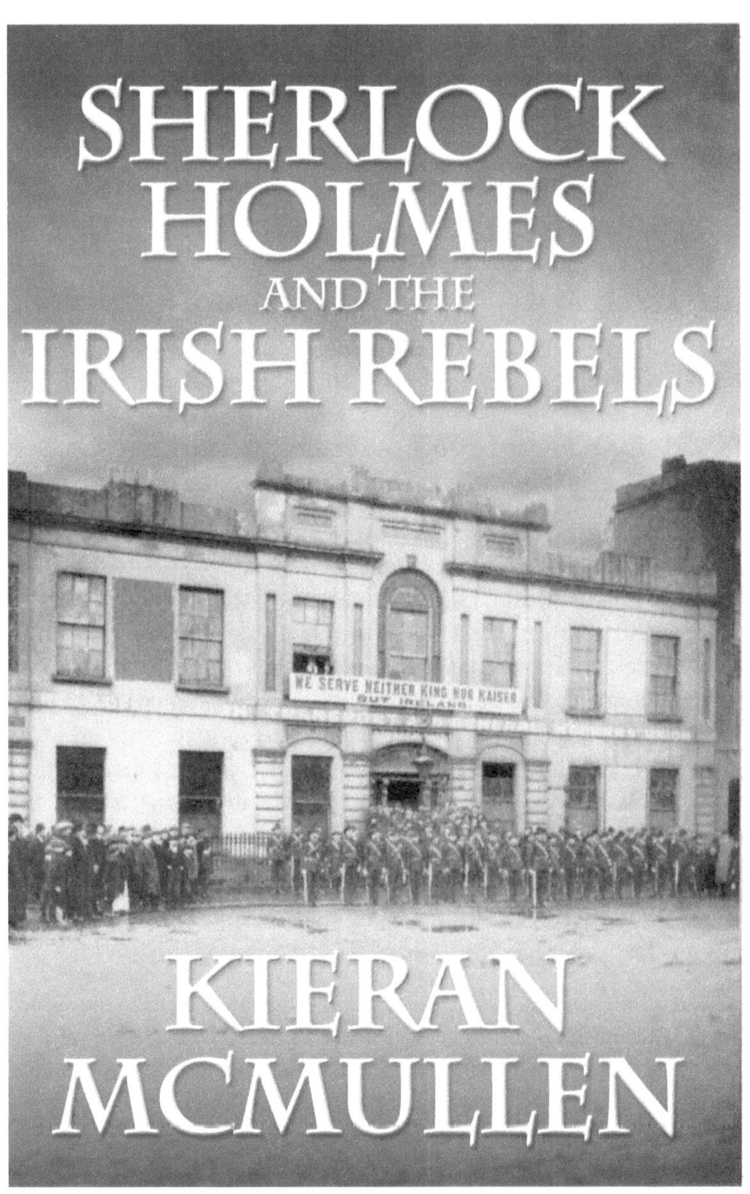
SHERLOCK HOLMES
AND THE
IRISH REBELS
WE SERVE NEITHER KING NOR KAISER
KIERAN MCMULLEN

Foreword

The episode which I relate in this book is the last adventure I had with my friend Sherlock Holmes, sponsored by his brother, Mycroft. While there was little mystery, there was much in the way of learning for me.

My stepmother had been Irish (as I related earlier in *Watson's Afghan Adventure*) and I had some sympathy for the land, though by no means was I truly cognizant of all its problems or its history. In fact, the schools of my day taught almost nothing about the island to our west. I knew more about America than I did about Ireland. This adventure changed my life and thinking probably more than my time in Afghanistan or my service in the Boer War.

Some will comment that I do not portray here the whole picture but merely segments of a bigger mural. That criticism is undoubtedly true for I was only involved in the smaller segments. Time and additional information give us the ability to see the broader view. We are later able to see all the actors on the stage. But when you're in the trench you can see only the mud and lumber walls, the slating under your feet and the barbed wire to your front. You are only worried about the man on your right, the one on your left and your enemy with his bayonet. All else - the politicians, the generals, the cannons to your rear, even though they impact your life - are out of your control and out of your thoughts.

So here I recorded what I saw and what I did during the war within a war. I came to it with few preconceptions and left it with grave misgivings.

Holmes had changed his role in life. He was no longer "the great detective" but now, since the adventure I recorded as "His Last Bow" he had continued to be "the great spy". It was a role he did not treasure. He performed it out of duty and he did it well, as he did all things.

As I write this, the Great War has ended and the victor nations are gathering in Paris. I understand that the Irish have sent a delegation to try and get recognition for an independent country. I'm sure no one will listen, not even the American President Wilson. I fear we are not done in Ireland.

John Watson, MD

Lieutenant Colonel, RAMC

Sherlock Holmes And the Irish Rebels

Chapter 1

Wednesday

12 April 1916

It had been a good year and a half since I had last seen Holmes. In fact, it had been since the day after we had captured the German spy, Von Bork, on the English coast in 1914. Von Bork had thought he was buying British naval codebooks from an Irish-American named Altamont. In fact, Von Bork bought a trip to his homeland and we had rounded up his entire spy organization. Not only had Holmes fooled Von Bork, he had even inserted Mrs Hudson in Von Bork's home as his housekeeper. It was a wonderful piece of work for the Home Office. I eventually related this case in a piece I called "His Last Bow". I was wrong to have done so!

Having heard nothing from my friend in over a year it was with some amazement that I opened a telegram from him on the 12th of April 1916: "Lieutenant Colonel John Watson, MD., 3rd Australian Auxiliary Hospital, Dartford, Kent. Come Dublin immediately stop. See Mycroft at Diogenes on way stop. Altamont."

I was puzzled, to say the least. Why was Holmes still using the name Altamont (he used Liam for a Christian name) and why was he in Dublin? Was he still working for the Home Office?

My own story since last seeing Holmes was quite simple. With the coming of the Great War, I had offered my services to the Army Medical Department. At first, I had been thanked but turned down. Surely, the war wouldn't last beyond Christmas. After all, it was England, France and Russia against Germany and Austria-Hungry. We had our foe caught on two fronts, and one might call our Italian ally the third front. We had very effectively divided his strength. His supply lines from overseas were cut off by our overwhelming naval power.

But as the months progressed and the war took on a world-wide aspect, the Medical Department found they had a use for me, a 64-year-old-former-campaigner. I had not seen service since my volunteer days in the Boer War. Back then, the Army had been stretched thin also, between the Boxers in China, disruptions in the Sudan and the Boers in South Africa, men were needed.

Now, however, in my more senior years, even the "New Army" felt I was of some use in the rearward hospitals. I had been assigned as Liaison

Officer from the British Army Medical Department to an Australian hospital that specialized in the care of shell shocked soldiers. It was a large facility in Kent that took care of 1400 men. These men had seen the worst that the trenches had to offer. My primary job was to make sure that the British Army Medical Department provided all support possible to our Commonwealth soldiers. To do this, essentially supply function, I had a staff of three exemplary non-commissioned officers, which gave me time to help with the overwhelming patient workload.

In later years, shell-shock would be a disparaging term so we would classify officers as having "neurasthenia" and enlisted men as having "hysteria". But for now, they were either "shell-shock: wounded" or "shell-shock: sick". Shell-shock: wounded was largely applied to those who had actually seen battle in the trenches. This was considered an honourable thing. Shell-shock: sick, for the most part, had seen no actual combat.

During their stay at our hospital, these men were treated with all the latest methods and all the finest care. They were given all the current treatments from sedatives to electric shock therapy. In many cases, merely a calming atmosphere was all that was needed, along with an understanding that fear was a natural thing. Fear, many times, is what keeps us alive and responding, but fear must be controlled and thought of as a useful tool.

Soldiers who stayed here were issued "Hospital Blues". It consisted of a medium blue suit and red ties. It seemed to give our patients a sense of unity and belonging. It also made them easy to identify if they decided on a private "vacation" from the grounds.

Those who recovered were sent to a Command Depot for re-assignment to an active unit. Those who did not recover but were capable of functioning in a society without cannons were given a silver war badge and discharged from service with the thanks of His Majesty's Government.

There were some who would never recover.

It was while I was pondering the telegram from Holmes that a corporal came to fetch me from my office.

"Commander needs to see you, sir. Said it was important."

I looked up, startled out of my thoughts. "Yes, of course. Tell Colonel Flynn I'll be right there."

The orderly was off almost before I finished speaking. I took a quick look at the mirror on my north wall before heading down the corridor to the Commanding Office.

“Nice old goat in the mirror,” I thought. “Still has a full head of reddish-brown hair, a grey moustache I admit, but still spry and presentable. Tie straight.” I looked down, “boots could use a brush. Ah, well, this is war. I wonder what Holmes wanted me for.”

I hustled down the corridor to the Colonel’s office on the west side. Entering his outer office, the orderly who had been sent for me came to attention behind his desk.

“Right in, sir. Colonel said don’t wait.”

“Thank you, Burton,” I responded, passing him and opening the door to Flynn’s office.

“John, come in mate,” came the booming voice of our Commander. “Sit down; you know I hate this military formality stuff. Be glad when all this is over and I can go back to private practice.

“Well,” he grinned, glancing at his papers as I took a seat next to his desk. “Looks like we’re losing you. Know what’s going on?”

“I’m sure you know more than I do, Colonel. I was just going to come and talk to you when I got your message. I’ve received a request from an old friend to come to Dublin post haste, though I don’t know why.”

“Looks like it’s you who knows more, John. All I got was a telegram from the Home Office and another from the Medical Department Headquarters, almost at the same time. Here.”

Flynn handed me two telegram sheets. The first, from the Medical Department, simply stated I was to be seconded to the Home Office, effective immediately. I was not to await my replacement but to report at once.

The second telegram, this from the Home Office, assigned me to Special Branch, Scotland Yard. “Report immediately to Mr Mycroft Holmes at his usual location.”

“What the devil do they want me for?”

“I’d hoped you’d tell me, John.” Flynn leaned back in his chair and looked at the ceiling as if trying to think of something. “Special Branch. Is that the outfit they used to call Special Irish Branch?”

“I believe so. Why?”

“Oh, nothing. They’re who I have to thank for my mum ending up in Australia is all.” He laughed and stood up from the desk. “Well you, my friend, had best make arrangements. Can you leave tonight?”

"No. I've got patients I must transition to someone tonight and I won't go off without doing that, even for Holmes. I've also got to pack a kit and arrange to store the rest. I'll take the first train in the morning. Mycroft can wait 14 hours for me to get there.

Flynn laughed again and coming forward, patted me on the back. "I'll be very sorry to lose you, John, you have been a tremendous help here. I only hope your replacement is half as good."

"Kind words, sir. I hope I'm not gone too long. I'm sure whoever they send to replace me will do just as well. In the meantime, Sergeant Locke will make sure your support line stays intact."

With that, we shook hands and I departed to make arrangements for the care of my patients.

Later that night I was packing the majority of my books and belongings into boxes that Sergeant Locke had procured for me. Not knowing what the mission was that required the assistance of an old fellow was driving me to distraction.

Why was Holmes still calling himself Altamont? Were there German spies in Ireland? Coast watchers perhaps, reporting our ship movements to Germany by wireless?

Then the thought suddenly came to me. Yes. It must be a German plot. After all, hadn't Martha Hudson moved to Dublin last year? And when I wrote to her, on receiving the assignment in Kent, she had written back that she had opened a rooming house on Talbot Street and taken to using her maiden name of McGuffey!

How stupid of me! I thought it odd at the time, but I had no idea Holmes was in Ireland. He had never returned the letters I had written to him in Sussex. And I had to admit that though I was too busy to look carefully, I had seen nothing in the newspaper about Holmes and any investigations or war work.

I spent the rest of the night visiting with two of my colleagues, discussing my current cases and the status of each soldier. I was concerned that in one or two cases the simple change of doctors would set the poor fellows back a bit. Having transferred cases, packed a traveling kit and boxed my belongings, I thanked Locke for his help and tried to get a few hours sleep. Unknown to me at the time, I was about to enter one of the most bewildering chapters of my life. For now, I would get a bit of sleep before catching the early train to London.

Chapter 2
Thursday
13 April 1916

Finding that sleep was useless, I was up especially early to make the train out of Dartford to London. With uniform on and bag in hand, I appeared on the train platform a half hour early. Taking a seat on one of the many empty benches, my mind continued to churn. Holmes, I thought, would not have this problem. He would merely say "One cannot make bricks without clay" and turn his mind to other things. I had never been able to achieve this.

Finally, the train came. Taking a seat in a smoking compartment, I drew out my pipe to pass an hour. Instead, it was almost two hours before we arrived at Victoria. However, much to my surprise, as I left the platform, I was met by a young Private (they all seemed so young) who saluted and asked if I were Lieutenant Colonel Watson. When I replied that I was, he informed me that he had been sent with a motor car to take me to my meeting with a Mr Holmes at the Diogenes Club[4].

It was nice to be back in London. As we drove through the streets I couldn't help but be amazed at the huge number of uniformed men and even woman. British, Australian, New Zealanders, Indian, French, Italian; soldiers, nurses, auxiliaries - it was astounding. As the streets bustled it seemed business as usual. Hard to believe that these same people were terrorized at night by the comings and goings of German LZ-90's[5] dropping their cargo of deadly bombs.

Our few minutes journey over, I walked up the familiar steps of the Diogenes Club and was ushered into the foyer before I had a chance to ring the bell. Having been reminded of the rules of silence[6], except in the stranger's room, and my hat taken, I was led by the major-domo to the Stranger's Room where Holmes and I had met with Mycroft on at least four occasions.

As the door opened, I saw nothing that reminded me of the old days. Instead, there was a bustling operation centre. Half a dozen uniformed men

---

[4] A club for "unclubable men" of which Mycroft was a founder.
[5] Baron Von Zeppelin's rigid air ships.
[6] No member was allowed to speak to another in the club.

were busy with tasks I knew would be critical to the war effort. The large windows had been covered with heavy curtains and on the far wall were two telephone switchboards, telegraph keys and tickertapes. Desks rowed both sides and on the wall opposite the window were bulletin boards filled with papers. In the middle of the room was a gigantic map board of Europe, Asia and Africa. The board was covered with coloured pins and two sergeants were busy reading telegraphs and changing pin locations. Mycroft, one hand on his hip, the other stroking his chin, was looking intently at the map.

"Sergeant, see if we can't get better information on the strength of Von Lettow. We're wasting far too many resources in Africa," said Mycroft.

"Yes, sir. I'll get the wire off immediately," replied the Sergeant.

Mycroft looked up and realizing I was present, came forward with hand outstretched.

"My dear doctor, how good of you to come so quickly. You're looking quite well. Being in harness is doing you good! Excellent. Excellent!" Shaking my hand vigorously, he continued, "But come, come. I have a little office to myself over here, used to be a coat closet, but it does for my needs. Come in and have a seat."

We crossed the buzzing room and entered a small cubby hole just big enough for a table to be used as a desk and three straight backed chairs. As we passed into the room, Mycroft rang for the major-domo and asked me to have a seat.

"Somewhere under all those papers there is a chair, Watson. Just pile it on the floor. Good Lad. Ah, Hancock, I know it's not quite noon, but bring the Colonel and me a brandy, will you? Sit, Watson, please. Let me just close the door. Hancock will knock when he has our drinks."

"Do your members approve of what you've done to the Stranger's Room?" I asked, smiling.

"Ah, well, all for the war effort. I needed somewhere to work where I wouldn't be disturbed constantly, and this is, shall we say, out of sight, out of mind."

Hancock knocked on the door and entered. After placing the brandies on the table he asked if there was anything else.

"No, Hancock. We'll have lunch in an hour, but nothing until then.

With that, Hancock departed. "To your health, Doctor," said Mycroft, lifting his glass. "And yours" I replied, doing the same.

Mycroft hadn't changed significantly in the years since I had seen him. A little heavy for his height, hair now white, and the hairline seemed to have receded significantly, but at 69, he seemed as quick and sharp as ever.

"Well, Watson," he finally said, putting down his glass. "Yes, I know I'm still overweight and have lost quite a bit of my hair, but you're right, I haven't lost a step when it comes to my job."

"But, I…"

"From your face and eyes. You must be a terrible card player."

"Yes," I smiled, "I'm much better at billiards."

"Well, down to business. Do you know why you're here?"

"Only that Sherlock is evidently still playing the role of Liam Altamont, that he is in Dublin, that Mrs Hudson, or should I say, McGuffey, is there also and that he has sent for me. Other than that, I know nothing."

"Excellent, Watson. Yes indeed. We have convinced Sherlock to stay on the job and Mrs Hudson has agreed to play a part as she did with the Von Burk affair."

"But how can Sherlock use a persona which the Germans must know is false if he's looking for German spies? Surely, Von Bork blew the whistle on him as soon as he got back to Germany."

Mycroft looked down at his brandy and swirled it in the glass. "Perhaps Watson, Von Bork never got back to Germany. Perhaps he has been held incommunicado for the last eighteen months just so Sherlock could continue to use his disguise as an English hating, pro-German, Irish-American."

I squirmed in my seat. "Is that legal? He was a diplomat."

"Let us say, necessary, shall we?"

"All right. I can accept that. But are there so many spies in Ireland?"

"Worse than that, I'm afraid," he said with a smirk. "There are so many Irish."

I sat looking at him for a moment, not knowing exactly how to take the remark. My confusion showed.

"How much do you know about the current situation in Ireland?"

"Not a lot, I'm afraid. I know we're not conscripting in Ireland and the number of recruits has fallen terribly since the war started. Also, that

Home Rule has been delayed until after the war. More than that, I'm afraid I've been too busy to notice."

"Unfortunately," said Mycroft, "Your understanding is all too common in Great Britain. Segments of Ireland are a boiling cauldron, both for the Union and for complete independence." He stood up and paced back and forth in the small space behind his desk.

"The problem," he said, turning to look at me "is the damned Irish won't be English and we can't be fighting there as well as everywhere else."

"Mycroft, you have surely lost me. Are you saying there is going to be rebellion? Why? Why now?"

"Because 'England's difficulty is Ireland's opportunity', as the saying goes. How many rebellions have we had there since Henry II made the mistake of invading? Just in the last 120 years there have been risings in 1798, 1803, 1848 and 1867. And believe me, unless we act, there will be another one soon."

"I'm afraid, sir, you'll have to explain it to me," I said. "I thought all was quiet, for now anyway."

"Let me give you the short version. In my opinion, since the incorporation of Ireland into the United Kingdom in 1801, we have made a great error. Ireland has been treated like a colony instead of an equal with this island. They've been in the parliament, yes. But we pass special laws which treat Ireland separately. Remember, they had their own Parliament until the Union. In recent years, there has been a huge revival of Irish games and music and the Irish language. And where Dublin was once the second city of the empire, it is now filled with decaying tenements. Tenements are rich turf for rebels. The industry has moved to the Northeast of Ireland which is heavily Protestant and heavily pro-union. The South is Catholic, nationalist and poor. Now that's a generality, but largely true. It's also true that most Irish want Home Rule, but those that don't are vehement in staying with the Union. The majority want a peaceful existence with dominion status like Canada."

"Why don't they just take an island-wide vote to see what the people want to do?" I asked.

"No, too many people have too much involved. It would surely go for Home Rule and the Ulster Unionists will take up arms to prevent that."

"What? Rebel to stay not rebel to go? I'm confused."

"Watson, in 1912, Sir Edward Carson formed the Ulster Volunteer Force, or UVF. They dedicated themselves to keeping Ireland in the Union even if it meant by force. They knew the majority of Ireland wanted Home Rule but were afraid of a Nationalist Catholic majority in Dublin. They claimed 'Home Rule means Rome Rule.' Not true of course, but to them, a real fear none the less.

"In April of '14, while you and Holmes were busy tracking Von Bork, Carson armed the UVF in violation of import and licensing laws. He imported 25,000 magazine rifles and 3 million rounds of ammunition and distributed them to a now well organized para-military organization."

Putting my glass back on the table, I turned back in my chair thinking. "And we did nothing?"

"Yes, Watson. Plans were started to take the weapons back but that would mean bloodshed and the army. And the army in Ireland was officered by Unionists who let it be known that they would not lead their soldiers in the task of disarming the UVF. The officers at Curragh, almost to a man, would resign their commissions rather than lead their soldiers against fellow Unionists."

"And the government permitted this type of behaviour?"

"Yes, in fact, large segments of the Parliament found it quite satisfying."

"But the Arms Act," I protested.

"The Arms Act has not been in effect in Ireland since 1906, old fellow. Another one of those ways we seem to have one set of rules for us and another set for Ireland. Since '06 it has been easier to buy and sell guns there than in England. Still, one needed an import license and a local license, but those were easy to get and you didn't need two magistrates to sign the license. But the fact is the law wasn't really enforced anyway. The outcome was this: you remember the labour riots in the larger cities in '13?"

I nodded.

"Yes, well," he continued, "the police badly over-reacted. People killed and injured, didn't look good to the working classes. Anyway, two men, Larkin and Connolly had been union organizers. When the disturbances happened, they formed a group called the Irish Citizen Army or ICA to protect the strikers from the police. For the most part they were unarmed but again in a Para-military format. Also, a man named MacNeill formed the Irish National Volunteers, still another group to contend with! Both the ICA and the Volunteers were for Irish independence. Peacefully, if possible, but violently if need be."

"But Home Rule is on the books," I said. "It's only held off until after the war."

"Home Rule, Watson, will not happen! Carson and the unionists won't stand for it. One way or the other, there will be bloodshed.

"But let me continue. Since the UVF imported weapons without consequence, the Volunteers decided they must arm also, and so they did. Not as well, I admit. They brought in 1500 single shot German Mausers to Howth and Kilcoole and I believe 25,000 rounds of ammunition. Now both sides were armed. But in the case of the Nationalists, there was an attempt by civil authority, using the Army, to take the weapons. They didn't get but eight or ten but the real tragedy was that the army opened fire on unarmed civilians at Bachelor's Walk on the River Liffey. Civilians were killed and the Nationalists could tell the people, 'see how England treats you!' Oh, the Army was provoked by the crowd. But their response played into the hands of the Nationalists."

"But where is the government in all this?" I replied.

"Nowhere!"

"What?"

"Both sides drill openly with weapons and posture about and the Irish government takes the attitude that it is better to do nothing."

"I can't believe all this."

"It's too true, I assure you, Watson. Once the war started, they believed things would calm down and the Irish would come to the defence of the Empire. At first it did. Carson's UVF enlisted en-masse. John Redmond, the leader of the Irish Parliamentary Party and who had orchestrated the Home Rule Bill had largely wrested the Irish National Volunteers from the more radical elements and offered the Volunteers for service with the army. He also agreed to hold Home Rule in abeyance. The decision to wait on Home Rule split the Volunteers. A good 80 percent went with Redmond. The rest went with MacNeill and became the Irish Volunteers, or IV, about 11,000 men."

"And it's the Volunteers who are causing trouble?" I asked.

"No end, I'm afraid. Marching about, telling young men not to enlist, seditious speeches and being generally a nuisance. Them and the ICA."

"And the Lord Lieutenant and other officials, what of them?"

"The current Lord Lieutenant is a fool named Ivor Churchill, Lord Wimbourne. Of course, his position is mostly ceremonial. No real power. The

Chief Secretary, who should really be running things, is Augustine Birrell, but since he is also a member of the cabinet and we've been at war, he spends most of his time in London. His sympathies are plainly with the Nationalists.

"The Undersecretary, Sir Matthew Nathan, is competent enough, but left on his own he is a 'business-as-usual' type who does not have the insightfulness to deal with the Irish. He too, I fear sympathizes with the Nationalists."

Mycroft sat back down at the table. "That, I believe is the big picture. Another brandy?" He lifted the decanter and I held out my glass without even thinking about it.

"Well," I said, sitting back again in my chair, "I would think that Redmond used exactly the wrong tactic."

"What would you have done?"

"Well, wouldn't he have been better off to withhold all the Volunteers until Home Rule had been implemented and provided them as a dominion force rather than playing the co-operative parliamentarian?"

"It's what I would have done in his place surely. Wait for the UVF to march off to war, decreasing Ulster's ability to resist Home Rule and put down whatever little trouble there was with Irish troops."

"Who supplied all the weapons?"

"Industrialists to the UVF. Irish-Americans supplied the money to the Volunteers. The Germans were happy to supply them to the Nationalists. Through the Dutch, of course."

"And the Volunteers, they're the same as the Sein Feiners?"

"No, Sein Fein is a political party which professes non-violent solutions, but since all Nationalists are lumped together by the government, the terms Volunteers and Sein Feiners are used interchangeably. The SF does hate everything English."

"Well, it's all very confusing, but what am I doing here?" I asked, leaning forward and putting down my glass.

"Doctor, Sherlock has need of a companion he can rely on with absolute certainty and he has asked for you. He has continued with his disguise of this person, Altamont, an Irish-American, English hater and has made himself a part of the Volunteers. He has worked himself up in their circles but has failed to get the information he needs.

"There is one more level to this puzzle, Watson. It's called the IRB, the Irish Republican Brotherhood. There are some who believe they are the ones actually in charge of what is going on. Sherlock and I know they are. Their leader is a man named Thomas Clarke. He has quite a history; bomber, prisoner, naturalized American and willing to do anything for the "Cause". It's this inner secret society that Sherlock has tried to infiltrate.

"There is going to be a rebellion in Ireland, and soon! On St. Patrick's Day last, the entire volunteer organization held a parade, a huge affair, in which they passed in review of their leader, MacNeill. We believe it was a dress rehearsal for a rising."

"And the RIC didn't stop it?"

"The Royal Irish Constabulary has no authority in Dublin. The Dublin Metropolitan Police do and the DMP is an unarmed force. But I'll let Sherlock explain all this to you tomorrow. What you need to know is this. Three days ago, a shipment of arms left Germany for Ireland. So did Sir Roger Casement."

"Sir Roger?" I was startled. "But he's a friend of Doyle's. What was he doing in Germany?"

"Your editor's friend did great service in Peru and in Belgian Congo, for which he was knighted. But he is also an Irish Nationalist and he has been spending the last few months trying to raise an "Irish Brigade" from among the POW's in German camps, to come home and fight for Ireland instead of England. He has been singularly unsuccessful."

"I would think so. Soldiers who have fought together, stay together. They don't go off with the enemy."

"Yes, well, not even Birrell knows of the arms shipment or Casement's movements. He'll be told when he needs to know. We can't let the Germans know we can read their codes, and that means not telling anyone who doesn't have to know. You, Doctor, are going to have to travel to Dublin on tomorrow's boat train. You will carry nothing that might be used to identify you as John Watson."

"Alright, but I'll need....."

Mycroft held up his hand. "Already done. From here you will go to your hotel, your room is here." He handed me a key. "In the room you will find clothes. They're not new, but they are all American manufacture and should fit you well. In the jacket will be dollars, a few pounds and an American passport. Sewn into your waistcoat, behind the breast pocket, will be a letter from the Home Secretary giving your true identity. Do not lose it."

"And may I ask who and what I am to portray?"

"You are Dr Thomas Elmer Ryan of San Francisco and a member of the Irish-American Clan na Gael and a friend of John Devoy, the clan's head."

"But I know Ryan. The last time I saw him was in San Francisco 25 years ago."

"We know," he smiled. "The two years you spent in San Francisco means you know the city. If questioned, you don't have to memorize or lie, you can answer from experience."

"But where is Ryan?"

"Dead. Died on a trip to Argentina a few months ago. He hadn't been active in the Clan in years and Devoy is probably unaware of his death. Since Ryan was educated in Scotland and lived in America, you'd best use your best American idioms." Mycroft smiled. "Leave your kit in your room, we'll collect it. You'll find everything you need there, all American. Even a Colt automatic pistol and some ammunition."

"Anything else?"

"Altamont will meet you at the dock, Dr Ryan," said Mycroft, extending his flipper of a hand and rising. "Best of luck to you."

I rose and we shook hands. As I retraced my steps through the now busy strangers room, I paused to look at the map. In Ireland were four red pins for troops in country: Curragh, Dublin, Belfast and Athlone. Maybe four thousand soldiers in all. *There best not be a rising*, I thought as I left the Diogenes Club.

On leaving the Diogenes Club, I found the same soldier who had picked me up at the Victoria waiting for me. But now he was dressed as a taxi driver and holding open the door to his vehicle.

"A man of many talents, I see," I quipped.

He smiled and saluted. "I'll be picking you up in the morning, sir, at seven to take you to the boat train. Here's your ticket." He handed me an envelope. "I'm afraid I'm taking you to a second class hotel, but it's the one we use for these sorts of things."

"Don't worry about me, son. I'm happy with just a blanket."

Within fifteen minutes we were at the hotel. It was not all bad, catering to the traveling businessman. Entering the room, I found a well-used traveling bag on the bed. In it was the usual underclothing and toiletries one would expect. There was also a note.

"Push down on bottom of bag. Spring latch."

I turned the bag on its top and pushing down on the corners of the bag, heard a faint click. The bag's bottom came off and in a narrow space I found the promised pistol and three magazines of ammunition. There was also an American passport in my assumed name, along with hotel bills, a Cunard ticket from the week before and a letter addressed to me at the hotel, all in my new name. Mycroft surely thought of everything. I removed the papers but returned the pistol to its hiding place. It was a .32 Colt pocket pistol, light and easy to carry. On the bed was a good set of American-made clothes. Not new, obviously worn, but not shabby. The labels were from a haberdasher on Mott Street in San Francisco. I tried on my new clothes - they fit very well - and packed up my uniform, placing everything in a large box I found in the corner of the room. It was already labelled with my name. You couldn't doubt Mycroft's efficiency.

I contented myself that night with reading all the newspapers I could find, looking for any clues to the problems in Ireland. Most of the news, of course, was about the war. It seemed that no one was paying any attention to the Irish question.

Chapter 3

Friday

14 April 1916

True to his word, my young soldier showed up with his taxi at exactly seven in the morning. "Euston Station, sir?" he said in a loud voice.

"Exactly, buddy." I said in my best pseudo-American. The driver laughed and shook his head as he opened the door. Inside, I found Mycroft.

"I didn't expect to see you again, sir." I said, sitting next to him.

"Just need to pass on a little bit of information," he said as the motor car started from the curb. "Our latest intelligence tells us that the rising is to be on Holy Saturday, the twenty second. Now, they already have a three-day exercise planned starting on Easter, so it wouldn't take much to move up the timetable a day. Let Sherlock know, though he probably already does."

"Certainly. Any news on the arms?"

"No, all we know for sure is that the ship has left port. The navy is searching for it, and they'll find it," he said confidently.

As we drove up to Euston Station, Mycroft touched me on the arm. "This is a more serious situation than anyone in the government wants to admit. Be careful, Doctor. We're not as young as we once were."

I smiled back as I exited the taxi. I was touched by Mycroft's concern. "And not as old as you might think," I smiled. Taking my bag from the driver I walked to the platform.

To tell the truth, I actually got more sleep on the train than I had the night before in the hotel. While the bed was comfortable enough, my mind raced all night thinking of what-ifs. Now with the rocking of the train, I fell into a deep sleep and it was only the calling of the conductor that woke me at Holyhead.

I transferred to the RMS Leinster, the Dublin Holyhead mail boat. (The reader may remember this vessel was some two years later torpedoed in the Irish Sea with the loss of over 500, almost all soldiers.)

The trip to Dublin Port was quite a miserable affair. The seas were rough this time of year and everyone watched the ocean's surface for any sign of U-boats. The chances were, of course, very slim indeed. None the less, there was always a nagging suspicion.

It was only an hour before sunset when the ferry finally docked at Dublin Port and true to form, there was Holmes, cloth cap, celluloid collar and of all things, a moustache. Raising his hand from across the street he shouted, "Hey Doc, how are ya?" He was indeed, still affecting his American persona.

We clasped hands and Holmes relieved me of my bag, slapping me on the back. "Great to see you again. Come on with me." Stepping back to the kerb he hailed a cab. "Talbot Street," he told the cabby and settled back on the seat. "We'll talk when we get to the roomin' house, Doc, okay?"

"Certainly," I said, and had a hard time not laughing at my friend.

As we passed through the city, Holmes pointed out places of interest. From Sackville Street we turned right at Nelson's Pillar onto Earl Street and in a minute, we were at "Mrs McGuffey's" rooming house, which was a walk-up over a grocers.

Coming up the steps we were greeted by Martha Hudson. "Oh, Doctor!" she cried, "It's been so long. How are you? I'll have tea in a moment. You have the room next to Mr Altamont and the next I've kept empty for you and him to use as your sitting room." With that she gave me a hug and as she scurried away I could hear her chuckling, "Altamont, what a name, couldn't you use O'Brien or something?"

"Well, come in, Doctor, come in," said Holmes, passing on along the hall to the sitting room. Throwing my bag under the table, I looked about at the comfortable, if under-furnished, room with its south window, bookcase, sideboard, table and four chairs.

"Not the lap of luxury, but it will do." I said.

"Sit down, Doc."

I looked askance at Holmes. "Really, do you have to?"

"Ryan, it's best to be in character at all times. That way at a critical moment you are less likely to give yourself away."

"All right, buddy," I said, turning a chair around and straddling it. I folded my arms over the chair back and grinned. Holmes could not help but laugh.

"All right, Doctor. You win. In here, we are ourselves."

"Fine. Fine. Ah, Mrs McGuffey, the tea, how nice of you." Mrs Hudson deposited pot and cups and biscuits on the table.

"I do hope, Doctor, that you'll hurry Mr Altamont along now that you're here so we can all go home."

"Don't you like it here?" I asked.

"Oh, it's nice enough, sir, but it isn't home, is it?"

"I understand Mrs McGuffey. I surely do."

Once Mrs McGuffey (for so I shall call her from now on) had left and Holmes had poured our tea I could hold my tongue no longer.

"Tell me, Holmes. What are we supposed to be doing?"

"How much did Mycroft tell you," he asked.

"Not enough about what you're doing. He said you'd fill me in. His was basically a broad brush. He did tell me to tell you that they believe there is to be a rising on Holy Saturday."

"Hmmm, possible but I doubt it. Much more likely for Easter itself. What else?"

"Well, the Germans are sending a boatload of weapons, and Sir Roger Casement is supposedly on his way here from Germany. I can't believe he was trying to recruit our soldiers for rebellion."

"Yes, I know he convinced your friend Doyle to be for Home Rule but it's a big jump to treason." He pulled out his briar pipe and started packing it from a pouch. "The German ship is supposed to have 25,000 captured Russian rifles, ten machine guns and a million rounds of ammunition."

"My God, what horror that could do!"

"True, Watson. But I'm sure our Navy is up to the task of finding it." He took a long puff, "And sending it to the bottom."

We sat quietly for a moment. Finally I took out my pipe (the one thing I kept from my kit) and started to fill it, waiting for Holmes to continue.

"Casement's efforts were fairly futile. He only got about fifty men to volunteer and most of them aren't worth a tinker's damn. One IRB man, named Montieth, made his way to Germany, through America, to help him recruit. Seems to be the only competent help he has."

"Oh, IRB?" I asked.

"Yes, Irish Republican Brotherhood. It really is a secret society. They are the ones planning the rebellion."

“Holmes, I really wish you’d explain things. I thought the Volunteers were planning the rising.”

Holmes grinned and took another puff. “Watson, nothing in Ireland is simple but let me see if I can explain our position.

“First, my name of course, is Liam Altamont. I’m an American and employed in Dublin Castle as a telegrapher. That gives me easy access to Major Price, the intelligence chief and my prime contact. My other contact is Detective Sergeant Burns of the Dublin Metropolitan Police, but we’ll get back to them.

“Because I’m an Irish-American with a Nationalist bend and a job that gets me in and out of Dublin Castle, I’ve been approached by members of the Irish Volunteers to supply them with information. This I have done over the past year. I even helped them unload rifles at Howth and hid them around Dublin.”

“No, surely not.”

“Oh, it wouldn’t matter one way or the other, they were going to import arms and Birrell wouldn’t make waves about it. After all, the Unionists had them. Anyway, I’m well trusted in the Volunteers though I hold no actual post. By the way, you, Doctor, have been employed by the military hospital which is now in the Castle. Major Price has arranged everything. He is the only one besides myself who knows who you are. I will, of course, introduce you around as my friend from the States and as a friend of Devoy’s, our benefactor in the US. You haven’t seen him in years. “

Holmes poured out the last of the tea before continuing.

“To finish out about your contacts, if you need to get a message to Price or to Burns but can’t get to the Castle, give it to Mrs McGuffey. She’ll take it to a fishmonger down on the quays from where it will make its way.

“Price is a good, honest fellow. You’ll meet him tomorrow. As to Burns, I’ll say nothing. I would like your impression when you meet him. He is a member of the G-division. There are only about sixteen members of that force. Besides investigating major crimes they are the ones who keep an eye on the Nationalists. Most work out of Great Brunswick Street but Burns has an office at the College Street Station.”

“You mentioned a secret group called the IRB, Holmes. Just who are they?”

“Now you get down to the crux of the matter, Watson. For it’s the IRB that’s planning the rising. Had I come here as a returning Irishman, I might have been accepted into the Brotherhood, but as it is, as an American, I'm trusted only to a point.

"Within the ranks of the Irish Volunteers are members of the Brotherhood. The IRB is for violent overthrow of the government, where even now, most of the Volunteers see hope for a peaceful solution to Irish Independence. Even the leader of the Volunteers, MacNeill, doesn't know that senior members of the IRB are using his organization to ferment rebellion behind his back.

"I also know that James Connolly, while not IRB, is in on the plot. I'll take you to Liberty Hall later tonight and introduce you to the 'players' in our little act. It's quite a varied assortment."

"Why doesn't DMP just shut all this down?"

"Because DMP can't get close enough to what's going on. Every DMP man is known as well as their informants. Not that the DMP doesn't also know all the Volunteers, of course they do, but each side knows not to talk."

Holmes looked out the window into the early darkness. "What say we go ahead and go to Liberty Hall now, Watson? No time like the present and it's only a few blocks."

As we rose to leave, Mrs McGuffey came in to get the tea service. "Need a late supper, Mr Altamont?"

"No, Mrs McGuffey. The doctor and I are going for a walk and we'll find something to eat while we're out."

"Very good, sir," she replied. "And Doctor," she added, stopping at the door, "like old times, it is."

Putting on my new felt hat, I started walking with Holmes back toward the quays. I looked about at everything, trying to orient myself to the new city. Holmes looked over at me.

"It is fairly easy to get around in Dublin, Doctor. Just don't go into that rabbit warren north of the Four Courts[7]. Dangerous and easy to get lost in the alleys."

"I'll remember that," I said. As we came into Beresford Place, I stood back and looked at the building called Liberty Hall, the headquarters of the Irish Citizen Army and the labour union they were formed to protect. Across the front of the building was a large banner "We serve neither King nor

---

[7] Area of slums north of the Administrative and Judicial Courts Buildings.

Kaiser, but Ireland"

I turned to Holmes. "Well you can't say you don't know where they stand, can you?"

"No," he replied. "Hopefully, some of the people I want you to meet will be here. The Volunteer Headquarters is across the river on Dawson Street. But the real leaders, the IRB members meet here with Connolly, or at the tobacco shop of Thomas Clarke over on Great Britain Street. Clarke is the real power behind this whole affair, and the money comes from John Devoy, the American Clan Na Gael leader. Neither Devoy nor Clarke know we read all their messages to their German allies."

"How?"

"Devoy gives his messages to the German Embassy in New York and the Germans send coded messages through South America to Germany. What they don't know is that we have broken their code. I have travelled four times between here and New York carrying messages to Devoy and many back. I'm well trusted now. But not enough to get in the IRB inner circle."

I shook my head. "I've never heard of any of these people."

Holmes grinned at me. "You never heard of Moriarty either!"

"Touché," I laughed.

"Well, Watson, let us enter the lion's den."

As we walked to the front door of the building, I saw a soldierly figure beside it. In the dark, the uniform colour was indistinct but he wore a slouch hat pinned up on one side, like a Boer or Australian and carried an antiquated Mauser rifle. As we approached, he brought his weapon to port arms but then relaxed.

"Ah, it's you, Liam. And how are things at the Castle today?" he said, showing a big grin. "And who is this with you?"

"Sean, this is a friend of mine all the way from San Francisco, America. Came to work with me at the Castle," Holmes said and nudged the man with his elbow. "His name is Thomas Ryan and he's a medical doctor."

"Well, glad I am to meet you, sir," said the guard, extending his hand to shake mine. "Nothing much going on tonight, Liam." He turned toward Holmes. "Just some of the big wigs having another palaver."

"Well, I just want to introduce the doctor around. Thanks, Sean." Sean held open the door as we entered. Inside was a small foyer. "Er, Liam" I said, "is this place always under guard?"

“Yes, Thomas. They’re concerned about a raid by the government. But neither Birrell nor Nathan would precipitate such a move. They know there will be bloodshed and neither wants to be responsible.”

We entered the main meeting room as some men were leaving an office on the far side. They were joking and smiling and appeared to be in a good frame of mind. I heard one say, “Ah, it will all work well. Nothing can stop it now.” He stopped talking and turned toward us on seeing that his compatriots were looking at something. Seeing the two of us, he approached with a quick step and a smile. “Liam, how are you? No meeting tonight, what brings you out?”

“Mr Connelly,” replied Holmes. “may I introduce a friend of mine and Mr Devoy’s, Doctor Thomas Ryan from San Francisco?”

Connelly looked me up and down a moment, then extended his hand. “A friend of Devoy’s is a friend of ours.” I shook his extended hand and nodded. He was of medium build and with a large bushy moustache. Not more than in his late forties I would guess.

“And how was Devoy doing when you last saw him?”

Cold panic ran through my veins. I’d never seen the bloody Devoy! “Well, very well, the last I saw him, but I’m afraid that was three or four years ago.” My mind was racing, remembering my Cunard ticket, I continued. “I just came in from Argentina actually. Liam had wired me he was here and that good work was going on. I could afford to come, so I did.” I smiled and hoped no one noticed the sweat on my forehead.

“Well, you’re a medical doctor, are you?”

“Yes. I’ve actually taken a job at the military hospital at Dublin Castle. Liam said that would be helpful.”

Connolly smiled over his shoulder at his companions. “Oh, Doctor, how rude of me. Let me introduce Mr Padraig Pearse of the Irish Volunteers. Mr Thomas Clarke, Mr Michael Mallin, my Chief of Staff and Mr Joseph Plunkett. Gentlemen, Dr Thomas Ryan.” There was a general round of hellos and handshaking, then Connelly continued. “Tell me, Doctor, do you think America will come into the war on the side of England?”

“How do I know?” I thought. I tried to look concerned for a minute while I searched for an answer. “Well,” I finally said, “the Lusitania sinking last year drove most Americans to believing that Germany was indeed the aggressor in this conflict. But most Americans still view this as Europe’s problem. They don’t want it. If Germany doesn’t sink US Flag carriers, I think we'll leave England on her own!"

Connolly looked thoughtful for a moment then grinned at me and patted my shoulder. "Excellent, Doctor. Excellent. I'm afraid, Doctor, we're just on our way to another meeting. Please come back soon so we can talk. Liam, good night." With that they turned to go.

A great sigh of relief shook me as they all departed out the door through which we had entered. As the door closed behind them, Holmes slapped me on the back.

"Sterling job, old fellow. Believed you myself," he whispered. "Now, let's look about."

There was nothing to be seen of an extraordinary nature: assembly room, offices, that sort of thing, until we reached the cellar. Down on one side was a large, locked steel door. "The armoury and explosives," said Holmes. And in a small side room was an antiquated printing press that might have been new forty years ago.

"The government has shut Connolly's newspaper down twice now for sedition," responded Holmes to my silent question. "He uses what he can get."

On the table next to the printing press was a piece of paper. Holmes picked it up.

"The assembly order for the Volunteers for Easter. Assemble at half six in the evening. If only I knew for sure it was the coming rising."

"But Mycroft's information says the day before," I argued.

"Yes, well, they're playing it close to the vest. Shall we go get a bite, Ryan?" He threw the paper back on the table. "I know a wonderful little pub over near Kingsbridge Station. The walk will help you get the lay of the land."

We departed Liberty Hall, into the night. I could feel the fatigue of a long day and the tension of wondering what would come.

Chapter 4

Saturday

15 APR 1916

I was knocked up early the next morning. It was barely half six when Holmes came in my room. "Up with you, Thomas! Martha will have breakfast ready in a few minutes then we're off to Liberty Hall again before the Castle. I go on duty at eight."

By seven, we had eaten and were on our way to Beresford Place. Everything looked different in the daylight and the city bustled with the life of everyday people going about their business. The traffic was that strange combination of push carts, horse-drawn wagons and motor cars that defined the changes of the early part of the century. Liberty Hall was not in the best nor worst part of the city and the early morning sea smell coming from the quays along the Liffey River was brisk and somewhat pleasant. It was a beautiful Saturday morning.

Sean was gone from the night before but the new guard at the hall was just as happy to see Liam Altamont and meet his friend. Passing inside, we made our way back to the office we had seen Connolly and the others come out of the night before. Holmes stepped to the door and knocked. In a moment the door was answered by Mallin. "Ah, Liam. We were just talking about you. Good morning, Doctor. Would you mind if we spoke to Liam alone a moment?"

I smiled and nodded. "I'll just have a seat by the window bench," I said, and the door shut behind them. I looked around the walls and studied the numerous Nationalist posters that covered them. There were also a lot of trade union posters and a bulletin board full of guidance to the members of the ICA. It was no more than a few minutes before the door reopened and Holmes called to me. "Thomas, come in, will you?"

As I entered, Connolly got up from behind his desk and came around to shake my hand.

"We're glad to have your services, Doctor. Liam speaks highly of you. Seems you have some military experience."

I glanced at Holmes. "Yes, not much, some work with the US Army. First in the Modoc War and then in the Dakota's against the Sioux, but by the early 80's I was in San Francisco. That's where I spent most of my time."

Connolly returned to his desk and sat down, indicating for me to take a chair.

"All I can tell you right now, Doctor is that someday we may have need for you. In the meantime I would like you to give me your opinion of the training and status at the Castle once you've had a chance to settle into your duties there. Will you do that for us?"

"Certainly, whatever I can do for the cause."

"Excellent, Doctor. Now I know you have to get to your new duties, so I won't hold you up." He rose from the desk and coming around again, gripped my shoulder. "We are going tonight to a performance of a little play I have written and I'd be delighted if you'd come back tonight with Liam and see it. It will be in the assembly hall."

"Of course, Sir. I'd be honoured. Now I must be off for I'm due at the Castle."

Holmes and I departed the hall and were not far down the street when I thanked him. "I'm glad we spoke of Dr Ryan's biography last night. I remembered he had served but I hadn't remembered where."

"It's not so much in the detail as it is in the consistency, old fellow. I might have been excused for not remembering if it was Sioux or Apache or whatever, as long as it was Indian wars. After all, we only met twice before Chicago." Holmes smiled.

"I take it they brought you in to talk about me?"

"Yes, one more review to see if you were to be trusted. If we could only break into the inner circle, we'd know for sure about the rising."

As we came to the Castle gate we joined a small crowd of people coming to their daily work, a half day for many because it was Saturday. Everyone seemed to know Holmes as he was greeted cheerfully by everyone we passed. The constable waved us over.

"Liam, who might this be with you?"

"Constable Flood, this is Dr Ryan who will be working in the hospital. Come all the way from America to help us out."

"Ah, that's fine, fine. You take good care of our boys, Doctor."

"I assure you I will do my very best, Constable."

We moved on and in the main foyer Holmes told me to follow him through a number of hallways until we came to a small office merely marked with the number 6 on the door. He opened the door without knocking. Inside was a long table and six chairs, no windows, no pictures, nothing except a bare room. Holmes closed the door behind me and switched on the single overhead light, then pushed a buzzer next to the door.

"Have a seat, Thomas. They'll be with us in a few moments."

"They? Who are they?"

"Major Price of the Army and Detective Sergeant Burns of the DMP."

"I take it you don't care for Burns," I said. "It tells in your voice."

Holmes looked at me out of the corner of his eye. "If it's that telling, I must watch myself."

At that moment, the door opened and two men walked in. The one in uniform was obviously Major Price. The other was in civilian clothes, a fairly expensive, well-tailored suit by the looks of it. He was tall, thin, with brown hair and hazel eyes and wore a perpetual smile which reminded me of someone with *Ricus Sardonicus*.[8] I disliked the man on sight. He was not to be trusted. I looked at Holmes, who I suddenly noticed had been watching my face intently. He smiled and nodded.

"Dr Ryan," said Holmes. "Let me introduce you to Major Price and DS Burns."

We did the obligatory round of handshaking and sat at the table.

"Well, Liam." started the Major. "Anything new?"

"No, unfortunately. The inner circle has continued to meet on a regular basis but that causes its own problem. An increase or decrease in frequency would tell us something. As it is, it tells us nothing. I will say that whatever is going on, I'm convinced that MacNeill, the Volunteer commander, is being kept in the dark by the others. He and Bulmer Hobson are never called to those meetings."

Price turned to me. "And Doctor, what is to be your piece in this affair?"

"As I see it," I replied, "as a medical man, I may have access to people and events that others won't. Anything I find, I will report to, ah, Liam, as quickly as possible. I can also feed information to the Nationalists that you, shall we say, want them to know."

---

[8] An abnormal, sustained spasm of the facial muscles that appears to produce grinning.

"Good. I understand you're currently an Army doctor?"

"Yes, auxiliary hospital in Kent."

"Seen any action?"

"Before your time, Major," I laughed. "Second Afghan War and Second Boer War."

Price nodded and I smiled to myself. So I'd passed the "what are your credentials" check!

Major Price went on. "We still believe they are planning a rising for Holy Saturday, but we must have more information!" He pounded on the table. Realizing what he had done, he sat back and smiled. "The good news is that Sir Roger's efforts in Germany have been a completely failed. He has but a handful of men." Price went on to review much of what I already knew. In fact, it looked like I knew more than he did for he said nothing about an arms shipment. The whole time Burns appeared to be terribly disinterested. I put it down to the fact that he had heard it all before.

When Price had finished, I told him I hoped I could add to their intelligence data soon and in a concrete way since there was only a week before Holy Saturday.

"I still think this is a tempest in the tea pot," Burns said. They were his first words since we met. "MacNeill won't give up control of the Volunteers and he won't allow a rising. And if we move to take their weapons, he will go for all-out war. But only then."

"You're wrong, Sergeant." It was Holmes. "MacNeill doesn't know it, but he no longer controls the Volunteers, at least not in Dublin. He is going to be as surprised as you will be!"

Price and Burns looked intently at Holmes. "There is something else working," he continued. "I'm convinced that the inner circle is working on releasing a document that will enrage the Volunteers. I don't know the content yet, but it is meant to cause further discontent with the government." Holmes looked directly at Burns. "And you, sir, need to get better informants. Every one of your men is known to the Volunteers and the Brotherhood. The game is being played on both sides."

Burns and Holmes looked at each other with unblinking stare. Burns held his painted smile.

"Whatever is going on, Mr Altamont, it won't cause a rising. They've been turning out their seditious trash for years, to no point."

"This time you're wrong, Sergeant. It's going to be something well thought out and powerful enough to take the kettle to the boil."

Price looked from one man to the other. "Right then, well, we have to explore all avenues." He looked at his watch, one of the newer wrist-watches that had become so popular since the start of the war. "Altamont, you're late for shift. I'll have to write you up again." We laughed and rose. "Liam, you and the doctor leave first. DS Burns and I will wait a few minutes. Doctor," he extended his hand, "here's to a short and successful association."

As we left the room, Holmes pointed me down the hallway. "You're not to report for duty officially until Monday, Thomas. Why don't you spend the day getting to know the city and spend some time back at Liberty Hall. I suspect they'll have more questions for you. Don't forget what we agreed to last night."

"Liam," I started. "This Burns…"

"Later, Thomas. Later." And he was off in the other direction. I was left to find my way.

I first asked directions to the hospital, where I found a well-organized set of wards. I did not make myself known since I did not want to be drawn into a day of handshaking and introductions. That would wait. I decided to take the long way back to Liberty Hall and walk the area as Holmes had suggested. As I left the gate, I waved to Constable Flood, then took out the pocket map of Dublin that Mycroft had seen fit to provide me. It was still early in the day and a long walk would do me good and help clear my head.

On leaving the Castle, I went past the City Hall and proceeded across the Liffey on the Capel Street Bridge. Then I went along the quays and up to the Parkgate by the Royal Barracks, where I made a circle across the river to Kingsbridge Station and then to the Royal Hospital. Phoenix Park was just a short walk from there back across the river, so I walked up the main road through the park. From there I could see the military headquarters, and to the west, the ammunition magazine. A short bit on and on my right was the back of Vice Regal Lodge. I started back toward the main part of town. I was impressed by the vast number of barracks in Dublin, but the lack of men would mean that a large force of rebels could run amuck in the city with the soldiers having to defend so many locations. I sat for a bit on a bench in front of the Ross Hotel, not far from Kingsbridge Station and next to the Royal Barracks. Spreading my map on my knee, I started counting.

I counted at least nine barracks, then there was the Castle to protect, the Vice Regal Lodge, a half-dozen hospitals, seven major railroad stations and yards, the Customs House, and the Bank of Ireland; how in God's name could you protect everything? And if what Holmes had said was true and there were 4,000 volunteers, they outnumbered us. Our only advantage was in weapons.

Somewhat disheartened, I gathered up my map and decided to head for Talbot Street for a bit instead of Liberty Hall. I walked back down along the Liffey until I came to Sackville and walked north toward Earl Street.

As I passed the new General Post Office, I thought, what a beautiful building. It had only recently been renovated and the statues of Hibernia, Mercury and Fidelity stood watch from the top of it. Then I noticed something else - dozens of telephone and telegraph wires. I shook my head. This would have to be defended too. It was a centre of communications and somewhere, I knew, there would be the central lines of the National Telephone Company. It, too, would have to be held. It all seemed impossible.

As I walked east on Earl Street, I continued to ponder. There were troops in Curragh and Athlone but that meant trains. If the countryside rose and they dropped the bridges a half hour train trip might be a day or longer through a hostile countryside. I wondered just how much support these potential rebels had?

By now, I had returned to the rooming house and Mrs Hudson and I spent a pleasant two hours talking about old times in Baker Street. She assured me that Holmes had not decorated any of her current walls with bullet holes spelling out GR. On finishing lunch I walked a few minutes down to Liberty Hall, determined to stay but a moment and then continue my walk of the city.

As I walked to the front door, I saw that Sean was back on duty and he greeted me as "hail fellow, well met." We were already friends forever.

"Busy lot in there today, Doctor." He leaned forward in a conspiratorial mode. "Mr Connolly and the lot are getting ready for his play tonight. Been rehearsing all week, they have." He leaned back. "Won't be much else going on."

I thanked my new friend, smiled and entered. As I did, I could hear quite a commotion coming from the assembly hall. I entered the hall to a number of looks from people standing about. Others were moving some furniture at the far end of the hall, setting the scenery as it were. Mallin came up to me and shook my hand.

"Back already, Doctor?"

"Yes, I'm not truly due to report until Monday so I decided to walk the city and get my bearings."

"Fine idea. We've got a few boys that know every ally, passage and building. Kind of like those 'Baker Street Irregulars' that Sherlock Holmes fellow had."

Panic screamed in my ears. Was he on to us? Were Holmes and I being played or was this just an innocent comment?

"Doctor, are you all right?"

"Oh, fine. Fine. I was just thinking about something."

"Come on back to the office," he said, taking my arm. "So you've been to the Castle today? Well maybe you can help me." We entered the empty office and Mallin indicated a couple of empty chairs. "What, Doctor, do you think of the Castle? Pretty solid place, eh?"

I looked at him for a moment. "Mallin, if you're asking me how defensible it is, the answer is very. Solid walks, gates, constables and armed guards and a barrack of about 125 soldiers according to my estimate. There is, of course, the hospital as well. They have food, water and a guard room with a dozen armed soldiers at all times and a supply of ammunition. Is that the answer to your question?"

Mallin looked at me intently before he smiled. "You've a good head on your shoulders, Doctor. I guess you do have some military experience." He leaned back a bit and shrugged. "Of course, this is only for my own personal curiosity, you understand."

"Of course" I smiled and offered him a cigar from my pocket case.

"Well, you're a gentleman, Doctor. I'll say that for you."

We both rose and started out of the office as he was lighting the cigar. "Coming back tonight for the play I hope. Sean Connelly from the Abbot Theatre will be playing the lead role. It's James' first play. I think you'll enjoy it and it'll give me a chance to introduce you around."

I thanked him and assured him I wouldn't miss it for anything. I left, thinking to myself, *exactly what Holmes said would happen, and our rehearsal was much more interesting.*

Having walked the area between the Liffey and the Grand Canal, I returned to Talbot Street about an hour later to find Holmes already there and Mrs McGuffey putting out tea.

"Ryan, you're just in time. I thought you would be back shortly. How was your walk?"

"Enlightening, Holmes."

"Liam."

"Yes, Liam. At any rate, I'm ready for some tea."

"Good, you can fill me in on your thoughts." He commenced pouring the tea as I sat down and started telling him of my discoveries. When I had finished Holmes walked to the window and looked down on the streets.

"You're right, of course, my friend. If there is a full rising and they get their German machine guns, there will be thousands dead, and it will play well for the Germans, as we will have to take troops from France. The end won't be in doubt. Only the cost." He shook his head. "And what of your time at Liberty Hall?"

"I told Mallin exactly what we rehearsed last night. He believes the Castle will be costly to take but I don't believe he's deterred."

"Yes, I was afraid of that. Pity there are only about two dozen soldiers in the whole place." He went back to looking out the window.

"Tell me about Burns," I said.

Holmes turned back from the curtain. "You first, Watson. What can you tell me about him?"

"It's Thomas," I smirked. "Well he makes my skin crawl. You can't trust anyone with such a make-believe smile."

Holmes laughed. "Anything else?"

"Well, he's Protestant, a Unionist and either has a source of income outside his DMP salary or has influential friends."

"Excellent my friend, and how do you know?"

"He had a signet ring with the Freemason crest. I'd recognize it anywhere, as you know, from my army days. Since Catholics or Jews can't join the Masons, he's not either. The suit he wore is well beyond what someone on his pay could afford, so he has separate income or well-placed friends."

"And Unionist?"

"In my travels south of the Liffey this afternoon, I saw him enter the Kildare Street Club, which I'm told is a Unionist stronghold. 'Nationalists need not apply.' At least that's what the tobacconist told me."

"Thomas, you never cease to amaze me! Correct on all counts. It may interest you to know that while the DMP and the RIC have plenty of Catholic constables, the hierarchy is almost exclusively Protestant Unionist. There are one or two exceptions of course. In fact the G-Division men must take an oath to join no secret society except the Freemasons. Their job depends on it. Does that tell you where their loyalties must lie? As you said, 'No Nationalist need apply'."

"I just don't trust that man, Holmes. There's something in the way he looks and carries himself."

"Your intuition does you credit, Thomas, but what is your reasoning?" I shrugged. "You really must learn to think these things out," he continued. "At any rate, I have to agree with you. He has discarded all my warnings and fails to follow up on information which I have been able to supply. He is playing his own game. But as of yet I haven't been able to determine what that game is. I appreciate your confirmation of my ideas."

Holmes filled his pipe and sat across the table. "I have not yet found his source of income but you may like to know that his house would be well beyond the means of most DMP Officers, even sergeants." He fell silent while he drew on his pipe.

My thoughts were racing. Why was the one man most responsible in the police force for listening to us, not doing so? Was he actually a Volunteer and we did not know it? Did he want the rising to occur because he hated the Volunteers and wanted them crushed by violence? Was there a third reason I could not fathom? My thoughts were broken by my friend's voice.

"Come, Thomas. We don't want to be late for the world premiere of Mr Connolly's play. He would never forgive us!" Holmes was standing at the door grinning back at me. Grabbing my felt, I was out the door and down the stairs right behind him.

When we arrived back at Liberty Hall it was not yet dark but the building was lighted like a great party was about to take place. People of all classes were gathered about, many in uniform of the ICA. Once again, Liam was well met by everyone. The only other time I had seen my friend display this kind of affability was years ago during the affair of Charles Augustus Milverton. At that time he was attempting to ingratiate himself with one of the parlour maids while in the disguise of a plumber. And that was what, more than 20 years ago?

"Stay by me Thomas, and I'll try to point out some of the key players in 'our drama'."

"Of course, Liam."

Holmes proceeded to point out one important person after another. To this day, I cannot remember all that were there. There were, of course, the men we had met the day before: Mallin, Pearse, Clarke and Plunkett. Holmes pointed to a far corner.

"There's DeValera, the tall one. He's legally an American, but hasn't lived there since the age of two. He's a battalion commander in the Volunteers but has not made it to their inner circle either. He's talking with Willie Pearse, that's Padraig's brother. Willie is a good man but is easily led."

Holmes went on naming names that meant nothing to me. I finally determined to try and remember faces so I'd at least know which side people were on.

As lights flicked on and off to tell all to take their seats, I noticed a very striking woman up toward the front of the assembly hall.

"Who's that?" I asked.

"Ah, Thomas, leave it to you to always ask about the women!" Holmes smiled out of the side of his mouth. "She's one you need to know. I'll introduce you later." We took our seats for the first scene of the one act play, "Under Which Flag", by James Connolly.

The play was a rather short affair, only three scenes. I will say that Sean Connolly put in an excellent performance as Dan McMahon (a little too alliterative to me). McMahon was a survivor of '48 and stirring up patriotic support for the rising of '67. It wasn't bad but it obviously was meant to raise Irish Nationalist ardour for another rising. The impassioned performance told me exactly where the ICA stood and where it was going.

The play ended with Sean Connolly holding up a green flag and saying something like, "Under this flag only will I serve. Under this flag, if need be, I will die." And the play ended. The crowd rose to their feet and Sean was called back for three curtain calls. Author James Connolly, came forward and held up his hands for quiet. He raised his right hand in the air and looked out over the crowd. "The next act of the play," he said, "will be written by all of us together."

The crowd erupted with cheers. I applauded heartily with the rest and turned to Holmes. "Is he saying what I think?"

"Exactly, Thomas."

As the crowd started to disperse, Holmes brought me forward to meet the woman I had pointed out to him earlier. Spying us approaching she held her hand out to Holmes.

"Altamont, old boy. Good to see you. And who is this gentleman with you? A supporter of the arts?"

"Countess Markievicz, may I present Dr Thomas Ryan, who has come to join the cause."

The countess was a tall woman, thin and while not beautiful, what is called, handsome. She was striking in energy and enthusiasm.

"I am delighted to meet you, Countess."

"I admit I've already heard about you, Doctor. Word gets around quickly here. But if you will excuse me, I must go talk to James. His play was so wonderful, don't you think?"

"Indeed, Madam."

The countess turned to go then evidently thinking of something, turned back to me. Putting a hand on my arm, she said "We may have great need of you, old boy," and walked away.

Holmes and I looked at each other as she disappeared in the crowd. Holmes motioned me to silence and I followed him out to the street.

"I believe it's time for a walk and a pint, Thomas."

"Yes, Liam, I think so."

It was during our walk that Holmes explained the countess' extraordinary position, having founded the Nationalist Boy Scout movement, Fianna Eireann, along with Bulmer Hobson and being an officer in the ICA.

"What? You mean to fight?"

"Yes, Thomas. A great number of women have armed themselves. The Cumann na mBan is the women's organization associated with the Volunteers. They, too, don't just act as secretaries or nurses but many arm themselves as well."

"Amazing," I replied.

"Quite, but we'll talk more about MacNeill, Hobson, and the others I pointed out after our supper."

Chapter 5

Sunday

16 APR 1916

It was a bright, if chilly, Sunday morning. I had been used to rising early at the hospital in Kent and so even without Holmes' knock on the door, I was already up and dressed at seven.

I met Holmes in the sitting room awaiting Mrs McGuffey's fine breakfast and reading the *Irish Times*.

"Ah, Thomas, good. There is not much we can do today. It is my day off and I have a few people I want to visit in the countryside. I'll be taking the train to Cork and won't be back until late. Coffee?"

"No, Liam, I don't think so. You know I'm not a religious type. I haven't been to Mass since I was 14 but for some reason I think I'll go today. St. Mary's has an 8 o'clock Mass."

Holmes looked at me quizzically. "Ah, yes, can't go eat or drink from midnight to go to communion. Well enjoy your walk. It certainly won't hurt your persona with Pearse and crew to be seen there. But, Watson," he said as I reached for my felt, "don't be going rebel on me."

"Ah, Holmes, I assure you that is not a worry."

It was a short walk to St. Mary's and I had plenty of time, so I diverted first down toward the Custom's house and then along the quays. Dublin was indeed, a beautiful city.

I will admit I felt a little awkward at Mass. It had been fully fifty years since I'd attended church. There was one Mass in a tent in South Africa during the Boer War, but it had been interrupted by some serious shelling.

Like most people, I sat toward the rear of the church. I actually found it somehow comforting that so little had changed in the conduct of the Mass and how well I remembered the Latin responses that had been drilled into me as a child.

When Mass was over, I found myself just outside the railings of St Mary's trying to decide how to best occupy my time.

"You're Doctor Ryan, aren't you?" It was one of the many men I had been introduced to the night before.

"Yes, I am and you are… I'm afraid I met so many people last night I didn't get everyone's name. I'm sorry."

"Pearse, Willie Pearse."

"Yes, of course and your brother is Padraig, is he not?"

"Exactly, everybody remembers Padraig."

"Well I just remember there were two brothers, Willie and Padraig."

"Are you after some breakfast now?" he asked.

"Yes, I was thinking the Gresham Hotel. I'm told they serve a marvellous table. Would you be my guest?"

"I'd be delighted," said Willie. "Let me get my bicycle and I'll walk with you."

"Live a long way from here?"

He pulled his bicycle off the railing. "Yes, a bit of a distance. I'm really not in this parish but I like the pro-cathedral. Especially Father O'Flanagan. So I come here for mass once in a while."

"What do you mean, pro-cathedral?"

"It means provisional cathedral. When the English took St. Patrick's from the Catholics and gave it to the Church of Ireland, the pope never gave up claim to it. When the Irish were once again given the right to have churches, the bishop needed a cathedral but since the government wouldn't give back St. Patrick's, St. Mary's was made the provisional cathedral. The same problem exists for churches all over Ireland."

"How interesting, I had never thought about that. But here we are. Please be my guest. Perhaps you can tell me more about the other sights in the city." Or perhaps, I thought to myself, you can tell me what I really want to know.

We had a delightful breakfast and I found my new friend to be a truly excellent and refined young man. He was kindness itself and he insisted on leaving his bicycle at Liberty Hall and escorting me about the city. We walked mostly to the north of the Liffey up to the Royal Canal and back before collecting his bicycle and having a late lunch back across the river and south to Trinity College.

I especially found interesting Willie's explanation of the importance of the General Post Office. It seems that Sackville Road and the area to the front of the GPO was a common area for speakers and demonstrators, a traditional site of assembly.

Down at Trinity College we were able to enter the library and look about.

"Did you go to school here, Willie?"

"Oh, no, Catholics can't go here. Neither Catholics nor Jews. It's legal now, but it's understood we're not wanted."

I put that in the back of my mind. Another case of separation. No wonder we had problems. It was near four o'clock when we parted and I thanked Willie profusely for his kindness. We shook hands and I watched him ride off down past Trinity and I turned to re-cross the river.

I supped alone that night then decided to visit our favoured pub. It was a fountain of information for those who wished to listen. I was given a pint of Guinness without having to ask and stood near the end of the bar.

The talk around me was general - the war, a job open at the brewery, cost of or lack of petrol, but here and there in corners sat men I had seen at Liberty Hall. They were deep in conversation.

It was close to nine and I was about to leave when Holmes walked in. "Thomas, will you share a pint?" We took our glasses and went to a table near the windows. The place had thinned out considerably and we talked quietly.

"Interesting trip?" I asked.

Holmes looked at his glass. "Yes and no. I went to Cork to see what I could find out. If there is to be a rising, none of the rank and file know anything. And their battalion commander gives the impression of one who suspects something but isn't sure. I tell you, Thomas, they've kept the date well hidden. Everything tells me Easter Sunday night, which goes against our intercept information of Holy Saturday. It's absolutely frustrating."

We sat for some time while Holmes smoked his pipe and I another cigar. Finally, he rose. "Well, Thomas, tomorrow is another day. Shall we be off?"

As we walked back to Mrs McGuffey's, I related all I had done for the day. I now felt I knew the main roads and thoroughfares and the principle buildings.

"Holmes, if they put 4,000 armed men in the field, they can overwhelm each outpost one at a time and take the whole city. That is, if the countryside rises too."

"Yes, Watson, I know. But Nathan won't move without more proof. So we must get it for him. Tonight however, a good rest. You, my friend, start work at the Castle tomorrow and must report early."

Chapter 6

Monday

17 April 1916

Holmes and I walked to Dublin Castle that Monday morning so as to arrive in good time. His parting advice to me as we went our separate ways at the gate was to concentrate on my duties, but to keep my ears open. Information could come from anywhere.

The hospital was actually in very pleasant surroundings. State apartments at the Castle had been taken over by the Red Cross and supplemented the city and government hospitals in the case of wounded coming home from the continent.

As a Red Cross hospital, much of the funding came from subscriptions. In fact, where regular hospitals received 4 shillings a day for each bed occupied, our hospital received only 3 shillings even though the actual cost was 3 shillings 11 pence.

But the hospital was well equipped to care for 250 men at a time. Another 50 could be taken care of in open air verandas. As it was, on the day I reported there were 182 beds occupied. Most of the wounded were those who might, with good care, return to duty in a few months. Some I knew would never return to duty but would have to be issued their silver badge. A few, I could tell, would have to go to a facility like the one I had just come from.

All the doctors and nurses were Red Cross volunteers and so, while paid, received far less than their services were worth. They worked for the good of the soldiers.

For my first day, we started with a tour of the "wards" and a discussion of our capabilities. I was very pleased with what I found, to include radiographs and a well-equipped surgery. I was assigned a case load by the senior surgeon and before I knew it, six o'clock had come. The doctors took turns spending the night on-call at the hospital but it was decided I would work a week before being assigned to the duty roster.

The one advantage to this hospital was that there was no daily intake. The bad thing was that patients came in boat-loads. About once a month the hospital ship, Oxfordshire, would appear in Dublin harbour with 900 or more men in need of help. From Dublin Harbour, the Irish Automobile Club Ambulance Service, R.A.M.C. and St. John's Ambulance Brigade would distribute the men throughout the city hospitals or take them to special trains to Belfast. Knowing that Holmes was by now off duty, I started for the gate when I was tapped on the shoulder. It was Holmes. He said nothing but walked past me and headed for Room 6. This time, when we entered the room, it was filled with people.

Mr Nathan looked up from his place at the head of the table, nodded and indicated two empty chairs.

"Gentlemen," said Nathan. "Let me introduce Mr Altamont, and I assume, this is Dr Ryan, both of Special Branch. I believe, Mr Altamont, you know everyone. Doctor, you know the Major and DS Burns. This is Mr Edgeworth-Johnstone, head of the DMP and Sir Neville Chamberlain, head of the RIC. We have much to discuss, so we best get about it."

I drew in a little as I sat. Surely Chamberlain wouldn't recognize me. We had spent three days next to each other in hospital after the siege of Kandahar, but that was some 35 years ago. He looked at me, then at Holmes as we took our seats. There was no spark of recognition.

"Major Price, if you will start."

"Of course, sir. There has been no significant change to our current situation. The Volunteers continue to make noise, interfere with recruiting and give speeches. Their parade on St. Patrick's Day gave us a chance to count men and weapons. It appears that they have over 13,000 men at this point but if you discount shotguns, they've probably got no more than 3,000 serviceable rifles of various types. The rumours continue about a rising in conjunction with the manoeuvres on Easter weekend but we have been unable to confirm this."

"Thank you," said Nathan. "I have a letter to share with you gentlemen. It comes to us from our Army commander in the south. He contends that the Navy has told him that they expect a landing of weapons by the Germans on our South West Coast and that they believe there is a rising planned for Holy Saturday. The Navy also says that Sir Roger Casement is on his way to lead the rising. What the Navy won't do is tell us how they know all this. Comments, Gentlemen?"

Everyone looked around the table. Holmes caught my eye and shook his head as if to say, "say nothing".

"Mr Edgeworth-Johnstone," continued Nathan, "Comments?"

The head of the DMP looked at the table for a moment and then at Burns. "As you know, Undersecretary, we have numerous avenues of information. None of these avenues have brought us an iota of viable information that would lead me to believe that a revolt is imminent. Why it would be preposterous," he blustered. "No rising by a few rebels could ever succeed and MacNeill knows that. He won't let it happen."

Nathan nodded. He turned to Chamberlain. "And the RIC's position?"

"Like the DMP," he said, nodding across the table. "We have numerous informants throughout the island. The Volunteers have been good at marching about. But a rising? Surely not. Though," he continued, a little uncomfortably, "I would like to know where the Navy is getting it's information."

"Mr Burns, would you like to contribute?" asked Nathan.

"As you all know, the Volunteers are riddled with our informers, all men whom I trust and are well placed. There has been no unusual activity either at Dawson Street or at Liberty Hall for the last month. I'll admit we have not been able to penetrate the IRB meetings at Clark's Tobacco shop but neither have our colleagues from Special Branch. Or have you, Mr Altamont?"

Everyone turned to look at Holmes.

"No sir, I have not. But let me assure you of this," Holmes leaned forward over the table. "I have been at Liberty Hall for the last two hours. The men who intend to lead this rising have been there also, sequestered in Connolly's office. Their mood is one of excitement. They have been working on the wording of some documents. One, I believe, they will release fairly soon. The other, I believe to be a Declaration of Independence, to be read at the start of the uprising. These men won't be stopped by MacNeill or anyone else. It will start this weekend and you need to confine all the King's forces to barracks to be ready to deal with the rising when it comes." Holmes leaned back in his chair, his right hand drumming on the table. Everyone was silent.

Burns was the first to speak. "Gentlemen, I completely and wholeheartedly disagree with Mr Altamont. If there were going to be a rising, I would know of it!"

"Forgive me, sir," said Nathan, looking at Burns. "This is not rivalry or pride speaking? You are convinced?"

"Yes, sir. I raise my right hand, and as God is my witness, there will be no rising."

"Well," continued Nathan, "Mr Altamont, I appreciate your input. But for now I must defer to the DMP. Major see if you can find out where the Navy is getting their information. I think that will be all for now. We'll meet again when we have more information."

With that, we dispersed. Holmes held me back in a corner of the hallway for a moment. By now it was almost half seven and dark outside.

"Should we get something to eat?" I asked.

"No, Thomas, I have a belief our friend Burns somehow intends to profit from this rising. I don't know how yet, but I will. We're going to follow him. I want to know more about him."

We stayed a good block back from our prey and followed as he crossed the river and headed for the Brunswick Street Police Station. As we trailed along, I mentioned to Holmes that I had known Chamberlain in Afghanistan.

"He gave no sign of recognition."

"No, Liam. It's been too long ago. He might remember the name Dr Watson, but I'm sure he didn't recognize me."

"He's the man who brought you and Thurston together, wasn't he?"

"What?"

"Invented the game snooker, didn't he?"

I had to admit he had and Thurston and I had spent many hours playing it at the club.

We had taken up a position in a doorway down the street where we could watch the entrance to the police station. We didn't have to watch long as in about fifteen minutes, he came out and headed east. Soon we were re-crossing the river and headed down near Trinity College and on to St. Stephen's Green. South of the green he came up to a group of six men standing near an alleyway. They all nodded as Burns approached and followed him down the alley. As they disappeared, we hurried to the top of the alley just in time to see the last one go through a red painted door, in what appeared to be a small warehouse.

"What now?" I asked Holmes.

"Now, we get your supper, Thomas. I've seen exactly what I want."

"And that was?"

"Later, Thomas. Later."

"Holmes, you are insufferable!"

He merely smiled and headed north up the street. "Were you able to overhear any more at Liberty Hall than you told Nathan?"

Holmes looked frustrated. "It's as I told them. They are preparing a declaration of independence. I distinctly heard Connolly demanding the inclusion of the equality of women in the document."

"Could it be just some general statement?"

"No, I assure you, it's more." He was quiet for a moment as we walked along. "I also heard Plunkett call Pearse, Mr President. Watson, they are forming a government and if the fools in Dublin Castle won't act, then they will be responsible for the coming bloodshed."

We continued a bit in silence.

"What of those men with Burns?" I finally asked.

"All in good time, Thomas. All in good time."

Chapter 7

Tuesday

18 April 1916

Tuesday was to be another disappointing day. Early once again, Holmes and I went to Liberty Hall but finding no one save the guard we walked down to Volunteer Headquarters. There Padraig Pearse was already in attendance and welcomed us warmly. Sean Fitzgibbon and a few others were about and Pearse was writing at his back desk when we arrived.

"Good morning, Liam, Doctor," he called from the chair. Getting up he handed two notes to Fitzgibbon. "You'll have to hurry Sean if you're to make the train."

Fitzgibbon seemed uncomfortable, fidgeted for a moment, looked up at Holmes and me and departed.

"What brings you gentlemen out so early?"

"Just checkin' to see what needs doin' Mr Pearse." It was Holmes's tolerable accent.

"I've never really thanked you properly, Liam, for all you've done. Your trips back and forth across the Atlantic to Mr Devoy have been a great help. Someday you'll know how much." He started walking back to his desk. "But right now I don't have anything of consequence going on."

"C'mon Mr Pearse, somethin' is goin' on. Everybody runnin' around like they are!? And all that hustle at the Castle? Somethin's up."

"No, Liam. Just the usual scurry when we're getting ready for manoeuvres. But what's happening at the Castle?"

"They've got the wind up over somthin'. DMP, RIC, Military Intelligence seems to be meeting quite a bit. Don't know why."

"Liam, it's important that you try to find out what you can. You know there is a real danger that they may come for our weapons. If so, I need warning of it."

As we were leaving the room, Pearse reiterated, "Remember Liam, anything you hear might be useful."

We hustled out onto Dawson Street and made straight away for the Castle, reaching there barely in time to start shift.

I was once again completely occupied for the day, not even breaking to eat but a mouthful at lunch.

It was after six when I made my way back to Mrs McGuffey's. There I found Holmes in the sitting room staring out the windows. The room was filled with smoke. It was suffocating.

"Holmes, do open a window," I gasped.

"Ah, Thomas, yes, go ahead if you wish." He left the window and sat at the table while I threw up the sash.

Holmes was in the midst of re-charging his pipe when I sat down.

"Your patients are doing well, I trust?"

"Yes, quite a fine group of men. I've referred a couple for special treatment, hysteric cases, but for the most part, they're doing well." I got some water from a carafe that was kept on the side table. "And you, Holmes? Is this a three-pipe problem?"

Holmes smiled and tossed a match on the table. "Thomas, I had another round with our know-nothing friends today. Lord Wimbourne, the Lord Lieutenant, is back from England. He called a meeting at the Viceregal Lodge with Nathan and Chamberlain. They went over the information from the Navy. Weapons are on the way and there is to be a rising on Holy Saturday. But since the information is second hand and not straight from the War Department, they refuse to listen. They then called in Burns who said, "If there were to be a rising, I would know" again! Even Major Price recommended waiting. Watson, they could end all this with a midnight roundup of a dozen men. Instead, we must get them more proof."

"Holmes, you can't expect them to just take your word for it."

"I suppose not," said Holmes and retired into one of his blue funks. I waited for a few moments.

"Liam, I'm famished. Shall we get something to eat?"

"Yes, well, we might as well. Usual place I suppose." He tapped his pipe out on the table, grabbed his cap and we went down the stairs to the street. As we came out on the darkening sidewalk, Holmes suddenly grabbed my arm and pulled me back into the doorway.

"What?" I started.

"Hush! Look, over there, on the other side of the street. The man walking west in the felt."

"Why, it's one of the men Burns met last night. You couldn't miss that hat."

"Let's follow him, Watson."

So we did, down Earl to Sackville, across the bridge to College Street Police Station, where he entered. We waited a bit down the street.

"Hol…. Liam, do you know who that man is?"

"Yes, Thomas. His name is Dowdle. He's one of Burns' informants. More than that, he's a cracksman[9] with an extensive history. He's been fairly active of late, but for some reason, all the cases against him fall apart. I'm sure you can guess why."

"Too valuable to Burns as an informant," I responded.

"That, too," said Holmes.

I was about to ask what he meant when Dowdle came out of the station.

"Thomas, I think we're going to a different pub tonight. The same one as Mr Dowdle." With that, we were back off in pursuit.

Dowdle led us to a small pub in the Temple Bar district. We let him precede us by a good five minutes, then entered. Dowdle was seated at a table on the far side of the room with two other men. They didn't look up as we entered but leaned in together over the table, intent in conversation. Holmes and I sat near the door and ordered food and a pint.

The drinks came and we sat in silence, sipping the brown stout. I found I was actually acquiring a taste for the stuff. Our food came and still Dowdle and his two companions were in close conversation. I had just started to eat when two more men came through the door to meet with Dowdle. The five men crowded around to the point where their heads must have been touching. They whispered to each other. I couldn't help but think of a comic scene in a bad play.

"Liam," I mimicked our friends in the corner, leaning close to Holmes. "Those are all the same men from last night, aren't they?"

"Yes. Only one missing, plus Burns."

"Do you know any of the rest besides Dowdle?"

"I do. The first two men who were with Dowdle are petty crooks

---

[9] Safe cracker.

named Murdock and Simple. I believe the other two are called Johnny Pepper and Phil Conarchy, both of whom are in the ranks of the Volunteers but hold no real position. And both are suspected of a number of burglaries in Rathmine. Actually, I gave Burns all the proof required to arrest Pepper of three separate burglaries."

As we ordered another pint, the men at the table started to leave - first Murdock and Simple, then a few minutes later, Pepper and Conarchy. Dowdle sat back in his chair. He was sitting so that he was looking toward the bar and having been lost in conversation until now, had not looked around to notice us.

As the door opened again, a man of middle height with a cloth cap and overcoat came in. Holmes leaned over and whispered, "Harry Malcolm. A competitor of Dowdle's."

Spying Dowdle, Malcolm went straight to his table where he was greeted as a long, lost friend.

"Not a competitor now," I smiled.

"Yes, Thomas, our sixth man. I now know what is going on. Or at least I believe I do. I think it's time we left It's almost last order and you have an early morning."

We paid for our food and stout and left the two conspirators sitting at their table.

Holmes walked silently for a while and when I could no longer stand it, I blurted out, "Well, what are they going to do?"

"I don't really have enough proof, Thomas," he smiled. "And you know how I love dramatic endings. But put your mind to it. Surely you will come up with the answer. If not, I will explain in good time."

He fell back into silence. The most logical thing I could think of as we approached Talbot Street, was that Burns intended to use these thieves cum Volunteers, to somehow hurt the organization from within, or discredit it to the point where they could gain no popular support.

We had reached Mrs McGuffey's and I was opening the door when I heard Holmes call out in a loud voice, "Good Night, Mr Dowdle." I looked at Holmes then in the direction he gazed. A hundred yards back stood Dowdle under a street lamp. He approached until he was but a few inches from Holmes.

"I know who and what you are, Altamont! You try to interfere with me and I'll expose you to all."

“Please do so. It will make my task all the easier.” They stared at each other. Dowdle was the first to flinch.

“Remember what I said,” Dowdle finally murmured, stepping back.

“Your plan counts on me continuing to be unknown. You’ll say nothing. Remind your boss at the DMP. Got it, mister?”

Dowdle’s fists doubled up and for a moment I thought he would strike Holmes. Silently he turned and walked away. We watched until he turned the corner.

“Holmes, what is going on?”

“Not yet, Watson, not yet.” And he went up the stairs.

Chapter 8

Wednesday

19 April 1916

It was now becoming difficult to be both a doctor at the Red Cross hospital and a spy. I felt the next two days things would move swiftly, and I was correct. Holmes left about half seven for the Castle and asked me to go by Liberty Hall for an hour. I had re-arranged my rounds so that I was not due in until ten and would work until six.

When I arrived at the Hall, Connelly was speaking to one of the ICA members, a man by the name of Robert Cacy. I knew Cacy was a trusted ICA man who had been there during the troubles of '13. He was known for both his loyalty and his love of poteen[10]. It was the second issue which kept him from rising higher in the organization. They broke up as I approached and Connolly wished me good morning.

Cacy was more voluble and asked if I'd care for a walk with him. He held a large folder full of papers and was off to deliver them. I accepted his offer thinking "here is a man that is always about, perhaps he has picked up some information he would unwittingly share".

"Surely," I replied after a moment's hesitation. "Where are we off to?"

"I'm to deliver this package to Mr MacNeill and wait to see if he has a response. I'm glad of someone to walk with. They're constantly sending me here and there and never a bit of company."

As we walked I tried to lead the conversation to the upcoming manoeuvres and the ICA's role in them with the Volunteers. My companion, it seemed though, was a dearth of information. If there was something to be known about hurling matches or the GAA, he was your man. But as far as the inner workings of the organization he belonged to, all he wanted to know was that Jim Larkin or James Connolly wanted something done, so he did it. It wasn't that he was unintelligent. He had thought things through, made a decision to follow these two, and he stuck to it. I had to admire him in a way.

When we arrived at MacNeill's it was he who answered the door and asked us in. Cacy presented him with the package and waited dutifully.

"Doctor," said MacNeill, tossing the package on the table, "would

---

[10] Alcohol usually made illicitly in small quantities from potatoes.

you and Mr Cacy care for some coffee?"

Cacy spoke up first. "Aye, Sir. But Mr Connolly says Mr Clarke wants you to read that straight away and I'm to bring back any response, so I am."

MacNeill smiled and picked up the package to unwrap it. "Coffee is on the sideboard, gentlemen. Please help yourselves." He sat at the table taking out papers. As Cacy and I took cups, he started reading and I could see he was becoming greatly agitated. He looked at me with a puzzled face. "Doctor, do you know what's in this?"

"No, Sir. I do not."

"Please, come here and read this. I want your opinion."

Putting down my cup, I took the top few papers from his hand. As I did, he started unfolding a map. I read the top paper with utter disbelief. How could this be? A document from the Castle proposing the arrest of all the Nationalist leaders and the possible execution of MacNeill himself! I read on. The document was a copy of an order from a secret file in Dublin Castle. The document was what I would have called a "warning order," i.e.: get ready but don't act until told to do so. It was to be carried out once signed by Sir Matthew and General Friend.

At first I thought the whole thing incredible: The DMP to be confined to barracks, the Army to take up patrols and stand pickets in the street, the Catholic Archbishop's house to be surrounded, whole groups to be arrested and houses and locations to be searched for arms. None of this seemed like Nathan.

But then I began to think. If I were the Army and in this same situation, would I not have such a plan? Wouldn't prudence demand such a plan? Not only dealing with the Nationalists, I'd also have one to deal with the Unionists. It seemed quite reasonable. MacNeill's voice brought me back to the moment. "Well, Doctor, your opinion?"

"I suppose this document could be real," I started. My mind was racing. How to play this? "But of course it purports to be a copy of a document. How close is it to the original, I wonder? And another question, is it for imminent use or a planning exercise?"

"Both good questions, Doctor. This makes no sense. They would be asking for blood to run in the streets. Surely General Friend doesn't mean to arrest leaders, confiscate only Volunteer arms, raid Liberty Hall and Fr. Matthew Park!"

“General Friend isn’t even in the country, Mr MacNeill.”

“What does it all mean? Mr Cacy, would you inform Mr Pearse I desire a meeting of the executive council at five o’clock? Tell him it is imperative that all are here.” MacNeill looked tired and indecisive. “Doctor, we’ve had rumours about these plans for a few weeks but I didn’t know they were so complete. I’d appreciate it if you would return tonight also. A third opinion may be useful.” He smiled as if to himself and Cacy and I left him sitting in his chair, shaking his head. Cacy went to find Pearse and I hastened to the hospital.

On arriving at the Castle, I sent an orderly to the telegraph office with a note asking Holmes to meet me as soon as possible. The orderly had no more than returned when I was asked to attend an accident patient in Room 6. Knowing what it must be, I discouraged taking any help and left the wards to meet with Holmes.

When I entered Room 6, I also found Major Price who appeared in a most serious mood. “Thomas,” said Holmes, “is this about the Castle document?”

“Oh, you already know,” I replied, disappointed. It seemed I could never get one up on Holmes.

“We’ve heard about it but not seen it yet. I understood Alderman Tom Kelly, of the Dublin Corporation, is even now reading a copy to the corporation and demanding answers. What do you know?”

I proceeded to tell Holmes and Price everything I knew about the document and about my discussion with MacNeill. I ended by asking Price if the document was real.

“From what you tell me, Doctor, I can say the document is a forgery.”

Holmes looked him directly in the eye. “But most of it is accurate, is it not, Major?” The Major looked uncomfortable.

“Certainly there are aspects which are accurate. We would be a poor Army indeed if we did not plan for contingencies. But I assure you that such things as surrounding the Archbishop’s house are ludicrous. This document has, shall we say, been enhanced.”

“You say MacNeill wanted you back with him for the meeting?” asked Holmes.

“Yes, at five.”

“I shall go with you. Hmm, what have we here?” Holmes was looking out the window. I went to join him. Below on the street I could see Connolly and Mallin. Connolly was pointing toward one of the Castle gates and Mallin was writing on a pad of paper. "I believe, Thomas, that Mr Connolly is making a last reconnaissance. "

"Mr Altamont," said Price, "I still believe that there will be no rising. Why even this fallacious document won't cause an armed conflict. It may be bogus, and it may rile them, but it would also put them on notice that there is a plan of action and so further deter them."

"You're wrong," said Holmes. "It will not cause a rising, but it makes it more likely. The Nationalists have always contended that the English do nothing but plot against the Irish and this will help confirm it."

"Thomas, you had best get back to your duties and I will meet you at the gate at four thirty. I'm sure the Major will arrange to have need of you on an errand of some importance so you can leave early. Correct, Major?"

"Of course."

So we broke up and I went back to the wards that I was beginning to feel I was neglecting. At half four, I was once again called back to help Major Price, but this time out in the city. Meeting Holmes just outside the gate, we headed for MacNeill's.

"Have there been any more developments?" I asked as we walked along.

"We were able to get Alderman Kelly's copy of the document," he responded, "and it appears it is a mixture of truth and falsehood, with enough truth to make it believable."

"Will the Castle refute it?"

"Yes, Nathan says he will but Burns has convinced him to wait for the moment to give time to prepare an adequate response."

"Ordinarily I would say that was reasonable, Liam. But to wait may lend credence. They must refute it now."

"I agree," said Holmes, "but as you know, Burns has his own motives for delay. Every moment now to him is critical."

"No, Liam, I don't know." I'm sure the frustration came through in my voice. "Why is delay critical?"

"Come, Thomas, surely you must have a hint of what his game is? No? Well think about it, man." He looked at me, out of the corner of his eye. "All right, I'll give you this: What do Trinity College, Dublin Castle and

Castle Street Police Station have in common?" He paused. "And what services do Burns' men provide? You should have the answers." We walked on a few moments. "Here we are, Thomas. Looks as though there is everyone of any importance here." Three motor cars were parked in front of MacNeill's and I could see Pearse's bicycle leaned up against the railing.

As we entered, we saw the room was truly filled with a Who's Who of the Volunteers. "If Price were to strike now, all he'd miss would be Clarke," whispered Holmes.

"Come in, gentlemen, come in," said MacNeill. The chairs all taken, Holmes and I stood in a corner to listen. I knew almost all there. Besides Pearse there was the O'Rahilly, MacDonagh, Joe Plunkett, Ceannt, Bulmer Hobson and others I knew by face but not name. Hobson and the O'Rahilly I knew were moderates and the most trusted by MacNeill. Pearse was his favourite, though, and Pearse was the most radical among them -well, except for Tom Clarke, and Clarke would never be acceptable to MacNeill.

Holmes now knew who the IRB men were and had warned me. MacDiarmada, MacDonagh, Ceannt, Pearse and Plunkett were all IRB and we assumed part of the plan. Hobson, the O'Rahilly and, of course, MacNeill, were not. The last three were the ones being played.

MacNeill started the meeting with a discussion of the Castle document and went through the order in detail.

"It can only mean that the English are set to move against us, quickly," piped up Plunkett as soon as MacNeill had stopped speaking. He was visibly excited. Plunkett was the son of a Papal Count, and part of a Nationalist family. There were no divided loyalties in his world. It was independence or nothing.

Pearse played a good game. He and the others of the IRB got all the concessions from MacNeill that were needed. They all agreed with MacNeill, oh yes, they would only fight if they were attacked. They would preserve their arms and ammunition and defend the organization, but only if the government fired the first shot. It was even MacNeill who recommended that the Volunteers buy supplies of food and medical stores and oil their weapons.

When the meeting broke up, the IRB men could barely hide their emotions of glee. Pearse nearly raced from the house. Hobson and the O'Rahilly hung back a bit and wanted to talk to MacNeill but he insisted he needed some time and so we all left.

Holmes asked Hobson if we could meet him in an hour at Volunteer Headquarters and he agreed. Holmes was exceedingly quiet as we sat at the pub. I ate a little and sipped my pint while he smoked.

At fifteen minutes before eight we started to our meeting.

Holmes startled me when he finally spoke. "They'll strike, no matter what happens, Thomas. The IRB's badly using MacNeill but they believe completely in their cause. To them, a small lie to gain a free Ireland is a small price. They are literally willing to give all, including their lives for what they believe is a great cause. You have to admire them. And who knows, perhaps they're right." He stopped and tapped his pipe out on a railing. "Nonetheless, Thomas, it's our job to stop them. I don't see much hope but perhaps we can convince Hobson and he can convince MacNeill. If they'll cancel the manoeuvres, we may at least delay the bloodshed."

We found Hobson in his office with Captain O'Connell. They were looking rather forlorn.

"Yes, Liam, what did you and the Doctor want to talk about?"

"It's about the Castle document, sir." Holmes went on to explain our concerns: the wording, the irrational sequestering of the DMP, surrounding the Archbishop's house, and the rest. He went on for a good ten minutes attributing his military objections to me and my Indian War campaign. When he finished, both men sat quietly for a moment, then O'Connell said, "It's Plunkett, man. He's taken some of the truth and made it worse. I can't prove it, but I know it."

"It's a wicked conspiracy to force a rising. You can be sure Clarke is behind it," replied Hobson. "We must go see MacNeill. There's more to these manoeuvres than just practice. I can feel it."

We left Hobson and O'Connell putting on their hats and coats for a return to MacNeill as Holmes and I departed for Liberty Hall.

"Let us hope, Watson, that they can get MacNeill to take some action, though I don't hold out much hope."

At Liberty Hall, we found the ICA alone for a change. They were having a drill night and Connolly was having a meeting with Mallin and three of his officers in his office. There was little to be learned here at the moment. It being late, we returned to Mrs McGuffey's.

Chapter 9

Holy Thursday

20 April 1916

I was now feeling that my taking a position at the Red Cross Hospital had been an error. I could not spend the time I thought I needed to gathering information. But it had been a way into the cause. Seen as useful by the Volunteers, Holmes spent time in the telegraph office I thought might be wasted.

Sir Matthew had issued a repudiation of the Castle document the night before and I was curious if it had any impact on MacNeill. We were now only two days from the planned rising and we were no nearer to verifying it. I knew it was to happen, so did Holmes, but without solid proof, it was just so much more talk. At least Holmes had convinced Sir Matthew to issue an alert to the DMP of possible trouble. Our friend Burns, of course, had objected most strenuously.

At four o'clock, I was once again sent for and reported to Room 6. Nathan, Burns, Price and Holmes were all present when I got there.

"Ah, Doctor, we can start." It was Nathan who led off the conversation. "I've had a report by an informer in B Company of the Volunteers that there is something to happen on Easter as opposed to Holy Saturday. Unfortunately, he can't say what. My question to you, gentlemen, is are we or are we not going to see a rising?"

Burns was the first to speak. "Absolutely not," he blurted out. "If there was a rising, I would know." With that, he slapped the table and folded his arms.

Poor Nathan looked rather stunned, but turned to Price. "Major, your opinion?"

"I don't know Sir. We believe that arms are on the way and the Navy has stepped up patrols along the coast to intercept. We also believe that Sir Roger is en route, but again, we've no certainty. If both of these things are true, that combined with the manoeuvres planned for this weekend can't be coincidental. However, I can't be certain."

"Mr Altamont?"

"There will be a rising!"

"How can you be sure?"

"Let me say that MacNeill, the Volunteer leader, has no knowledge of the rising. He's a good man and will only fight if attacked. But don't doubt he's for independence! The IRB will use the Volunteers and the ICA to start a rising this weekend. I guarantee it. The timing is what I lack."

"Where's your proof?" spat Burns, his eyes glaring.

"I admit I have nothing in a concrete form not a letter or an order, nor even an overheard conversation."

"Ha!" cried Burns.

Holmes turned to Sir Matthew. "If you do not take all the leaders, all at once, by Monday there will be a revolution. I believe the Navy reports."

Holmes was playing a two sided game here. He knew that the Navy had broken the German codes and was aware of the arms shipment. He also knew that neither the Army, nor the Irish government, had been told anything official by the Navy for fear of compromising their position and the Germans realizing their codes had been broken. Admiral Bayly in Queenstown had "hinted" to General Stafford about what was happening but the Army had no sources to confirm the "hints".

The air was now still. "Well Gentlemen," said Nathan. "I will not act without proof that can be taken to a court of law. Bring me that and I will act."

"Then, sir," said Holmes, "Burns will have his revolution." The two of us left the room as Burns started a tirade against us.

"Come, Thomas, we've been invited to the Countess's for tea and we must grab a trolley."

As we rode the trolley south toward Rathmine, I asked Holmes why he did not go back to Liberty Hall and look for more proof.

"Because, even though I'm considered a friend and Clan Na Gael, Irish Americans are still somewhat outsiders. However, at the Countess's, we might be able to pick up the conversation we need in an unguarded moment. After all, she and about twenty other women are actually members of the ICA. Connolly is very progressive."

As we rode south, I noticed a motor car which seemed to be moving with the trolley. It would pull ahead each time the trolley stopped and would pull over to the kerb then start up again once we had passed.

"Yes, it's two of the six." It was Holmes. He had been watching me watch the motor car.

"What should we do?" I asked.

"Nothing. Let them stay with us. They are harmless where they are."

"Why doesn't Burns just give us away to the Volunteers? I mean, if it's like you say, and he wants the rising, why not just turn us over?"

"Because, if he does, it may all be called off. They won't know how much we know, so how can they be sure their plans are not already known? He would chance losing his opportunity."

"Holmes, you are frustrating! Opportunity for what?"

"Is it possible you still do not see? Let me expand my clue. What do College Street Police Station, Trinity College, Dublin Castle and the City Hall, and the telephone exchange all see in common?"

With that, he would say no more until we reached Rathmine.

When we arrived, we were welcomed like old friends of the family. We were brought to the countess who was in the dining room with other guests.

"Oh, you'll introduce yourselves in a moment, old dear." She said, taking my hand. "But right now we have great need of you. Doctor, grab that edge of the bed sheet over there and pull it taut. Mr Altamont, keep stirring this pot. It's my own mixture, gold paint and mustard. All I could find, I'm afraid. You must keep it stirred."

She had a green sheet spread across the dining table and four guests held the corners tight while she, with Holmes stirring the pot, wrote in great letters, Irish Republic. All the while she talked of the future face of Ireland, women's suffrage and the like, while a brown cocker spaniel ran at her feet.

I must say, I found the Countess somehow intimidating. She was excited, alive, outspoken and a true equalitarian. I was completely fascinated.

With the new flag drying in the pantry, we had tea and the countess insisted on knowing all about the Indian Wars in America. I cursed myself for not having spent more time reading up on what I had done. I vaguely remembered a few of Ryan's old tales of the Modoc War and what I didn't know, I filled in with what seemed reasonable.

Holmes tried to move the conversation to the ICA and the Volunteers, but while she was expansive on politics she was silent on any action to be taken. In an hour Holmes and I were taking our leave as the Countess had a meeting at Liberty Hall to get ready for.

As we left the Countess's, the same motor car sat a block away. Holmes and I caught a passing trolley and our friends continued their leap frogging.

Having crossed O'Connell Bridge we got off and walked east on the quays toward Liberty Hall. The motor car drove on.

At Liberty Hall we found Sean on guard again. "Hello, Sean, all quiet tonight, eh, no drill?" asked Holmes.

"Not tonight, but lots going on I guess. People been coming and going all afternoon. Robert's just back from Cork. He's inside." I offered Sean a cigar which he took and slipped in his pocket with a "Thank You, Doctor. I'll be using it later."

As we entered the hall, I could see Cacy sitting on one of the benches near Connolly's office. He looked up from his pipe as we approached.

"Been busy, Robert?" asked Holmes.

"That I have. Yesterday they have me all over the country delivering papers from Mr Plunkett's house and today it's Cork and back and a 'hang on a bit, Robert, we've more for you'. You'd think I had nothing of me own to do."

I looked at Holmes and he nodded. So it was Plunkett who printed the Castle document! Holmes sat next to him on the bench and started charging his pipe. "Why to Cork, Robert?"

"I'm sure I don't know now. It's just take this here, and take that there. I never look. A gentleman doesn't look at another's message, ya know!" He pointed empathically with his pipe stem.

"You're right, of course. I wasn't saying you would."

We smoked for a while with Cacy when Holmes looked at his watch. "Doctor, you ready for a pint? Good, then we're gone. See you later, Robert." And we started for our favourite pub.

"Holmes," I finally said, "you really have to work on the accent." It was then I felt the blow to my head and I sprawled across the pavement. It was now quite dark and the attack had come from the shadows. I rolled over on my left side but as I did I received a kick to the stomach. I heard someone shout, "Some help here!" and the attack on me ceased for a moment. I could now see two attackers trying to pin Holmes against the wall and punching him. As I scrambled to my feet, one broke off and came at me but seeing the Colt automatic in my hand, he ran without a word, leaving his fellow attacker. Holmes had placed the other in a choke hold and whispered something in his ear. The man nodded and when released, ran after his companion.

"Watson, you're bleeding. Come, we'll get you cleaned up at home."

Mrs McGuffey was all attention and concern when we arrived and asked for hot water and some towels. She insisted on cleaning me up and, not wanting to go to the hospital, I allowed her to put a few stitches in my head while she thoroughly chastised two "old men" for running about the countryside doing dangerous things, "God knows what!"

"And, Mr Altamont," she continued, "there's a man in the kitchen who's been waiting for you half the afternoon."

"Mrs McGuffey," chimed Holmes, "bring him here, please."

Mrs McGuffey gave him a foul look. "Everything in its own time, Mr Altamont. We take care of the Doctor first."

"Yes, yes, he's taken care of. Now, the gentleman in the kitchen, please," and he shooed her out. "Are you all right, Watson?"

"I'll live. I suppose it was our friends from the motor car?"

"No, two others of "the six" as you call them. I suppose they thought to just put us hors de combat and so solve their problem."

There was a knock on the door and it opened. In walked a man of medium height and build who was dressed as a tradesman and holding his bowler.

"I was hoping you'd get back soon, Mr Altamont." He stopped speaking when he saw me and quickly looked at Holmes.

"It's all right Cusack, he's with us. What have you got?"

Cusack seemed to relax a little and went on. "It's as you said, sir. We've been told to parade Easter at seven at night but the word is it's not just a manoeuvre, it's the real thing. Our lieutenant say's we'd best make Easter duties as some of us won't be coming back. Word came to Cork today."

I could see the excitement in Holmes's face though I'm sure Cusack could not.

"Do you have anything in writing, man? Did they give you anything?"

"Well, no, sir," our informant looked slightly downcast. "Wasn't I right to come to let you know?"

"Of course, man, of course." Holmes reached in a pocket and took out two five pound notes. "Here's for your travel. You've been wondrously helpful."

"No, sir," said Cusack, "I really couldn't. It's for Mr MacNeill after all. I'll fight if they come for us, but just going out and starting it, well, I'm not for that."

"Mr MacNeill would want you to take it Cusack. Here, if anything changes, send me news."

Cusack reluctantly took the notes and departed.

Holmes turned to me as soon as the door shut. "Thomas, are you up to a walk?"

"Certainly, Liam, where to?"

"We're off to see if Hobson is still at work."

Hobson was indeed still at Volunteer Headquarters. We had been in his office but a moment when Captain O'Connell and another burst through the door.

"Just a minute," Hobson said to O'Connell. "What can I do for you, Mr Altamont?"

Holmes reflected a moment, looked at O'Connell and decided to proceed. "Mr Hobson, you guys need to know that I've been told that the Volunteers down Cork way are saying these manoeuvres ain't manoeuvres at all. It's to be a regular American Revolution this weekend and what I want to know is, what's goin' on! I don't mind a fight but let's have the deal!"

It was O'Connell that spoke first. "That's what I've come to tell you Bulmer. O'Duffy here, and I have been told that several of the companies outside Dublin have been told to prepare for an insurrection on Easter Sunday!" O'Duffy nodded and Hobson sat still.

"I've been talking to Managham from Limerick and he had some strange questions about an 'imminent crisis'. I didn't know what he meant."

"Then there's the inconsistencies in the Castle document," chimed in Holmes. "It made no sense from the Brit's point of view. And because of the manoeuvres, the whole Volunteer force will be in arms. Can ya think of a better time or place for a revolt? Can you?"

Hobson sat back in his chair. "So it is to be a rising! They've been planning it all along. Come on then, the bunch of you. We've got to see MacNeill."

O'Connell had a motor car and we piled in and headed for MacNeill's.

Hobson was the first to the door and started knocking as we tumbled out of the car. It was now getting close to midnight.

MacNeill himself opened the door in a dressing gown and pyjamas. "Quiet, please, Gentlemen. Come in to the study. Now what can it possibly be that brings you here so late? More on the Castle document?"

Holmes let Hobson take the lead. Hobson laid out the information he had received from us and O'Connell. He reiterated his fears about the Castle document and the close ties between Connolly, Clarke and Pearse. MacNeill listened intently. "Sir," he finally said, "we've been betrayed! These manoeuvres are just a way to cover for an open rebellion!"

"Pearse would never do such a thing," MacNeill paused, "or would he? It's that old Fenian Clarke! He must have convinced the boy that this is the way. O'Connell, that your car? Yes, of course. Let me get dressed, I'll be with you in a moment then I want you to take me to Pearse."

Chapter 10

Good Friday

21 APRIL 1916

We drove quickly to Pearse's home and knocked. His sister answered the door. She said Padraig was asleep but we heard him call out to his sister that it was all right, he was awake. He waved us all toward the side room.

No sooner were we in the room then MacNeill started. "I want to know what the meaning is of your orders to the companies! Have you told them to attack police barracks and railroads?"

"We had no choice. You had to be deceived. You never would have agreed to the rising."

"This is insanity," stormed MacNeill. "You send men to their deaths like this was one of Connolly's plays on a stage! We can't hope to win. Do you think England will not act? Do you not understand they will bring their soldiers home from the front and stop this? You have no weapons or ammunition worth speaking of, and most of all, the men in the countryside are not trained to use arms even if they had them. How can you do this to our men? Have you no soul? No conscience?" He paused but no answer came. "And what of our word that the actions of the Volunteers would be open for all to see? Yet you do this in secret!"

Pearse was silent, lost in some thought of his own with half a smile on his face.

MacNeill's rage was spent. He now spoke quietly. "And worst of all, you, a man I trusted, deceived and lied to me."

"The rising will happen, with you or without you Professor. The orders have been sent and the IRB will see that the Volunteers respond. Hobson here is held by his oath." Pearse looked to Hobson.

"No," said Hobson, "our call is for force if Ireland is ready and it is not."

"No, Hobson, they will rise and if we fail, it will not be like you to want of trying."

Pearse looked at Holmes. "Altamont, was not the American Revolution started as a rag-tag type of fight?"

"Mister Pearse, they did it in the light of day with a declaration and a trained militia, what they turned into an Army. Do you intend to do the same?"

"Yes, my friend, I do. I know that we are outnumbered, lack arms and training but we must strike now. It may be our only opportunity. Even if we fail, we will have won."

"The country will not be with you," went on MacNeill. "There are nearly 150,000 Irishmen in uniform. Will their families be with you? All you want is a blood sacrifice."

"It will be enough to make a change."

"No, Pearse, I won't let it happen. You'll not sacrifice boys and old men in a senseless fight they can't win. I'll do everything I can to stop you, short of calling Dublin Castle."

I'll do that, I thought to myself.

MacNeill rushed out of the room and straight through the front door. We hustled to catch up. "I want all manoeuvres for this weekend cancelled, now, tonight!"

O'Connell volunteered to head to Cork as soon as he dropped off MacNeill at his home. When we arrived, Holmes held back as the other three entered.

"It's over, Holmes. Cancelled, or it will be in a few hours."

"No, Watson. I seriously doubt that. Pearse may have to write off the countryside but he and Connolly may still have the power in Dublin to rise here. And we still don't know where or when the weapons are to be landed. Pearse will have to talk to Connolly and the others. We must know what they're planning next."

O'Connell came back out of the house. "Liam, can you find Cacy and send him to Volunteer Headquarters?"

"You bet, mister. I'll go right now."

"Tell him to report to Hobson immediately. You come along too."

"Can't do that, boss. Have to be at the Castle at eight or they might start askin' questions. Doctor here, too. I've got that telegraph to listen to."

"Yes, you're right of course. Well I'm off to Cork." He disappeared down the street in his motor car.

"What now, Liam?" I asked.

“We send Cacy to volunteer headquarters. Then you head to Mrs McGuffey’s. Get a few hours sleep, then stop by to see Hobson at Headquarters before going to work. I’ll see you at the Castle sharp at half nine. Room 6.”

“But Holmes, what about you?”

“I have other things to do at the moment. Remember, Thomas,” he said, walking off. “Half nine, sharp.” He nearly trotted into the darkness while I returned home to attempt some sleep.

As it turned out, sleep was almost impossible. My mind would not be quiet. There was to be a rising, now there wasn’t. There might still be a rising, but there might not. I had met good men, men who all wanted the same thing, an independent Ireland. Some only by peaceful means, some who said 700 years under England was enough and violence must come. I had always been for Home Rule but were the Irish ever to have it? And what of the Irish who didn’t want Home Rule? I felt for Sir Matthew. No matter what he did, he would have the enmity of thousands.

I finally gave up the hope of sleep about six and rang Mrs McGuffey (for somehow the name seemed to fit her better.) for hot water and coffee. Within a half hour, I was walking to Dawson Street to see if Holmes was there. As I walked in, I could feel a great heat and going back to Hobson’s office, I found the man busily going through files and throwing papers into a blazing stove.

I knocked and when Hobson turned around he looked startled, then relieved. “Doctor, you’re just in time. Give me a hand here. I’m afraid our friends have made a great muck of things.” He turned back to the file cabinet. “Grab those papers on the table and throw them in the stove, will you? Good man.”

Almost without thinking I complied. The door to the stove was open and I started feeding the fire. Others were coming in now and as each arrived, Hobson told them, “I expect the Brits will raid us. Go through your files and desks. Burn everything that they might use against us or our friends.”

I took up a position as stoker. Men would pile papers upon the table and I would feed the fire. It was impossible to discern all that was being consumed by the flames. At nine, I was about to make my excuses and leave when MacDiarmada came in with a note from MacNeill. He gave it to Hobson, who read it once, looked at MacDiarmada and then read it out loud. “Take no action till I see you. Am coming in. MacNeill”

Hobson looked at MacDiarmada. “Keep burning boys,” he said and turned back to his file.

I left and walked to the Castle. Constable Flood said good morning and I made straight for Room 6. Holmes was already there. Price, Nathan and Burns followed in quickly before I could speak to Holmes.

"Mr Altamont," started Nathan, as he sat down "DS Burns has been filling me in on your discussions of last night, but I'd like to hear the news from you."

Holmes explained what had happened: MacNeill's cancelling of manoeuvres and his fear that Pearse was still able to do something. "You must move against the leaders tonight," he finished.

"Do we have any proof to use in a court beyond what you and Doctor Ryan have heard?" asked Price.

"No," said Holmes.

"And you won't," I added. "Volunteer headquarters has been burning documents since before dawn." I then added what I had overheard and what Mac Neill had written to Hobson.

"See that!" Burns added. He was smiling but seemed angry. I could not figure the man out. "MacNeill has sent word to cancel the manoeuvres and told his men in Dublin to do nothing. I think any danger there might have been is past. And with Pearse's reputation and good standing in the community, you'll never convict him in a court for doing nothing." He sat there with that artificial smile that made me despise him.

"If," said Price, "there is still to be a rising as Mr Altamont says, we must look at where they would strike, especially with a reduced force. Should I prepare an order to move men from Curragh to Dublin?"

Nathan sat quietly for a moment. "No, Major. I'm not prepared to do that. It might precipitate exactly what we are trying to avoid. The Shinners would claim we were about to attack them and the fight would be on. As long as we hold the railroads, we can move them quick enough. Anything else?"

Holmes was frustrated. "Sir Matthew, if you don't act quickly, you will have a rising, at least in Dublin. When it happens, it won't be just the Volunteers. The ICA, Fianna Eireann, Cumann na mBan, the Foresters and the Hibernian Rifles will all gather. It won't be an event you'll want to deal with, I assure you."

Nathan looked at Holmes somewhat uncomfortably. He finally rose and said, "Yes, well thank you gentlemen. Oh, Price, any word on the arms boat?"

"No, Sir."

"Right, well, good day Gentlemen." The three of them trooped out.

I told Holmes that I had to get to the wards. He nodded and I left him alone sitting by the table.

It was just six when I saw Holmes again at the gate.

"Come, Watson. We have some decisions to make." We walked north toward the bridge. "Hobson has been kidnapped."

"What?" I cried.

"Yes. My people say that Hobson was visited by Neal Daly and Sean Tobin about two and the three left in a motor car. Hobson did not seem to be a willing participant. That can only mean that Pearse and his men intend to continue with or without MacNeill. Pearse has also sent orders for the four city battalions to parade on Sunday at 4."

"What has MacNeill done?"

"They've convinced him to fall in with their plans. They've surely told him about the arms and Casement coming with men.

"What do we do now?"

"I've men out trying to find Hobson, Whether Nathan wants to face this or not, this is far from over. Just before I went off shift I took a message about a man taken prisoner near Tralee who might be a German spy. I think they'll find it's Casement coming here for the rising. We'll have to wait and see. Now, Thomas, a pint and we'll be off to Liberty Hall to see what we can find."

As I had suspected, Holmes' favourite pub was also where he received messages. His contacts had, so far, been unable to find where Hobson was taken but word was he was to be held unharmed. No word had yet come as to who the prisoners were from the sea, for now there was more than one, but worst of all, word of countermanding orders had been sent to the countryside.

"So in less than 24 hours the rising is on, it's cancelled, and it's on. At least that should confuse them all," said Holmes.

"And make them wonder if their leadership knows what they're doing." I added. "Do we go back to the Castle?"

"No, I think not, Thomas. I think we let things play out for now. If it was Sir Roger who was taken, then surely the Navy can take the arms also."

He raised his glass to finish it but stopped with it at his lips. “Or so we shall hope!”

Though we stayed till nigh on midnight at Liberty Hall, all was quiet and we departed.

Chapter 11

Holy Saturday

22 April 1916

By Saturday morning even I was confused. I had no idea who was really in charge of the Volunteers or whether there would be a rising or not. The secret society, the IRB, had infiltrated everywhere. But did they control things? Would the Volunteers follow MacNeill or Pearse? The ICA would follow Connolly and the IRB would follow Clarke no matter the consequence. But in all truth, their numbers were inconsequential. Who, I wondered, really held power?

I met Holmes at breakfast and we walked together to the Castle. He already knew the prisoner from Tralee had been transferred to an Army escort and was about to depart for London. We were not to have an opportunity to question him.

A little after 10 o'clock, I was called again to Room 6. I had already tired of what I saw as endless meetings with no resolution. I was not to be disappointed.

Sir Matthew was in a splendid mood for a change and he informed us of the fate of the German arms shipment. The Navy had not only intercepted the shipment of some 25,000 rifles and a number of machine guns, it was at the bottom of the sea. The German crew had, with capture imminent, scuttled the ship in Queenstown Harbour. They had tried to, at least, block the harbour channel but had only been partially successful.

The rebel weapons were gone, at least one of their spies captured. How could there possibly be a rising? Holmes informed them of Hobson's kidnapping and his belief that the rising would still occur.

"I talked with Lord Wimbourne a few moments ago," said Nathan. "He is still insisting on immediate raids on Fr. Matthew Park and Liberty Hall, and arrest of all leaders. I believe, however, that we'd best wait." He looked around the table, smiling with his thumbs in his waistcoat pockets. "I want proof that links the leaders to the arms and spies. We think there are two others still on the loose. Mr Burns, you will work directly with Major Price on putting the information I require together."

Burns nodded. "No danger of a rising now. Even Clarke knows a rising without arms can't succeed."

Holmes rose from the table shaking his head. "Sir Matthew, defeating the Crown forces was never possible. Pearse, Clarke, Connolly, they all have always known that. They see the rising itself as a victory. They are ready to be martyrs to the cause. Unless you do as Lord Wimbourne advises and do it with overwhelming force, I fear you will regret it. Come Thomas, we have things to do." He turned and I scrambled to follow him.

I closed the door and hustled after Holmes, "Surely," I said, grabbing his arm, "with the weapons gone and their spies on the run, even Pearse will call this off."

"No, Watson." He stopped and looked back down the corridor to the closed door. "Now, they'll surely rise. MacNeill may yet be convinced but the rest will believe that with the guns gone, the Crown will feel more confident and come for them and their arms. And MacNeill has always pledged a fight if that happens."

"Then there is no hope?"

"Wimbourne is not a complete fool. Not as big a one as Nathan and Birrell. I'm afraid, old friend," he patted my shoulder, "the Shinners will have great need of you."

I left Holmes and went back to the wards. The only hope left was if Holmes could somehow intervene for it was certain that Nathan would not act.

Leaving the Castle that evening, I noticed that there were few soldiers about and asked Flood on the way out where everyone was.

"All leaves and passes were approved for the weekend, sir," he smiled back. "Won't be much of anyone around till Tuesday. Monday's a bank holiday and the big races. Most everyone likes a bit o' holiday."

I thanked him, wished him Happy Easter and started to the pub where I assumed Holmes would be gathering information.

I had not entered when Holmes came out the door, turned me around and we headed toward MacNeill's residence.

"It was worse than they thought, Thomas. It is Casement who was caught! The arms, as you know, are gone; one of Casement's companions is also caught and singing like a bird; arrests of Volunteers have occurred in Tralee and the men who were sent to steal precious wireless equipment to aid the rising are drowned in the river."

"My Lord!"

"Yes, and as for us, the critical time for action is passing. Soldiers have been released for the holiday and Nathan has convinced Wimbourne they should not act.

"And why are we headed to MacNeill's?"

"To see if we can one more time get Mac Neill to cancel the manoeuvres. Perhaps we can at least minimize the damage."

We walked in silence until we reached MacNeill's. We had just rung the doorbell when a motor car pulled up and out got the O'Rahilly, Sean Fitzgibbon and a third man. The door was opened and we all entered.

MacNeill took us into the study, where Holmes told him about all that he had already explained to me. The O'Rahilly explained how Pearse had kidnapped Hobson, and Fitzgibbon told how Pearse had always made it appear that MacNeill was behind all the orders.

MacNeill was horrified; no arms, men dead already, Castle documents bogus. His whole life's work was crumbling in front of his eyes.

"Can we stop it?" He looked around the room.

"We must," said Holmes.

The O'Rahilly was confident. A message to all the Volunteers in Ireland, an open statement to the world from MacNeill that he and his had nothing to do with the arms, and a declaration that he believed the Castle document bogus. It had to be tried.

MacNeill sighed. "To waste lives in a war that is unwinnable is the height of insanity. Worse, it is immoral. Pearse seeks his blood sacrifice."

We waited quietly while MacNeill sat a moment lost in thought. "We must call off this insanity." He turned back to the O'Rahilly. "Take me to St. Enda's school. I must see Pearse. Liam, gather some men who can travel tonight. Meet us at O'Kelly's in Rathgar at nine o'clock." With that they left and Holmes and I started walking toward Volunteer headquarters.

"We've less than twenty four hours to stop this, but it seems that MacNeill has finally settled on a course of action." I ventured.

Holmes was paying no attention to my words. He was watching a man up ahead crossing the street. I followed his gaze and realized it was Dowdle.

"Watson, go to the headquarters, gather three or four men and meet MacNeill, I'm going to follow Dowdle. I'll meet you later."

"But Holmes, you may…"

"Not now Watson. Your duty is the men. I'll find out Dowdle's purpose."

"He's just reporting to Burns," I said to myself out loud, for Holmes was quickly half a block away.

By the time I gathered men and we trolleyed to Rathgar it was close to nine o'clock.

When we reached the doctor's house, the study was already full of men. Many I recognized. Arthur Griffith, founder of Sinn Fein was there, as were other men who were not volunteers. There were also our earlier friends of the evening, plus Joe Plunkett (whom we now believed had printed the bogus Castle document) and Thomas MacDonagh (both IRB men of the first water).

As I was admitted, MacNeill was summing up the situation to all in the room. He was visibly emotional about all that had happened in his name. Griffith stood and looked around the room. He was appalled by what was happening. It was a war of "self-destruction". The argument went back and forth but it was only MacDonagh and Plunkett for the rising, the other eight or ten against. Finally MacNeill raised a hand in the air and slowly fell silent.

"Gentlemen, we shall have no useless slaughter. I am cancelling tomorrow's manoeuvres."

MacDonagh and Plunkett rose together and left the room with the sombre warning that the rising would still happen and those present had added to the slaughter. MacNeill let them go.

MacNeill took out pen and paper and wrote a moment. "How's this?" he cleared his voice, "Volunteers completely deceived. All orders for Sunday cancelled." He looked around and heads nodded. "Where's Liam?"

"He'll be here presently," I said. "I've men here to carry the messages."

"Ah, thank you, Doctor. I'm going to add a note for the Major Commanders. Let's see, how's this? 'Every influence should be used immediately and throughout the day to secure the faithful execution of this order, as any failure to obey may result in a very grave catastrophe.'"

Copies were made and messengers left, but still I knew this was far from over. I left in search of a trolley and Holmes. Not finding him at headquarters, I moved on to Liberty Hall. The place was a beehive of activity. Though near midnight, the place was filled with men in a holiday mood. Here, at least, there was no confusion. James Connolly was in charge and what he said, went! Guards were on the doors as usual and lights blazed throughout the building. Connolly himself was not to be seen nor was Holmes. I finally decided to head for Mrs McGuffey's and some sleep. As I left the building, Holmes was approaching.

"Ah, Thomas, I had hoped to find you. Come, I think it best we get a few hours' sleep."

We started the walk north to Talbot Street. As we walked I related the events at Dr O'Kelly's then asked Holmes what he had learned.

"Dowdle met his cronies and Burns at that warehouse we saw them at a few days ago. I'm sure he was just reporting back what little he knew. However, once their meeting ended, they went out to the four corners of the city. Since some are Volunteers, I wondered what their roles and they moved with a purpose."

"And the purpose?" I prompted.

"Ah, well, to stir up support for the rising. Talk it up, so to speak."

"But the rank and file hasn't been told," I protested.

"True, but if you build discontent, when it is announced, you will have support."

"I don't understand. What has Burns to gain? Some plan of promotion, some sort of revenge?"

"You hold all the clues, Watson. It would not be fair for me to just give you the answer. Besides, I have no proof that Burns could not talk his way out of. It will all come in time. But for now, I believe, some sleep will do us well. Tomorrow may be busy."

As we entered Mrs McGuffey's, events unknown to us were developing. Mr MacNeill would be more resourceful and intuitive than we or his opponents ever dreamed he would be.

Chapter 12

Easter Sunday

23 APRIL 1916

It was Easter morning and as I looked out on the street, I could see the early churchgoers on their way. I was tempted to join them but knew today would be a turning point and I had best await developments.

"Watson, look here!" Holmes had been looking at the morning paper as he drank his coffee. Throwing the paper down on the table, he stabbed his finger at an advertisement.

"*Owing to the very critical position, all orders given to the Irish Volunteers for tomorrow, Easter Sunday, are hereby rescinded, and no parades, marches or other movements of the Irish Volunteers will take place. Each individual Volunteer will obey this order strictly in every particular.*"

It was signed, Eoin MacNeill, Chief of Staff.

"He has certainly bearded the lion in his den." I remarked, pushing the paper back. "Or the Clarke in the tobacco shop." I chuckled at my own sense of humour.

"I believe," said Holmes, "that we have somewhat underestimated friend MacNeill. So have the IRB."

"Surely, it's done then."

"No, Watson. I understand you think me a pessimist but I think this, in the end, will only embolden our opponents. Pearse will only see it as another betrayal of the Irish cause. He will press on to become a martyr." He stopped to relight his pipe. "And we must not let them have martyrs.

"It's sad in a way, Watson." He went back to the window and looked out. "I truly feel for their cause. Were it up to me, the island would be a dominion like Canada or Australia." He shook his head. "Politicians and power."

"Should we try to see what effect this has had?" I tapped the paper.

"Yes, let's go to Liberty Hall. That's where the nest will be."

By eight o'clock we were entering the Hall, Sean greeted us. "Something is astir," he whispered in his best conspiratorial tone. "Big meeting in Connolly's office." He started naming those who had come through the door: Clarke, Pearse, Mac Diarmada, Ceannt, Connolly and

MacDonagh. Plunkett was to be ushered in as soon as he came.

“It’s what they call the Military Council,” Holmes whispered to me.

“Sean, what’s with all the police? There must be twenty of them all around the place,” said Holmes.

I looked over my shoulder up and down the street and of a certainty I saw police half a block down on both sides.

A giant grin spread over Sean’s face. “It’s glorious it is. Two hundred and fifty pounds of gelignite the boys got this morning. Stole it from the quarry. Brought it here they did and those peelers know it. But don’t you worry, I won’t let them in.” He picked his rifle up in both hands.

“Quite a haul, Sean.” Holmes returned the grin and patted him on the shoulder as we passed on in. “We’d best see if the bosses need anything. Come on, Thomas.”

As we entered, I tugged his arm. “Liam, with that much gelignite they could destroy two or three of the railroad bridges needed to bring the troops in or drop bridges across the river.”

“I understand, but that isn’t all the explosives they have. I wonder if they got the detonators.”

“Liam, Liam, come here.” It was Connolly calling from his office. We went straight over. Connolly pulled us into his office where other members of the Military Council were waiting. “Can you get a message out for us at the Castle? It’s very important.”

“It’s my day off, boss. But I ought to be able to get it done without any problem. What ya got?”

“This message must go to our friends in Philadelphia. They will understand its meaning. I don’t expect a reply right away so come back when you can.” He handed Holmes an envelope.

“Sure boss, back in a jiff.”

We left the office, and as we did Holmes instructed me to stand fast and gather what information I could in his absence.

“This will give me an opportunity to talk to Nathan. I’ll be back as soon as I can.”

While Holmes was gone, I spent my time listening to every conversation I could and trying to keep mental notes on it all. Holmes later told me of his visit to the Castle. He was able to send the wire without any problem. “A fairly simple coded message which detailed the loss of the arms ship and asking for replacement arms from America. Even Clan na Gael couldn’t make that happen.”

After sending the wire he was able to meet with Nathan, Price and Burns.

“Burns was beside himself with rage. Of course I knew why, but he had to pretend as to his delight with what was happening. Price, of course, wanted to delay until he could bring in troops to Dublin, and Nathan had convinced himself that nothing is going to happen and we should all just smile and go about our business. Never mind the ICA has hundreds of pounds of explosives and a leader willing to use it! All my arguments are to no avail. They will not act!”

It had been near on noon when Holmes returned to the hall, and I had much to report. Members of the ICA had been reporting in all morning. The atmosphere was more like a county fair than a unit about to do battle.

“Well, since you’ve been gone we’ve had three men, whom I’m told are printers, brought in. Captain Partridge told them they’re under arrest and took them down to the printing press in the basement. They’ve been hard at it ever since and it’s some kind of proclamation. I haven’t been able to get a copy yet but the first few words were in Irish in big black letters. The printers have complained freely about a lack of type and decent paper.”

“I imagine the boys are ‘under arrest’ so if things go badly they can claim they were forced to print the document. It’ll be their declaration of independence. We’ll soon see.”

“They’re drilling the ICA men and their little council of war has continued all morning. They called me in and asked me numerous questions about the guard mount at the Castle but I’m not sure they completely believed me. I kept to our story of 120 men. I must say I felt a little foolish.”

“Don’t worry, Thomas. You can always say that’s what you saw yesterday. Today they’re letting men off for the holiday.”

We continued to wait throughout the early afternoon. At one point Mallin asked me to do a review of their first aid stores. It was a miserable lot. They had few bandages and almost no medicines. Some iodine was about the limit. I was horrified at the lack of planning. No unit could see combat with so little preparation. It was if they had no thought of casualties. I reported back to Mallin my findings of their deplorable preparations. “What would you recommend, Doctor?” he asked.

The moment I opened my mouth, I regretted it. "You need to raid every chemist in a mile for supplies," I blurted.

"Give me a list, Doctor, and we'll see what we can do. We won't take anything unless we have to, and then we'll pay for it."

I sat down and started on as extensive a list as I could, imagining a force of a thousand men and their needs in combat. Mallin left me to fall in with the rest of the ICA who were readying themselves for a march around Dublin. Connolly evidently was planning a march to check the defences of different points in the city. He would watch the response of the different sites to the appearance of 250 armed men. This would give him a better idea of how to take each site. Actually, it was quite a good idea.

While the soldiers of the ICA were gone, the Military Council had broken up. I continued to refine my list and Holmes made his way to the print room to see what he could learn.

It was not overlong before Holmes was back, having confirmed his original thesis that the document was indeed a declaration of independence, proclaiming an Irish Republic. He had not, however, been able to gain a copy.

"Well, Doctor, it appears your information was accurate." It was Mallin, they were back from their march. "When we passed by the Castle, the gate was closed and the guard called out a dozen rifles."

"I don't make a mistake about such things."

"No, you don't. Have that list? I'll get some men on it." He took the list and departed.

Holmes recommended we depart. It was now late afternoon and he wanted to stop into the pub and check for messages. We had but sat down when one of the men I knew to be a contact stopped by to ask Holmes for a light. As he handed back the matches I could have sworn it was the same box he'd been handed. It was not. Our friend had palmed Holmes's and switched it for one of the same make but containing a small slip of paper.

"It appears Lord Wimbourne won't take Nathan's 'no' for an answer. We've been summoned to the Viceregal Lodge at 10 tonight for more talk." He threw the paper in the fire. "Will they ever stop talking, Thomas?"

We drank for a moment before I ventured to bring up the problem, to me yet unsolved: What was DS Burns up to?

"Ah, Thomas, while you would believe me our friends at the Castle would not. In fact, if I told them my suspicions they would put us on the side-lines and make an end of using us. No, I had best keep my own council."

On returning to Liberty Hall we met quite a sight. The Hall was filled with men. Instructions had been given that all ICA men were to spend the night at the Hall. Connolly was busy with men coming and going and the women were in a joyous mood. In the basement, a few rooms down from the printers, men were busy making bombs - some from gelignite, some from powder - and then stacking them in boxes.

Holmes and I decided to split up to see what we could learn. I was near the front door as the sun was setting and came upon our friend Cacy.

"Out running some errands?" I asked.

"Aye. They had me taking messages to the Volunteers. Seems we're all to parade at twelve noon tomorrow. Though they still haven't said why."

"Never mind, Robert. It'll all be plain enough tomorrow."

"I'm sure it will be, Doctor. But my holiday will still be ruined," with that he went on into the hall. "And me stuck here all night with a bunch of tea-totalers!"

Holmes approached from inside. "Time for our walk, Thomas." Off he went, down the street. It was now well dark and as in most cities the streets were, in most areas, poorly lighted. The moon, I knew, would not be up until well after midnight. So in the deep darkness we headed toward Phoenix Park.

The park was probably the most beautiful in the United Kingdom--1750 lush acres, and in the middle of it, the Viceregal Lodge. It was toward there we walked. As we passed through the park gate, all light seemed to disappear into the inky blackness. Holmes touched my elbow and held a finger to his lips. I listened intently, trying not to let my footfalls make noise. There were other footsteps. I felt my muscles tense. Surely they would not try again? Were they that desperate to be rid of us? Holmes guided me off into the grass and behind one of the trees that lined the avenue.

Four men passed us by along the road, but even in the darkness I could recognize them as four of "the six". We waited for them to be swallowed up by the darkness, then, using the meadow instead of the road, continued our trek to the Lodge in silence.

From the direction we had taken, we came upon the rear of the Lodge and so made a long sweep to the right to gain the front.

We were admitted to an extraordinarily large study with a massive table. We were evidently the first to arrive.

"Holmes, some days I think I'm getting a little old to be avoiding ruffians trying to do me harm." I threw myself in a chair.

"Never mind, old friend. I'm sure the two of us could have taken them." He smiled as the far door opened. I had not yet met all the players to our coming tragedy, but surely here were the principals: Lord Wimbourne, Nathan, Burns, Colonel Cowan (who represented General Friend of the Castle Guard), Price, Captain Robertson (of the General Staff) and Chief Commissioner Edgeworth-Johnstone of the DMP. Introductions were made of me and Altamont and the meeting started.

Holmes was first asked about what was going on with the Shinners. He explained we had just come from Liberty Hall and everything we knew including the declaration and the assembly for noon tomorrow.

"Lord Wimbourne, we must move quickly or their rebellion will be upon us," he concluded.

"Rot!" cried Burns. "Their arms are in the ocean, Casement is in gaol in London, and MacNeill has cancelled their parades. Even if Pearse calls for a parade tomorrow, no one will come. And Connolly isn't so stupid as to think 250 ICA men can start a revolution." He slammed his hand on the table, again. This seemed to be his favourite antic.

"Mr Altamont," said Wimbourne, "is right. Seize Liberty Hall tonight. Then round up about 60 or 100 of the Shinner leaders and we'll nip it in the bud."

"The Dublin Battalions have been ordered to assembly," I interjected. "Action must be taken."

"Rot!" cried Burns.

"Gentlemen, please. Sir Matthew." Wimbourne stared at the undersecretary. "Act now, in the dark, without delay. By two in the morning you could be ending this whole farce."

"Your Lordship," replied Sir Matthew, "we should end up the farce. We have no proof yet that will stand up in a court of law. I have not yet received any instructions from Birrell and I will not be the cause of an insurrection, which such a move surely must spark." He leaned back in his chair. "I will not have another incident like Bachelor's Walk. Why we might have Shinners rioting in the streets."

Wimbourne looked to the Chief Commissioner. "And you, Sir?"

The Commissioner had been sitting back, his shoulders slumped and appeared lost in thought. Now he threw off his reverie, and sitting up straight, looked around the table. He looked daggers at Burns.

"Lord Wimbourne is right," he started. Wimbourne grinned.

"How should we proceed?"

The Commissioner cleared his throat and continued.

"Your Lordship, we should surround and occupy Liberty Hall, Volunteer Headquarters, and Father Matthew Park and seize all their weapons. At the same time, we should make arrests of all their leaders, forbid drilling, and start a house by house search for weapons."

"And when should we do this?" Wimbourne was obviously enjoying this unexpected support.

"Tonight. We must start immediately." The Commissioner now looked uncomfortable. All was quiet for a moment. Burns was blood red.

Nathan stared directly at the Commissioner. "Can you do this by 2 a.m.?"

"By two?"

"Yes, Commissioner. It will be light by four-thirty. Sunrise is at five, and we must act in the dark."

The Commissioner sat back. "No, I can't. Especially with an unarmed force."

"Colonel Cowan, what forces have you?"

Cowan took a paper from his pocket. "Seventy-six officers and 1465 other ranks of infantry and 35 officers and 851 other ranks of cavalry. With those men, I have to garrison five barracks, the Castle, the Lodge, of course, your Lordship," nodding to Wimbourne, "the magazine, the Royal Hospital and the bank.

"Those numbers leave few men for a round-up of the size you infer. What if our installations were attacked while we were out marching in the streets?"

"There are about 250 to 300 men assembled right now at Liberty Hall," I put in.

Cowan eyed me a moment, then went on. "If what the gentleman has said is true, and they have the gelignite, we'll need to bring in infantry support from the Curragh and perhaps artillery from Athlone." He took a breath. "And it would have to be done in secret or the Shinners will be out and shooting."

"It can't be kept a secret," said Holmes. "Informers are everywhere. The moment you move, it will be known."

"You have a better idea?"

“Yes. You can end this by arresting eight men. Cut off the head and the body will be confused long enough for you to move up the men you need. Dr Ryan and I will return to Liberty Hall and start trying to find the locations of the leaders, for some will be staying in places other than their homes. If you don’t strike now, it will be too late.”

Nathan turned to the Commissioner. “Do you still say you can’t make this happen?”

“Sir Matthew, you know that the only armed part of the DMP is G-Division of which DS Burns is a part. They are only sixteen men. I must have military support.”

“Well, your Lordship, I believe that puts us back where we were. I will not arrest without proof or permission from Birrell, which I have already asked for. I hope to hear in two or three days. In the meantime, Major Price would you meet me at the Castle tomorrow, say at noon?”

The major nodded.

“And DS Burns? I would like you both to help me construct an arrest list.”

“I might be a bit late, Sir Matthew, but I’ll be there. I’d scheduled a meeting of my men for noon. Won’t take but a moment.”

“That’s fine, Detective. Is there anything else, Your Lordship? If not, I’ll wish you all a good night.” We all rose and started to depart. As we left the study, Holmes stopped in front of Burns.

“You really need to employ men with a little greater intelligence, you know. Dowdle and his three friends missed us again.”

“I don’t know what you mean, Altamont, but I think I’ve only one more need for them,” he paused. “Tomorrow.” He smirked and walked off.

“What now, Liam?” I asked.

“For me, Liberty Hall. For you, Mrs McGuffey’s. I’ll meet you at breakfast.”

“But, Liam.”

“In the morning, Thomas.” He departed into the darkness.

Chapter 13

Easter Monday

24 APRIL 1916

"Come, Watson. Breakfast is ready and I fear today you may not eat much else." Holmes was shaking me from my heavy sleep. It had been near dawn when I had finally been able to close my eyes to the outside world and fallen into a dreamless rest.

The sun shone behind my curtains. It was half six by my watch as I gathered myself together. Holmes was almost finished eating when I finally got to the table and as I sat there was a knock on the door. It was Cacy. He and some others had been given a mission to arouse people and get them to their assembly points by noon.

"I'd offer you some coffee but I'm sure you're in a hurry," I told him

"We've always a moment for a cup of coffee, Doctor. It's my only vice you know."

Holmes and I looked at each other and smirked. I poured a cup and handed it to Cacy. "Have you a bit of something to warm it? No? Well, that's fine, any coffee is good coffee."

"Do you have a particular message for me?" I asked.

"Yes, sir, you're to report to Connolly himself and to bring whatever medicines you have with you. He wants you too," he continued, nodding at Liam.

"How is your work going?" Holmes asked, packing his pipe.

"Not finding too many, I'm not. Between the manoeuvre being called off and all, folks have gone on their holiday." He put his empty cup back on the table. "Thank you, sirs, most welcome and refreshing. I'd best be off to see if I can find more folks for their parade at noon." With that, he waved and left.

"Holmes, he still doesn't know what's going on!"

"No, Watson. I left the Hall just over an hour ago and they still hadn't told the rank and file. Some of them have it figured out but for the most part, they are still ignorant of where their leadership is taking them today."

"What were you doing all night?"

"Mostly watching."

"Oh, who?"

"Burns and his men," he fiddled with his pipe. "Can't seem to get it packed right."

"Really, Holmes, can't you just answer a question?"

"Burns and his six minions were surveying their target and I was surveying them. They were also collecting equipment. Uniforms mostly, some weapons, rope, drills and other tools and taking them to their warehouse."

"What uniforms?"

"Volunteer uniforms."

"Do they intend to infiltrate the Volunteers?"

"Watson, Watson. You still do not see. Well, today all shall become clear. Come on," he rose from the table. "Connolly wants you and you can tell him I reported to work at the Castle as usual but I'll make some excuse of illness and come along presently."

As we left the lodgings, Holmes stopped me for a moment at the door. "Have you your identification papers?"

"Still sewn in my waistcoat."

"And your pistol?"

I patted my pocket.

"Good. Be a good fellow and tell Mrs McGuffey to go this morning and lay in enough provisions for a week. She'll understand what I mean. I'll be at the Hall quick as I can."

Holmes left and I went in search of Mrs McGuffey. She only sighed and nodded and I departed for Liberty Hall. "Doctor, do be careful," she called as the door closed.

When I arrived, the Hall was in a state of organized chaos. I sought out Connolly who smiled but seemed very serious.

"Doctor, good morning. Is that your whole supply?" he pointed to my medical bag.

"Yes, what's happening?"

He grabbed me by both shoulders and now truly smiled.

"We're making a republic, Doctor, and you're part of it. What do you think of that?"

I put forward my best grin. "Let's have at it, I say!"

"Good man. Many of the women here will be working with you. I've got some carts coming and I need you to supervise the loading of our medical stores."

"Is Dr Lynn not organizing that? After all she is your medical officer. First rate one, too."

"Ah, Doctor, she has other things to do this morning. Kathleen will have her hands full so I need you to supervise for the headquarters."

"Of course. I'll go find the ladies now." I went to find my charges. It seemed I would be needed in a professional capacity. I found the ladies packaging their meagre stores. Some had a fair idea of first aid, and others were nurses or students in training, so I saw some hope.

By now, word had spread generally all through the Hall that today was to be the rebellion. The full strength of the ICA was there, about 250. There was also a large group of Volunteers. Some had travelled from Plunkett's down in Kimmage by loading themselves and their weapons on a trolley and paying the two pence fare.

There really wasn't much for me to do yet. One lady appeared to be well in charge and had the women stacking boxes by the door awaiting transport. I decided I could better use my time by trying to gain information to pass to Holmes when he returned. So I went to Connolly's office.Tthe door stood open and I heard voices so I entered. Half the military council was in the room. A map of Dublin lay on the desk. It was Pearse who noticed me first.

"Good morning, Doctor. Come in, you may have need of this information before the day is through." Clarke looked at me, but did not speak. He was not the open trusting kind like Pearse. Mallin smiled and shook my hand, then turned back to the map. Ned Daly was also present.

Mallin's map was covered in dots from various coloured pencils. The colours were grouped in different areas. Mallin explained that each colour represented an area of responsibility for the four city battalions and the ICA or headquarters.

"Once more," said Clarke, "I want there to be no misunderstanding."

Mallin shrugged and with his pencil pointed out locations and named units.

“ICA and headquarters at the GPO. 1st Battalion under Ned goes from Blackhall Place and takes the Four Courts and the area west of GPO.”

“I’ll send D Company under Sean Heuston to the Mendicity to keep the Brits busy until we’re set up,” said Daly. “I told him he only has to give us three hours.” Everyone nodded and Mallin continued.

“MacDonagh takes his men to Jacob’s Biscuit Factory and covers the southwest. He’ll have to slow any troops coming from Portobello Barracks. He’s going to take Davy’s Pub down by the bridge. He’ll also be responsible for sending food supplies from the bakery.

“DeValera and his third battalion will take Boland’s Mill. The towers will give him great advantage. He’ll also take the rail yard, Westland Row Station and have to find a way to hold Mount Street Bridge. It’s the most direct route for troops being landed in Kingstown and marched north.

“Ceannt and the 4th Battalion take the South Dublin Union and will have to hold against any reinforcements from Richmond Barracks. I think that is it.”

“And 5th Battalion?” asked Clarke.

“Ashe will have a really tough job. He’s basically got the whole north side of the city. And I will take 100 men and hold St. Stephen’s Green.”

“What of communications?”

“We’ll have the GPO of course and Michael King and his men will take over the telephone exchange.”

“Do we have any numbers yet on how many men are mustering?”

Pearse answered the question. “Not yet. I’m afraid MacNeill has sorely hurt us but we’ll have what we have and no more. Surely once we start, the City and the Countryside will come to us.”

It was the pragmatist Clarke who broke the silence that followed Pearse’s statement. “We’ve modified the

3
8
7
2
4
5
6
Liffey River
13
A
F
1
10
1. Richmond Barracks
2. Magazine Fort
3. Viceregal Lodge
4. Military HQ
5. Military Hospital
6. Royal Barracks
7. Constabulary Barracks
8. Marlboro Barracks
9. Dublin Castle
10. Wellington Barracks
11. Trinity College
12. Customs House
13. Kingsbridge Station
A. Mendicity
B. Four Courts
C. City Hall
D. Jervis Hospital
E. Jacob's Factory
F. South Dublin Union
G. Davy's Public House
H. Mount St. Bridge
I. Bolands
J. St. Stephen's Green
K. College of Surgeons
L. Bank of Ireland
M. Liberty Hall
N. Pro-Cathedral
X. General Post Office
Dublin 1916

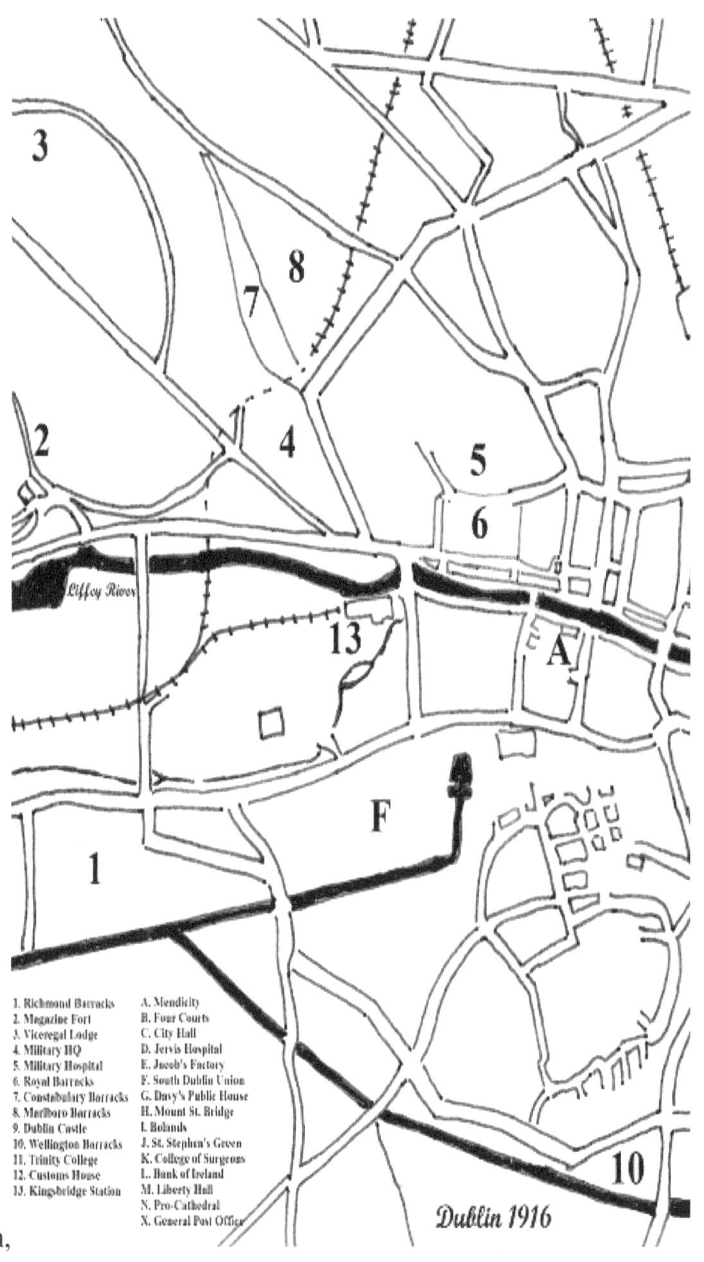

plan,

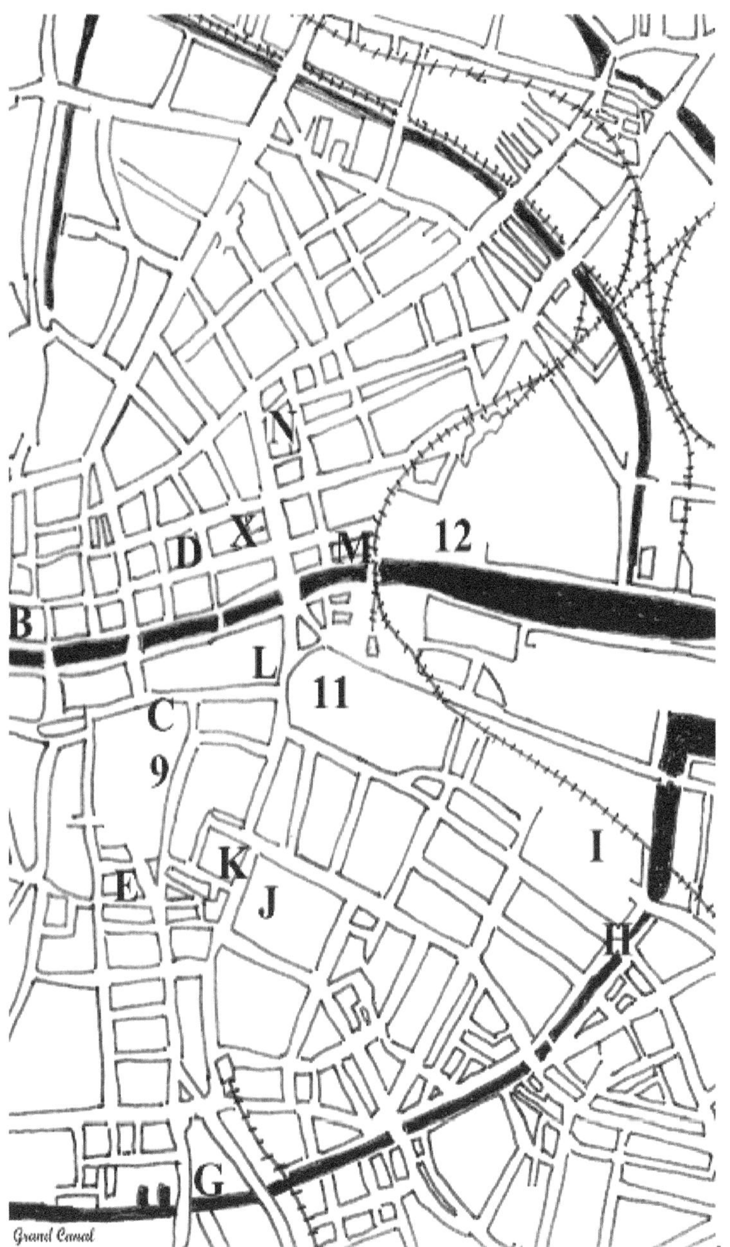

we're only taking key buildings and we here all know we can't hope but be defeated in the fight. But we will have risen and we will have done what is right for Ireland. Now, gentleman, let us shake hands and be about the people's business."

As we were about to leave, Cacy came in with a piece of paper, saluted and gave it to Connolly.

"It seems the first numbers are in, gentlemen. 1st Battalion 125 of 350 men are reporting, 2nd Battalion 150 men, 3rd Battalion 130 of 500 and 4th Battalion 130 of 1000. No numbers on 5th Battalion yet."

It was a sombre group that walked out of Connolly's office. Out on the steps, I could hear cheering and quite a commotion. I hustled to the door to find the Countess standing on the steps and reading, in a loud voice, the Proclamation of the Republic. When she finished, she waved the paper about to more cheers. Not only had they declared their independence, they had declared equality for all, both men and women. The cheers continued a moment, then their Lieutenants sent them back to work.

The Countess was ecstatic. She looked quite a sight in her ICA uniform. Breeches, tunic, Boer hat, Sam Browne and pistol. The ICA was the one unit that allowed women in their ranks and the Countess was one of the officers. I had to smile as I thought, "Mrs Hudson would never approve of the trousers, dear lady." But I must say I found the Countess an exciting woman.

It was now eleven o'clock and only 45 minutes before the Irish Army (such as it was) was to step off. I could not decide if I was watching a comedy or a tragedy. I knew that Nathan would be surprised. Even now while I knew he was meeting with Major Price to start an arrest list, he would be thinking a rising impossible.

The men joked and sang and appeared in high spirits. Their weapons were a motley collection. Most carried the single shot Mauser rifles that had been openly smuggled in at Howth. They were long barrelled affairs that fired an 11mm cartridge (about .45 calibre) and while they could not fire as quickly as a magazine rifle, the large heavy bullet meant substantial damage to anything or anybody who was hit.

There was a smattering of Enfield rifles in .303 calibre with 5-shot magazines, hunting guns, a few American Krag and German Mauser rifles left over from the Boer War, and lots of shotguns. This little Army would find its hands full in a fight. They little knew that Nathan's hesitancy, a liberal Army leave policy for the Holiday, and the need for the Army to protect so many sites, would all work to their benefit. Swift reactions might have crushed them in a day.

As the men were called to fall in a green touring car pulled up at the door. It was the O'Rahilly. He fairly leaped from the car and walked straight to Pearce. There was a moment of tension. Would the O'Rahilly confuse the whole situation? Would he stand on the steps and exhort the men to return home? I could see Pearse hold his breath. But it seemed that even the O'Rahilly felt there was nothing to do now but stand with the men he had trained. He thought the whole affair despicable, but how could he do other than stand with his soldiers? He held his hand out to Pearse. "I've helped wind up the clock. Might as well hear it strike." Pearse took his hand and thanked him. They may not agree but they would stand together.

We were able to load our few supplies in the O'Rahilly's car along with rifles and ammunition and bombs. The men were formed up. Sean Connolly, whom I had seen in the play a week before departed, with a force of fourteen men and nine women. His job was to keep the Castle from reinforcing or being reinforced. The women were well armed with pistols.

Mallin departed a moment later with 100 ICA men to take control of St. Stephen's Green. It was as he was leaving a man came up to Connolly. It was King, the man who was supposed to take over the telephone exchange. This was crucial. Telephones must be cut to keep the barracks from communicating with each other and coordinating an attack plan.

King had his back to me but I could hear him. "Sir, not one of the men detailed to take the exchange had appeared. I must have some others."

Connolly was looking straight at me. He knew I could hear. "Don't worry, Michael," he patted him on the shoulder. "We'll take it later. Right now we have use of everyone at the GPO." King's shoulders sagged as he walked off.

Connolly took a step toward me. "We know there is no hope, Doctor. But it's a start." He turned and walked toward where the columns had formed up.

Holmes had yet to return as our little Army started it's short march to the General Post Office. For the moment I walked along side of the O'Rahilly's touring car. The best I could estimate was that there were about 150 men and women altogether. Most were ICA, close to 100. The next were Volunteers including the Kimmage men. One tall fellow named Collins walked with Plunkett. Plunkett was recently out of surgery and in his weakened condition should not have even been with us. He would not let his men go without him.

It's but a three minute walk to the GPO from Liberty Hall and waiting for us were Clarke and MacDiarmada. It was just then that Holmes came up to me.

"We're in it now," he said.

"Nothing from Nathan?"

"No. He and Price would only work on the arrest lis., Burns has not appeared so Nathan sent for Norway, who is in charge of the Post Office to come help."

"Charge!" The cry rang out from Connolly at the head of the column. With a rush, the men broke ranks and ran through the doors of the GPO from Sackville and Henry Streets.

"I'm back to the Castle, Thomas," Holmes whispered, and flew down the road as fast as he could run.

The crowd in the Post Office at first took the whole melee as a joke. That is until Connolly fired a round from his pistol into the ceiling. Patrons and workers alike poured out the doors.

"Doctor," said Connolly. "Find a good place for your dispensary. Probably somewhere in the back."

There was a commotion in the centre of the Post Office. Collins had two men at gunpoint, one a constable, the other an Army Lieutenant. The constable stood quietly, hands in the air. The Lieutenant was going on about his status in life and his thoughts about the Volunteers. When Collins felt he'd listened to enough he grabbed down some telephone wire, tied the fellow up and dumped him in a telephone booth, closing the door. Even the constable laughed.

"Where would you like the equipment, Doctor?" It was one of the nurses. I hadn't yet learned names.

I spent the next bit of time deciding on the Postmen's Sorting Room at the far back of the building. It had windows for light and water in two small closets and a passage out to Prince's Street.

Having organized the nurses and given instructions, I went back to the Public Office. Men were busy all around converting the building into a fortress. Windows were smashed now to avoid injury later and then barricaded with whatever was at hand. The building had only been opened to the public six weeks before after a renovation that had taken years. Now the non-supporting walls were being smashed down to make new passages and arms and bombs were being stacked in the general sorting room.

Upstairs there were shots. It took me fully a minute to find a set of stairs and make my way to the floor above. Seven or eight soldiers were under close guard and their sergeant wounded. Up here was the main telegraph office, something the rebels surely wanted to control.

"Let me see the Sergeant," I insisted, and pushed my way through. It was a head wound, not bad, but in need of stitches.

"Is there a hospital close by?"

"Yes, Doctor, Jervis Street Hospital. Just a minute's walk," replied a Volunteer.

"Sergeant, you need stitches and it would best be done there." I turned back to the Volunteer leader. "I'm sending him."

"Of course, Doctor. We'll take the rest downstairs."

"I'm no goin'" cried the Sergeant. "I'll no leave my men nor quit my post until 1800 as ordered."

"Sergeant, you go get treated and we'll let you come back to your post," remarked the Volunteer.

The men shook hands and the Sergeant and his men were escorted out.

I asked the Volunteer as we descended the stairs why there hadn't been more casualties, both sides at close quarters and heavily armed. He stopped on the stairs and turning to me grinned. "They had rifles but no ammunition! Lucky for us, eh?" The squad leader was Michael Staines and I found him to be a fine man.

Back in the Public Office I caught sight of Holmes coming into the building. Spying me, he motioned for me to come outside. I joined him by the columns.

"I was too late, Watson. They had already attacked the Castle and one of the constables has been killed. The gates were closed when I got there."

"Not Flood?" I asked.

"No, another man named O'Brien."

"Still, surely he was unarmed."

"Yes, but the soldiers had weapons. He must have been killed while closing the gate."

Men were passing us as they came out of the GPO and, once on Sackville Street, started running toward the Liffey. I knew they meant to take up positions by O'Connell Bridge. They would use Kelly's Pub and Hopkins on the other corner. Men were now in the Imperial Hotel across the street and a cheer went up as they raised the Starry Plough, (the flag of the ICA), over the hotel. There was a responding cheer and the men in the Imperial were pointing at the GPO. Holmes and I walked out into the street and, looking up, saw the Countess's green flag and the tricolour of the Republic flying where the Union Jack had been.

"What now?" I asked. "We've failed miserably."

"No, Watson, we didn't fail. They would not listen." He reached in his pocket and pulled out his pipe. "Now we at least try to stop Burns. Something good must happen."

"But you still haven't told me what it is. You are really frustrating Holmes!"

"All will be clear by tonight, old fellow." He stopped to light his pipe. "Now, shall we see where the great rebellion stands?" We walked back into the GPO.

As men worked feverishly, Pearce, Connolly and Clarke were gathered together by the counter. Collins was with them, as was Cacy.

"Plunkett has sent someone to the Archbishop?" It was Clarke asking.

"Yes," said Collins. "He wants to be sure the Archbishop is informed. He still thinks we should have kept him informed."

"No word from the battalions yet?"

"Too early, they'll be just getting into position. We do have more men reporting in. Word is getting about already."

"What have we left out?" asked Pearse. "We've sent men everywhere we can reasonably expect to hold, I think."

Holmes took the pipe from his mouth. "Give me a dozen men and I can hold the South side of the O'Connell Bridge."

Connolly thought for a moment. "No. Liam, I appreciate the offer, but we haven't enough men to hold Trinity College and that would be the place to hold. Now come, Padraig. It's time you read our proclamation to the world." They walked off, out of the GPO, and toward where Pearse would announce the Irish Republic.

"Look here, Liam! What's this about a dozen men?" I asked.

He slowly took his tobacco pouch out to recharge his pipe and, while Pearse declared the Republic, Holmes explained. "What buildings are around the Castle? You've walked the city, describe what's there."

"Let's see, Ship Street Barracks, the Daily Express Office, City Hall of course, a hospital, the Telephone Exchange. Trinity College is a block east."

"And across the street from Trinity?" He threw his spent match down.

"The Bank of Ireland!"

"Exactly, old fellow. And it is the bank that is the object of Mr Burns' desire."

"Of course, the uniforms, the weapons. He intends to rob the bank and blame it on the Shinners. But why haven't the Volunteers taken the bank?"

"Well, first off, they know that it's a depository of the People's money and they don't really want to do more harm than necessary. Secondly, the bank is of no strategic value."

"But it covers the bridge and looks into Trinity and it has historical significance. The Irish Parliament met there before it was dissolved."

"Yes, but it has no windows and does have thick walls. You can't shoot from it."

"No windows?"

"It was built when windows and fireplaces had special taxes. It has no windows to avoid the tax."

I thought for a moment. "But we must stop Burns. How?"

"We shall solve that problem. He won't strike before dark and sunset is not until half seven. In the meantime, we best get back and help the rebellion."

The initial chaos and adrenalin rush of the charge had faded and now men moved with calm and purpose. I decided to check on Plunkett. He had found a stool in one of the offices and sat quietly by a counter, Collins stood with him. He acquiesced to my insistence on checking him. He was fatigued already. I recommended he take himself to the Imperial Hotel across the street and lie down, but he would have none of it.

Hearing constant banging I asked Collins what was going on. "Tunnelling, Doctor. We'll be knocking holes in all the walls that connect with another building. It will allow us to move up and down the streets from inside and not expose our men to travelling openly on the streets where they can be shot."

"A wise device."

"We'll soon be able to move from here to Jervis Street hospital, or down to the river and back, with little exposure - except when we have to cross an intervening road. At those we'll have barricades to help."

I looked about. "Have you seen the O'Rahilly?"

"He's been given charge of the upper floors. The boys will have a tough job."

I could feel movement at my back. Men were running to the doors and windows, rifles at the ready.

"Lancers in the street!" cried someone. I rushed to the doors with the rest. "Keep back, they're forming up at the top of the street," came another voice. All was excitement. I decided to go to the second floor. Where was Holmes? In moments we would be in a shooting war. I found a window from where I could see toward the top of the street.

Lancers in bright uniforms mounted on fine thoroughbreds were formed into line two deep all across Sackville Street. They actually carried lances! This wasn't pig-sticking in India! These men I was with were armed. Antiquated weapons surely but they could kill. "You fools!" I wanted to scream.

Word was being passed around the floor. "No shooting until men and horses are in front of the GPO, per Connolly." Somehow I had to stop this. Taking my pistol from my pocket, I waited. If I could fire a shot just when they were in good rifle range, it might be enough to warn them to fall back. I could claim I was over-anxious.

Now they were moving, lances and polished leather shining in the sun. Damn fools. Closer and closer they got. I held my breath, pointing my pistol in the air, I got ready to fire. They were close now. I must fire now or they were lost. But there was an explosion! The lancers hesitated, general firing commenced from roof tops and windows. The Lancers fell back, up the street and out of range. They left dead men and dying horses but not near what could have happened. I ran as fast as I could go, back down the stairs. I must get to the wounded.

"Hold on, Doctor." It was Holmes. "Those men are dead. But we've a couple wounded of our own. Cut by glass coming in the windows."

I went to our little dispensary where I started treating some bad cuts. One man had shot himself in the belly with his own weapon by accident. I grabbed two able looking fellows and had them carry the fellow to the hospital. As yet, the streets were still fairly safe. That was not to last long.

I went back to the Public Office, searching for Holmes. There I found him with Connolly, Plunkett and Pearse. I could tell we had more men in the building than two hours ago. Plans were being revised. Messengers, mostly boys and girls, were coming and going with reports and instructions.

It was a bit after two and the map that Mallin had left had more markings. Holmes motioned for me to accompany him outside. "Let me bring you up to date, Doctor." He was using me to clarify his own thoughts. "We had our little fight, and we've lots of boys raiding the food stocks and chemists about for supplies."

"It was fortunate someone's bomb went off early," I said.

"Perhaps the poor fellow was handed one with a fuse cut too short?" Holmes whispered to me. "At any rate, there is already general fighting. Some telephone lines were cut but without taking the exchange, they have left communications intact for the Army.

"Sean Heuston has the Mendicity[11] and shot the Army up pretty badly trying to come down the quays. The men at Jacob's Biscuit weren't able to hold Davy's and the bridge, but have stopped any men from Portobello barracks for the moment. The Castle is not taken and soldiers are already arriving in Dublin from the Curragh at Kingsbridge Station. Trinity College is held by the students and some soldiers who were in the area. They've closed the gates and can fire on the Volunteers all the way to the GPO. No real word from Boland's Mill but Mallin is digging in at St. Stephen's and the Countess has stayed to help him. Oh, and MacBride has evidently fallen in with us. Good man to have in a fight."

"MacBride who led the Irish Brigade for the Boers?" I asked.

"The same," replied Holmes.

I made a few excuses about getting back to the dispensary and Holmes tagged along behind with some questions about a blister.

I talked lowly to Holmes as we walked.

"Holmes, this is insanity! They have a score of little Maiwands[12]. These rebels can't hope but to be defeated. Where is the honour in this?"

"It's not the honour, it's the martyrdom, my friend."

"Liam!" It was Collins calling. We re-entered the GPO. "Connolly

---

[11] A stone building across the river and slightly East from the entrance to the Royal Barracks.

[12] Maiwand was the disastrous battle where Watson was wounded in the Second Afghan War. See *Watson's Afghan Adventure.*

wants you to try and take a message to Ceannt at the South Dublin Union."

"Come, Doctor, let's talk to Mr Connolly."

Connolly was back at the counter. "Never mind, Liam. I've sent Seamus. The City Hall wants more men, now Sean tells me that Heuston is already surrounded by machine guns at the Mendicity. I've no help to send." He walked to the windows. "And now we've the poor to contend with."

I followed his gaze. Crowds were gathering in the street and already the first stores had been broken into. "They've nothing and now a chance to have everything," he went on, "or so they think." He shook his head. "Excuse me. I'll have to see what I can do to stop this." He walked off.

Sean MacLoughlain was about to bolt out the door and return to Mendicity when Holmes grabbed his arm.

"Hey, Sean, buddy. I need you to do somethin' for me, would ja?"

"If I can, Liam, but I've got to get back."

"Tonight 'bout seven-thirty, I need you to do a job. Go by the main building of the Bank of Ireland. I want to know who's there. Then come tell me."

"Why?" asked Sean with a serious scowl.

"Because I think some rats are gonna take advantage of this and try to break in. We have to stop 'em. Get it?"

"We wouldn't do that!"

"Not us! Some rats!"

Sean looked doubtful. "Well okay, but it'll be on the way back here. I've got my duty too."

"Sure, you betcha. But I'm relyin' on ya!"

"Alright," replied Sean, and he was gone.

"Holmes," I whispered. "Shouldn't you get to the Castle and see what you can do to help?"

"No, Watson. This is a military affair now, and besides, no one will want to see the people who can say 'I told you so'."

"No, I guess not."

"But we should be able to get you out of here."

"You jest! I can't leave. We've already got wounded and injured. I must stay."

Holmes just smiled. "I'd best see if I can help with the looters. I'll be back."

I returned to our little dispensary. We were still able to get to the Jervis Street hospital so I evacuated all I could.

It had finally gotten dark, close on to eight o'clock. Runners were still making regular reports. The Mendicity and Jacob's Mill had evidently had the most of the fighting. The raid on the ammunition magazine at Phoenix Park had been terribly botched. Four Courts had seen some fighting with Lancers. The Castle had been reinforced as had the Viceregal Lodge and soldiers were pouring into Dublin from the Curragh and Athlone. Athlone meant artillery!

Here, tunnelling was still going on. Soon men would be able to travel under cover from the GPO to the Liffey and out the back all the way down the block west. Soldiers were on top of Trinity College and able to snipe the GPO. It was a long shot with iron sights, but random bullets would hit a mark. I would later learn that these were Australian and New Zealand soldiers who had merely been on leave in Ireland and came to the College's aid. Despite the threat of death by the new Republic, looting continued unabated. Pearse might threaten, but he had no heart for shooting the poor.

I had agreed to meet Holmes in the Public Office just after eight and found him there in conference with MacLoughlain.

"Ah, Thomas. Good. We've got to find Pearse and Connolly. I'll fill you in on what the lad has told me when we find them. I think they're with Plunkett in the Bag Room."

As Holmes had said, the three along with Collins were in the bag room conferring.

"Gentlemen," said Holmes, not waiting to be recognized, "you need to hear what this boy just told me."

"Well," said Connolly, looking to Sean.

"Ah, Liam here asked me to check on the bank on me way back next time, so I did."

All looked at Liam but said nothing.

"Well," the boy went on. "I did and we've taken it."

"What do you mean, we've taken it? We don't have anybody there!" shot Connolly.

"There were two men by the door with Volunteer uniforms. There were having to hide pretty good because of the soldiers at Trinity but they were ours."

"What can this mean?" said Pearse.

"It means someone is trying to take advantage of the rising for their own gain, sir. And they'll blame us," replied Holmes. "Give me six men and we'll put an end to this."

Connolly looked at Pearse for a moment. "All right. But I want your man Collins to go also, Joe. The men know him better."

"Of course. Michael, pick five good men. If the bank has been taken by our men, order them out."

"Yes, sir," replied Collins. His dower disposition seemed to disappear. He was a man of action and being constrained as he was in this building was trying on him.

"Doctor," continued Holmes. "I'm most afraid we'll need you also."

"Of course," I replied.

We took our leave of the leaders and Collins went to gather up his men.

"Tell me, Sean," Holmes asked the boy, "can you lead us a good route?"

"Sure, I can. We can still get across Ha'penny Bridge with no problem, then it's the alleys to the west side of the Bank."

With Collins and his men, we started to work our way through the streets toward the river. We left the looters behind. The streets were deserted and dark. DeValera had turned off the electricity to the trams early in the day, but now all the electricity was off. Keeping low, we hustled across the bridge and past the turnstiles. The British had not yet moved down the Quays but were assembling in Trinity College. We passed down turnstile alley, the dark and the height of the buildings in front protecting us from the view of snipers on the roof of the college.

There was a stillness to our west, to the east came the sound of an Army in motion as men and equipment poured into Trinity. The British were also making use of the early hours of darkness. Only a few hundred yards away men were moving down the roads between the Castle and the College, men who fortunately did not know the area and chose not to leave the main roadways.

We were headed for the west side of the building. Formerly it had been the Irish Parliament (dissolved by the Act of Union in 1801) and now the Bank of Ireland. Holmes already knew where the vault was located on the west side of the Bank. As we neared the bank, we kept to the east side of the alley, moving slowly. Holmes was a few steps in front of me with Sean. Behind me came Collins himself. As we reached the northwest corner of the building, Holmes stopped and motioned everyone to get down and wait. Slowly, he and Sean disappeared into the darkness. We waited there, listening to the noise of soldiers preparing for the next day's fight. It seemed we waited forever but in truth it could not have been more than a few moments. A figure came toward me, slowly out of the darkness. I gripped my pistol until I was sure it was Holmes returning. He whispered for the men to close up and listen to his instructions.

"Sean is watching their one man, who is in the shadow on the far end of the west portico. You can see the glow of his cigarette. He's in a Volunteer uniform, but in the dark it's hard to tell between British and Volunteer.

"Collins, the doctor and I are going to take him. Don't worry how, but when you hear the scuffle, come on. Send two men down the street below. They'll have to make sure no one comes up. Leave one man here and send one to the alley going west. No shooting unless you have to, got it? If you're attacked, hold as long as you can, then make a run for the bridge. You and your other men follow me and the doc here in once we've got their guy on the outside. All you mugs understand? Good. C'mon doc." He stood up straight and walked to the middle of the alley. "Count to 20 then follow us."

Grabbing my shoulder, Holmes started stumbling and singing in a moderate voice. He laughed in a booming voice between choruses of a song I had never heard and half dragged me forward toward the bank. We passed Sean hidden in the recess of a doorway. I could see him grin as I and my drunken friend went by.

Holmes stumbled and sang and as we came abreast of the portico, I saw the glow of a cigarette being flicked to the ground.

"I want me money, Thomas," cried Holmes, in a voice to wake the dead. "These beggars have me money and I need it. What say we go ask, eh?" And we stumbled toward the entrance. A figure in uniform and holding an Enfield rifle stepped out of the darkness.

"Hold up there," said the figure. "Get the hell out with you. The bank is closed and if you don't leave I'll have you arrested." I recognized one of "the six".

"But they have me money!"

"Off with you, I said," hissed the guard. And as he did, took one step too close. With that cat-like reflex Holmes had always possessed, he struck a tremendous blow to the man's jaw, laying him out on the steps, his rifle falling with a clatter.

With a rush, Collins and his partner were there. Our guard was trussed, gagged and dragged into the shadow. At the same time, I could sense the other four take their places and Sean came hurrying up. He gathered up the guard's rifle and melted back into the shadows across the alley.

By now Holmes was at the door listening to find if we'd been given away. He quietly opened the door and we followed him inside. In front was a counter which we followed around to the right. The darkness was horrible. Moonrise would not be until two in the morning, so even with the large door behind us open there was only blackness.

As we came around the corner I could see a dull light from under a door. In here, there would be no danger of someone outside seeing it and investigating. Holmes stood, charged the door, and burst in. The guard here must have been standing with his back to the door, for he was thrown onto four other men who were lying, bound on the floor in front of him. Before our victim could recover, he found Holmes on his chest and a pistol in his face. A candle glowed on a small table. We had the second of our six in hand and tied up with four British soldiers on the floor. Holmes instructed Collins' man to stand guard on our prisoner, then he, Collins and I went on down a corridor to a large double door. I knew we must be outnumbered now. Surely Burns and Dowdle were here with their other three minions. As we slid through the double doors, Holmes whispered to me, "Remember, it's Burns we want. The rest we can always have."

We moved along a second corridor to a stairwell. I could barely see at all when Holmes flicked on an electric torch. "Someday I must thank Mr Hubert for his invention," whispered Holmes. We moved down the stairs, all three pistols in hand. The vault would be below.

We exited the stairway and Holmes switched off the torch. Down the hall, to the right, we could see the glow of lamps and hear men working. We tip-toed down the corridor and, almost as one, the three of us gazed around the doorway. Inside the room were six men. Burns was chastising his thugs to hurry and fill Army kit bags with money while Dowdle held a gun on the man I imagined who had been "persuaded" to open the vault.

"That's it boys," said Burns. "That's all us rebels can carry," he laughed, as the men picked up the bags.

"And him?" asked Dowdle, pointing at the banker with his pistol.

"Why, he died trying to save the bank's money."

Dowdle smirked and cocked the hammer. I didn't wait. I stepped into the light, my own pistol pointed at Dowdle.

"I do not believe that would be advisable Mr Dowdle," I said. "Now put that weapon down."

For an instant, everything stopped. There was no movement anywhere. Dowdle must have thought me alone, for he merely smiled.

"Why, sure it is, doctor," he replied. But I had learned long ago to watch a man's hands, not listen to his words. Instead of dropping the pistol, he pivoted toward me, weapon level. His shot went wide, mine struck home, followed by another. Afghanistan and South Africa had both taught me to make sure my foe was down and not able to make a second effort.

Holmes and Collins were now in the room. Burns and his three friends all had their hands in the air. The banker still stood in terror, his back against the vault wall. I went to Dowdle, but he was already gone. "It didn't have to end like this," I said, to no one in particular.

"Never mind, Doctor. " It was Holmes. "Let's get these others out of here."

"Sir," he addressed the banker, "we are going to remove these men. Would you be kind enough to re-close the vault door?"

The banker nodded. I could tell he was in shock but for now, at least, he could function.

"Collins, if you'll go first, these four gentlemen will follow. Doctor, grab the lantern. I'll come along with Mr….?"

"Brooks." Stammered the banker.

"First, let's get this man out of your vault. Grab a hand there, that's it. Now shut the door please and lock it. I'm sure you can put all that money back on the shelves later."

I had moved into the hallway with the lantern and it was here I made my mistake. Collins was moving slowly in front, then Burns' three men, then Burns. All had their hands in the air. I walked up behind Burns, pistol in one hand, lantern in the other. I knew I was too close when, with one motion, he turned to his left and caught me in the face with his left hand. I went sprawling, still clutching both pistol and lantern.

A rifle is a fine weapon but not in a close space. As all four made a run at Collins, it was more use as a club than a firearm. He was thrown to the floor in the rush and the gun went off. Another man down and Burns and the other two were sprinting up the stairs three steps at a time. Holmes passed before I or Collins could get off the floor. Collins followed Holmes as I looked to Burns' man. He was dead, the bullet having entered the chin and gone through the top of his head. Brooks was beside me in near panic. Holding the lantern and pistol in one hand, I took his arm and guided him up the stairs.

At the room where we had left all the prisoners, I found Sean, Collins, the men we had left, and Burns' companions who had followed him up the stairs.

"Where's Liam?" I asked.

"Gone after some gent," replied Sean. "They moved too fast for me, but I got these two trying to come out," he gestured with his newly acquired rifle.

"Which way did they go?"

"Over toward direction of the Castle."

I pondered for a moment. What was I to do? It was pointless and dangerous to go after the two of them. I didn't know where they would run. And the soldiers were likely to shoot any civilian in the dark.

"Doctor," said Collins. "We'd best do something with these men."

"Sean, untie the soldiers."

"What?"

"Untie the soldiers. Tie up this lot." I pointed to Burns' men. "First stack all the rifles over here by me. Now just tie their hands behind their backs. Collins, re-call your men. We'll be taking these imposters with us."

Collins had his men gathered in moments.

"Mr Brooks, I put these four soldiers of the King in your care. You will not be molested again. I assure you these men were bandits and no part of the Volunteers. I think that once we are gone, these men will be able to re-arm themselves over at Trinity College."

Seeing that we had all the arms and our four prisoners, I asked Sean to lead us back. We moved swiftly back across Half Penny Bridge and north to the GPO.

As we entered, I could see a line of men waiting to say their confessions to Father Flanagan, but I had more need of some rest. Wherever Holmes was, his battle with Burns was now his. It was just now half ten and Collins took charge of our prisoners. I could hear firing in the distance. The firing would go on all night. It was left to me to explain our adventure.

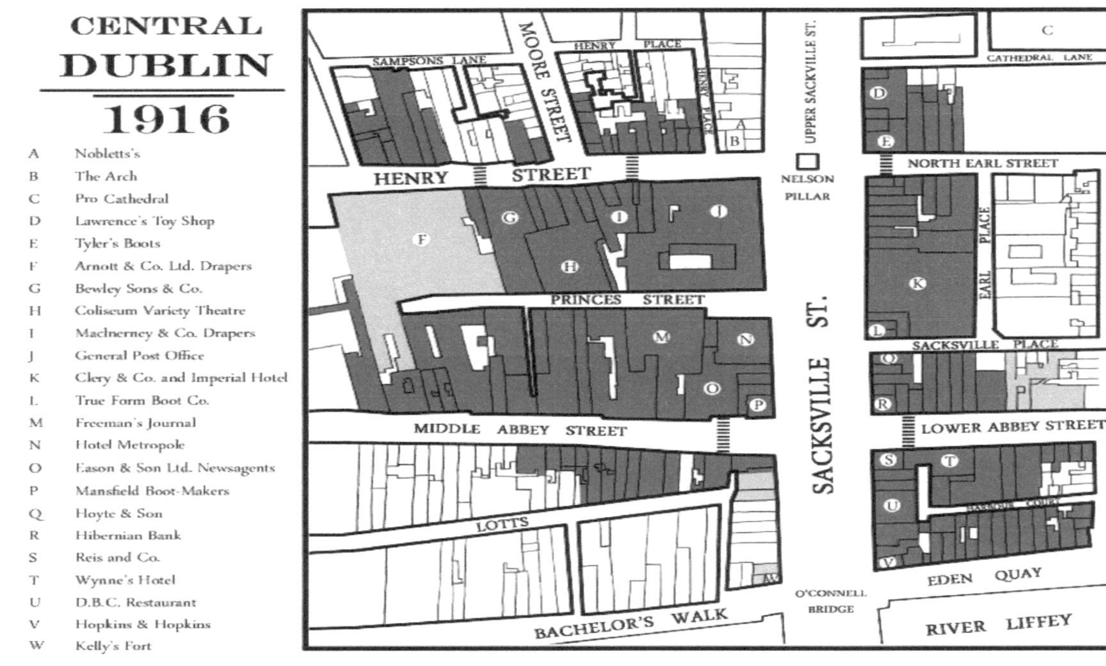

CENTRAL
DUBLIN
1916
A Nobletts's
B The Arch
C Pro Cathedral
D Lawrence's Toy Shop
E Tyler's Boots
F Arnott & Co. Ltd. Drapers
G Bewley Sons & Co.
H Coliseum Variety Theatre
I MacInerney & Co. Drapers
J General Post Office
K Clery & Co. and Imperial Hotel
L True Form Boot Co.
M Freeman's Journal
N Hotel Metropole
O Eason & Son Ltd. Newsagents
P Mansfield Boot-Makers
Q Hoyte & Son
R Hibernian Bank
S Reis and Co.
T Wynne's Hotel
U D.B.C. Restaurant
V Hopkins & Hopkins
W Kelly's Fort
SAMPSONS LANE
MOORE STREET
HENRY PLACE
HENRY PLACE
UPPER SACKVILLE ST.
CATHEDRAL LANE
HENRY STREET
NELSON PILLAR
NORTH EARL STREET
PRINCES STREET
EARL PLACE
SACKSVILLE ST.
SACKSVILLE PLACE
MARLBOROUGH STREET
MIDDLE ABBEY STREET
LOWER ABBEY STREET
LOTTS
EDEN QUAY
O'CONNELL BRIDGE
BACHELOR'S WALK
RIVER LIFFEY

Chapter 14

Tuesday

25 April 1916

It had taken past midnight to explain to Pearse, Connolly and the rest what had happened. I thought it best not to tell all I knew. I explained how we had found the seven men trying to rob the bank and had stopped them, how we had turned the bank over to the now disarmed guard and how Liam had gone after their leader. Burns' men were quite morose without their leader and kept quiet. At least they understood that to admit their complicity with a G-man would only make their plight all the worse.

I could tell that Collins thought there was more to the story than what he knew, but said nothing and asked no questions. I went to check on my little dispensary. Considering our meagre supplies, the ladies had done admirably with our few patients who had not been evacuated to the hospital.

By one in the morning, I had found a nook and fallen to sleep. I knew I could not impact whatever Holmes was doing, and somehow I now felt my age. Many's the time I had slept to the sound of gunfire.

It was just past three when I was awakened. "Thomas, time to get up old fellow. We've places to go." It was Holmes. I wiped the sleep from my eyes and looked at his face in the candle light. Even now, I marvel at his energy.

"I see you wasted no sleep on worrying about me," he grinned.

"Fairly pointless, old fellow. I'd no idea where you went, but I had faith in you."

Holmes laughed and sat back on a pile of mail sacks.

"And Burns?" I asked.

Holmes face did not lose its smile. "Dead, I'm afraid."

"Did you?"

"No, not me, old friend." He reached in his pocket and retrieved his pipe. "Soldiers of His Majesty's Army meted out the punishment."

"But how?"

"Oh, they thought he was a rebel I suppose. I chased him west toward the Castle, then up to the Quays and back east and finally south toward

College Street. I suppose he was trying to make it to the police station." He stopped and lighted his pipe.

"And?" I prodded.

"Well," he drew in some smoke. "I suppose the soldiers in Trinity College took him for a rebel. I mean, in the dark, civilian clothes, running down the street. Pretty valid assumption at most times. Once he went down, I watched some soldiers go to him. They left him there on the street. No point in bringing in a dead man."

He leaned back further into the sacks and closing his eyes, puffed slowly on the pipe.

"So without knowing it, they have served out the King's justice," I mused.

"Quite, and we, my friend, should be off." He stood up and looked at where I sat. "Dawn comes at five, it's near four now and it'll be lightening in the east. Our mission is done and we need what little darkness is left to get to the Castle and not end up like friend Burns."

I stood for a moment and looked at the dispensary. The ladies had formed themselves into shifts and, while some slept, others tended the wounded.

"No, Holmes, I can't go." I looked at Holmes, who only nodded.

"I thought you might say that."

"I know warfare, Holmes. This is going to be very bloody. All they have is a few nurses and a medical student. Good lad by the name of Jim Ryan."

I paused, thinking. "I can't say I'm not in sympathy with their cause. The country has been treated shabbily. I just don't approve of their method. But I can't leave men who I know need what little skill I possess. Can you understand, Holmes?"

Holmes put a hand on my shoulder. "It's what I expected, Watson. Exactly what I expected. But I had to come and give you a chance to get out. By tomorrow, the men north and south of the Liffey will be cut off from each other."

"I appreciate it, Holmes. But my duty now is with the wounded. I'll be careful and I still have my papers." I patted my waistcoat.

We shook hands and Holmes turned to go. "How will you get there?"

"Oh, for now, across Capel St. Bridge, then through the alleys to the Castle. I'll have no problem."

"And what will you tell them about Burns?"

"That I haven't decided. Well, Watson, be careful." With a quick wave, he was gone. I went out into the Public Office. Things here were quiet for the moment. Plunkett was asleep on a cot that had been brought out for him. If anyone had no business being out in this mess, it was he. He should have been convalescing at home from his surgery.

It was now near dawn and the streets were dangerous again. The snipers at Trinity College could drop rifle bullets all around us. I could hear a roar of gunfire down by the river and to the southwest just a bit. The Army must be attacking city hall. They needed to drive the rebels out so they could have free movement in the Castle yard and civil government have a place to work. The thought kept coming back, "a score of little Maiwands". I suppose our American cousins would call it "little Alamos". I shook my head. Had the war in France taught these men nothing? A static defence against overwhelming power? To me it made no sense. And soon we on one side of the river would be cut off from those on the other side. Their very plan had meant disaster. Had all the men been between the Liffey and the Grand Canal, how much better for command and control it would have been. Or between Liffey and the Royal Canal, at least then they could escape into the mountains. But it was not my job to fix their deficient plan.

Dawn had come. It was about five in the morning and the firing was dying out from near City Hall when I heard the rattle of machine guns. I approached Collins and asked what he knew.

"Not much, Doctor, I do say I don't like being in this box for the Brits to shoot at."

"Nor I. Any word from outlying points?"

"Our people are moving quite freely still. I fear the City Hall has probably fallen, but we've other men in the buildings in the area. Worst is that Mallin is catching hell. Brits have put machine guns in the Shelbourne Hotel and are cutting him up pretty badly."

Connolly walked up to us and asked Collins to check on the tunnelling efforts. The tunnel from the GPO to the west had just started. But work should be progressing from the Liffey.

"I'm sending men over to the Metropole Hotel, Doctor, and we'll be putting up some barbed wire across the road. With the sniping from Trinity, I expect some casualties."

"I see our looters are out again," I remarked. "You'd think they'd stay in from the bullets."

"What more fear have they of bullets than of everyday life? No, Doctor, they don't fear death. For these people, death is a relief." He looked down and started to walk away when an ICA man stopped him.

"Excuse me, sir, but I need to leave for a bit. I've got to get to work."

"You what? This is a war, man!"

"Oh, I understand, sir. But I'm the only one with the keys to the warehouse and me mates will lose a day's pay if I don't open up."

Connolly looked stunned, then looked at me and laughed.

"I understand," he replied, "but once you've opened up, remember we need you here."

"Course, sir, thank you."

The man gave a salute and scurried toward the Henry Street door as he checked his watch.

The morning continued with sporadic fire from Trinity, looters in the streets, tunnelling, and the building of barricades. For me, there was a constant flow of minor injuries, mostly glass cuts, or misdirected shovels and picks.

Our British prisoners were put to work in a make-shift kitchen and actually seemed to be having a good time. The nearby hotel kitchens had been emptied of supplies. There appeared to be adequate food to go around. Burns' men had been taken to the basement and locked in a small room to be dealt with later. There had been sporadic fire in the looted buildings and the fire brigade had been risking both irate looters and occasional bullets trying to put the fires out. So far, they were successful. It was going late morning when Sean O'Kelly brought the first bad news. City Hall and the Express Office had both been taken and British troops had free movement in and out of the Castle. There were but a few Volunteer snipers left in the area.

About noon, a large number of re-enforcements arrived, about 65 in number. They were immediately divided up and put to work. A barricade went up on lower Abbey Street and the tunnel from Sackville Place to Lower Abbey Street was finished. On into mid-afternoon things around the GPO were still fairly quiet.

I could imagine Colonel Cowan's plan, if he was still the senior man present. I speculated that Brigadier-General Lowe would probably be here by now. There was no need to rush. We had bottled ourselves up. Cowan only had to gain strength then take out each strongpoint one at a time. He'd probably concentrate around the Castle first and the Viceregal Lodge. Then St. Stephen's to be sure of a route from the boats for more troops. All he really had to do was make sure we stayed put and ran out of food and ammunition.

It was mid-afternoon when Sean MacLoughlain ran into the GPO. "Doctor, have you seen Mr Connolly? Ah, never mind, there he is."

I walked over to where Connolly stood next to Pearse.

"Sir," went Sean. "I can't get back across the river. We're fairly cut off. Without swimming it in the dark, I'm not sure how to get across."

"Can we still communicate with Ned Daly at the Four Courts?" asked Pearse.

"Yes. sir." He looked at me. "And we've got a hole yet to the hospital, doctor. I knew you would ask." He smiled. This was without a doubt, the bravest 15-year-old I had ever met.

"You've done well," said Connolly. I could tell he truly liked the boy. "Stay close, we may need you to run more messages soon." I went back to my dispensary. There sat Holmes on a pile of sacks.

"Liam, what…?" I asked.

"Couldn't leave you alone, don't know what you might do."

I knew he could have stayed out of danger and yet he came back to help a friend. I didn't know what to say.

"Well, where do you need me?" he continued.

"I do need more supplies, so anything you can go out and find would be appreciated." I moved closer and whispered, "How the devil did you get back?"

"All the way up by the Grand Canal and then south," he whispered back. "Plenty of open ground if you're willing to leave the main roads. They're moving around in an arc all across the north side. If our friends don't decide to get out soon, they will not get out."

"Liam!" It was Connolly, "Where have you been?"

"Out scoutin', boss. Like Sherman through Georgia. Pickin' the place clean for the Doctor here."

“Excellent. Listen, I’ve just heard from Fergus O’Kelly. The wireless is up and running at Reis’s. I need this message taken there and sent to the world. Everyone must know that there is now an Irish Republic and that the Republican Army holds Dublin. Come back and tell me when it’s sent.”

“Right, boss,” replied Holmes and started to leave only to be stopped by a rush of men entering the building. It was a dozen or more with four or fiveprisoners.

“Mr Connolly, sir,” said one, “we’ve had to fall back. They’re using artillery on us now. Blew up our barricades by north Circular Road Bridge and kept moving south, they did. We picked up these boys along the way.” He pointed at the prisoners with his rifle.

Holmes looked at me with a stare that said, “I told you so.” Shrugging his shoulders, he turned to the door and was gone.

Connolly had been busy questioning his men about the situation to the north. I recognized one man instantly as an Army doctor, a Captain.

“Captain, I see you’re an Army surgeon. How did you come to be here?”

“Home on convalescent leave,” he said with the thick accent of County Cork.

I extended my hand, “Doctor Wa….Ryan. I may have need of your help, sir.”

“Captain Mahoney,” he replied, taking my hand. “I’m a doctor first and will do what I can.”

Connolly had ordered the prisoners to the kitchen, but quickly acceded to my request to leave Captain Mahoney with me.

By seven in the evening, our casualties in the GPO were still minor, more accidents than anything else. Holmes had long returned from the wireless school and ensconced himself in the dispensary as my orderly. It was he who told us Pearse was to speak outside and deliver a message as to the state of the Republic. Leaving Mahoney, Holmes and I went to the street. There I was to hear a man I had respected, Pearse, tell bold-faced lies to the crowd. We were winning, Ireland was rising, Irish regiments of the British Army were refusing to fight. All of this he knew was not true. Truth was not convenient. It was discouraging to hear.

“Who does he think came from the Curragh and Athlone, Russians?” whispered Holmes. We returned to the dispensary.

The rest of the evening I spent going about the upper floors checking on the men. Those on the roof were most exposed and I knew that by morning the British would probably be in a position to make their lives hell.

A runner came in after dark looking for Connolly. He found him in the General Office with Plunkett and Pearse. Holmes and I were listening to their plans for victory. It all seemed hollow. They knew what would happen. But the runner made it worse.

"There's a gun-boat on the Liffey, Mr Connolly." He was a young man of the Fianna Eireann. There was silence a moment.

"They'll be able to place artillery fire directly on Liberty Hall from the river," I exclaimed. I couldn't help myself.

Plunkett looked up from his cot. "He's right you know."

"We've nobody there now but the caretaker," said Connolly. "There's no need to fire at it. Besides, a capitalist army will never fire artillery at shops and businesses in their own city. A few of our barricades to the north here was one thing. But their own city centre? Never!"

Collins was standing nearby and listening. I could see him shake his head and walk off. He was angry. He hated this "box" he was in.

"Let us hope so," said Pearse. "Liam, go above and ask the O'Rahilly to have his men watch carefully for the gun boat."

"Right, boss," he replied and started to move away toward the stairs. "Feel like a walk, Doc?"

"Coming, I need to check on the men again anyway." I followed him.

"Connolly is wrong, you know." Holmes said. They'll burn the city to the ground before they let the rebels have it."

"What do we do?"

"We do what we can to save lives."

"Do you report back to the Castle?"

"Report what, Watson? That nothing's changed and that they are winning? That these men are determined to be your 'little Maiwands?' They already know that. No, we must try and influence things from within here. Ah, there's the O'Rahilly."

Holmes communicated his message and we returned to the floor below. Sixty more men had come in. Connolly was busy dividing them up among the GPO, the Metropole and the Imperial. For a little while I watched the flow of burning buildings and the shadows of the fire brigade as they fought to extinguish the flames. Finally Holmes and I went back to the pile of mail sacks to try to get some sleep.

Chapter 15

Wednesday

26 APR 1916

I made rounds about three in the morning to check all our wounded. At the moment they were fair, so I returned to my mail sacks. Young Ryan and Captain Mahoney would be more than able to handle things. Holmes was awake and smoking another pipe.

"Have you decided how to influence things?" I asked.

"Curious problem, Watson. We cannot be overly strong to stop the fight or we shall be written off as cowards and our words ignored. If we do nothing, things will resolve themselves, as we know they will, with great loss of life. No, we must play the middle path, trying to make them see their foolishness but preserve their pride." He grew quiet for a few moments and I sat back down.

"I believe, Watson, we must make sure they have all the information we can give them and let them come to the final conclusion. They are intelligent men. Soon they have to realize they must save lives. They've made their blood sacrifice. It's time to stop."

"How will you get the information?"

"I intend to go to the Castle or the Royal Barracks, find Nathan, get all the information I can on the troop strengths and disposition, and return here."

"How will you explain how you got all this information?"

"Ah, well, Mr Pearse is going to send me on a reconnaissance mission." Holmes winked at me. "He just doesn't know it yet."

I shook my head. "He'll know it shortly, I'm sure," I muttered.

Holmes got up and brushed himself off. "I'll be back in a bit. I need to talk to Pearse alone."

I pulled my hat back down over my eyes and listened to the occasional rifle fire in the streets and how it echoed. Trying to sleep was useless, so after a few moments I went to the floor above and made my rounds of it and the roof. I could get the first sign that the end was in sight. As I moved among the men in the growing light, one called my attention to the Liffey.

"Look at the city crew," said one of the men pointing across the river. "They're working on the street. The fools are likely to catch it." He shook his head.

We all strained to see in the early light. Sure enough, they were tearing up cobblestones in the roadway across the river. The men talked among themselves and made sure no one would fire upon the work crew. I dared not tell them what it really meant. I decided to find Connolly and explain what was happening. This was the kind of information that was needed to stop the fighting.

I found Connolly and Clarke as usual in the main office. The increased crack of rifle fire could be heard with the first light. There would be another day of bloodshed.

"Mr Connolly, have you heard that road crews are digging up the street?"

"Yes, Doctor. Life must go on, I suppose. It would be better if they had rifles instead of shovels and picks."

"Then you don't know what it means?" I asked. But I knew he didn't.

"Means?"

"Yes," I looked hard at the two of them. "It means cannon! It means they're bringing up the artillery to shell us into submission!"

The two looked stunned for a moment and then, to my horror, began to laugh.

"Don't you understand?" I asked. "It's time to evacuate, disperse, move to the mountains. To stay here and be destroyed by artillery would be folly."

"Doctor," replied Connolly, "I thank you for your advice, but they will no more fire into the city than they would burn it. The capitalist owners would not stand for it. Believe me, it's one thing to blow a few barricades, but not the city centre. Now, let's hear no more of it."

"But what an honour it would be James," said Clarke. "It would mean they took us seriously."

I now knew that I could never get through to these men. The cause was all there was. I would have to save those that I could, one at a time. A cry came down from the roof. "Gunboat!" We raced past the upper floors and then to the roof. Indeed, the gunboat that had been reported at the mouth of the Liffey was approaching the Customs House. She was a small ship, a single funnel craft. I was later to learn that her name was *Helga* and that she had been used in patrolling the fisheries before the war. Now she patrolled the coast looking for German submarines. She sported what appeared to be a 12 pounder cannon fore and 6 pounder cannon aft. She had a Holmes searchlight near the bridge for night time use.

She anchored by a Guinness boat but as she was moving up I could see more activity from down near Tara Street. The O'Rahilly was by me at the upper window. I pointed to the men. "Two 18-pounder cannon. I'm afraid Mr Connolly is wrong. The capitalists will shell the city. They've dug up the road so the spade of the pole trails could dig into the dirt. They'll be able to fire in a moment."

The O'Rahilly seemed lost in thought. "I tried to tell them," he said quietly. "But now we must do our best. Hold on long as we can, then perhaps, go to the mountains."

"It looks like they've laid to fire on Liberty Hall."

"Yes. They probably think we'd not give it up without a fight." As if a man shaking off the doldrums, he shivered a bit, smiled and slapped me on the back. "We've a real war now, Doctor. A real war. You'd best get back to your dispensary."

"Time enough for that yet." The occasional crack of sniper fire was all that was to be heard at the moment. I could see the artillerymen readying their cannons.

The first shot came from the *Helga*. It completely missed Liberty Hall and hit an intervening railroad bridge.

"Too direct a shot," I said to the O'Rahilly. "They'll have to fire under the bridge. Those naval guns shoot too flat a trajectory."

He was as fascinated by the scene as I was. He nodded and continued to stare at the river. Now the two cannons on the street opened up. The 18-pounders roared and bucked, their spades digging into the ground where the cobblestones had been removed. The *Helga* now had the range and was firing more rounds into and around the hall. The *Helga's* sighting was poor and as many shells landed on the buildings around the hall as on the hall itself. The machine guns started playing their tune on the empty hall. The firing came from across the river. There was also rifle fire, but I could not tell from where it came. I decided to go back below and await development.

Captain Mahoney and Jim Ryan were in the dispensary when I entered. Ryan was anxious for news of the shelling, so I sent him to the front of the building.

“I thank you for your help, Captain. This can’t be easy for you.”

“It’s a sad situation, I agree. But if we concentrate on saving lives, that’s what’s important.”

“Doctor!” Ryan rushed in with a wide grin. “Cannons, machine guns, rifles, and old Peter ran through it all. They never touched him!”

“What are you talking about, Ryan?”

“Old Peter Ennis, the caretaker at the Hall. He answered the door when the *Helga* “knocked” and ran through it all. It’s a good sign, Doctor.”

I hoped, in my heart, that he was correct. The shelling was like a flame and all the citizens of Dublin moths. Both soldiers of the Republic and citizens of the city were attracted to the sound and fury. They were fascinated by the oncoming destruction, just as I had been, the first time. Everyone rushed to the windows save Mahoney and me.

“I don’t suppose our friends have any artillery to respond?”

I had to laugh. “No, Captain. I’m quite sure they don’t.”

“Well, that’s something anyway. Surely it will end quickly now.”

“Not if they keep shelling empty buildings,” I replied. I was occupying myself checking supplies for the hundredth time; they were still meagre.

“Ole Spence here has been sloppy with his work. Can I get a bit of help here?” Two men had entered, one holding up the shoulder of the other as he hobbled in. Both Mahoney and I went to them.

“What have we got?” I asked.

“We just finished the tunnel up from the Liffey and Spence here puts a pick in his leg with the last swing. What a clown, eh?” He smiled at his companion and we put him up on a sorting table.

“Well,” I said, looking at about a four-inch superficial tear in the calf. “That’s pretty serious. We’ll bind it up and then I want you to take him to the hospital for some stitches. They can do it better there.” Mahoney looked at me out of the corner of his eye. “Right you are, sir,” continued the companion. “I’ll get him there in a jiff.”

I tore away Spence’s trouser leg, used some peroxide and put a bandage on the wound, sending the two on their way. Mahoney came up to me once the men had left.

“Two less rifles?” he whispered.

“Two less dead men.” I replied.

Leaving Mahoney in the dispensary, I went back to the General Office. The cannons were still shelling an empty building and the machine guns were still rattling hundreds of rounds into barren windows.

Connolly and Clark couldn’t be happier.

“If they’re willing to destroy their own shops and businesses, we must be winning, eh Doctor?” cried Connolly.

“No, it’s a war, sir. They’ll do what they need to do to end it. That’s all it means.”

“Doctor, the whole world is at war. Why? For Belgium and the right of small nations to exist, at least that is what they say. Had they given Home Rule as promised, I doubt they would be here. There would not have been the need. We’d eventually get complete independence by parts. At least that would have been the general wisdom. But they won’t give us peace or our country back. We must fight. We’re taxed greater than England itself, our patriots are deported, and they want to draft us into their army to fight for their cause but not our own. At some point we must say ‘no’. At some point we must fight. This is that point.”

I looked around at the many men in the GPO. “I understand, Mr Connolly.”

“These men will fight because it’s the right thing to do.”

“Excuse me, Mr Connolly.” Cacy approached without so much as a sound. He was fumbling with his cap. “I’m supposed to report to you with some information, Sir.”

“Yes, spit it out.”

“Well, Sir, they’re landing at Kingstown. Hundreds of them.”

“You see, Doctor! They do fear us. They fear the people will rise with us.” He turned back to Cacy who was still fumbling with his cap. “Is there something else?”

“Yes, sir. Mr Heuston, sir. He’s surrendered the Mendicity. Low on ammunition and surrounded by machine guns.”

“He did much more than was asked, Cacy. He was to hold for three hours. He fought them for three days. He did well. Now, Cacy, find me Mr Collins. I want him to make sure our tunnelling is proceeding to the west. Do you think you can get through to DeValera?"

"I can try, sir. But I doubt it. I'm willing to try."

"Then do it. He must stop those soldiers from crossing the canal. The longer we hold, the better our position. No, on second thought send Sheehan. He lives in that area and can give an excuse for being there. See him off and come straight back."

"Aye, Sir."

All was quiet at the GPO for the moment. Mahoney and I were discussing the casualties to come. The looters were still on the streets, though there was less and less for them to rummage through. What hadn't been carried off was being set on fire here and there. In fact, around noon, there was a large fire in Henry Street, but the fire brigade dealt with it fairly quickly.

It was early afternoon before the attack came directly toward the GPO. By mid-morning, the Army had stormed Liberty Hall and found no one in attendance. The shelling had temporarily stopped but I could see the 18-pounders being manhandled toward a grassy area south of O'Connell Bridge. If I was right, they'd start by firing directly into Kelly's or Hopkins and start north, one house at a time. But what was happening in other directions? It was Holmes who answered that question for me.

I had been making my rounds to check on those who had been slightly injured. On returning to the general office, I found Holmes in conference with Pearse and the rest.

"Ah, Doctor, you're just in time. Liam was about to tell us what he's found out. Continue, please." Pearse turned to Holmes.

"It's like this, boss. Ya got lots of soldiers coming into Kingsbridge Station. They're going to the Royal Barracks, then in a big ring around us to the north. The Castle is full of soldiers too. So is Trinity College. Must be thousands there. Your man DeValera has some of his boys by Mount Street Bridge. When I left, they was trying to hold up the whole British Army coming from the boats. Half the soldiers gettin' off the boats is just goin' around them straight to Kilmainham or the Castle. They have a least four cannons, that gunboat, and more machine guns than I've ever seen. All that ammunition in Phoenix Park is still there. Your guys didn't damage a bit of it when they tried to blow it up." Holmes looked around at the assembled leaders. Each stood quietly, thinking his own thoughts for a moment.

"Let me tell ya, gents," he continued, "if you're going to get to the mountains, you'll have to do it before dark 'cause by then they'll have you like rats in a trap. Then all they gotta do is wait. We'll run outta food and ammunition. I might be able to get back south and tell the rest of the boys to just disperse as best they can."

"Not time for that yet," said Connolly. "I hope DeValera gives them hell. We still have direct contact with Ned at the Four Courts." He turned back to Holmes. "What about the rest?"

"Well, Ceannt and MacDonagh are holding on but they're each surrounded. The Mendicity is gone, so is City Hall and Mallin is shut up in the College of Surgeons. No one can move. Bunch of little Alamos, eh Doc?" He winked at me.

"Have you noticed the cannons south of the bridge?" I asked.

"Yes," replied Connolly. "I've ordered our men to fall back through the tunnels when the artillery starts. They've nothing but a rifle and a few shotguns down there. They'll come back to the Metropole."

It was Collins who seemed the most distraught. Here, I thought, was an ally. He wanted to fight, but not here in this box. He wanted to go out and take the fight to his enemy. Maybe we could get him to make the others see the light. Their mission had been accomplished. Ireland had risen. Why waste lives? Fight later on better terms.

"Collins," I ventured. "Could you get these men out of here and to the mountains?"

"No!" cried Clarke. "We stand and fight! Ireland must come to her senses. She will come to her senses. We must show that a just cause will win out!"

I could see that Holmes, Collins, and I would be the only dissenters. The O'Rahilly I thought would be with us but he had put himself in exile on the upper floors. He rarely came down.

The roar of cannon dispersed our little group. So close were the cannon to their targets that the sound of the firing was almost simultaneous with the explosion of the shell. That target was Kelly's at the end of the street on the corner of Bachelor's Walk.

"Cacy!" called Connolly. "Anyone seen… ah, there you are. Across to the Metropole, friend, and make sure our men got out of Kelly's. Let me know, off with you."

"I'm back to the dispensary," I said. Machine guns were now pouring thousands of bullets into what we hoped was an empty building. "Liam, I could use a hand."

Captain Mahoney was waiting for us. I explained to him, Ryan and the ladies what was happening. None seemed concerned and in fact, the ladies seemed elated. They were making the British enemy fight for every street. To them, this was success. I had to admit, from their perspective, in a way, they were winning. They had declared their independence, formed a government and were fighting a fair fight.

The afternoon dragged on with a constant crack-boom from cannon and shell and the buzzing of machine guns. Holmes and I had retired to our mail sacks to discuss our next move. The truth of the hopelessness of the situation seemed to gain us nothing. What were we to do? I had seen this before, both in Afghanistan and in South Africa. It seemed the more hopeless the cause, the more desperate the fight.

For more than two hours the cannon and machine guns played on the empty building. I had decided to go to the roof to peer down the street when someone came up on my shoulder, Collins.

"Are they ever going to attack?"

"Not yet," I replied. "They want to cross the bridge and since they have plenty of ammunition and time is on their side, they'll destroy both sides before they try and cross. At least, that's what I'd do."

"Me, too, Doctor." We knelt behind the statue of Hibernia and watched for a few more moments.

"Ah, look Collins, they're traversing the cannons. They'll start on Hopkins now. Once they're sure the other side of the street is destroyed and abandoned, they'll cross."

"The boys upstairs will have something to say about that."

"What's that?" I asked, hearing a machine gun.

"Another machine gun."

"I know, but it's coming from the west."

I was right. The Army had placed a machine gun on the top of Jervis Hospital and was pouring down fire on the GPO. We rushed below to pass the word, but they already knew.

"Liam! Liam!" I could hear Connolly calling at the top of his voice. "Someone give me a pencil and paper! Find Liam!"

I turned to Collins. "He's in the dispensary." Collins went off to get him.

"Blackguards know we won't shoot at a hospital," railed Connolly. "We'll obey the rules of war, even if they won't."

Holmes came in with Connolly. "Yeah, boss. Whatcha' need?"

Connolly was writing furiously. "Can you get through the hole in the wall into Jervis Street Hospital?"

"Sure, boss."

"Take this message to whoever is firing that machine gun. They know we can't shoot back, but we can do something else. If they don't stop, we'll start shooting prisoners."

"But you can't!" I blurted out.

"Of course not, Doctor. I wouldn't even think of it. But they don't have to know that." He looked back at Holmes. "Do you understand, Liam? You must make them believe it."

"Don't worry, boss. I can do it. Let me get my cap, Doctor, I'll be back."

Holmes was gone for more than an hour. The others worried but I realized he had taken the opportunity to get to the Royal Barracks or the Castle. It hadn't been twenty minutes before the firing had stopped from the roof of the hospital, so we knew he had delivered the message. By the time he was gone 90 minutes, they had decided that his mission had made him a prisoner, so when he appeared after two hours, they were all amazed. The word he brought was both good and bad.

"The boys at the hospital have been hidden by the good sisters," he told Connolly. "The Brits believe them to be regular patients. The bad news, boss, is that they've got armoured cars."

"Really, have they now?" Connolly was joyous. The worse the odds, the better it looked for us if we hold out, was his thought.

"They've mounted steel boilers on some lorries and put gun ports in them. They're using them to cut us off from the Four Courts." He looked at the floor, then back up at Connolly. "We're surrounded, boss. One man might get through at a time, but other than that, we're caught."

"How do you know?"

"I went lookin'. Only reason them cannons haven't blown us sky high is they can't get a clean shot from across the river cause of the buildings."

Holmes took another long breath. "Only chance I know might be east, then north, once we cross the rail lines."

"Thank you, Liam. We'll take that into consideration. Doctor, would you and Liam like to get a bite? Tell the kitchen to send some tea if they can. Thank You."

Holmes and I had obviously been dismissed so the council could talk. We went to the makeshift kitchen where I delivered the message and then out to our little sanctuary of mail bags. We sat on the sacks, tea in hand, listening to the cannons destroy the jewellers on the corner opposite Kelly's Pub (another now empty building), while machine guns rattled between cannon rounds.

"Think they'll listen, Holmes?"

"No, Watson, not so long as Connolly and Clarke are running things. Pearse is the weak link here. He's willing to die for the cause but he's a pacifist at heart. He doesn't like to see others injured or killed. He's the one we have to work on. His poetic soul makes him vulnerable. You can see that the minor suffering so far has already caused him pain." He took out his pipe and started to charge it. "Yes, Pearse is the one to get to. Problem will be that the others will cause him to stiffen his backbone. He won't want to appear weak. We have to convince him that they've made their point, it's time to stop." He lighted the pipe and leaned back.

We sat for a few moments, quietly, in our sack-filled closet. I was startled by voices by the door. It was Connolly with his teenage son, Roddy, and an ICA man. Connolly was talking quietly but firmly to the boy.

"You must get through to Bill O'Brien with this message, Roddy. That's why I'm sending the two of you. Once you've delivered it, stay with Bill, he has work for you."

"But, Da," protested the boy. "I'm needed here."

"You're needed with Bill. Those are the orders."

"Yes, sir," replied the boy and turned to go.

Connelly and the other men shook hands and a knowing look passed between them. Then the ICA man turned to follow the boy out the Henry Street door as Connolly walked back to the front.

"Holmes, did you…"

"Yes, Watson. I'm afraid it's a bad sign for us. He sent the boy out of harm's way. He means to stay at all costs." He kept drawing on the pipe. I sat, thinking there was some way to stop things. Nothing came to mind.

Suddenly I realized that the cannons had stopped firing and even the machine guns were quiet. It was just an occasional popping of rifle fire. I got off the sacks and went to the front of the building. I could see that Hopkins Jewellers was on fire, as was Kelly's, I assumed. I couldn't see Kelly's but there was smoke. I wondered if the 18-pounders were using incendiary shell instead of high explosive. Either could cause a fire but the incendiary was designed to. Of course, I reasoned if they could destroy the buildings that blocked the GPO, they could shell it also. I wondered how all the other "little Maiwands" were doing as I returned to the infirmary. Night was starting to fall and I could feel the first emanations of a fatalistic turn in our little garrison.

With the dark came relative quiet from outside the GPO, but inside was quite different. As I made my rounds that evening the men were together in small groups singing songs. Pearse was philosophizing to a few and Clarke held a group enthralled with stories of the old Fenian days. By the time I had checked patients and seen to the men on the roof, I was feeling tired. I went in search of Holmes. He was gone, so I turned my sacks into a couch and tried to sleep.

Chapter 16

Thursday

27 April 1916

It was just before four o'clock that I awoke to movement. Holmes had returned and was seated across from me, pipe still lit and a sadness on his face that I will never forget.

"What news?" I murmured, not moving.

"They've done exactly what you predicted, Watson, though it hasn't gone all the way of the Crown." He tapped the doddle from his pipe on to the floor. "Each little strong hold has been surrounded. They're not going to pay much attention to any of them, just keep them bottled up. They made a try at the South Dublin Union and got bloodied for it. The worst was down by Mount Street Bridge over the Grand Canal. They marched men up from Kingstown and tried to cross a bridge that they could easily have bypassed." He started to recharge his pipe, his head shook back and forth and he let out a small sigh. "Over 200 dead and wounded in one spot. Of course, they're claiming there was a whole company of rebels, but I doubt there were more than a dozen who cut them up in a nice crossfire."

"What next, Holmes? We're cut off from everywhere. I'd think they'd come after us, then, with the headquarters gone, They'd call for the others to surrender."

"Oh, exactly right. Lowe is still in charge and he's planning on taking the GPO. Today if he can, but he's willing to wait. Soldiers are pouring in and he has no desire to be accused of wasting lives. By dawn he will have cannons north and south, armoured cars in the streets and the ability to grind us down slowly." He looked at me for a moment and taking the pipe from his lips, looked down at the sacks. "I don't suppose you'll agree to leave now? No, of course not, but I had to ask."

"Do you know what's happened to the Countess?"

"Ah, well, I should have known you'd ask that. She and Mallin are surrounded in the College of Surgeons. They can't move without machine guns tearing the place up. As for the rest, Four Courts is surrounded, as is Jacob's Biscuit Factory, Boland's Mill and the South Dublin Union. They're all ineffective at this point. They can be starved out, if need be. Oh, Lowe will have his men harass them, have no fear. Some cannon and machine gun fire will keep them awake and on their toes. But he'll wait it out until he's taken to the GPO. But now" he stood "let's get some tea and see what we can do to convince our rebel friends to concede."

It was as we took some tea in the kitchen with our prisoner workers that the renewed assault began. By half four it had started in earnest. From the upper floor and the roof, movement could be seen all around us as Lowe closed his forces ever tighter. The machine gun and rifle fire were sporadic but heavier than through the night and seemed to come from everywhere. As yet, there was no cannon fire.

Holmes went to pass all the information he had gathered to Connolly and Clarke. His knowledge was explained by his night reconnaissance. But what should have made them see it was time to stop just made them dig their heels in all the more.

"The longer we hold on, the better our place at the table when the war is over. How can they claim they fought for the rights of Belgium, a small country, and deny us?"

As it would turn out, after the Great War, even the American President Woodrow Wilson would not listen to them at the Paris meeting in 1919.

At six o'clock, another call came down from the roof. The three stacks of the destroyer HMS Dove could be seen drawing into the Customs House. Did it mean more troops or just more cannon? We did not know at the time it was the return of Birrell. His time left in Ireland could be measured in days.

Holmes spent the rest of the morning with the hierarchy while I attended to the infirmary. By mid-morning, the cannon had added in their bark and it was not long before the surrounding buildings were starting to blaze. Now, however, there was no fire brigade. It was far too dangerous for the men to try to put out the flames with machine guns raking the streets. I continued to be amazed at how comparatively few casualties we had.

The coming of the cannon fire brought new machine guns. The bullets came from the Gresham Hotel to the north and Lower Abbey Street to the south. The rebels sniped away, hoping to make them keep their distance. In this they were most successful.

It was shortly after this, while I bandaged another glass cut, that I heard a cheer from the Public Office. Clarke had sent a young girl (Leslie Price) to the Pro-Cathedral for Father O'Flanagan to hear confessions and take notes to families. Putting on his traditional stove pipe hat so he could be identified as a priest, he and the young girl had dared cannon fire and machine guns crossing Sackville to the north and then down Moore Street and through the tunnel to the GPO. Here were two true acts of bravery. One might fault rebels or the Church in many things, but bravery was not a shortcoming in either. The Archbishop had been irritated at the fact that he had not been advised before the rising of what was to come or asked his permission. But when the British asked him to interfere on their behalf he had sent them off with a flea in their ear. In fact, as I was to find, some of the Church were the biggest supporters of the rebels.

I found Holmes in with Connolly, Plunkett and Pearse. Holmes had been a wealth of information to them. But no matter the darkness of the picture he displayed, they hung to an unreasonable combination of hope and fatalism. Holmes knew he could not demand they listen to his continuing words but he must win them over with the argument of saving lives.

"We've had a few casualties here," Clarke was saying. "Each a tragedy, yes, but some blood is always lost."

"And you've lost quite a few at Mount Street, the Mendicity, and the Union" Holmes said. "Ask the doctor here. He's fought the Indians in Californy when they was hold up. Comes a time to go, eh, Doc?"

"Er, ah, yes, certainly. If there is a way to slip out we ought to save the people from harm and save their homes from destruction. I'll tell you it's getting very hard to get through to Jervis Street Hospital and we can't do a lot for the wounded here. We have stretcher cases now that should have gone."

I could see we were getting through to Pearse. He was wavering, starting to ask himself at what point do we stop. It was Plunkett's aid Collins who spoke up. "I, for one, believe we should try for the mountains. It's a long time until dark, but we should get out of this trap and keep the fight going in the countryside."

"Sorry to interrupt, sirs." It was our friend Cacy. He looked tired, his eyes sunken from the lack of sleep, and he kept rotating his cap in his hands as had become his nervous habit.

"Yes, Cacy," replied Connolly.

"You Gentlemen need to come see this. They've got lorries what are bulletproof."

"Ah, yes, Mr Altamont had been telling us. Where are they? Show me."

"Right, Sir. One's on Henry Street and the other is by the bridge.

Haven't moved this way yet."

We all, save Plunkett who was lying on his mat, started for the front of the building. It was just as we moved that there came the crack of a cannon to the north and the slam of a shell into the Metropole Hotel across the street. It was indeed all too late now. Cannon north and south, armoured cars in the streets and machine guns in all four directions. The lid on the box was closed and we all knew it. It was a stand to the end, a bloody fighting withdrawal or surrender. Those were now the only alternatives.

The machine gun fire increased, but most bullets went high in the windows, hitting the back wall. The cannon, whether north or south, still couldn't get a good angle at us yet. Our own men in the outlying buildings poured fire out as best they could. While the lorry on Henry Street was stopped by one of the rebel barricades, the one on Sackville slowly moved north, bullet after bullet slapping the sides of the boiler turned armoured plate. As dozens of rifles tried to shoot into the gun ports cut in the boiler and meant to shoot out of, the lorry rolled to a stop. It was deluged in a thunderstorm of bullets which seemed to last forever but had not been more than a minute. As suddenly as the storm had started, the firing stopped. What had happened? The iron creature sat still. Had they shot up the motor where it could not run, had the transmission gone out, or had the driver been killed with a lucky shot through the eye slit?

We could not go out to the iron lorry and any soldiers inside dare not come out. The men in the boiler were trapped as surely as we were.

"We've got to improve our barricades," Connolly muttered looking about, he grabbed a half dozen men to follow him out on the Prince Street side. I went back to the infirmary. Holmes came with me. He was as near to exhaustion as I had ever seen him. His inability to impact the situation, I knew, was infuriating to him.

"You can't control everything, Liam. Emotions don't lend themselves to logical resolution." I could see him breathe deeply and look down at the floor.

"We should be able to control these things. But it's like the greater war, each side will only stop at 'victory' no matter the cost or the logic of it. Look outside, Thomas, the second finest city of the empire is burning. Why? Because, each side sees violence as the only answer."

"Sometimes it is the only answer," I sighed. "Submission is against human nature, and wrongs, or perceived wrongs, cannot be dismissed. Sometimes it has to be washed away in blood. At least, that's how humans feel. In a way, it's a shame the good Lord gave us both reason and emotions. They are so often contradictory."

Holmes was looking directly at me with a quizzical smile. "There are times you astound me, Watson." He walked toward the Henry Street door and gazed out. "I'm off to the Castle. I can have the most impact there."

It was odd how the rattle of machine guns had become just noise. It was the crack of the 18-pounders that brought me out of thought and back to reality.

"How Holmes? We're surrounded. Wait until dark at least."

"I'm certain I can get through the tunnel, over the rooftops then through the hole to Jervis Street Hospital. They're not firing from there anymore."

"Holmes, please, just this once listen to me. Wait for darkness."

"Dr Ryan! Dr Ryan!" Cacy was racing toward me. "Mr Connolly has been hit, come quickly!" Connolly was walking calmly behind him, as if nothing was wrong, but holding his left arm wet with blood.

"In the infirmary, sir. We'll soon take care of you." Turning back to where Holmes had stood I saw nothing but empty doorway. Holmes was probably halfway to Jervis by now. I followed Connolly and Cacy into the infirmary, still shaking my head.

The wound was not at all critical. It was more blood than damage. Our medical student, Ryan, did an admirable job cleaning and tending it. There was little for me to do but watch. Our nursing staff swarmed the poor man. It was no wonder he wanted to get back to the fight and away from the attention. This he did as quickly as possible. In the space of twenty minutes he was thanking everyone and, putting his jacket back on, went to the Public Office. I decided to once again make a round of the upper floors, but first made a tour of the ground level.

Our numbers had swelled since we first came to the GPO. It was hard to estimate how many we had now. Men were tunnelling through walls half a block away, they were barricading at a frantic pace on the ground floor. (Clarke was as positive that there would be a final bayonet charge by the British as I was sure that there would not be.) I was certain that Lowe had learned something from the Great War, and that would be "don't waste soldier's lives in foolish charges against even antique firearms." There were more men in the surrounding buildings, especially at the Metropole and the Imperial Hotel, the other two strong points. But volunteers were spread from

Lower Abbey to Cathedral Lane and Henry Street to Middle Abbey. Men and women bustled all about me.

Leaving the frenzy below, I went to the upper floor. Here there was more of a calm. I was greeted with the usual good humour of the men. Except for some complaints of not being relieved and going for long periods without food, all seemed in good spirits. Every minute or so came the crack of a rifle from a southwest corner window. I went over to a young volunteer kneeling at the sill.

"What are you shooting at?"

"Oh, that tin can on wheels there, Doctor. Every now and then I pot at it. Just to remind them that we're out here." He smiled up at me chuckled, "And they aren't!" He turned back to the window and fired off another round. The clang of the bullet hitting the disabled armoured car was clearly heard. I put my hand on the boy's shoulder.

"There are men in there, you know. Men like you and me. I understand the need to keep them where they are, but try not to enjoy it. It could be you someday."

The boy looked at me as if I were some museum oddity, then looked out at his target. Without looking back at me, he replied, "I understand, Doc. Don't worry, I'll just remind them now and then that we're still here."

As I continued my round of the floor, I saw Connolly, and it looked like young MacLoughlain, lead a large group of men onto Princes Street, which was fairly well protected with a barricade on the east side and dead ending into a wall of a building on the west. I watched as they continued south down an alley about mid-block, which led to Middle Abbey Street. I wondered their purpose. Too many men for a reconnaissance. Was it a flanking attack of some sort? In fact, Connolly had taken the men out to work on fortifying a barricade, but I would only learn this later.

Having finished my round of the first floor, I continued to the second. My reception here was much as the floor below. There was a certain tenseness in the air, but the men were still in good humour and looking for the final fight. Here I spent a little time cleaning a few cuts. It was as I finished that I took the time to look out of the south-facing windows. There, on the ground by the alley where Connolly had led his men, I saw an arm stretch out from the side of the intervening building. The hand clawed at a piece of cobblestone and pulled so that the next moment a head appeared from behind the brick. Leaving my vantage point I sprinted down the stairs to the ground floor, across the Postman's Sorting Office that served as our dispensary and out the Princes Street door. The only thought in my mind was that Connolly must be saved. He was the logical leading force. If he were lost all would be chaos, and surely it was his head I had seen appear. As I crossed the infirmary, I called for Ryan to follow, and bolted across the narrow street to the alley. As I knelt next to Connolly, he nearly smiled. "Can you give me a hand, Doctor? I need to get back to headquarters."

"In a moment. Let me take a look here."

Ryan was now with me, as was Captain Mahoney. Connelly had been shot in the ankle and there was no way but to carry him to the infirmary.

Once inside, the poor man was once again surrounded by those wishing to help. I'm afraid I made few friends with my demands that people leave and stay out of this. I had Ryan find Cacy and had him give instructions to keep everyone out until we could deal with the wounds.

Mahoney was a fine doctor. I deferred to him. I placed a tourniquet on the leg while he cleaned the wound and Ryan got the pieces for a splint. The ankle was terribly shattered. We had no morphine for the pain, little antiseptic, and no anaesthetics.

"Ryan, my boy, send anyone you can to the chemists shops they can safely reach. We must have some morphine."

"Yes, Doctor, right away."

"Captain Mahoney, I must admit you're younger and steadier than I. I'll loosen and tighten the tourniquet as required. Would you see if you can extract the loose bone chips?"

"Of course, Doctor."

Connolly must have been in severe pain, but he refused to show it. Many were the men I had treated in Afghanistan and South Africa, but never had I met one who dealt so well with his suffering. Though the tears of pain were in his eyes his smile stayed and he spoke words of encouragement to those around him. Even severely injured it was clear all would turn to him for guidance. The women crowded around him until the press of bodies became such that I had to demand they leave the area. But no matter my words, they would not go. I changed strategy. "Mr Connolly, would you be good enough to remind my helpers here that we have other patriots in the room."

Through his agony, he had the ability to laugh. "Ladies," he announced in a booming voice, "I thank you for your concern but I'm not badly done. Please help the others that are here while the good doctors look to this minor injury of mine. Please, ladies."

With some additional prodding on my part, they dispersed. One lady refused to go and I did not press the issue any further. Ryan's men had worked quickly and some morphine had been found. It wasn't much but it would have to do.

The crash came without warning. Plaster and dust cascaded around us as Mahoney threw his body between the debris and the open wound. As the dust started to settle, Mahoney raised his head to me. "They've re-laid the cannon, Doctor."

"Yes, they've found the range. We're in for it now." I gazed up at the ceiling. "Upper floors and roof I think."

Another artillery round crushed above us. Again we were enveloped in dust. "Mary," I asked of one of the ladies, "get us some hot water from the kitchen and see if we have an umbrella."

"Umbrella?"

"To help keep the ceiling from falling in the wound."

"Oh, of course, Doctor, right away."

"You have some fine people, Mr Connolly." I paused and peered at the man on the sorting tables. "Be sure you remember to take care of them." Mahoney stopped in his work. He and Connolly both regarded me for a moment.

'Doctor," replied Connolly with a slow meaningful nod. "I know what you are trying to say. I know that while you are with us your heart is not in the fight. You think this has been an error. It hasn't been." He looked about him. "Never fear," he sighed. "It'll be over soon." He smiled and placed his head back on the table. "We've won, Doctor. You'll see."

Mahoney shrugged and went back to cleaning the wound.

"I'm afraid we've done all we can, Doctor. He needs to go to the hospital."

"No, I won't go! I stay with my men!" Connolly's look was intent.

"Never thought you'd do anything else, sir" smiled Mahoney, patting Connolly's arm.

"Let's get him off this table and onto a cot, Captain."

We took him out and placed the cot near Plunkett in the main room where he was immediately surrounded by the men, each more concerned than the next. I returned to the infirmary and left them to their task. The ladies were working down the sorting tables as I entered. We now had nearly a score of injured. I needed to triage so that I could get the worst men out to the hospital. Mahoney made no arguments to my decisions as he too knew we had to move men safely. The artillery was coming more frequently now, both here and among the buildings south.

The O'Rahilly came into the infirmary and looked about.

"Any prisoners in here, Doctor?"

"Just Captain Mahoney, but he's more help than prisoner."

"Well, I'm moving them all to the basement for safety. We don't want them injured by their own shells."

"I'm needed here," piped up Mahoney.

"Yes," I affirmed. "He's of great value here."

"All right, but we must protect the rest. The rules of war demand it, and it's only the right thing to do."

I took the O'Rahilly by the elbow and walked to a far corner. "We've been able to put the fires out and no one has been badly hurt so far. But the fires toward the Liffey are out of control. Clery's store and the Imperial Hotel are on fire. Men are coming in the best they can from the outposts. We've no way to fight the fires."

I looked intently at him and he smiled a crooked smile. "I know what you're thinking, Doctor." He straightened his body and lifted his shoulders. In a loud voice he continued, "Yes. We're doing quite well. If you see them bring in any more prisoners, send them down, will you Doctor? I'd best be above to my men." He patted my shoulder and walked off to the stairs to the upper floors.

"Ryan," I called. "Make a round of the basement, will you? Mahoney, you stay here. I'll start around."

Men were still working steadily at barricades and re-dividing ammunition amongst themselves.

"They're running for it," shouted a voice from the front. With the call came a deafening roar of machine guns. There must have been a half-dozen guns streaming 600 rounds a minute, pouring up and down Sackville Street. Despite the noise and danger, men rushed to the windows like moths to the flame. Bullets popped the inside walls, but all seemed to be high. The men yelled encouragement as six volunteers made the insane charge across the broad street from the burning Imperial Hotel to the GPO. As each man reached us he was cheered, but then there was a collective moan. The sixth man had gone down in the street and did not move. In the midst of celebration was sadness. It was a horrible let down. I forced my way to the front at the call for a doctor. One man had cut himself badly leaping through the broken windows. The machine guns continued for a few seconds then fell silent. I checked my new patient. Lots of blood and he'd need stitches. I stood up to ask for some help moving him to the back, when, from the corner of my eye, I saw movement. It was from the street. The man we thought dead was up in a moment and running for us. It took the machine gunners by surprise also, for he was fair in the building before they got the first shots off. He was being pounded about the back and shoulders by his comrades and heartily cheered. It was all I could do to force my way to him.

"Are you all right, my boy?"

"Yes, sir. But I learned a valuable lesson." He looked about with a broad grin. "Don't fall down when people are shooting at you!" There was a general laugh and cheer at this. I made my way back to the infirmary.

Mahoney had our latest casualty well in hand so I decided to go above and make my self-imposed rounds.

Above were the signs of fires that had been recently extinguished From the windows I could see a short distance north and south. Across the street, the Imperial Hotel was going up in flames as were most of the buildings on that side down to Upper Abbey Street and on down toward the river. Connolly and Clarke couldn't have been more wrong about the "capitalists".

It was close to dark before I finished. The shelling at the GPO was intermittent and the 18-pounder shells made little impact on the solid outside walls. The flames of the explosions constantly started fires which had to be quickly extinguished. There was now no need for lights on the upper floors for the burning buildings that surrounded us made a glow that must have been seen for a dozen or more miles.

It was fairly quiet in the infirmary. In the Public Office, great activity continued unabated.

Explosions were coming from down the street. Seeing Sean Duffy at the door, I went to find out what was going on. He stood guard at the door of the GPO as he had the first time I'd seen him at the door of Liberty Hall.

"Busy night, Doctor," he smiled, showing his distinct lack of teeth.

"Are you alright, Sean?"

“Fine, Sir, but I do thank you for asking.”

I looked about and took in the activity. “What’s Mr Clarke organizing?” I asked. “I see he’s quite occupied.”

“Oh, he’s putting together his own fire brigade. Try to keep us from burning like those buildings out there. I’ll take the guard, thank you. Never could see running into burning buildings.” He paused to look outside again. “Men coming in,” he called. A dozen or more men flushed through the door like quail in the light of a grass fire.

“That’s everybody but the boys at the Metropole,” shouted someone.

Pearse appeared by my side and started dividing the newcomers up. Some were sent to move explosives to the basement to better protect them from the shelling. Others were detailed to join a party already in the basement trying to construct a tunnel under Henry Street to the buildings on the north side of the road. At least, I thought, they are finally thinking of escape. But escape to where? We were completely surrounded. Maybe, if they could go under Henry Street then up and through the buildings along Moore Street, then out at Great Britain Street and away. Yes, it could work …. if the Army could be drawn closer to the GPO and the Volunteers came out behind them. But the badly wounded couldn’t go, that was certain.

“You’re right, doctor. The whole thing is foolish!”

“What? Oh, Collins.”

“You’re quiet transparent you know. You’re thoughts I mean. We’ll make a try tomorrow. Pearse and Connelly have been working on a plan for an escape from our little box, but you and I both know it’s too late.”

“I just hope we won’t waste lives.”

“So do I, Doctor. Next time we won’t. Next time we’ll know more and we’ll fight on the move.” He paused and looked around. “Yes, next time.” He walked off and I thought about having a seat on my favourite mail sacks. But first, one more round through the infirmary.

Chapter 17

Friday

28 April 1916

I had again been unable to sleep, so I made continuous rounds. The men worked desperately, but the upper floors were now burning steadily. Try as they would, spots were put out only at great risk. The men exposed themselves to the intermittent fire of the snipers to slow the flames. For the moment at least, the cannon were quiet. Finally I succumbed to age and lack of sleep. Having made one last check of the ward, I barely remember laying back on my mail sacks in the darkness as men passed and smoke started to fill one's lungs from the burning street.

"Today, there will be an end to it." Holmes's voice came to me as if in a dream. I rolled over on my mail sacks and tried to find a more comfortable position.

"Come, come, Doctor. You've been sleeping for almost three hours; it's time to get up and about."

"Holmes, what the devil are you doing back?" I rubbed my eyes and sat up.

"There will be an end of things today, I think. By tomorrow at the latest. New man is in charge, General Sir John Maxwell."

"I thought he was in Egypt."

"No, he was in England and at rather loose ends, I suppose, for he's been sent here with full powers to do whatever he thinks he should."

"And what does he think?"

"Ah, well. I was able to participate in the meeting a few hours ago. Maxwell is at the Army Headquarters in Kilmainham Hospital. He's left Lowe in charge of Dublin and has approved his method - surround and reduce."

"Well, there is no change there. It's the logical course."

"Yes," agreed Holmes, pulling on his pipe. "But there are some changes. First," he tapped his pipe on his boot, "he has signed a proclamation that he will destroy any neighbourhood or area where he finds rebels. There will be no questions. Second, he has ordered a pit dug at Arbour Hill Detention Centre."

"A pit?"

"Well, a grave, if you will, large enough to hold one hundred bodies."

"What? Surely not!"

"Think not?" Holmes pulled out his tobacco pouch.

"Well, of course I believe you, but surely he does not mean to just execute people."

"Oh, of course not, they'll get a fair trial," he lighted the pipe, "then he'll shoot them. He intends to give Pearse his blood sacrifice in spades."

I sat quietly for a few moments. "Anything else?"

"Yes, no organization shall be left to exist in the open. Not the Volunteers or the ICA, not even the Hibernian Rifles or the Foresters."

"I understand that, of course. But doesn't he realize that executions will only give them martyrs?"

"Yes, that's why he intends to bury the leaders in quick lime. No bodies!"

"What can we do?"

"The same as we've done, old fellow, try to keep people alive as best we can. Neither side will listen to us openly.

"Everything is fairly well situated as far as Lowe and Maxwell are concerned. The GPO will be the big push come dawn. The rest they'll just hold in place." He continued to puff on his lighted pipe.

Struggling off my bags, I suddenly felt old. "I'm sure there'll be some tea in the other room, Liam. I need some."

"Of course, Thomas, I could do with some as well." We had just entered the makeshift kitchen when the first cannon of the morning fired and the building shook. I looked Holmes in the eye. "I'm getting my tea!" I asserted.

"As I, Doctor," grinned Holmes.

I took a china cup from one of the ladies, thanked her, and drank hastily as another round hit the upper floors.

"Come, Thomas, it's time to see if we can intervene." Putting down his cup, Holmes walked toward the Public Office while I swallowed the last of my tea and hastened to follow. Between the fall of shell, was the buzz of the machine guns like thousands of bees telling us to leave.

Connolly was on a new cot, this one with casters. Two ICA men were pushing him about as he continued to direct the construction of defences. I peeped out the windows to see all the buildings around us burning or already smouldering bulks. The streets themselves were littered with debris and devoid of human life. It was too dangerous even for the looters. One saving grace was the large amount of ammunition the soldiers were wasting on empty buildings as everything had now been abandoned except for our own position. I despaired at the scene before me. Leaving my vantage point, I went to where Holmes stood talking with Connolly, Pearse, and Plunkett. It was a surreal scene I would have expected out of some novel by Mr Wells. A man on a mattress, one on a cot, a dreamer and a spy, all arguing the fate of hundreds of people - none but the spy knowing, or should I say, admitting, the truth of the situation. It was Holmes who was speaking as I approached.

"Boss, if we don't get out now, we're goin' to get run over like Custer at the Little Bighorn."

"I appreciate your opinion, Liam, but we can hold out a while yet, and the longer, the better," replied Pearse. "The men are doing quite well."

"The men will do what you and Mr Connolly ask, Mr Pearse, which gives you a responsibility I wouldn't want." Holmes turned to Connolly, "And you, sir, the doctor here says you gotta get to a hospital or you'll be dead. Then what good will you be to your men?" We all looked, involuntarily, at his leg. "And Mr Plunkett there, he should be in the hospital too."

There was a pause before Connolly replied. "No, Liam, I know your council is well meant, but we're all right for now. I think the fires are under control for the moment and they're not in a position to rush us yet."

"But the fires are getting worse up above, sir. I've been up there."

"At least send the women out, for God's sake, man." I interposed. "We can't have them here when the end comes."

"I can see you don't know our women, Doctor. There will be hell to pay to force them to leave. They won't do it willingly." Taking a deep breath, Connolly was thoughtful for a moment. If I could get Pearse alone, I thought, we might make the evacuation happen, or even surrender.

"We're staying and that's the end of it. At least for now." Clarke had come up behind without my notice. He was a stern figure. Though slight and somewhat bookish looking, his presence was one that was felt. His quiet spoke more than a thousand books. His would be a force I knew I could not overcome, but try I would. "And the women and wounded?"

"We'll deal with that in due course."

"Sir, the King's forces are within a few hundred yards of us in all directions."

"True," replied Clarke, "and we haven't been able to tunnel under Henry Street, but for now at least, we stay here."

"If you don't act, the deaths of women and boys will be on your soul not the souls of the soldiers who are without!"

With that, I stormed off to the infirmary, leaving all behind save Holmes, who nodded to the group and followed. I consoled myself that I had done my best. While Holmes left for the upper floors to make another assessment, I once again made my rounds and talked to each man. Father Flanagan was also making round of each man in our little ward, hearing confessions, giving absolutions and stuffing notes from the men to their loved ones in what must have been pockets that reached to his knees. He held a constant smile. Every man got a hearty handshake, a quick prayer, and assurance that messages would be delivered. How he would be able to get out safely any more than we would I could not see. Perhaps the stovepipe hat would be his safe passage.

It was just before noon when the O'Rahilly brought our prisoners up from the cellar to feed them and then send them back below for their own protection. Among them were the men from the Bank of Ireland. One, a man named Harry Pepper, was talking to our friend, Sean Duffy, who evidently had been detailed to the guard mount. In a moment the two of them approached me as I was bandaging another volunteer with burns.

"This prisoner wants to address you, Doctor. Is that all right?"

"Surely, Sean." I looked up at him from my work. "What is it Pepper? Are you ill?"

"No, sir." He held his hat in his hand; his eyes looked down toward his boots. "It's this, Doctor. These men here have treated us right and we've always been with them in their cause." He glanced up and then back down at his boots. "It's just, well, we got caught up in the other thing, you know. We got selfish like, and we know there's going to be consequences but right now we want to help." He looked back at me with a pleading face. "All of us do, sir. We'll give our parole and take what's coming. But for now, couldn't we be let up to help?"

I scrutinized the man's face. I believed him, I didn't trust him, but I believed him.

"I'll do this, Pepper; I'll speak on your behalf. I'll recommend you be allowed to help, unarmed, in fighting the fires or working with me. I promise nothing else."

"That's fine, sir. I trust you to do your best. Me and the boys appreciate it."

"Take him back to his friends in the basement, Sean. I'll let you know what's decided."

By now the fires were growing worse. To touch the walls of the building meant burning your hands. Still, men and women went about their tasks: nursing, cooking, fighting the fire that surrounded us from four sides and above, and returning shot for shot to the snipers at the Gresham Hotel. In three wars now I had seen such bravery. How sad.

Holmes returned from above. "Hopeless, Doctor. They'll never put out the fire."

"And evacuation?"

"Connolly has agreed. The women must go. They're to gather here and be sent out under a white flag."

"Will it be honoured?"

"One can only hope."

It was Pearse who assembled the women. It was perhaps 30 girls that crowded around. MacDiarmada and Fitzgerald were with him as he addressed the assembled. He looked at them and smiled. He looked more like a kindly priest than a combat leader.

"When the history of this week is written, the highest honours will be paid you. You have taken part in the greatest armed attempt to liberate Ireland since 1798. You obeyed the order to come here. Now I ask you to obey a more difficult one."

There was a sudden chorus of "No" shouted from the assembled women. "What was all that stuff about equality?" cried a lady in the back.

Pearse had been ready for the discord. He held up his hand and looked about until quiet prevailed. In a slow, well-modulated voice, he continued. "I am not asking you, but telling you to leave. I know it's not easy and some of you might be shot. But you showed your readiness for that when you came. Now go and God be with you."

The women were not at all happy with the decision. Neither was MacDiarmada, who pulled Pearse over by me and in a whisper argued against sending the women out. But Pearse was firm.

Fitzgerald went over by the door and called for order and a white flag, which he gave to one of the girls. Fitzgerald, like the O'Rahilly, had been against the rising, but once started felt it his duty to participate. He had spent the week in charge of stores and the kitchen, and so in close contact with many of the ladies he was about to send out. His concern for them was obvious. I too, feared for those who had helped me so.

"You heard the order ladies," cried Fitzgerald sternly.

A white flag secured, it was given to the first lady in line and tentatively held out the door. The firing started to quiet and the ladies, all save three, exited into the street as the machine guns fell silent. Connolly's secretary, Winifred Carney, and two others, Grenan and O'Farrell, refused to go.

We all waited, silent, expectant, until the ladies were brought behind the British barricade. Whatever their fate, they were at least out of harm's way. The street remained silent for a few moments until a single shot from way of the Gresham renewed the onslaught of bullets.

"We've made some progress, eh, Thomas?" Holmes was now hopeful that the surrender would not be far off.

"Some," I replied, "but now they've less reason to quit."

"The women's surrender worked, why not the rest?" He seemed puzzled by my comment.

"Warfare doesn't work logically all the time old fellow. You box. It goes against man's nature to give up in a fight. They know they're down, but they'll go on for a while yet."

"Lunch, Gentlemen." It was Fitzgerald calling. "It may be our last here so we've a fine chicken dinner."

"But it's Friday," replied a volunteer.

We walked into what had been the mess for the last week and there before us was a mountain of food, perhaps the best some had ever seen. In the centre of plenty lay platters of freshly cooked chicken. The men looked at it but no one would touch it. That is, until Father Flanagan, knowing the men needed to eat, stepped forward. While everyone watched, he retrieved a piece of the fowl and with great zest, bit down. The men started to cheer and eat a hearty meal. He had given them dispensation to eat meat by action instead of word. All the while, the shooting continued. I joined in the meal. One thing the army had taught me was to eat when the opportunity presented itself. Who knew where the next meal would come from or when? Holmes, of course, satisfied himself with another pipe instead.

"You really should eat, Liam."

"Yes, I know, but I'm satisfied with this. You however, want to ask me something."

"No, just tell you that I've need of help in the ward and our four friends of the other night have offered their assistance. I'm going to take them up on it. Objections?"

"None."

"Indeed? I thought…"

"No, Watson, I've no need to see them punished in a formal court. With Burns dead, they'll return to their old ways, perhaps, or they may use this to find their own redemption."

"But surely you've reported the whole episode to the DMP. They'll want these men."

"Why report anything? No, the right people know and the Castle does not want it known that one of their own used this whole unfortunate occurrence." Standing, Holmes started to the front of the building. "Use them as you want, old fellow."

I had to admit it all seemed the best way out, so I went in search of Pearse to whom I explained my need to use our four friends below. To this he readily agreed. With his permission I sent for Pepper and the others. Duffy brought them up for me. They were somewhat dejected looking in their stolen IV uniforms but listened attentively as I explained their situation.

"Mr Pepper has told me you all wish to make amends for your recent actions by assisting here as you can. I'm going to give you that chance. Here are your choices. Work here with me caring for the wounded or return below as a prisoner. If you choose to help, when this is over, you'll be free to go your own way as far as we're concerned. However, should you claim you want to help and then in any way try to betray us or to run off, you will be found and dealt with." I paused and looked in the eyes of each man. "Do we understand each other?"

As I looked from face to face, each man nodded.

Pepper stepped forward. "We're all with you, sir. We want to help with the good work. It's our country too."

"All right then. Ryan," I called. "take these four men if you'd be so kind and assign them duties as you need."

"Of course, Doctor. This way men. We've plenty to do. You two men go over to Captain Mahoney, you other two stay with me."

I went to find Holmes. He was on the first floor from where he could see the streets burning from the river to the Pro-Cathedral. Even the Metropole across the street was fully engulfed in flames. Men were everywhere fighting the flames. While Pearse tried to make cohesion out of chaos, he had not the force to make it work. The O'Rahilly was the one who now directed the overall attack on the flames as Clarke and MacDiarmada tried to organize the use of hoses. While the fire took control, men continued the fight at the barricaded windows to keep the British foe at bay. The fire was now in the lift shafts, spreading from basement to roof. We all knew there was no hope.

"We'll be done by nightfall, Watson. The fire hoses have burned away. There's little water pressure and the roof and the second floor are abandoned. The soldiers won't come. They only have to wait for us to come out."

"That's why I've come, Holmes. I could use some help when we get ready to evacuate. I've got about two dozen wounded. Litter cases and walking and you've been in and out of Jervis Hospital. Can you lead us through?"

"Of course, old fellow. Let's go see what we have, shall we?"

Together we descended to the ground floor and through the chaos of 400 men trying to battle the enemy without and the fire within. It was young Ryan who informed me that we were to get the wounded fit to move by sunset. Mr Fitzgerald had been put in charge of evacuating the wounded and was off drafting men to be litter bearers.

"This will be difficult, Thomas. It's not easy to get to Jervis through the tunnel, but we'll make do," declared Holmes. Spying our former prisoners, he left me to supervise them in constructing litters suitable for our coming journey. Ryan, Mahoney, and I revisited each wounded man, doing what we could to ready them. So the rest of the afternoon proceeded as each floor was abandoned and the few rooms left to us crowded with men.

It was half seven when the O'Rahilly brought our prisoners up from the basement. Lieutenant Chalmers was the senior man among them. He was addressed by the O'Rahilly as they stood near the door to Henry Street.

"It's up to you now, Lieutenant. You and your men can stay with us while we remain or you can take this white flag and leave now. The choice is yours. You and your men are safe from us in either case." The O'Rahilly was a sight to see. His hair was scorched and his eyebrows burned away from fighting fire. As he talked he had men moving the explosives from the basement to a small concrete room near the ward. And while confusion reigned, Father O'Flanagan was checking on the wounded as if he were strolling about his parish yard. What a strange scene.

"We're out," said Chalmers. Taking the hand of each man, the O'Rahilly wished them luck and the Lieutenant led out, white flag held high. In a moment, they were gone down Henry Street then up Moore Lane toward their own barricades. Later I would learn that the Lieutenant had been wounded and one man killed, shot down by their own men.

I went to the O'Rahilly. "What now, Sir? What is the plan?"

"We try to go north, through the barricade on Moore Street. There's a factory on Great Britain Street which will do well for us. Then we'll try to link up with Ned Daly at the Four Courts. At least, that's the plan."

"But the wounded?"

"I believe MacDiarmada has told young Ryan to get them ready. You can take them to Jervis as best you can." He looked out toward the Henry Street door. "Connolly and Plunkett will be coming with us."

"But that's madness. Connolly has to get to hospital. Besides, the two of them will only hamper the escape of the rest."

The O'Rahilly shook his head. "We've little enough chance of getting out. Besides, the men love Connolly. He's better off with us. Don't worry, Doctor. It'll all be fine." And so saying he walked toward the door. I returned to our little ward where Mahoney and Ryan had things well in hand.

Here we had a short conference. It was decided that the three of us would go with the wounded and would return if possible. Father O'Flanagan was coming too but the three women would go with the main body: Carney, Grenan and O'Farrell, would go with the main body in their attempt to escape. There was no dissuading them.

Holmes and our four friends were busy making litters from anything handy - blankets, thin mattresses, whatever was at hand - while all around us fire and debris fell from above. And still the artillery threw cannon shot into the upper floors, each shot drowning us with burning timber. Under Fitzgerald's guidance, we organized our evacuation, most badly injured first behind Holmes, who knew the route, then the less severely injured. Ryan,

Mahoney, and I would spread ourselves out to deal with emergencies.

"All right," said Fitzgerald, "we move as soon as the O'Rahilly takes out the advance party. Are we ready?"

"Yes," was all I could think to say. Holmes, Fitzgerald, and I went to Henry Street door. The O'Rahilly was to take about 30 men with him. He was rising from his knees in front of Father Flanagan when I saw him. He had received absolution. He bid the good father farewell and took out his Peter the Painter. Looking about at those who were praying for him, he shouted, "Cheerio," but Pearse stopped him. Not a word passed between the two men as they shook hands. The O'Rahilly now stepped back, looking at his 30 men. "Now!" he yelled and they flooded out the door behind him.

"Time to go Doctor." It was Fitzgerald calling. Holmes was already through the back wall of the GPO and men were passing litters through one at a time. Passing behind one of the litters, I entered through a hole of broken brick to the house beyond. A hand reached out to pull me through and another grabbed my elbow. I looked up into the smiling face of Cacy. "Here you go, Doctor. On to the far wall and keep your head down under the window as you go past." He reached for the litter behind me. I crossed two small rooms and found myself at the next tunnel. Here I stopped to help Pepper manhandle two litters through. I had almost gotten use to the smoke-filled buildings, but now the extra exertions made my lungs burn. I went on behind the last of the litters as Pepper continued to help the walking wounded. We passed across some type of shop up a stairway and out onto a roof. There we bent low for Moore Street was straight north of where we gathered. Above us was a ladder to a door leading into the Coliseum Variety Theatre. The litter cases were in agony as they were tied to their litters and handed up and in through the door. I scrambled up the ladder. As each man arrived, Ryan, Mahoney or I checked for re-opened wounds. It had taken almost a half-hour to move half a block and the fire was following us.

Here Fitzgerald decided to rest for a bit. We had no sooner laid the men on the carpet when a runner arrived asking for Captain Mahoney. Connolly's protective cage, over his leg, had been damaged. Could he come back and fix it? Mahoney didn't hesitate but went straight away. He was back in what seemed like moments.

It was Holmes who suggested a Red Cross flag be flown from the pole on the roof but to do so arms must be taken out. Fitzgerald insisted that the rules of war would be followed. "We need to dump our arms back at the GPO," he insisted. "Let's pile them here and two of us can take them out."

There were not more than a dozen weapons. It was with great

reluctance I added my pocket pistol to the pile. That action made me involuntarily pat my vest for my letter. When I looked up, I could see Holmes smiling at me.

"Doctor Ryan." Jim Ryan was tapping me on the shoulder. "I'm going back to look after Mr Connolly. They may have real need of help when they fight through. You and the Captain have no need of me now."

I was about to volunteer to go along. "Well, I think that I…." Holmes was looking sternly at me and shaking his head ever so slightly.

"Yes, Doctor?" Ryan was appraising me quizzically.

"Oh, I was just going to say, if we don't meet again, be sure to finish medical school. You'll make a fine surgeon." I reached out my hand, the two of us shook, and he was gone out the door.

Holmes approached as I stared at the empty doorway.

"I'll have need of you, Watson. All we can do now is save what lives we can. And that will be in the offices of our friends in the khaki uniforms."

"I understand, Holmes, but I don't like letting that boy go off like that. I want him alive, not martyred."

"Yes, I know."

Cacy had approached and grabbed Holmes by the elbow. "There's no putting up a flag, Liam. It's suicide to try and get on the roof."

"Well, don't worry 'bout it. We can use it when we go out to the hospital."

"Liam, Cacy, come here." Fitzgerald was standing with Father O'Flanagan by the weapons pile.

"Yes, sir."

"Father and I are going to take these weapons back to the GPO. We'll be back in a few moments. Maybe there's someone still to take them."

"But sir, I can…" started Cacy.

"No, I want you two to find a way out of here. That fire will be here shortly and we'll need to get these men out. I'm relying on you."

He bent over to pick up the stacked rifles. Slinging them over his shoulder, Father Flanagan doing the same, the two of them made an awkward retreat through the door and down the ladder. Cacy and Holmes left to find an exit that would not lead to further destruction and I went back to the wounded.

I was convinced that all would recover if given prompt attention save one who worried me. He was a slight lad who had been unconscious for the better part of the afternoon.

Fitzgerald and the priest were back quickly. The tunnels were now a conduit for the fire, and as fires do, this one was creating its own wind to force the flames toward us.

Holmes, of course, had been through the building now numerous times and knew well where the only unlocked door was. But he played the game and allowed Cacy to "discover" the only door without a padlock. Later, he would tell me there was actually a window, hidden by draperies, which he had used before. The unlocked door, which opened into a passageway, led to a locked gate that opened on to Princes Street.

There was now a scramble to find a tool to open the gate. A pickaxe was procured from where the tunnellers had worked and Cacy made haste with his trophy to open the gate.

We had now been at rest for nearly an hour. Fitzgerald insisted we must press on to the hospital. The men picked up their fellows on their make-shift stretchers with the greatest care. We started down the stairs to street level and out the unlocked door to a narrow passage. One man carried our make shift Red Cross flag in front with Father Flanagan at his side. We all followed to the edge of the passage. Here we hesitated. Prince's Street ended to the west at the wall of Arnott's Drapery Store. To the east, it opened to Sackville Street but faced the burning Imperial Hotel. So here,, though the fires lighted the sky like an artificial sun, we were able to cross with relative immunity. It was only the occasional stray bullet or shrapnel that came our way.

We crossed Princes Street and entered an alleyway partially blocked by a burning barricade of what appeared to be rolls of newspaper. We passed the wounded in their blankets over the flames and continued down a narrowing passage to Middle Abbey Street. From here we peered around the sides of the buildings. To the east a barricade of our own was in flames blocking the way to Sackville Street. To our west were Jervis Hospital and a British barricade of sandbags manned with soldiers and machine guns. And from windows all about us volunteers were trading shots with the British forces. It seemed that only the fires consuming the buildings on both sides of the street would move them.

Fitzgerald knew all too well the danger of our situation.

"All right then, hold that flag out high soldier. Listen men, we're going out and right to Jervis. Move slowly, no running, no sudden moves.

We've got to make them understand that this is a mercy mission." He looked about at the faces around him. This was our most dangerous moment yet. Both sides needed to cease firing; our only hope was respect for our little flag. In a moment we would be easy prey. I sucked in my breath involuntarily and gazed at the Red Cross, so plain, in the light of the fires.

The call from Fitzgerald brought me out of my thoughts.

"Out then, boys."

We started out of the narrow passage at what seemed a snail's pace and turned right toward the hospital. Everything in me screamed "run for cover." I looked to Holmes, who was across from me helping to carry one of the stretcher victims. He merely smiled back. Somehow, that made me feel better. It was then as I staggered into the street that was lighted like noon that the firing died away. I had a sense there was a thousand angels holding their breath as we slowly passed down the pavement toward Liffey Street. Beyond stood the British sandbags. We moved without a word. The sudden silence of the guns gave an eerie feeling. One could now both feel the heat and hear flames crackle as the fire was consuming the city. We continued forward, the only sound the shuffling of feet as we picked our way through the rubble of a week of devastation.

I now wondered what had happened to the rest of the men. Were they already in the mountains? Fighting their way through to the west and south to the Four Courts? Or dead in the streets?

"Halt where you are!"

It was a shout from behind the barricade. We could see a row of rifles and a Lewis gun with nervous soldiers peering at us over the sights of their weapons. A captain and a major were off to the right in deep conversation. While they talked, they kept looking at us. They were surely wondering if this was some sort of trick. The captain sent a runner off somewhere while they conversed. It seemed forever but was probably about five minutes before the captain finally called to us.

"Man with the flag. You and the other come forward and be recognized."

Father Flanagan now had the flag and was about to start forward when Captain Mahoney's hand restrained him. "I'll go with you, Father. Maybe they'll take my word for things."

"Thank you, Captain. I surely hope they'll take the word of a man of God and one of the King."

The two started forward, but were stopped a good dozen paces short of the barricade by a command to halt.

"Holmes," I hissed, "we might…"

"No, Watson. It would just confuse the situation. Later, once we're in the hospital."

I thought that our identifying ourselves might be a boon to our situation, but as usual, Holmes was correct. I could hear a discussion between the captain and Father Flanagan and Captain Mahoney. I could not make out what they were saying from where I stood, but it was plain that the officer wasn't sure whether to believe our two representatives. The captain sent off another runner and a moment later two young men in civilian clothing appeared. The two were quite animated and pointing at Father Flanagan. Their heads bobbed up and down. The captain also nodded. With a wave from Mahoney, we picked up our burdens and moved slowly toward the side entrance to Jervis. Nuns, nurses, and medical staff poured out to help us carry the wounded inside.

"Mr Altamont," came the booming voice of the Major at the barricade, "this way for you. I remember you, sir. Spied at the Castle did you? Well, never mind, we'll take care of that."

I was near panic. If Holmes were taken this way he might be tortured or worse. I started to step toward the barricade, but Holmes laid his hand on my sleeve. "Easy old fellow, I'll be fine," said Holmes, and winked at me though he had a scowl on his face. "How do you think I've gotten back and forth," he whispered.

"Don't worry, Doctor. I'll be fine," he shouted and waved back as two soldiers grabbed him and pulled him across the sandbag wall.

I turned back to the wounded as we entered the hospital. Mahoney was still with us. He and I explained each case to the medical staff. The hospital was filled with patients - civilians, military and Volunteers. Many of the supposed civilians I knew to be Volunteers whom I had treated during the week and we had smuggled through to Jervis.

I had been there not more than 30 minutes when a soldier came into the triage room asking that I and Captain Mahoney report to the Major at the barricade. We left Father Flanagan with the wounded. I knew that Holmes was safe and I still carried my safe conduct papers, yet still I worried. That is, until I saw Holmes and the Major taking tea in a room just off the foyer of the hospital.

"Come in, Doctor, Captain. Tea?"

"Yes," I sighed as I sank into a chair. I looked at the clock on the far wall, just a bit after eleven. The end of the fifth day of the rebellion and I was still in one piece.

"Understand it was a tough go out there, Doctor."

"Yes, quite, Major. Though I suspect you haven't had a good time of it."

The Major gave a crooked smile. "No, very bad show down the road toward Kingstown. They bloodied our noses fairly badly. We've over two hundred dead and wounded. I'm told up north of town there's been a bit of a brawl too." (Later I found out he was talking about Mount St. Bridge and Ashbourne.) "But all's in hand now."

Mahoney was staring at me.

"You mean, all the time…"

"Yes, Captain," replied Holmes. "We've been working for one reason, to save lives."

"You, too?" He was incredulous, "and you sound British, not American."

"I had always found that good theatrical training is a distinct benefit in my line of work. And the Lieutenant Colonel here has been of immeasurable help, not only here, but throughout my career. Let me introduce myself. My name is Sherlock Holmes and this is my good friend, Dr John Watson of the RAMC." Holmes bowed with all the drama of an actor taking a curtain call. It was the kind of theatrics I needed. The tension was broken and I laughed until tears came to my eyes. I'm afraid my two fellow officers thought me on the edge of a nervous breakdown.

"I've heard of you, Mr Holmes. The Colonel here has written stories about you, hasn't he?"

"Ah, time has passed, Watson. I'm afraid you're not as well-known as you once were."

"That's all right. Doyle still sends me royalties enough," I quipped. We were all quiet for a moment and I sipped the tea. "What of the stretcher party?" I asked. "What becomes of them?"

"Gaol in the morning. We'll hold them here until light."

"And the women who came out?"

“Were they part of the game?”

“I don’t think so,” I lied, “pressed into service.”

“Well, we’ll see.”

“And Father O’Flanagan?”

“Ah, well, unless he actively fought, we dare not hold a priest. We’d surely have a rising over that. No, he’ll be sent on his way.”

“Good.” I looked to Holmes. “I’m afraid I’m suddenly a tired old fellow. Can we find a place to sleep?”

“Already arranged, Watson, but we’ve more to do before we sleep, old friend. We’re off to see General Maxwell. Unless, of course, you’d rather not. I can go alone.”

“No, Holmes. In for a penny, in for a pound.”

“Yes,” replied the Major, “I’ve a motor outside, the driver will take you to the Royal Military Hospital. I believe that’s where the General is at the moment. General Lowe is to meet with him tonight. You may leave any time you wish.”

Chapter 18

Saturday

29 APRIL 1916

We followed a fairly straight route to the Hospital, down Parkgate, past Kingsbridge Station, and quickly over to Army Headquarters. An occasional shot was heard in the distance, but mainly my impression was of the glow from the fire. Holmes and I sat in the town car as the driver moved swiftly down the streets.

"Holmes, what about Martha? Has she been all right? Do you know?"

"Yes, she's been in England since Monday night. I instructed her to go to Kingstown and take the ferry as soon as I sent word it had started."

"Well, thank heaven for that. You do think of everything, Holmes."

"No, old fellow, if I had thought of everything, none of this would have happened."

"Holmes, you did all you could. When the world has gone mad, one man cannot set it right."

"Thank you, Watson, but had I been able to truly get within the inner circle, things might have been different."

"If you'd been in the inner circle, the rebels might have won. Then where would we be?"

Holmes laughed for the first time in days.

The yard of the hospital was filled with soldiers. We drew up to the front door. With sidelong looks from those around and the sentries at the front, we were escorted through the halls and into a large conference room. Here we found a half-dozen staff officers.

On the table before them was a map of the city and in it were pins of various colours. The arrangement of the map was almost identical to that which the rebels had used a week before. Interesting, I thought, how all armies worked so alike. The wall clock was striking one as Maxwell looked up from his study of the maps in front of him.

"Ah, you must be the spies I've been told to expect. Well, what have you?"

Holmes bristled instantly. I could see the change in him as he stood straighter and his eyes pierced at the general. Maxwell was not an easy man to deal with and he obviously did not relish his position. He had a hard reputation in Egypt as to his dealings with the natives, and I instantly saw that his attitude toward the Irish would be no different.

Lowe, who I much more respect to this day, stepped up.

"General, let me introduce Mr Sherlock Holmes, the consulting detective. He has spent almost two years in working within the Shinners organization for us. You might remember the Von Bork Affair? It was Mr Holmes who solved that situation for us. And this is Lieutenant Colonel John Watson of the RAMC. He was recently brought in to assist Mr Holmes."

At the mention of Von Bork and then being told I was an Army man, Maxwell seemed to relax a bit. Like most military men, he took a dim view of civilians and spies were to be loathed. But, Holmes was proven and I was one of his own so he would listen to what Holmes had to say.

Holmes gave a quick overview of the week. He told them of his estimate of the strength of the men who had abandoned the GPO, of their northerly course, and their intent to double around to the Four Courts.

"Connolly is a litter case you say? Well, they're cornered in some buildings not two blocks from the GPO from what we can tell. They certainly haven't broken through our lines." Maxwell walked back to the table and once again inspected the map.

"I see no reason to rush in, Lowe. Your strategy seems to have done well so far. No waste of men or equipment. We'll make the beggars come to us. With the countryside generally quiet, we can continue to concentrate."

"Dr Watson, what's the prognosis on Connolly?"

"He'll need a hospital or he'll be dead in a few days. That's as plain as I can say it."

"He'll be dead in a few days anyway. And their will to fight, Mr Holmes?"

"Connolly and Clarke would just as soon fight to the death, which they might do if left to themselves. But they've made Pearse the Commander and he'll surrender so that you can kill him. Martyrdom appeals to him."

"We'll have no martyrs, but there will be payment for this. When I'm through, no one will think of doing it again for a hundred years."

I was amazed at the contradictions in his statement that he himself seemed to be unaware of. The man had no concept of where his thinking would take a country that had re-awakened to its identity.

"Come, Watson. It's time for us to exit the stage. This play for us is done." My friend looked tired but his eyes told me that he had something in mind.

Lowe came over and shook our hands. "Your information has been a great help, Mr Holmes, and saved many lives."

"I'm afraid it has not saved this island for the Union, sir, and I regret that. I will be returning to London tomorrow. Dr Watson, I believe, will want to return to his other duties in Kent."

"Holmes, I feel as though I should stay a few days yet. They'll have need of extra hands at the Castle Hospital for a while."

"Of course, Watson. Goodbye General." He turned and we left without a word from Maxwell.

Our driver was still waiting outside. He had been instructed to take us to Ross's Hotel just next to the Royal Barracks where rooms were available to us.

We rode the short distance in silence. I thanked the young private, who drove us and entered the hotel to find that my whole kit, which I had left in London, was waiting for me.

"Yes," replied the desk clerk to my question. "It arrived about a week ago with a note that you would be calling for it, sir. The note was from Mr Mycroft Holmes. It was odd though."

"Odd? How so?"

"Well, sir, the note had the annotation that you would call this morning before five a.m. for your bags. Nothing comes into Kingsbridge Station that time of morning." The clock behind the desk said 4:30.

"Holmes, how could he know?"

"I don't know, Watson. Truly I don't."

As we walked to the stairs to go up to our rooms I could still hear firing from a short distance as it echoed between the buildings; light shown through the windows as the fire still raged.

"It's about over, Holmes."

"Yes, Watson, all but the killing."

"Maxwell will think better of it. You'll see Holmes."

"No, Watson, he won't. He'll have his pound of flesh and give Ireland away." He stopped on the stairs and took my hand. "Thank you, old friend, for helping me to try. I'll be gone in the morning when you get up. I need to see Mycroft. If anyone can influence what is to come, it is he."

"I won't tarry long here, Holmes. I don't think I can stand much of this."

"Good old Watson!"

He entered his room and shut the door. I entered mine and lay my head down just as the first rays of sun were over the horizon. I thought I would be unable to sleep but as soon as my head was on the pillow, I must have been dead away.

A hard pounding at my door awoke me. I had only been asleep two hours by my watch. "Coming, coming, who is it?" I opened the door. "Holmes, I thought you were leaving?"

"Yes, but I want a crack at Nathan and Birrell first. I understand they're at the Castle. Perhaps they can influence Maxwell. I doubt it but I must try. Well, come on, man. Get dressed."

I hurried a shave in cold water and donned my uniform. By just after eight o'clock we were entering the castle yard. There I was relieved to find Constable Flood. He looked much the worse for wear, but smiled as we entered.

"Joined up, have you, Doctor? Didn't recognize you for a moment, Liam, good to see you."

Flood leaned toward me and, in a conspiratorial tone, allowed as how Liam had been going in and out all week at odd times. I grinned and Flood winked back.

We made our way through a large encampment of soldiers in the courtyard, through the foyer, down the hall and into Room 6. Here sat a solitary soldier of the signal corps. He leaped up from his chair, dropping a book as we entered.

"Morning, sir. Mr Altamont. Who do you need to see, sir?" Holmes instructed him as to our need to see Birrell and Nathan. The young man departed.

I looked at the title on the book. "*A Tourist Guide to Ireland*." I noted. "At least the young man wants to see something of the countryside."

"Let's hope he doesn't have to do it with a rifle, Watson."

When the two men who had run Irish Affairs for so long entered Room 6, I was shocked. Rarely had I seen such an utter change in men. The two had the look of men under the gallows, which, I suppose, in a way they were. They were haggard and drawn. Nathan especially had the hollow eyes of one who has sat in the trench during long hours of shelling. They knew that their careers had gone up in flames with the city, a city that they truly loved but could not protect. They now realized they had been doomed from the time that the Ulster Volunteers had formed, the officers of the Curragh had mutinied, and the government in England had failed to act. They are where the Fates have dictated. The three hags must have laughed at their work.

"You bring what word, Mr Holmes," asked Nathan.

"We all know, sir, that this rebellion is all but over. What I have to ask is about your status and that of Mr Birrell. Do either of you have any influence with Maxwell?"

"Ah, as to that Mr Holmes," Birrell sat heavily behind the table, "I'm sure you know the answer to your own question. We have neither control nor influence over the man." He looked up at Nathan, and then continued. "He thinks us fools of the worst order. If it were up to him, we too would be tried and executed. He's no use for civil authority. He is in charge, and, unless replaced, will not even listen to the Prime Minister. No," he lowered his head and looked at his hands. "No, Matthew and I will be sacrificed on the altar of government and sent away with all the blame, whether it is ours or not. Whatever your idea Mr Holmes, we cannot help you."

"Fair enough, sir. I appreciate your candour. I'll leave on the mail boat and hope to be in London tonight. Watson, you won't come with me?"

"No, Holmes. I'm off to the ward to see what's to be done."

Holmes thanked the two men and we left them, silent and morose, in the quiet of the room.

I said goodbye to Holmes at the foyer and we parted company. He was off to Kingstown and I to the hospital ward. It was barely half ten in the morning.

The wards were filled, not only with our patients from the Great War, but also patients from our little one. The entire Castle, with its few hundred soldiers and patients had been on short rations. Only now was food starting to come through. Medical supplies I found rich in abundance, compared to my work of the last week. I was heartily welcomed back by the staff that was curious about both my absence and my new status. To their enquiries I merely replied that I had been on a special assignment for a short time as I would need to return to Kent and my usual work.

It was at rounds in the early afternoon that word spread like wildfire. The Rebels were surrendering! Cheers resounded through the Castle, but now, I thought, we must deal with the aftermath. Some of that aftermath was not long in coming. About mid-afternoon I was drinking tea and looking out the window toward the courtyard. There was quite a commotion at the gate. Seven of Connolly's men had carried him to the Castle and asked that he be put in the hospital. I rushed, unthinking, to the gate. Connolly was the first to recognize me as I bent down to check his leg.

"Ah, Doctor, you seem to have changed sides."

"No, sir, I've always been on the side of reason." I stared into his eyes.

"Well said."

"The leg?"

"Not so bad as it could be."

"We'll get it properly treated now. You'll be all right." I wasn't at all sure of that myself and I could tell he didn't believe me anyway.

"Bloody Hell! It's Doctor Ryan!" The outburst came from Sean Duffy who stood half at attention by Connolly. He had helped to carry him in.

I stood up. "Hello, Duffy. It's actually Dr Watson."

"And I thought…"

"I'm glad you're all right Duffy. I was worried about you."

"Not likely!"

"Believe it or not, my friend, I was."

"I think," said Connolly, "it would be best if you did not attend to me Doctor. I'm sure there are others here who can help."

"I understand, sir." I stiffened a bit. "You're probably right. Good luck, sir, and may I shake the hand of a brave man?"

He hesitated a moment then lifted his hand. Without a word, we shook and I left. Connolly was taken to the old Royal Suite away from the hospital wards. I was never to see him again.

By late afternoon word had filtered down; Pearse was a prisoner at Arbour Hill and he and Connolly had both signed a surrender. Daly and the men at the Four Courts had marched in and the girl Elizabeth O'Farrell was being used to carry the surrender message to the other garrisons.

The night grew strangely silent. It was queer not to hear the guns that had fired all week. Lowe's forces had been told to stand fast, so now there came only the rare sound of a single sniper. I chose to spend the night at the Castle, immersed in treating the wounded. Somehow, there was relief in that work. I did not want to think of the men who I felt I had abandoned. When I finally lay down on a cot, I could not sleep. I knew there were men out there who didn't even know that their leaders had surrendered. What would happen in the morning?

Chapter 19

30 April 1916

Sunday

By dawn, which was about a quarter to five, the entire Castle was swarming with messengers coming and going. I was sent for and asked to see Major Price over in Room 6.

"Ah, Doctor, thanks for coming. We have need of you. Could you come with me to the Rotunda Hospital? We are identifying the leaders among those that have surrendered. Since you were on the inside, your assistance would be greatly appreciated."

A chill went down me as Price made what should have been a simple request.

"No, Major, I don't believe I can be of any assistance to you. I'm sure your G-men are more than capable of identifying the leaders."

Price appraised me rather quizzically for a moment, then shrugged. "All right, Doctor. But, speaking of G-men, do you know where Sergeant Burns is? We've looked for him for days. I thought he might have made contact with you or Mr Holmes."

"I have no idea where he might be now." I was truthful about that. "I can honestly say, the last time I saw him he was fine. But that was the first day of the rebellion. I haven't seen him since."

Price stared at me. As our eyes locked I could tell he thought I was either lying or at least not telling all that I knew.

"Right, then. Thank you, Doctor. Do you know if Mr Holmes will be returning?"

"I'm afraid I don't know that either," I smiled.

"Well, no matter. We've plenty to do for the moment."

With that I went back to the wards.

All day word of more surrenders came in. Miss O'Farrell was sent into the most dangerous areas, sometimes alone, sometimes with the help of one of the priests.

It was two in the afternoon when I saw the Countess for the first time in a week. She and Mallin had marched the Citizen's Army men who had fought at St. Stephen's Green and the College of Surgeons to the Castle in surrender. Even in defeat, she held herself like a queen, unbowed and unbroken. I never got the opportunity to talk to her, for no sooner had they arrived than she and Mallin were put in a lorry and taken to Kilmainham Gaol. The men were marched off toward Richmond Barracks.

By evening, it was over. All the outlying units had surrendered. Men were already being loaded into cattle boats to be taken to England or Wales and prison. The leaders had been separated out and were spread among the local gaols. I stayed in the wards and did the only thing I knew to do.

Late in the evening I walked to O'Connell Bridge and north, across the Liffey. The fire brigade was once more out and doing what they could. The streets were filled with curious onlookers. It had almost the feel of a macabre carnival. People were picking through the ashes either for souvenirs or anything of value. Soldiers were everywhere but interfered little with the crowd and once more the DMP were on the streets. The second city of the empire was a smouldering ruin.

I walked on to the GPO. After fire, artillery and a week of fighting, there she stood above the pediment, Hibernia with her spear and harp. To her left and right were Fidelity and Mercury. The three still stood guard. I could not help but feel that this was a sign. Ireland still stood, faithful to her cause, proclaiming it to the world. I shook myself. I was becoming morose. Afghanistan, South Africa, Ireland; I was suddenly very tired of the fighting.

I walked back along Middle Abbey Street and West past Jervis Hospital - past the barricade that had stopped us just the day before - still manned but now allowing anyone to pass. I walked past the back of the Four Courts and the Royal Barracks and turned into Ross's. Stopping only for my key I went straight to my room. There were plenty of other doctors in Dublin. Tomorrow I would go to London and then on to Kent. I must see what Holmes had been able to accomplish. Yes, I thought, tomorrow I go home.

Chapter 20

1 May – 13 May 1916

I was delayed one day from my intended departure. I've no doubt it was intentional. Price was still trying to find Burns and he believed I knew something about the disappearance. Burn's body was identified on the first of May by fellow G-men. He'd had no identification on him when he went to raid the bank, so his body was placed with other dead Shinners to be looked at later. His death was put down as an accident of war.

It was now the second of May and I was determined to leave.

I took the mid-day ferry from Kingstown. I had nothing but the uniform I wore, my few things in a Gladstone and my medical bag.

I had made it a point to make a last round at the Castle and to say good-bye to Flood. It's interesting that it is always the common man who most fascinates me. He was a good man and I wished him well. I had no desire to see Maxwell, Lowe, Price, or any of the key players in our theatre of the absurd. Nathan saw me leaving. When I told him I was off to London, he wished me well. I did the same to him. For a moment I thought the man mad as he grinned and started to laugh.

"Ah, Doctor. We'll be joining you soon. Birrell and I will have to resign and I suspect Wimbourne will also be made to go. Though, in fairness, he was more right than I, but when it's a question of the government standing, they'll need to make a clean sweep of it all. Best of luck to you, Doctor. I've got to get with the arrest list."

"Arrest list?"

"Well, we can't let men like MacNeill get away."

"But he didn't fight. He tried to stop the uprising."

"No matter, he was involved and that's all that will count. We've got a few hundred around the country to get. I'm afraid we may have more fighting yet."

"What will happen to Pearse and the others?"

"Now, Doctor, you know the answer to that."

"He never even fired a pistol!"

"Those who led are the most guilty." He looked down at his boots. "Or maybe it's those who failed to lead." He seemed to drift off in thought for a moment. “Well, anyway, good luck to you Doctor.” He offered his hand and we shook and parted. I felt more regret over Nathan than any of the others.

By nightfall I was in London and fortunate enough to find a hotel room. Though it was late, I planned on making a visit to the Diogenes Club to find Mycroft and perhaps Sherlock. I had much I wanted to talk about with them. I found the two brothers in Mycroft’s makeshift war room. Both had obviously used the room to its named purpose. The antagonism was palpable.

The Strangers Room was a bee hive of activity. Men were moving pins on maps of France and Turkey; telegraphers were busy sending messages; the teletype rattled. Nowhere was there a map or sign of Ireland.

It was Sherlock who saw me first and waved a hand to Mycroft’s closet. Taking his brother by the arm, he moved him inside.

“Close the door, will you, Watson? Thank you.”

“Ah, Doctor, I thought you’d stay a few days,” remarked Mycroft, placing himself in the chair behind the desk.

“I doubt that,” I replied. “You knew I had no stomach for what’s coming.” Sherlock smirked as Mycroft looked up through his bushy eyebrows. “No, Doctor, you’re right. I didn’t think you’d stay.”

“Has it started?”

“By dawn, the first will be done.”

“Who?”

“Pearse, Clarke, and MacDonagh.”

“And there will be more?”

“Oh, undoubtedly Doctor. This needs to be ended for the duration of the war in Europe at the least. We can’t be distracted by wars inside our own borders. I should think a half-dozen or so will do.”

“Holmes,” I turned to Sherlock, “Is there nothing we can do?”

“I’m afraid the blood lust is up in England, Watson, at least among the politicians. They won’t listen to me or Mycroft.”

“But surely, Mycroft, you see what the result will be? More martyrs, more songs, more stories. Spank them yes, and then send them home like little boys. People will laugh at them. If you kill even a half dozen you’ll make them heroes.”

“Doctor, just because they ask my advice doesn’t mean that they’ll take it. The great politicians are looking a little foolish to the world right now. They want to regain control with an iron fist and let the world know they are not to be trifled with."

"Surely they know that this will cause problems with the United States."

"True, but not with the companies selling munitions and war goods. There is too much money to be made to let a little trifle in Ireland upset sales. We may be unpopular with the common man, but the common man doesn't sell artillery shells."

I sat in the chair by the right of the desk. There was an intense sadness in my soul.

"What of Casement?" I asked.

"He will be hanged, surely. Your friend, Doyle, is trying to help him. Evidently they are great friends but the Crown Prosecutor won't let Sir Roger live. There are things about the man neither you nor Doyle know. Casement will be destroyed."

I looked beseechingly to Holmes. "Sherlock?"

"Watson, I've been to the Prime Minister himself. I fear it's time two old men went home."

Denouement

I read of the first executions the next morning as I was boarding the train for Kent. The newsboys were hawking the headlines as Holmes and I walked toward the platform.

"You should come stay with me for a few days, Watson. Martha would like to see you, now that we're out of character."

"Thank you, Holmes, I'd like to take you up on that in a month or two. Right now, I think it's best to get back to my patients. The work will do me good."

"Yes, I think it will, Watson."

We walked on to where my train waited.

"We stopped a bank robbery and we kept innocent men from being blamed for it. We made the best effort we could to stop unnecessary bloodshed. You saved the lives of wounded men." Holmes shrugged and put his hand on my shoulder. "We did what we could Watson. But both sides were against us."

"Perhaps after the war is over, some solution can be found."

"Good old Watson."

"I'm not giving up on it, Holmes."

"Nor will I."

We shook hands. Without another word I boarded the first class carriage.

I watched from the window of the train as it pulled out of the station. Holmes had already turned and was walking away. I meant to keep my promise and see him again.

By the twelfth of May, Maxwell had finished his executions. In all, with Casement, sixteen would be shot or hanged. Ireland had its new martyrs, England would have more wars, and Holmes and I would be called for again.

Links

Save Undershaw www.saveundershaw.com

Sherlockology www.sherlockology.com

MX Publishing www.mxpublishing.com

You can read more about Sir Arthur Conan Doyle and Undershaw in Alistair Duncan's book (share of royalties to the Undershaw Preservation Trust) – An Entirely New Country and in the amazing compilation Sherlock's Home – The Empty House (all royalties to the Trust).

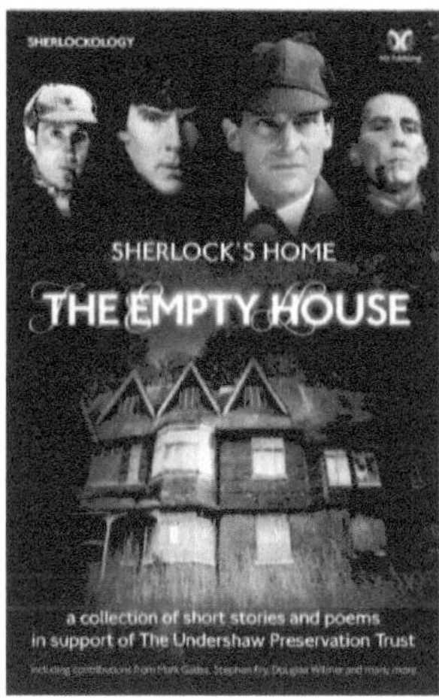